SUNSHINE AND SHADOW

She heard him move again, a little closer to her. Then she felt a hand on her arm. Her heart began to race and she opened her mouth to speak, but she shut it again, not sure what to say or do. His touch was exciting, and despite the heat she felt a shiver along the length of her body. In a moment he would want to kiss her. Oh, she wanted to hold him! She wanted someone this night.

She heard him sigh heavily and she felt his hand draw away. He stood up. Then, to her dismay, the form retreated as he picked his way along the roof. He had not wanted to take advantage because he thought she had been sleeping.

Oh, it was just as well, she thought. Involvement with a man like Michael would be disastrous. A poor man, an angry one – and with family problems. His going was a stroke of good fortune. But it was hard to remember how lucky she was as she lay there with a body that wanted so much to be touched.

D1386401

SUNSHINE AND SHADOW

Antonia Van-Loon

A STAR BOOK

published by

the Paperback Division of
W. H. ALLEN & Co. Ltd

A Star Book
Published in 1983
by the Paperback Division of
W. H. Allen & Co. Ltd
A Howard and Wyndham Company
44 Hill Street, London W1X 8LB

First published in the United States of America by
St Martin's Press, 1981
First published in Great Britain by
W. H. Allen & Co. Ltd, 1982.

Printed and bound in Great Britain by
Cox & Wyman Ltd, Reading

ISBN 0 352 31269 6

Acknowledgments

Many people helped me in the writing of this book. I gratefully acknowledge my agent, James Seligmann; my editor, Hope Dellon; and my family and friends: Clifford Van-Loon, Jennifer Van-Loon, Christopher Van-Loon, Frank Smith, Leona Thompson, Marguerite Schall, Roni Finkelstein, Sheila Ceder, Dorothy Shiff, Kathleen Bartlett, Rosemary Moore, Dorothy Keefe, and Lillian Brown.

In memory of my brother,
Benjamin Smith

Part

One

Chapter One

Tracy Sullivan stood with the shivering crowds on a platform high above Third Avenue waiting for the El to come in. It was February and bitter cold. The wind slashed and shoved against the people as though to say, "Get out of my way!" She held her hands over her exposed ears and bounced up and down on her freezing feet. Where was the train? What was the engineer *doing*, for pity's sake? He was probably in the next station up, sprawled across his cab, a bottle of whiskey in his hand and an idiotic grin on his face. The thought brought on a wave of rage that caused her to jump higher and faster.

She was dressed in an absurdly inadequate black straw hat and a typical shopgirl jacket, which was fashionably cut but cheap and frayed at the cuffs. She was eighteen years old, of average height, and thin, with light brown hair, hazel eyes, and a fair complexion that in weather like this brought high color to her cheeks.

An old man in a ragged greatcoat glanced with amusement at Tracy who, he thought, jumped like a spectator up at the Polo Grounds. But most of the weary immigrants crowded on the platform didn't turn their heads. In the New York of 1895 one had to do something truly outlandish in order to be noticed.

Up ahead could be seen at last the lights of the oncoming train. A sigh of relief swept through the crowd, and there was a whoosh of movement as people arranged themselves to be the first into the cars. Tracy shoved her way to the edge of the platform, managing to outmaneuver men twice her size.

"Watch it, miss!" thundered a hefty laborer who was dressed in a warm-looking jacket and a hat with earflaps.

"I was here first," Tracy snapped.

"*I* was here first."

"Oh, no, you weren't!"

The train screeched to a stop. The doors opened, and the man put a foot in Tracy's path. Tracy stepped over it, holding her arms out to keep him back, and pushed her way into the train.

She had once been taught ladylike manners by her mother, but that had been long ago in another world. Her mother was dead now and so were most of the manners. Now Tracy lived in a three-room Monroe Street flat with a grandfather, a father, two brothers, and two sisters—an atmosphere not conducive to cultivating social graces. But she often vowed that when she got rich she'd learn to act like a lady again. That would be the first thing she'd do, she had promised her mother's ghost.

At least the car of the train was an improvement

over the platform, Tracy thought. She could stand many things—even the press of people moving back and forth against her, emitting fumes of onion and stale sweat—but she couldn't stand cold. When she dreamed of being rich she dwelt longest not on thoughts of gentle manners but on thoughts of a house with a stove in every room.

The train rumbled down Third Avenue and then ground along the tracks over the Bowery. From the windows of the train she could see directly into the flats that were perched over the stale beer dives, vaudeville theaters, and ten-cent lodging houses of this infamous thoroughfare. It was said that there were prostitutes who crooked fingers in the windows in order to solicit interested riders of the El. Tracy had never seen this. All she had seen in the upper-story windows were families much like her own. People eating or fighting or hanging out wash—it was all very dull to Tracy. But she would sometimes peer into the windows wondering if she could spot a fancy lady. Tonight she was standing in a dense crowd and had no view at all, so she looked instead at the faces of the men who were closer to the windows. Most of them didn't even turn their heads. They were probably too weary to get off the train, much less to go chasing up the Bowery after the beckoning women. They had been up since dawn laboring on docks or in sweatshops, and Tracy guessed that the only thing on their minds right now would be the food waiting at home.

Food! Tracy had been thinking about it for most of

the day. It was food, in fact, that defined her days. Her oatmeal breakfast was scarcely finished before she was counting the hours until her sandwich lunch. Then all afternoon, as she waited on the chunky customers at Midridge's Shop, she dreamed of supper. Her sister Mary usually served potato soup and bread, but Tracy was generally too hungry to notice the sameness of the fare. It was food, and it filled her up.

Much of the money for this and for the other Sullivan meals came from the six dollars a week Tracy earned. And today she had nearly jeopardized that. She shuddered as the memory of that perilous moment assaulted her. A fat customer, who had insisted on buying a shirtwaist two sizes too small, had gotten furious when Tracy said that she'd surely pop the buttons. The buxom matron had flounced over to Tracy's employer, and the incident had nearly resulted in a fining. Luckily Tracy had escaped with a stern lecture on how and how not to treat customers.

"One *never* suggests that a lady might be too corpulent, Miss Sullivan."

"But she was two sizes too big."

"One never says nor implies that. One simply suggests that another waist might be more flattering."

"Yes, ma'am."

"I should think that after a year in my employ you might have grasped this essential fact."

"Yes, ma'am."

"I'll let it pass this once. But in the future you will remember that no customer is too corpulent. *No* customer, Miss Sullivan."

Hah! Tracy had thought. About everyone coming into Midridge's was too fat. Tracy sometimes imagined those spoiled ladies seated at their supper tables cramming so much food into their mouths that the excess dribbled down the front of their new clothes: roast beef in pan drippings, baskets of biscuits running yellow with butter, fresh salads even in winter, bowls of fruit, desserts on silver trays that were gooey with frosting, crunchy with nuts . . .

She was daydreaming of one of these meals when the train steamed into the Chatham Square station and disgorged Tracy and a gray-looking army of fellow neighborhood people. Chatham Square was in the southwest corner of the Lower East Side. It had once been the stronghold of Irish potato-famine victims, but it was now home to many Jews as well and even a few Italians who were moving down from Mulberry Street. A newsman named Jacob Riis had written a book about this square and the rest of the East Side. He had meant only to stir more comfortable New Yorkers into an awareness of conditions down here. But, though well-intentioned, he had managed to insult many proud Europeans and Asiatics who saw this area only as a stopping-off place in their journey from the village or the shtetl to the promised land.

Tracy was not a reader but had nevertheless been interested enough in Mr. Riis's *How the Other Half*

Lives to look at a copy that her sister had gotten from the library. Instead of cheering the fact that someone wanted to clean up the slums and give the poor a better life, she had raged over some of the descriptions of the people who lived here. Why, Riis made it sound as though all the streets were filled with illiterate, filthy lice-carriers! Before taking the book back to the library, Tracy had scrawled a comment that ran all around the white space of one page:

My family's not dumb or dirty either! Even my little sister and brother can read and write and spell and we always wash in the morning and wear fresh linen most of the time. So there, Mr. Riis, you old blatherskite!

At that moment she had vowed once and for all to get her family out of the East Side. It had taken a lot of thought, but her plan was ready now, and tomorrow she would take the first step.

Tracy charged down Catherine Street, propelled by the cold, looking like a Confederate assaulting Cemetery Ridge. She whipped around the corner onto Monroe, where she lived, and her mouth began to water as she thought of supper. The street was almost deserted this evening. Even the hardiest street vendors, who normally peddled their wares near flaming ash barrels, had taken shelter from the piercing wind.

She passed Mednick's bakery and inhaled the fragrance seeping through the cracks of the door. It

14

was too much for Tracy, coming as it did in the middle of a reverie about food, and so, on impulse, she darted inside, foraging for a penny in a handkerchief she kept in her pocket. Ruth Mednick was behind the counter, a young woman of about Tracy's age. The two didn't know each other well, and for that reason they disliked each other, but in a passionless way, since they had no reason for enmity other than coming from different cultures.

"Two sugar buns," said Tracy, swallowing back the accumulated saliva and shuddering. "No, don't wrap 'em up. I'm gonna eat 'em here."

Ruth shrugged and handed her the buns. Tracy seized them and inhaled them without bothering to take off her gloves. Ruth stared at her with amazement. Oh, the manners of the *goyim!* But there was understanding mixed into the sneer, for Ruth remembered what it was like to be hungry. On coming to America, her father had chosen the bakery business over some other endeavor because in bakeries you could always stay warm and fed—even if flour wasn't the most nutritious food around.

"Is that all?" Ruth said as she watched Tracy brush the sugar off her gloves.

"That's all." But Tracy didn't move. She wanted to savor the warmth of this place for a few more minutes before walking the remaining half-block home.

"So how's the family?" Just as Tracy was instructed with regard to her uptown customers, so Ruth was educated for service on this block. "The family you should always ask about," her mother

15

had said in Yiddish. "The customers should know you care."

Tracy said, "You don't even know my family," because the Irish usually patronized McGinty's bakery over on Market Street. Only occasionally did one of them venture in here, and Ruth knew no more of Tracy's family than the name.

Ruth said, "So what difference does it make if I know them or not?"

"The difference is, you don't care how my family is, so why are you asking?"

"My mother told me to," said Ruth, with a candor that would have appalled that good woman.

"Oh," said Tracy. "Well, save your breath."

"Whatever you say," Ruth muttered, baring her teeth. "Customer's always right."

Tracy had been warming for an acid retort, but at this she found herself smiling. At first Ruth glared at her, then her expression became quizzical, and then a tentative smile played about her lips as she sensed that the skinny Irisher wasn't laughing at her but with her. "What's so funny?"

"That's all I hear all day," Tracy said, "how the customer's always right."

Ruth had heard that this Tracy was a shopgirl, but she didn't know any of the details, so she asked Tracy what she meant and Tracy, who wasn't normally given to reliving her experiences (preferring to forget them as soon as possible), stood there basking in the warmth and telling Ruth about the fat shirtwaist customer. It was the longest conversation she had ever had with this fellow resident of her block, but Tracy did not realize this. She simply stood there, savoring the warmth, licking the sugar that had lingered on her lips, and described for Ruth this big tub of lard who couldn't breathe in her shirtwaist. Tracy had a way of embellishing stories, though she would have denied that there was anything fanciful about her, and thought of herself as the only one in her family with any common sense whatsoever. But such phrases as "tub of lard," "yelping at my boss," and "waddling out the door with her seams splitting left and right," were not exactly the language of common sense and Ruth, laughing, was glad of it. She liked being entertained.

As Ruth stood there listening to Tracy, she thought that this slim, red-faced *shiksa* had lived in the neighborhood for at least three years, and she wondered why she had never known her better. But it was a crowded block of alien cultures, each wary of the other, and Ruth had learned in infancy never to trust Gentiles, who, no matter how appealingly they presented themselves, were all potential Cossacks, even the women. Still, there was no harm in listening, and especially in hearing Ruth's own nasty thoughts put into words. Ruth had been trained by her mother to be understanding, and a phrase like "tub of lard" would have incited her mother to anger even if applied to a waddling Gentile. Ladies didn't have ugly thoughts, Mama said. Ladies did not ridicule either the poor or the gentry. Ladies realized that there was good in all creatures, even the Cossacks.

"So did you get fined?" Ruth asked.

"No, not this time." On previous occasions and in previous jobs Tracy had been fined part of her wages for various infractions. But not this time, saints be praised. She'd bring home the full six dollars this week.

"You were lucky," said Ruth.

Tracy just shrugged.

"Or maybe not," said Ruth.

"Huh?"

"I mean living like that. Never sure if you'll have a job tomorrow."

Tracy narrowed her eyes. Though insensitive about many things, she reacted like a bloodhound to the merest hint of pity. "I'm no worse off than you are, I guess."

"Of course not," Ruth said hastily, reluctant to jeopardize this precarious relationship, for though she liked Tracy only a little better than she had liked her ten minutes earlier, she'd been amused by her for a while, and actually laughed. In the bakery such moments were rare. Most of her customers were worn women reciting their medical woes or complaining about their husbands and children. To Tracy she said, "I meant that *none* of us are lucky, living the way we do."

"Well, there's no use thinking about it," snapped Tracy, who thought about it to the point where she sometimes wished she could erase her brain.

"Sure there's a use," Ruth said. "You got to know where you are to figure out where you're going." This was one of her father's favorite pronouncements.

"I know well enough where I am," Tracy said.

"So what about where you're going? Ever think about that?"

"Twenty-four hours a day," Tracy said. She had concluded that there were only two ways out. Either you married a rich man or you became rich yourself. Since there were no rich men in her circle and since she didn't think herself beautiful enough to trap one, Tracy had decided on the second course. Of the ways that one might become rich she had immediately discarded the idea of being employed by someone else. No one ever got anywhere that way. She took into account *all* employment, including that in uptown parlor houses where the wages were said to be excellent. But moral considerations aside, this was out of the question for her because the owners and Tammany collected most of the earnings. No, the only way out was to be your own boss—but not in a business like Mednick's bakery. The people down here were as poor as the laborers they traded with. And the ones with hearts, like Ruth and her family, were the worst off of the lot because they extended credit to anyone with a hard-luck story, and half of them ended up worse off than their customers. Just last week old Minsk, a grocer on Market Street, had been dispossessed. Neighbors had passed the hat around, but there hadn't been enough for another month's rent, and now poor Minsk was boarding like a beggar with a family he had once kept off the pauper lists.

No, she didn't want to open her business in the slums, but if for some reason she was forced to, she would never extend a nickel's credit. No, not even a penny's. The only way people made money was to lock up their hearts, stretch forth their arms, and grab, grab, grab.

Tracy shared none of these thoughts with Ruth. Her ideas about business she wouldn't even share with her family, though Luke, the cousin from whom she hoped to borrow the money, would want to know the reason. The thought of approaching this rich relative made her nervous, and she didn't want to think about it sooner than she had to, so she thought instead of the cookies Ruth was placing in the display case.

"Give me a dozen," Tracy said impulsively, then remembered that just this morning she had given another stern lecture to the family about their wastefulness.

"A dozen?" Ruth said.

"No, never mind." Tracy shook her head, and Ruth seeing a familiar struggle going on, handed her one gratis.

"Thanks, but I don't take charity."

"Listen to her. Charity yet. All right, so pay me."

"I'm on a budget."

"Don't think of it as charity. Think of it as if a

neighbor dropped in and bought you a sweet."

"No, thanks."

"You're a strange one," Ruth said.

"And you're crazy. How do you expect to make any money if you're giving food away free?"

"We get along."

"I don't believe it."

There followed, though Tracy didn't quite know how they got onto the subject, a brief lecture by Ruth on the evils of capitalism and the virtues of something called socialism—terms Tracy had heard of but had not the slightest interest in. Pa was always saying that the Jews were as political as the Irish, but he felt that where Jews went in for wild foreign philosophies and wanted to overthrow the government, the Irish were democracy lovers and good Americans. These distinctions didn't interest Tracy any more than the politics did. She had a thorough distaste for such abstractions, and she judged politicians, when she judged them at all, by what they had actually done and not what philosophy they espoused. But she watched Ruth raptly, while not hearing a word, because she couldn't remember ever meeting a woman who was concerned with political matters, and certainly never one of her own age. Eighteen-year-olds were supposed to be busy looking for fellas.

Ruth spoke with a trace of an accent, for she had lived in Poland for the first seven years of her life, and Tracy was intrigued by this and by the animation in her eyes.

Ruth was saying, "... my father doesn't like it because he says it's not for ladies, but I go to the meetings anyway. My neighbors get mad. They say, what kind of business person is this, supporting factory workers yet? But I tell them if we don't do it who's going to do it? That's what I tell them. It's the cause that's important." She looked at Tracy expectantly, the gleam in her eyes matching in intensity the gleam of her black hair.

"What did you say?" said Tracy.

"The cause. Don't you support the unions?"

Tracy sighed and said half to herself, "The only cause I care about is Tracy Sullivan's cause." She recalled that the original issue had been a cookie and couldn't remember how they'd gotten from that to unions. Her impulse was to yawn and go, but there was something about this young woman that kept her here. Not common sense. This Ruth obviously had none of that. But something different. She didn't analyze further. She just stood there a while longer until she finally broke down and took the cookie.

"Come again," Ruth said, as Tracy headed for the door.

It was one of the friendliest remarks Tracy had ever received on this block, and she didn't know what to make of it. "Sure," she said, though she wasn't sure she would. But as she walked out into the cold she felt much warmer.

Chapter Two

Home was a three-room flat on the third floor of a tenement that, though it was less than ten years old, looked ancient enough to have been erected in the era of the first Dutch settlers. As Tracy hurried toward the entrance, she nearly collided with Michael Ryan, her neighbor across the airshaft, who was bound for the adjacent building.

"'Lo, Michael."

"Tracy."

"Cold tonight, huh?"

"Yeah," he said.

"Night, Michael."

"So long."

This was the extent of their conversation, though they had known each other for four years, their brothers and sisters visited back and forth, and she hadn't seen Michael around since Christmas. He was two years older than she, a lordly twenty, black-haired and attractive, if one preferred scowls to pleasant smiles. Which Tracy did not. When it came to men, she had a hard time deciding what to do about them. On the one hand, she was drawn to the smiling young charmers who winked at her as she passed in the street or told her she was pretty (which she didn't always believe). On the other hand, the word "weak" might have been stamped on the foreheads of these blarney boys, for she'd never known a charmer who wasn't also a drinker and/or philanderer, money-squanderer, and scrapper. But the quiet types like Michael were even worse. They were more honest and reliable, but they were often bad-tempered and rude as well. If she had to choose, she would probably choose the blarney, but it would have to be the blarney of a rich man.

She plodded wearily up the three flights and into the kitchen, which was packed with family: Her grandfather, her sisters, Mary and Kerry, her brothers, Patrick and Tommy, all sat guzzling their soup. Everyone was here but Pa, who was either still working or down at Flanagan's hoisting a few. Tracy had given up hoping that Pa would tote his load. She, Tracy, was the full-time breadwinner, and Pa could be relied on only for surprise windfalls. Her sister Mary ran the house, while Pat earned a few dollars peddling papers. He, Kerry, and Tommy were still in school and too young to be taken out of it, though Tracy wouldn't have hesitated to pull Pat out had she not made all sorts of deathbed promises to Ma.

"Shhh," Tommy said to his younger sister. "The crab's home."

"That's not nice," chided his older sister Mary. "Tracy works hard and needs her quiet."

In this family Tracy played the role of the mean old father, Tracy thought. But at least real fathers had saloons to run to, liquor to drown themselves in. Nothing like that for her. If Tracy was the father, then Mary (a year younger) was the mother, and their real father became one of the kids. Gramp was the only one who filled the expected role, handing down fatherly advice from time to time, telling stories of the old country, soothing them all when they were unhappy. Gramp and Mary were the only ones Tracy really loved. There had been Ma, of course, but Ma was long dead and Tracy could love only her memory.

"Make sure the children are staying in school and going to church," Ma had said before she died. "And make sure your father's marrying again. . . . There, there, Tracy, none of your pouts. He'll be needing a woman and you'll be needing a mother and that's the fact of it."

In those days they had lived in a charming Connecticut factory town. Here Tracy and the others had been born and raised, Pa and Gramp had had steady work at the factory, and Ma did fancy work and mending for the gentry. The children had attended a fine common school, had spent afternoons strolling through the hills (one of which afforded an exquisite view of the Connecticut River), and had come home to balanced meals and smiling faces. Of course it would have seemed reasonable to Ma that they would prosper even after she was gone. After all, they had lived comfortably, if frugally, in a nicely kept two-story company house. And they knew many people in the town. Even the prospects for marriage had been good, for in this place the children of factory people could actually marry into the gentry. A lawyer's son had claimed for his own the tawny-haired daughter of a janitor, and few who knew the girl had found many objections to make.

It had been a fairy-tale life, though Tracy, having been born to it, did not realize this at the time. And then, bit by bit, it had all been taken away. First Ma had died of the great white plague, consumption. How she had contracted that foul disease in the clear and clean Connecticut hills no one could guess. Pa, though grieving, had plodded on somehow, and the children, as promised, stayed in school. Then, six months later, in 1890, the first Italians began coming in. Hungry and willing to work for low wages, they had one by one replaced the native and Irish workers. Pa had never expected his own job to be taken away. The factory owners were more like friends than bosses. Didn't he go up to the big house at Christmas and Easter and partake of toasts to the Savior with his whole family in tow? And hadn't his bosses shed tears and sent flowers when his Delia, God rest her soul, was called to her reward? Folks like that wouldn't turn their backs on a man just because some dago wanted to work for a few pennies less. Folks like that, who'd watched over him and his kin for thirteen years, would watch over them forever like the lords in old Europe. And a good thing it was too, for he was grieving too much to be worrying how he was going to feed the children.

But America wasn't Europe, as Tom found out on the day he received his notice. When America discarded its nobility it did away with paternalism too. There were no other towns to go to, for adjacent milltowns were either laying off or replacing the Irish with Italians and Poles. Nowhere to go except back to the city of his youth where at least there were pals and some family and Tammany to send a basket when the going got rough.

So it was out of the picturesque company house with the garden out back and the view of the hills, out of the town with the rambling trees and the rosy-cheeked children. Into the train and down to the city and onto the noisy Els and creaking trolleys. Past the pushcarts and up, up, up to the third floor of a crumbling tenement building that reeked of fish and urine.

That had been four years ago, and Tracy had thought she would never survive the change. Yet she had learned some valuable lessons about people and about how the powerful treated the weak. They were truths that she never, even in relaxed moments, forgot. But they were also truths she was glad her mother had been spared. And now, as this eighteen-year-old girl playing father took her place at the table, she saw her mother's face in her mind, and thought, Thank God you never lived to see this, Ma.

The talk flowed around her as it did every night. Foolish talk of school lessons and childhood gangs and how Danny McGarrity got sick and the teacher sent him home. Mary was silent, preoccupied with serving and clearing away the dishes, and Gramp said little, for he was relishing the last bit of soup. Tracy was silent too, but it was not the silence of contentment. It was pure fatigue mixed with a little anger. She was annoyed by the silly laughter of the children. As though there were anything to laugh about. Didn't they realize that their Pa would be coming home drunk, and their oldest sister's job was in jeopardy, that the landlord was threatening to raise the rent, and that the toilet down the hall was blocked up again? Of course not. All they did was laugh or quarrel or accuse Tracy of being a crab. Yet a part of her welcomed the laughter. The part that was her mother was saying, "Don't be fretting about the troubles. The important thing is the family's together, and that's all I ever wanted."

"I need a new ribbon for my hair," Kerry said.

"Need?" Tracy said through gritted teeth.

"Yeah."

"You mean, 'want.' What's wrong with the two you have?"

"They're awful and old. Can I have a penny?"

"Oh, hush up and let me finish my soup!" Tracy snarled.

"Well, you don't have to have a duck fit."

"One more word out of you and I'll smash you against the wall."

"You been working out in boxing rings?" Gramps said with a smile.

"Oh, quit teasing!" Tracy cried impatiently,

28

though she seldom spoke shortly to her grandfather. Always a hardworking man, he was now frail and beset by rheumatism that was often extremely painful. Yet he rarely complained or got drunk as his son would have done. Even now he had a job of sorts—whittling pipes for a local shop. The amount he earned was so negligible as not even to figure in Tracy's budget, but he did earn some and he gave of it generously, and without his steadying presence the household would have been chaotic.

She closed her eyes briefly, in part to shut her sister Kerry out, then opened them slowly, sighed, and sipped more of her soup. "I'll be late getting home tomorrow," she said to Mary.

"Oh? Why?"

"Overtime," she lied—and her heart fluttered as she considered her true mission. Suppose cousin Luke wouldn't loan her the money? Suppose he said she was too young? Or suppose—perish the thought—he just turned her away?

She didn't know Luke very well. He was one of a hundred distant cousins living in and around New York. Gramp knew him better and Pa knew him best of all, since there had been long-ago adolescent capers in which both Luke and Pa had been involved. Luke had risen from the slums and was now an uptown swell, a doctor with an office near Washington Square who occasionally donated time to a settlement house down here on the East Side. This was where Pa had run into his cousin again, two summers ago after twenty-some years. Ran into him

29

and hated him thoroughly for being so successful where he, Tom, had failed. Yet Pa had called him to the flat to tend Gramp during one of his bad spells. And later Tracy had met Luke again at the wake of a mutual relative. A middle-aged man, attractive and decent too for al! Pa's tales of Luke's checkered past: street gangs, involvement with the Tweed Ring, false high school papers, using connections and Tammany money to bluff his way through medical school. He had married into the lace-curtain gentry and done well for himself professionally and financially, but she'd overheard Pa saying to a cousin that Luke had once jeopardized everything for some mistress everyone but his wife knew about.

How true these stories were Tracy had no idea. Nor did she care a whit. She knew only that she had a rich relative and that as things stood now he was their only link to a decent future. She would present her plan first and then ask him for the money. Then she would offer him a share in the business. Or should she offer the share first? And should she plead the poverty of her family or pretend that things weren't so bad? She'd been raised to be proud and she'd long resisted the idea of asking a farthing from Catholic Charities or the city tills. But pride too had its limits and she wasn't about to starve for it. Besides, Luke was family. Distant family, but still blood—and with the same last name of Sullivan. That ought to mean something to him.

"You finished, Tracy?" Mary removed the soup bowl and placed a cup of coffee on the table. The children had gone to the flats of friends to be free of the glowering presence of their oldest sister. Gramp, having finished his soup, had limped to the next room and rest. Tracy took the coffee and sipped, warming her still-cold hands on the cracked cup. She looked around the bleak crowded room. The coal stove, the shelves of cheap dishes, the laundry tub, the window facing the airshaft, the sink, the peeling walls with the crucifix and a sketch of President Cleveland cut from a newspaper, the thin curtain leading to other rooms. The kitchen in a tenement was the room a family actually lived in. During the winter everyone clustered here because it was the only place that was warm. Here families ate, did homework, cooked, washed and mended clothes, washed their bodies, and in some cases made a living sewing or making paper flowers. The "parlor" was the kitchen table. Sitting on worn rickety chairs around the oilcloth-covered tables, families traded news, argued, dreamed, gossiped, greeted guests, celebrated holidays, congregated after funerals, planned for the future.

The two rooms behind the kitchen were used as bedrooms. In the Sullivan household the room that faced the street was euphemistically called a parlor. It even featured one straight-backed chair to symbolize gentility, but it was actually the bedroom of Tracy's father and the boys and was strewn end to end with bedding. Tracy and her sisters shared the back part of a middle room, and Gramp, separated from them by a curtain, got the front end, which was closest to the kitchen and heat.

Tracy was content to sit alone at the table with Mary, for Mary was soothing, as their mother had been. She was a quiet girl who spent what little leisure time she had devouring library books or writing poems. Tracy didn't understand her sister, but she respected her. Mary didn't whine or plead for hair ribbons or come in drunk. Instead, she used Tracy's meager earnings to buy potatoes, celery, day-old bread, onions, salt pork, tripe, or soupbones, which she cooked into edible if not delicious concoctions. And she rarely asked for extra because she knew that if there had been anything to spare Tracy would already have handed it over. Tracy did not tell her sister about the wolfed-down rolls at Mednick's. True, it had only involved pennies, but pennies added up, and according to their strict budgeting plan every cent was to be accounted for. She felt a twinge of guilt, then chided herself for her foolishness. Would that fat pig in the shirtwaist have felt guilty about sneaking two buns after ten hours' work and a walk from the El in the February cold? Not likely.

"Tell me about the world out there," said Mary, who saw enough of it in her daily marketing trips. But this block wasn't glamorous Fifth Avenue where Tracy worked.

Tracy did not repeat the story of her customer. No sense letting Mary know how close to losing the rent money they had come. To say nothing of jeopardizing the job itself. She said, "Same old world," and

32

yawned loudly, not bothering to cover her mouth. Then she said, "I saw Michael coming in. When did he get back? Or is it just a visit?"

"He's back. Day before yesterday, I think Maureen told me."

"Where was he, do you know?"

"You'd know as much as I do."

"Yeah." One of the girls on the street had said that Michael had been living since Christmas with a woman in Hell's Kitchen, another New York slum. The husband had run out on the woman and she couldn't divorce because she was a good Catholic, so she'd taken Michael in as a roommate. It was a nice arrangement, the gossip had said, and convenient to Michael's job. Hell's Kitchen was a few miles away, though, and the rumor had not been substantiated. Still, it was a juicy story. "What if he leaves her with a baby?" Tracy said.

Mary shrugged. "Let's hope he doesn't."

"But I wonder why he's back home now. He hates his father so much. Maybe I'll ask him."

But she didn't think she would. She didn't know Michael well anymore, though they'd been close when she had first moved here. He'd grown silent and sullen a lot of the time, and he spent so much time away from the neighborhood that these days she knew him no better than she knew Ruth Mednick.

She said to her sister, "Do you know Ruth Mednick?"

"Not too well. Pa likes me to shop at McGarrity's."

"Oh, Pa!" Tracy made a face. Everyone deferred to

33

him though no one respected him much. It was a habit instilled in them long ago by Ma and one that was hard to break.

"What about Ruth?" Mary asked.

"I went in there today to get warm. We talked for a bit."

"She's nice, isn't she?"

Tracy shrugged. She was not as generous as her sister and nowhere near as trusting of people.

The two went to bed early, snuggling together under the blankets in the bed they shared. It was cold and they shivered until the body heat was trapped in the blankets. Across the room eight-year-old Kerry babbled in her sleep. Tracy, who was having trouble sleeping anyway, got up and tiptoed through Gramp's part of the room to the kitchen. She lit a kerosene lamp and warmed water for tea, rubbing her hands over the stove to thaw what felt like ice on the tips of her fingers. After a while Pa came in, weaving slightly but not as drunk as usual. He greeted her amiably, said he'd worked a construction job today, and presented her with two dollars, which she put into Mary's tin can till. It was his only contribution this week, though more had probably been drunk away down at Flanagan's.

Mary had urged Tracy to try to understand their father. He'd not been himself since Ma's death. He needed patience and sympathy, and if they'd just bear with it he'd come round again and be his old ambitious self. But patience was not one of Tracy's virtues. The best she could manage was to keep from screaming at him.

"I could do with some of that," her father said.

"Tea, Pa?"

"Warm my insides."

Mother of God! she thought. As though they weren't warm enough already. She sloshed some tea into a cup and set it on the table. His large hands looked strange holding the delicate vessel. They were designed for steins of beer. He was a big man but thin, and the effects of alcohol were beginning to show in his too-red face. His brown hair was graying, and he resembled Gramp more and more, though he was only forty-two. But a weaker Gramp with vacant blue eyes and a mouth that trembled.

She decided to use the subject of Gramp as an opening wedge to get Pa to the subject of Luke. The more she knew about this legendary rich cousin the better off she would be. She said, "We must get what's his name, our cousin who's a doctor, to come look at Gramp more often."

"Luke?"

"Yeah. Luke. How's he related to us?"

"His great-grandfather and mine were brothers in Galway."

"When did you find that out?"

"Years ago when Luke and his folks were living on Elizabeth Street. Him and me . . ." Pa trailed off.

"Bagged money for the Tweed boys?" she prompted.

"Everyone done it in them days."

"Anyway, he seems like a nice man."

Tom shrugged. "Got a swelled head if you ask me. Stuck up and lording it over his old pals. I was always wondering if his wife knew the truth about him. She's a grand lady. I met her years ago. A great beauty—blonde and dressed like a princess. Luke didn't deserve her."

"He deserved a chance with the gentry, same as everybody else."

"Well, maybe, but he's still low-class and he showed it. All but booted the lady over for some silly piece used to work in the settlement with him."

"The Henry Street Settlement?"

"Elizabeth Street. His old neighborhood."

Tracy wondered how a man who would give his time to a settlement could be the stuck-up swell Pa described. She said, "How do you know about his other woman?"

Normally Tom would have clammed up at this point. Where matters of sex were concerned Tom, like many Irishmen, was prudish. It wasn't a subject for discussion in any mixed company, much less with a nubile daughter. But he'd been drinking, and to him Tracy wasn't much of a daughter. She was pretty, but she wasn't gentle and feminine as her mother had been or his daughter Mary. She was hard and practical to the point of irritation, to the point where he felt less manly than she. So, fogged by alcohol as he was, he went on discussing Cousin Luke's peccadilloes as though Tracy were a chum at the saloon. His language remained proper, for he was not given to coarseness even when drunk. But the substance was most improper indeed.

"Well, he had this office near Washington Square. It's the house of some other doctor—a surgeon or something—and Luke rents the office from him. The surgeon has a sister. A young widow. They say she owns a mill in Massachusetts, but you wouldn't believe it if you saw her. Twenty-five or so and not a sensible bone in her body. And I never believed she ran no mill. Anyway, she came down to the settlement with Luke a couple o' summers ago when I had that job on Canal Street. I'd watch 'em prancing up and down the street looking into each other's eyes, all but kissing and hugging. The folks in the neighborhood they wondered how the mill was getting on while she was here in New York chasing around with a married man."

"But you said they worked at the settlement. They must have *worked* once in a while."

"Maybe they did, but the only time I saw 'em was when they come by Canal Street. And there was one other time I saw 'em leaving a hotel together. Bobby—that's Luke's brother—he was with me. Bobby was always out of work, never two nickels to rub together, and I thought he'd use it. There would've been money in it."

"Blackmail? His own brother?"

"He didn't use it, though."

How kind of him, thought Tracy wryly. "Is the girl still around?"

"One of the coppers I know in the Sixth, he said she went back to Massachusetts. Maybe someone found out about them. Maybe there really was a mill."

"And Luke's still married to the princess?"

Tom nodded. "They have a couple of boys. Both of them spoiled rotten, I hear."

Spoiled indeed, Tracy thought. They had probably just had a normal life. The poor had a regular bag of sour grapes to explain away their lot in life. The favorite slogan, of course, was that money was the root of all evil. But there were many other ways of saying the same thing, and spoiled children was one of them. Tracy understood this. She too had enjoyed making fun of the wealthy. But she was more eager than most to trade in the sour grapes for the type of life she had always poked fun at. Convictions weren't sacred to her, but money was. And tomorrow she was going to start going after it.

Chapter Three

Before leaving for work the next morning she went to a great deal of trouble with her hair. Normally she wore the pale brown hair pulled back with a ribbon, but today it was important that she look older. She was going to tell Luke she was twenty-one. With Mary's help they got the mess up and anchored with hairpins while the front tendrils went through the tortures of a curling iron. She had told Mary only that shopgirls were treated better if they looked mature. No one in the family knew of the scheme she had in mind.

There was nothing to be done about her clothing. Her boss had sold her two nice shirtwaists on discount and the white one was very rich-looking and appropriate, but the one blue poplin skirt was all she had to complete the outfit. For a wrap, she had to settle for the old gray jacket she wore all winter long. The hat was a dreary navy that Mary usually wore for Sunday mass. When Tracy finished her lengthy toilette she sighed in dismay. She looked older but just as shabby.

She had made the appointment the week before at

Luke's office on Tenth Street off Fifth. Thursday at 6:15, which gave her fifteen minutes to get from the shop to his office—and her nose had better not be shiny or her hair in disarray. At six she dashed into the washroom, worked quickly and furiously to get herself in shape, then tore out the door and down Fifth, holding onto her hat and her hair and praying that neither would fail her now.

The house in which Luke rented an office stood on a street full of similar dwellings. Smug four-story brownstones, some with little fences in front and steep stairways leading to the main entrance, which stood well above street level. A hanging sign proclaimed the offices of Douglas Wilson, M.D., and Luke Sullivan, M.D. Douglas Wilson must be the brother of Luke's mistress. He either knew nothing of what was going on or he knew full well and for some reason tolerated it. Tracy wondered if she'd ever learn the full story.

She entered through the imposing doors, her heart hammering in her ears, then walked into the doctors' waiting room, which was empty and abundantly provided with well-thumbed magazines. Last week, when she had made the appointment, a portly receptionist had been at the desk. But she wasn't there now, so Tracy must have the last appointment. She heard someone moving in one of the three rooms opening off this one and she wondered if she should knock. Normally, she wouldn't have hesitated. Tracy believed in taking risks, reasoning that even if you lost it was better than doing nothing at all. But now she sat down and twined her hands together. Her future and her family's future depended on this moment, and she'd better remember what she was about. Suppose he had a patient in there and she disturbed his concentration by banging on the door? It would put him in a mood that might affect all his attitudes this day. Better to sit and wait.

It was fifteen minutes before the door opened, and when it did no patient emerged. Only Luke, looking thin and very tired. He was coughing and moving wearily toward the coatrack. He stopped when he saw her and said, "Did I have another appointment?"

"Yes," she said. And then added, "doctor." It was plain that he didn't recognize her. And why hadn't the receptionist entered her name in the book? The name Sullivan might have meant something to this other Sullivan, even if it was one of the most common Irish names.

He walked over to the receptionist's desk, looked at the appointment book, and said, "Oh, yes. Theresa Sullivan. The nurse must've forgotten to remind me. It's after hours."

"Yes," Tracy said, disappointed because the surname had still failed to strike a responsive chord. "You took care of my grandfather Dan once."

"Dan?"

"Sullivan. He's your cousin. We're distantly related."

"Dan?" he said again, coughing.

"Tom's father."

"Tom's father," he repeated. "Which Tom?"

She gave the address of the family's flat, and his confusion vanished at once. "Oh, *that* Tom. Monroe Street Tom. I've got a lot of relatives named Dan or Tom." He paused. "So you're his daughter?"

"Yes. We've met before."

"Have we? Well, we meet again. Now what seems to be the trouble, young lady?"

"It's not a medical problem."

"I see." He brushed at his graying black hair. "Well, what sort of problem is it then?"

"More of a well—well—a family problem."

He studied her for a moment, his brows knit. He was certainly attractive, she thought, for all that he was middle-aged. Tall, black-haired, and dark-eyed with enough gray in his hair to make him look distinguished and yet not old. He said, "In that case, why don't you come into our consultation room."

She nodded and stood, smoothing the dreary poplin skirt. She followed him in. He sat behind a desk and she on a leather chair facing him. He poured himself some brandy and apologized because he did not have a suitable refreshment for young ladies.

He said, "Now then, to the business at hand."

"Yes." Her heart raced like a drum roll.

He coughed again, sipped some more brandy, and looked at her inquiringly.

She cleared her throat. She had rehearsed this scene a dozen times and had decided during the first few rehearsals that there'd be no sense in beating around the bush. She launched into her speech, which had

42

been carefully memorized, with special attention given the vocabulary and the grammar. "Well, doctor, I have a business venture in mind and I need to borrow money. I intend to repay it at the standard interest rate, but I preferred to deal with a relative in lieu of a bank."

He was silent for a moment, though his mouth twitched—whether in amusement or with impatience she could not determine. He said, "You're rather young to be dealing with a bank, much less a business."

"I'm twenty-one," she said, looking directly into his eyes.

He looked skeptical but said, "May I ask what sort of business you had in mind?"

She resumed the rehearsed speech that consisted of sentences it had taken some time to compose. She hoped the grammar was correct. "There are many working girls in New York, as you know, and it had occurred to me that they might enjoy a pleasant establishment in which to take their noonday refreshment. There are few such in the city." (Pause.) "After some thought, I came upon the idea of a tearoom for working girls. That would be the name of it, I decided. The Working Girls' Tearoom." (Pause.) "I would serve tea and some pastry, but the patrons could bring their own lunch, for most of them cannot afford a lunch out." Perfect delivery, she thought, feeling more confident.

He considered her proposal for a moment, his expression inscrutable. Then he said, "Then business hours would be confined to the noon hour?''

"Oh, no. Anyone could come in at any hour."

"But not many working girls are free to do that,"
he said. "Not to discourage you, Miss Sullivan, but if
you're going to go into business, you ought to try to
make the venture as profitable as possible."

"But this would be—"

"No." He shook his head. "Working girls would
have only a half hour at lunch to spend in your place,
so most of your business would have to come from
ladies of leisure. And they'd demand watercress
sandwiches or biscuits imported from England or
some such, which would make operations rather too
complicated for your purposes. If you want working
girls, you don't open a tearoom. You set up a
pushcart for the hour between twelve and one."

She could see his point, though she didn't want to.
Her head grew light as she realized that things were
going very badly.

His voice seemed to come to her from a distance.
"Miss Sullivan?"

"Yes?" she said dully.

"Do you see what I mean?"

She didn't answer.

"Theresa—may I call you Theresa?"

"Yeah. Uh—yes, doctor. But Tracy's what most
people call me."

"Tracy then. My name's Luke. You can omit the
'cousin.' Call me Luke."

She nodded.

"I'm going to ask you again how old you are."

44

"Twenty-one."

"You don't look it."

"But I am."

"Tell the truth," he said in so sharp a tone that she winced.

"Eighteen," she whispered.

"That's more like it." He paused. "I suppose people have told you you're too young to open a business?"

"I haven't told anyone my plans."

"Well, you are," he said. "Much too young. Did you finish grammar school?"

"Yes."

"Any high school?"

"No, but—"

"Still, you're well spoken. No accent either. You don't sound like the"—he had been about to say "slums" but chose the more diplomatic "city."

"I grew up in Connecticut," she said.

He remembered someone telling him that Flannel-Mouth Tom (the name by which Tracy's father was known in the family to distinguish him from other Toms) had lived for a while in a factory town and then fallen on hard times. He said, "That explains the accent. And your early education was good, I imagine?"

"Oh, yes. Excellent."

"That helps, but it's not enough."

"Yes, it *is*," she cried, forgetting that she had promised herself to be composed no matter what he said.

He took a deep breath. "Tracy, you want to borrow money. If you want me to consider giving it, you'll have to listen to what I have to say."

She wound her hands together to still her panic. "All right."

"I have a few ideas, but I need time to consider them and I have a lot of questions to ask you. Now it's well past six and I imagine you're as hungry as I am, so why don't we continue this discussion over dinner?"

"In a restaurant?" she said, looking with dismay at the frayed sleeve of her jacket.

"Of course in a restaurant. Let me ring up my wife to tell her I'll be late. Will your family be expecting you soon?"

"I told them I'd be late too."

"Fine." He rose slowly and she noticed again how very tired he looked. She hadn't realized this the two previous times she had seen him.

They dined in an elegant Broadway restaurant with a white damask tablecloth, gigantic chandeliers, and well-dressed people bound for the theater. She had never been in such a place before and was worried that he might notice her clumsiness with silverware and napkins. She knew he had once been a slum boy himself and that he'd be more likely to sympathize than sneer, but the future proprietor of a tearoom ought to know something about these things, and she made a determined effort. She would wait for him to pick up a spoon and then try to follow his lead. This wasn't easy. She had never seen so much food even at Thanksgiving Day dinners, and she longed to gobble it down. But she demurely sipped her soup and consumed the biscuits in dainty nibbles as though long accustomed to such feasts. Over the roast beef he finally resumed their discussion, asking her to explain to him the reasons she wished to open a business. She told him the truth: that in her opinion business was the only way out. He nodded, saying he'd once felt that way too. "After all," he said, "a doctor is a man in business for himself."

He asked about her family, about her childhood in Connecticut, about her mother's death, her father's dismissal from the factory, the move to the city, her current job and responsibilities at home. It was hard for her to answer, and at one point she was afraid she might cry. So she pretended that she was talking about some other family and managed to project a dispassionate air. It worked very well, though she could no longer taste her wonderful meal.

Luke wasn't tasting anything either. As Tracy unreeled this distressing story, his thoughts went back to his own youth. They were very much alike, Tracy and he, though he had been living in New York when his parents, a sister, and brother had died in a cholera epidemic, leaving him in charge of what remained of the family. Thirty-some years had passed since then and still the city brutalized its children. Here sat this thin slip of a girl who would be old before she was twenty. A pretty girl too, though she probably didn't realize it. She ought to be dressed in velvets and giggling over boys instead of sitting here putting up a preposterously brave front, her brain frantically working as she calculated the moves she must make in order to stay in his good graces.

"Would you like some more wine, Tracy?"

"Yes. A little."

He poured her some wine. He wanted to see her relax. She was young enough to be his daughter, he thought, yet she'd lived the life of a fifty-year-old woman. What would she have been like if Tom had pampered her? Toys, sweets, tickets to the circus, pretty clothes, a ladies' seminary, a good college. She'd be like Kathy . . . But he didn't want to think of Kathy. A year and a half had passed since they had planned to run away and then realized that it would never work. A year and a half had passed, yet a night didn't go by that he didn't long for her.

Luke drank the wine but pushed his plate aside. He wasn't feeling well. A cold, he preferred to tell himself. But he'd been a doctor too long not to know what was probably wrong with him: the rheumatic fever of his tenement years making good on its promise. He could see himself being written up in a textbook. "The disease remained quiescent for thirty years and then at the age of forty-one, the patient began experiencing edema and shortness of breath. This is the typical history. . . ." So many years, so many accomplishments, and yet the slums reached across it all, determined to beat him. Would he be the winner instead, he wondered? Not likely with rheumatic heart disease, but he would fight.

He tried to smile at Tracy, and she smiled back, warily. She had lovely hazel eyes and smooth fair skin. If she made it out of the slums, he wondered, would they chase her down the years as they had chased him? No, he wanted to believe she'd get away over some invisible border where the past could never reach her.

He felt the pressure of tears and fought them back. Odd that she'd affected him so strongly. In this city alone he had scores of relatives, many in circumstances more straitened than hers. And there were his patients too, the bulk of them impoverished East Siders. He heard stories like Tracy's every day and managed not to listen too hard. For he knew he couldn't save them all even if he were a Carnegie. And he was anything but that. Many of his stocks had melted away in the Panic of '93. He wasn't exactly starving, but he had his wife and his sons and the future to consider and if he gave money to one cousin, every third cousin once removed would be holding a hat out. In order to be fair, he'd have to give so much away that he and the family would end up in the street.

He said, "Tracy, I'd like to help you, but I want you to promise me something first."

Her eyes widened and she nodded.

"That you won't tell anyone who gave you the money."

"But if people ask me how—"

"You found it in a pouch in the gutter."

She smiled. "But it would only be a loan. I will pay you back and with interest too. I'm going to offer you a share in the—"

"I know it's a loan," he said, "but other people may wonder why I'd loan money to you and not to them."

"Oh, I see."

"I have a nephew who'd like to own a saloon and a sister who thinks she should buy stocks while the market's down and—but you get the idea."

"Yes sir. I promise I'll never tell." Dare she ask what amount he had in mind? She'd been hoping for three hundred, but maybe he was thinking in terms of fifty.

"That's settled then," he said. "Now I'd like to discuss the business itself."

He told her that the tearoom idea hadn't sounded promising but that he did agree that the working girl market was a good one to tap. "Some say it's a passing phenomenon, the idea of women going out to work, but we all know industry's here to stay and it's a fair bet that women won't be returning to the farm again."

He told her that a patient of his believed that one machine in particular would revolutionize women's lives. Not the sewing machine or the telephone as might be expected. No, the miracle machine would be the typewriter. It would change the face of business, this patient had said.

This device had been in commercial use since the seventies, but only in recent years had it begun taking hold. It had been mainly a gadget for male secretaries in big businesses, but Luke reminded Tracy that female secretaries, called shorthand-typists, existed too. Not many, but their numbers were increasing at a geometric rate; and by 1900 there would be an even greater demand for them. He asked if this suggested anything to her.

"You think I should be a shorthand-typist?"

"Well, you'd have to start as one, yes. And then?"

"I'd be promoted and get to be president of the company?" She grinned, feeling more at ease with him now.

He smiled too. "No, you'd leave the company and go out and buy some typewriters. Then you'd open a school. *Voilà*, your own business. Sullivan's Office-Skills School. Typing, stenography, filing skills taught."

She knit her brow. "But I don't have any of these skills, so how can I teach them? And where would I learn to work a typing machine?"

"Some typewriter companies train girls. Or you can learn from a fellow clerk. There are places that teach stenography too. You'd have to learn that."

She thought for a moment. "But if people are already teaching those things, how would my school be so special?"

"You wouldn't teach just skills. You'd teach dress and demeanor, grammar, telephone manners too. The telephone will be in very wide use pretty soon. And even if your school is identical to someone else's, what difference would it make? People haven't

51

stopped opening restaurants just because someone else thought of the idea first."

"How do you know so many things? I thought doctors spent all their time chasing germs."

He smiled. "I'm like you. I've always had an ear cocked for new ways of making a buck. We have similar backgrounds, Tracy."

It wasn't until the end of the meal that he mentioned an amount. "I'll give you four hundred for the future business and another hundred fifty to get yourself some clothes, some training, and to keep bringing home the bacon. It's all I can spare, I'm afraid."

"All?" she gasped. He'd promised more than she would have dreamed of.

"Typewriters cost a fortune. Rent costs a lot. And there'll be advertising expenses, equipment, employees, nonharassment for the cops, and expenses you can't even imagine. But do it the way I tell you. The clothes first, the training next—and then I'll find you a job with one of my grateful dyspeptics. Most of my financially successful patients are dyspeptics—which ought to discourage you but won't."

She studied his face, slowly shaking her head in disbelief. Five hundred and fifty dollars!

He said gently, "You've never quite believed there was any good in the world, have you?"

"I did once. But not in a long time."

"There's good around, Tracy, but it comes up rarely, so don't ever expect or depend on it." He was immediately sorry he had said this, for she was already a little too hard and didn't need him to give more lessons in cynicism. But he couldn't in conscience withdraw the statement either.

Through dessert they discussed typing and stenography instruction and he promised to get her not only the money (in cash) but also the names of places where she might learn her skills. As they were leaving he said, "My sister Alison still lives on the East Side. On Elizabeth down near Bayard. Never had any desire to leave, if you can believe that. She's one person I wouldn't mind knowing our secret. She keeps secrets well, Alison does." He gave Tracy the address. "She's a teacher. She might have advice on educational techniques, so feel free to talk to her." He paused. "I'll have the money for you tomorrow. Come over to the office at about ten."

"I'll be working then, but as soon as—"

"Not anymore. You're going to school and lying about where you've been all day."

"You mean I can quit tomorrow?"

"Tomorrow."

"Thank God."

"You're very welcome," he said.

The two of them laughed and clinked wine glasses.

Chapter Four

No new acquaintance observing Tracy in the months of March and April 1895 would have believed that she had ever been short-tempered. Fired with plans, resplendent in new (though economical) attire, she was the essence of sunny good humor as she bounced toward the El each morning on the way to her classes. Everyone who already knew her was amazed. Her sister Mary, her father, and her grandfather had not seen Tracy so happy since the carefree Connecticut days before her mother had died.

"It's spring," she would say to whoever asked. "No, I'm not in love . . . no, I haven't gotten a raise . . . it's just that it's spring."

The family, of course, knew nothing about her loan and nothing about the courses she was taking. Every Saturday she came home with her weekly wage of six dollars, and no one had a clue that she wasn't earning it at Midridge's Shop. Someday soon she would coolly announce that she'd gotten a job as a secretary and if anyone asked how she'd acquired the skills, she would say she'd been trained on the job.

Luke had asked her to keep him posted, and she dropped into his office once a week to tell him of her progress and of her ideas for the future. She had also made the acquaintance of his sister Alison who played her part in the charade, even going so far as to offer Tracy her flat as a place to study stenography when she needed the quiet.

On the street she said hello to people she had ignored these four years, and she became more trusting too. Ruth Mednick became a bona fide friend and the butcher traded jokes with her. Even her brothers stopped fleeing the kitchen when she came in the door.

At the end of April, having mastered the skills required, Tracy accepted a shorthand-typist position with Thomas and Rand Associates (Rand was one of Luke's dyspeptics), an advertising agency. She had no idea at first what such an agency did but learned quickly. There were companies who paid Thomas and Rand for writing and sketching advertisements and seeing to their placement in newspapers, magazines, the walls of buildings, and the sides of trolleys. Tracy's job was to type up letters sent by her boss to the client company covering such subjects as the advisability of using the word "grand" rather than "good" in describing a tooth powder, the estimated cost of advertising a patent medicine in three major papers over the length of two months, the question of how detailed a sketch should be drawn of such items as ladies' corsets, and the question of where her boss might take the client to dine next week. For this she earned the princely wage of eight dollars a week. Moreover, the company was small and jolly, numbering only fifteen people who, when they weren't busy, actually joked away the hours. Unbelievable! Too good to be true! Every morning when she came in she surreptitiously knocked wood.

The wood failed her within three weeks. The company lost a major account and the last to be hired was the first to be fired. She was out on the street again but not daunted. At least she'd actually been a shorthand-typist and could say she was experienced.

It was while she was looking for another position that Luke told her he was leaving for an extended holiday on Long Island. She had stopped in his office at lunch hour and he said, "This blasted bronchitis has hung on all spring and the only place to get rid of it is at the shore. My wife's family has a place on Long Island."

"Then you won't be here for my weekly progress report?"

"I'm afraid not, Tracy, but take notes, huh? I'll be interested in hearing whether your next boss prefers 'good' tooth powders to 'grand' ones."

"You don't take my job seriously," she teased.

"Oh, I do. I do. In any case I'm glad to see you smiling."

All she'd needed was hope. She wanted to tell him that and also to tell him she wished he'd been her father, for she loved him very much. But he seemed not to be in a serious mood and anyway it would be hard to explain why she'd rather have him for a father than Tom. So instead she laughed and said, "Take you to lunch, mister?"

"You can't afford it."

"Yes I can. It's your money I'm using."

Over a fish and chips lunch he told her to wait at least a year before taking the fatal step. "If you're going to do it, Tracy, do it right. Learn as much about the business as you can. Make sure you've got money in reserve just in case you fail. But don't go into business *expecting* to fail."

It was two weeks before one of Luke's contacts came through with another position. This one was a lot drearier—she was a shorthand-typist for a purchasing agent for a men's cloak and suit manufacturer in a run-down building on Canal Street that looked like a firetrap. The office employees—most of them tired old men—were a sober lot. But the place was within walking distance of the flat so that she could save carfare, the wages were $8.50 a week, and her boss said that the work was steady and that industry would be rewarded. What with Luke's absence and the dullness of the job, the excitement of early spring gradually subsided. She settled into a routine again, but it wasn't so deadly as it had been in years past, for now she had something to look forward to.

IN SUMMER on the Lower East Side, the entire population moved outdoors. Stoops filled up with housewives and small children, and at night the men joined them, swilling beers. Older children ran in the streets, turned hydrants on, darted away when a cop came in view. Peddlers came forth with their pushcarts, adolescent gangs (quiescent during the winter) resumed old battles, prostitutes and gamblers came out of back rooms for a breath of air, and little boys played ball under the clotheslines in the alley while their older brothers played dice or tortured cats on tenement roofs.

The aromas of summer would have offended those not long accustomed to them. Everywhere the smells of horses and their excrement mixed in with those of cheeses, fish, and other pungent foods sold from pushcarts. Garbage that was thrown down airshafts fermented in the heat. Perspiration seeped into clothing, and since bathrooms were unknown in the slums, people either had to rely on the public baths, which cost money, or manage to get rid of their families long enough to bathe in the kitchen washtub. Often it was easier to learn to tolerate the smell of perspiration. In the flats the scent of kerosene was strong. Needed to exterminate lice and bedbugs as well as to light lamps, it was used everywhere, presenting severe fire hazards. When a fire did break out, access to fire escapes was often blocked, since at night people slept on them, bringing their bedding out of the steaming rooms. Sometimes they slept on the roof or the stoops. Sometimes on the sidewalks. On hot nights the East Side was an open-air dormitory.

With all those people living and sleeping in full

view of their neighbors, privacy vanished and behavior changed. Unwed couples found each other and mated on dark rooftops or in alleys. At three in the morning, when the gaslight was down or turned off altogether, even parents who happened to be awake couldn't see what sons and daughters a few feet away were up to. Yet many of the girls had a point beyond which they would not go. Religion, the fear of hellfire, the fear of being disowned by their families were too strong in the girls if not in the ardent boys.

In her years in the slums, Tracy too had had her moments on rooftops. She had learned to kiss and to fondle and even to let boys climax in her hand, but she'd also learned how to avoid actual intercourse. At eighteen her virginity was still intact, partly because of the fear of hellfire but mostly because of a horror of pregnancy. It enraged her to hear a boy complain that she was hurting him by her refusal to give in. Hurting *him*, was she? It was *she* who'd end up with the baby while he went dancing off to stick his seed into someone else.

Some girls had told her that it was impossible to get pregnant the first time you did it. This was just an old wives' tale, they had said. It took three times at least to get a baby started because a woman's insides had to be made wide enough for the white stuff to get through. Tracy had no reason to doubt this, though she'd known a girl who had sworn that a child had started the first and only time she'd lain with a man. But most of the girls who ended up with a child had

59

indeed slept with men many times. And the girl who had claimed it had been only once was probably lying.

Tracy didn't want to risk that first time, however safe it might be. Try it once and the boy would expect it ever afterward. And if he didn't get it he'd tell the whole street that Tracy was easy.

It had been a long time since Tracy had been kissed. Because of her preoccupation with survival she didn't think much about courtship. It wasn't that she didn't want marriage; she just didn't want to marry an East Side boy. Time enough for weddings when she was successful, elegant, and worthy of the charming college swells she sometimes saw on Fifth Avenue. In the meantime it was all right to like the local boys provided that they understood that she cared only for their friendship, not their love.

On a sultry July night when Pa and the younger children were sleeping on the fire escape, Tracy, finding no room there, decided to go to the roof. She didn't bother to wake Mary, who was too modest to sleep in public, so she had to leave the feather mattress behind and take blankets instead. She put her cotton skirt on over her drawers but omitted a petticoat. Then she tiptoed past Gramp, wondering how he could sleep in such a furnace. Lighting the stub of a candle, she made her way out of the flat and up the reeking stairway to the roof.

In the dim city light it was almost impossible to see anything but forms. Here and there a baby whimpered or a child talked in her sleep. The candle helped Tracy avoid stepping on anyone, and she picked her way to the edge of the roof where she would have some privacy. She laid down her blankets and herself on top of them, then stretched out, spread-eagled, hoping that the faint breeze would cool her.

From somewhere in the vast black dormitory came the sounds of lovemaking. Soft moans, a gasp, the steady slap, slap, slap of body on body, a grunt, a whimper, and then silence. She had heard it before, from across the airshaft—Michael's father taking Michael's mother. She had also heard it on fire escapes and had once stumbled across a copulating couple—both of them drunk—in an alley.

As the couple started up again, she knew she'd never get any sleep in this spot. Rather than picking her way back toward the stairs, she decided to go to the adjacent roof, hoping things would be quieter there. Climbing over the ridges of the roofs, dragging her blankets behind her, she descended with a crash on the roof of the next tenement. In the blackness a voice shouted, "Watch my arm, willya?"

Tracy recognized the voice. "Is that you, Michael?"

"Yeah. Tracy?"

"Yeah. Fancy meeting you here."

"But it's my roof," he said.

"Well, I couldn't get any sleep on mine. Are you decent or should I go somewhere else?"

"I'm decent. Grab a spot."

So that he can grab me? she wondered, recalling the actions on the roof next door. But Michael

61

wouldn't. At least he'd never gotten fresh before. She spread out the blankets once again and lay down. But she couldn't sleep, and from the sound of his tossing it was plain that he couldn't either. After a while they began to talk—in low voices so they wouldn't wake anyone up. She rarely spoke to Michael anymore because there wasn't much occasion to and because he was generally remote these days. It had been different years ago when she'd first moved into this tenement. He had been sixteen and she fourteen, and it was easier at that age to be friends. She had met him when another boy had tried to paw her in an alley. Tracy had shouted, Michael had heard, and he'd sent the boy scurrying with a few well-placed punches and a threat. She had been grateful to him and had thereafter made it a point to smile when she saw him. They had talked occasionally about their jobs or their families and at times had been very close.

She had gotten to know his family too. The father, Joe, was a tyrant and the mother was a shy and self-effacing woman who submitted to the man's beatings meekly. There were eight children in the family. The two oldest girls had married as soon as they could and Michael had lived away for extended periods. But he always came back. Though she hadn't been on close terms with Michael in more than a year, she couldn't help asking him why.

He was silent for a while before he answered. Then he said, "Someone's got to look out for them."

"For your mother?"

"And the twins."

He meant Matthew and Annie, the youngest children, who were only three years old.

"But you don't look out for them all the time. You're always going away."

"If I didn't go away, I think I'd kill him."

The flat tone in which he said this made her wince. Across the airshaft she had often heard Michael and his father arguing. Once, when Joseph had started beating up his wife, Michael had pulled him off shouting curses so shocking that Mary had run to the bedroom and covered her ears with a pillow. And there had been one time when Tracy had heard Joseph beating the twins. Michael had come down to the street holding one child in each arm. Both had been screaming and the boy had been bleeding. Michael had bandaged the boy with a handkerchief, then taken the two to a vendor for some ice cream.

Wife beating and child abuse had been rare in the town where Tracy had lived and after four years here she still could not get used to it. In the months since Michael had been back things had been quiet in his flat. Perhaps he had actually threatened his father. Or maybe he didn't have to threaten but only to glare.

He said, "Mary told me you had a new job."

"Yeah. A cloak and suit place on Canal."

"Good money?"

"Enough. How's your job?"

"All right." He was still, after all these years, working at the bicycle repair shop in Hell's Kitchen, a big slum in the West Thirties that differed from this one only because the majority of the residents there were Irish. She was reminded of the rumor about Michael and the married woman in Hell's Kitchen and she wondered if it was true.

She asked, "Where did you stay the last time you moved out?"

"A room."

"Near your job?"

"Yeah."

"Cost a lot?"

"No."

I guess not, she thought. They had probably shared the rent. But further probing failed to yield any more information, and she still didn't know if the rumors were true. He had never had a reputation as a ladies' man, not on this street at least. But that was true of many of the boys who preferred girls from out of the neighborhood, girls they wouldn't have to meet in the stairwell on the morning after sparking all night in an alley. There were several young women who were interested in Michael, who cut a fine figure, especially on Sundays when he was dressed up. Taller than average, with black hair, dark eyes, and good features, he was one of the better-looking men in the neighborhood. But he seldom noticed his admirers. As a former street gang member he maintained a casual alliance with some of his old comrades, but other than this he had little to do with the people on the street. His heart, she thought, was somewhere in Hell's Kitchen.

As they lay in silence with only two feet between them she wondered what he'd be like as a lover. It wasn't the first time she'd imagined it, though generally she didn't think of him that way for there were others on the block who were more charming.

With his failure to give any details on the Hell's Kitchen situation their conversation sputtered out and she lay gazing up at the stars, wishing a breeze would come up, wishing she could fall asleep. She had to be up early for work tomorrow and it must be one or two in the morning by now. Her work was not in itself very challenging, but she was proving herself to be a good shorthand-typist. With Luke's four hundred dollars safe in the bank and the skills she was sharpening every day, she did not doubt that her plans would see fruition, perhaps in as little as a year.

She had not heard from Luke in more than a month and she wondered if the rest on Long Island had cured his bronchitis. There was a great deal she wanted to tell him and a number of questions she wished to ask him, but it was possible that he'd extend his holiday until September—which meant another seven-week wait.

Michael still wasn't asleep. She could tell by his breathing and shifting around. She herself didn't move very much; she'd learned that the best way to sleep was on one's back with the hands stretched out over the head. It was necessary to do this when one shared a bed with a sister.

She heard him move again, a little closer to her. Then she felt a hand on her arm. Her heart began to race and she opened her mouth to speak, but she shut it again, not sure what to say or do. His touch was exciting, and despite the heat she felt a shiver along the length of her body. In a moment he would want to kiss her, and she didn't want to discourage him even though she knew it might lead to a situation in which she'd have to throw him off. Should she let him know that she wanted to be kissed? While she thought about it, she sighed, for the fingers stroking her arm were gentle yet exciting. Oh, she wanted to hold him! She wanted someone this night. When they got to the danger point there'd be time enough to tell him it was wrong. Meanwhile . . .

She heard him sigh heavily and she felt his hand draw away. He stood up. She could see his dark form standing over her. Then, to her dismay, the form retreated as he picked his way along the roof. Damn! He had not wanted to take advantage because he thought she had been sleeping. Why hadn't she let him know she was awake? Why hadn't she touched his hand with her own free arm?

Oh, it was just as well, she thought. Involvement with a man like Michael would be disastrous. A poor man, an angry one—and with family problems that made her own life look like a Louisa May Alcott novel. His going was a stroke of good fortune. But it was hard to remember how lucky she was as she lay here with a body that wanted so much to be touched.

Chapter Five

She actually blushed the next evening when she saw Michael slouched against the lamppost in front of his building talking to a new tenant named David Litvak. Fortunately it was dusk, so Michael didn't see the blush. She knew she ought to go straight upstairs but lingered there awhile, keeping her eyes fixed not on Michael but on David, a big broad-shouldered young man of about nineteen who apparently didn't understand the unwritten rules of the neighborhood. Here he was talking cheerfully to Michael, a former member of a band of toughs that had grappled with Jewish gangs on many a summer night. Not that Michael had gone in heavily for this sort of thing, but he had been involved—and if David knew that, would he be standing here chatting so amiably? To her surprise, Michael didn't even seem to be suspicious of the young man and was just as friendly as David was. That might be because of the topic— which was the phenomenon of the horseless carriage. Both of them apparently felt that the new invention was the most exciting development in years, and Michael was telling David about some article he had read. Normally Michael talked in the manner of every self-respecting street kid—muttering out of the corner of his mouth and using as few words as possible. Tonight, as he described for David the mechanism of something called a piston, he actually seemed enthusiastic, and she realized that he had a vocabulary after all. But the subject was boring, and she was a little annoyed by the fact that he was ignoring her. Not that she wanted a repeat of last night's performance. She wasn't sure what she wanted.

David and Michael talked on and on, and finally she went upstairs, looking once over her shoulder to see if Michael was following her progress. To her satisfaction, he did look at her. David did too—and he smiled and said good-night. She had promised Ruth that she would keep an eye on David. The new man on the block had captured Ruth's fancy, and when she'd found out he lived next door to Tracy she was delighted. Not the type to flirt or to make obvious overtures, and too far down the block to watch him herself, Ruth had asked Tracy to watch David for her, find out what sort of things interested him. Then perhaps if he came to the bakery Ruth would have a topic of conversation. But how bored Ruth would be, Tracy thought, when she heard that the topic would have to be horseless carriages.

Tracy was just settling down at the table with a glass of cold tea when there came a knock at the door. Mary answered, and a small boy came in saying, "Tracy Sullivan live here?"

"That's me," Tracy said.

"Alison Sullivan says could you come to her flat."

"Who's Alison Sullivan?" Mary wanted to know.

"A cousin of ours. Lives on Elizabeth." She didn't add that this was Luke's sister, for this would lead to a string of questions. How well did Tracy know Luke? Why did she know him so well? And so on.

Mary said, "I don't know any cousin named Alison."

Tracy ignored her sister and said to the boy, "Did she saw what it was about?"

"Nope, just said to come over."

Tracy rose and turned to Mary. "I met the woman last week. By accident. She—uh—she fell getting out of a trolley and sprained an ankle. I helped her back to her flat and we got to talking. I found out she was related to us on Pa's side. Anyway, she was grateful, and I guess she's asking me over for tea."

Mary still looked skeptical. Much as she loved her sister, she was not unaware of Tracy's faults. In a situation like the one described, Tracy would have left the good samaritan duties to another passerby. But Tracy did not bother to embellish the story. She rose and followed the boy out, wondering what was going on. Maybe Luke had come back to the city earlier than planned and wanted to see her. Or maybe Alison had found a secondhand typewriter that was too good a bargain to resist. In setting up the school, Tracy would need several typewriters, and though the business venture was to be some time in the future, she was already looking around.

The boy, having completed his mission, skipped on ahead and darted around a corner. Tracy moved more slowly than he but at a very brisk pace. A few blocks up Catherine Street and then along the Bowery under the El. Here was the center of the Lower East Side's night life: vaudeville theaters, parlor houses, gambling places, beer dives, music halls. A man standing in a group followed Tracy's bustling figure and shouted, "What's the hurry, honey?" But she was quickly beyond his view, swallowed into the dense crowd that glutted the Bowery night and day. There were uptowners slumming for the night, policemen looking for protection money, accordion players pumping hurdy-gurdy tunes, women searching for venturesome children, beggars jingling cups, garment workers plodding home from work, girls looking for fellas, fellas looking for girls, and laborers looking for the nearest saloon. She crossed under the El tracks, gagging as she passed a fly-ridden dead horse, and went a block along Bayard Street, the border of Chinatown. Then she turned right onto Elizabeth, a crowded block that was becoming more Italian every day.

Alison lived five flights up, and few could make the ascent without becoming winded. But Tracy was young and agile, and by now so convinced that Luke was here that she bounced up the stairs without breaking momentum and arrived at Alison's door only a little bit breathless.

Alison was formally dressed this evening. She

greeted Tracy, but not with her usual smile, and motioned her into the kitchen. Alison looked a little like her brother Luke, though she was a year older and much grayer. It was something in the shape of the mouth, Tracy thought.

Alison said, taking a chair, "It's about Luke."

"Is he here?" Tracy also sat down.

Alison bit her lip and studied the table. "I didn't want to send a telegram or a message. I thought it would be better if—" She broke off, swallowed, and then said quickly, "Luke died last night."

At first Tracy stared at her blankly, unable to absorb it. Then she felt the shock like a physical blow that hit somewhere in the region of the chest, then radiated to the ends of her hands.

Alison said, "I knew how much you admired him and I wanted to be the one to tell you."

Alison continued to talk, but Tracy wasn't listening. When her mother had died, she had at least been prepared, but this had come so unexpectedly that she could not at first absorb it. Luke dead? Never again to see him, listen to his advice? So much of her recent life had involved Luke that she could no longer imagine a world in which he did not exist. He had been so many things. Her benefactor, her confidant, her link to the future. And she had loved him like a father while respecting him as a successful man. And now, just like that, with no warning, he was gone. It was outrageous. No life—not even her life—could be so outrageous. She turned back to Alison and asked, "How did he die?"

71

"It was his heart. He had rheumatic heart disease. He didn't tell us about it, so it was a shock to me too."

Tracy still could not believe it.

Alison continued. "He was on the island, but he came to New York yesterday to be best man at the wedding of his colleague. Then he came to visit me." Alison swallowed. "It was the stairs. He had to climb all those stairs. . . ."

"You mean he died here?"

"Yes."

Tracy hadn't been able to picture Luke dying but now she believed it. Yes, of course it would be here on the slum street where he had been born. She had no way of knowing that these had been Luke's own thoughts just prior to his death. And she had no way of knowing that he hadn't wanted it that way, that it had been sheer coincidence and not his plan.

Alison told her more of the details. That Luke had come here with the sister of the groom for whom Luke had stood up, that Dr. Rosen from the settlement had tended him at the end, that Father O'Donnell had given last rites, that his wife and sons had been summoned from the island but had arrived too late, that the wake would begin this evening, and that she, Alison, must be getting uptown for it soon. But the funeral, a high mass, would be held downtown where so many had known Luke.

Tracy said, "In this parish?"

"Yes. Tuesday morning." Alison had had quite a time persuading Luke's wife, who had wanted an elegant uptown ceremony, that many of Luke's old friends and patients would find an East Side service more fitting. Luke's wife had been persuaded only because she'd had no real interest in dealing with the tedious details. "Whatever his family thinks," she had finally said. For the death of her husband had been less a tragedy than a monumental inconvenience. She'd loved him no more than he had loved her, and the important business would come later—when the will was read.

"I must be getting to their house," Alison said, drawing on her gloves. "If you'd like to come with me. . . ."

Tracy shook her head. She did not want to attend the wake. She'd seen enough wakes to have learned to detest them. And never could she make herself look at Luke dead. Nor did she want to meet his wife, sons, or any of the people in his circle. He had existed for her as a man, not a circle, and she wanted to remember him that way. But she would go to the funeral on Tuesday. She owed that to Luke.

Tracy could not later recall her actions after she left the flat. She must have walked, eaten, undressed, slept, dressed, gone to work, made small talk. Only one incident registered strongly enough to be remembered afterward. This was when Pa learned of Luke's death from another cousin. At the table the next night he remarked upon it as he remarked on the deaths of all his relatives. "My cousin Luke passed away. His heart gave out, they tell me." A sigh. A bite from his pickle. And then, "One by one, they're all dropping off. They're all dropping off."

That was all. Pa didn't mention it again or go to the funeral. Nor could Gramp go, for his rheumatism was acting up again. Tracy went by herself, asking her boss for the hour off and not telling her family where she was going.

The church was packed. There were lace-curtain uptowners, shanty downtowners, Jews, Italians, two Negroes, and one Chinese man. There were representatives from the police and fire departments, the health department, Tammany, City Hall, the clergy, and the press. There were rich men, poor men, beggarmen, and not a few thieves. Either Luke had been a much-loved man, Tracy thought, or else New Yorkers loved funerals. Probably both. Tracy took her seat and looked toward the front of the church where Luke's wife, whose beauty was concealed by heavy mourning, sat beside the two sons who looked to be in their mid-teens. The long mass was sung by Luke's childhood friend, now a priest, and by a chorus of urchins dressed up in their Sunday best. The coffin lay under a mountain of flowers, as did the altar. It was an East Side funeral to the core, Tracy thought, with prostitutes trying to look dignified, and cops staring them down, and women weeping for the sake of weeping, and children shushing other children, and politicians looking at their watches because they had a wedding or a shiva visit scheduled next. Luke would probably have liked the service, though. He'd spent so much of his life down here.

Somehow it ended amid mumbled prayers, and the pallbearers came into the aisle for the coffin. As the

74

six men marched slowly out, Tracy looked away.

On the street, behind the hearse, the coaches, carriages, and wagons were lined up for the length of a block and around the corner. Where were they taking him? Brooklyn, probably. She was glad she would not see him lowered into the ground. Someone touched her arm, and she turned to see Alison, who had not gotten into a coach yet. Alison was standing with a young man and a woman whom she introduced to Tracy. The man was Dr. Douglas Wilson and the woman was Douglas's sister Katherine Madison.

Dr. Wilson, Tracy thought. Luke's colleague. So this Katherine must be the one Pa thought was Luke's mistress, the mill owner. Now she remembered Alison saying that Luke had come into the city to be his colleague's best man. Hadn't she also said that after the wedding the sister and Luke had come down to the flat? Did the doctor know of his sister's involvement with Luke? Did Alison know? Did anyone know and was the story even true? Maybe Pa had misunderstood. It looked as though Luke had been so close to Katherine's family as to be almost a part of it. He and Katherine might have been no more than close friends. Pa had seen the two coming out of a hotel, but for all anyone knew they might have gone there one day for lunch and nothing more.

All the time Tracy was thinking, she was being introduced to people by Alison. To Douglas, to Katherine, to Katherine's mother, Beth, and several others. Tracy nodded and said her pleased-to-meet-yous, but she kept looking over at Katherine thinking that she was young for Luke. Ten years younger at least. She didn't even look thirty. Her hair under the black hat was auburn. She was tall, slender, brown-eyed, and wore spectacles. She had a pretty face, though she wasn't beautiful, but her expression was strained from grief. Tracy tried to picture this woman with Luke—holding his hand, smiling into his face—but it was hard to imagine Katherine smiling. It was hard in fact to believe Pa's story at all.

Alison and the other mourners moved on toward the waiting coaches. Tracy watched until the procession got under way. Then she walked toward her place of work thinking that all she had left of Luke was the money. If only she could return it and get Luke in exchange.

Chapter Six

Somehow, daily life went on. Discipline in the flat had become lax in the months of Tracy's other preoccupations, but after Luke died, the reign of terror came down like a hammer. She boxed the ears of her brothers for not doing their chores, her fights with eight-year-old Kerry grew more frequent, curfews were made more strict, and she refused to give the children their allowance for Saturday candy unless the week's behavior had been sterling, which it never was. Mary was spared Tracy's rages, though she was just as unhappy as the others. What was wrong with her sister these days? She was worse than she had ever been, Mary thought.

Tracy missed Luke desperately. She had been storing in her brain all her adventures and all her plans, waiting for the moment when she could share them with him. Now he was gone, and only his sister Alison was left to provide her with even a measure of the understanding Tracy had come to rely on. Alison had been apologetic about the fact that Tracy had not been mentioned in Luke's will.

"He wanted to," she said. "But other relatives

would have been hurt. And at that there was barely enough to maintain his family. The boys' schooling alone—"

"He already gave me more than I ever expected—"

"But he told me once that he wished he could slip you more. He said you were special to him. Not a whining relative but a girl with a head on her shoulders. He used to say—"

"Please don't tell me. It'll make me cry, and I don't want to cry."

She didn't cry. Not then or for a long time afterward. She went through the days trying to pretend that nothing had happened. Arguing with Ruth down at the bakery was a diversion she came to look forward to after work and on Sundays when Tracy had the day off. The topics varied but the attitudes could be reduced to the ongoing argument that had characterized their first meeting: Ruth's idealism versus Tracy's practicality. Always in these conversations Ruth managed to work in the name of David Litvak. And after a while the bakery discussions consisted of nothing but thinking up ways for Ruth to get David's attention.

One Sunday afternoon in October conditions seemed ideal. Tracy rushed down to the bakery to tell Ruth that her *mensh* was down on the street again talking to Michael. David and Michael had become pals of a sort. Their common interests ranged from baseball to electricity, though they were still mainly interested in the horseless carriage. Tracy was surprised at Michael. In the old days he hadn't been able to sustain such conversations and had preferred to spend his leisure time with his street gang pals—smoking rather than reading, grunting rather than talking. But now he was down on the street heavily engaged in this conversation with Ruth's idol, and it looked like they'd be there the rest of the afternoon.

"He's in front of the stoop with my neighbor Michael," Tracy said. "Get your father to watch the bakery and come over. I'll start talking to them and then you can come up and pretend you're there to see me and sort of fall into the conversation. Now for pity's sake, don't say silly things or choke up. Just be the way you are with me."

But the meeting was disastrous. Tracy felt awkward with Michael these days, and David, who didn't want to bore Tracy and her friend but could think of no topic to interest them, fell silent too. Ruth, who was normally a provocative conversationalist, could find nothing better to talk about than her mother's geraniums. She spoke solemnly, her mouth scarcely moving, her dark eyes looking not at David but at the stoop railing behind him. Her black hair was pulled back severely into a single braid. No hat was on her head and no curl was there at the temple to indicate a little frivolity. Tracy groaned inwardly. David would think she was an old maid.

The four stood stiffly outside Michael's and David's building. Michael kept looking off down the street, obviously planning his escape. David was glassy-eyed, lost in thoughts far removed from geraniums. Ruth looked anxious and nervous and it got worse and worse as she became aware that she was failing in her mission. And Tracy, annoyed with all of them, looked disgusted.

Into this tableau wandered Gramp, coming back from a post-mass visit with some pals and limping with his cane. He said hello to the dismal assemblage and then sat on his own stoop where he was soon joined by two little girls. It wasn't long before he was telling the children of his childhood in Ireland. The little girls had never heard his tales before, but Tracy, Michael, and the older children on the block could have recited them like a litany. The verdant land, the cliffs of Kerry, the cattle lowing in the hills; then the coming of the famine, the potatoes rotting in the ground, the work projects and soup lines, the families starving and dying, the departure for America in the holds of rotting ships. Why did he dwell on it so? Tracy wondered. Why didn't he try to forget his hurts as she did?

When he told his stories, Gramp always included in the script a rendering of "Danny Boy." There were many explanations of the meaning in the song, but the version Dan Sullivan favored, because he had actually lived it, was the version where a father is seeing his last son off to America at the time of the famine. He explained the meaning to the little girls. Then, over the clamor of the street, came the sound of Gramp's strong baritone, and people turned to listen.

Oh Danny boy, the pipes the pipes are call-
ing
From glen to glen and down the mountain-
side.
The summer's gone and all the flowers are
dying.
'Tis you 'tis you must go and I must bide.
But come ye back when summer's in the mea-
dow,
Or when the valley's hushed and white with
snow.
'Tis I'll be here in sunshine or in shadow,
Oh Danny boy, oh Danny boy I love you so.

David walked over to Gramp and murmured,
"That's the saddest song I ever heard. And it could be
about any nationality, I think."

Gramp nodded. "The Jews, the Greeks, the
Germans, Italians, they all know what it means."

David said, "All the parents who saw their sons
and daughters go away from the shtetl, the old people
who saw children sail out of Naples. Everyone who
ever handed over his dreams to the young."

Michael and Tracy exchanged glances. Many
times had they heard this song, but never had they
heard any of this in it. And they hadn't realized that
David was possessed of such emotion. Michael
looked a little uncomfortable, but Tracy was moved.
She was thinking of Luke saying good-bye to her.

"Could you sing it again?" David asked.

"There's yet another verse," Gramp said softly,

and he continued:

> But should ye come when all the flowers are dy-
> ing
> If I am dead as dead I well may be,
> Ye'll come and find the place where I am ly-
> ing,
> And kneel and say an "Ave" there for me.
> And I shall hear, though soft you tread above
> me,
> And all my grave will warmer, sweeter be,
> For you will bend and tell me that you love
> me,
> And I shall sleep in peace until you come to
> me.

Tracy stood rigid, fighting the tears. But it was no use. She cried so hard that she could scarcely stand up, and Ruth guided her over to the stairs of the stoop. Everyone else looked on. Gramp, at a loss for something to say, finally murmured, "She feels things sharp, she does. 'Tis the Irish in her." And Michael, who could not abide sentimental scenes like this, walked away.

"Tell me what's wrong," Ruth said to Tracy.

"Later," Tracy said. And she fled up the stairs to the flat.

On the stoop, Gramp explained to the little girls gently that some songs made people cry and that it was nothing to be fretting about. Ruth walked over to David, who was standing there looking awkward, and said, "I have a feeling it was more than the song."

David shrugged. "I don't know. My father breaks down over songs from the old country. Some of them are even happy tunes that you'd think'd make him smile."

"Yes," Ruth said. "My mother's like that."

They talked for a while about their parents. Both of Ruth's parents were alive, but David lived alone with a widowed father. His mother had died some years earlier of what David said was a broken heart. He was a little uncomfortable using such a cliché with Ruth, so he said, clearing his throat, "I mean a bad heart. Congestive heart failure."

"No," she said. "You mean a broken heart. I think sometimes it really does break in a way. It's from all that pressure of thinking of people and places you'll never see again."

He nodded. "It's hard sometimes to try to guess what they're thinking about. We're Americans. I mean, we were born in the old country but—were you born on the other side, Miss Mednick?"

She nodded. "In Poland. I know what you mean, though. We were so young when we got here, we don't really understand a lot of things about them."

They continued to talk while on the stoop Gramp tried to cheer the two little girls by singing more spirited ballads, though even tunes with a beat, like "The Kerry Dance," had a sad message to deliver. But Ruth and David were no longer listening. They were discussing their parents' generation and their own, and comparing notes as to how each of them dealt with the matter of simultaneously pleasing parents and getting along in the New World. Ruth wanted to be a teacher. And David, who worked in a factory while going to night school, longed to be a writer. Both were having problems persuading traditionally oriented parents to approve of these ambitions. David also confessed that he had conflicts between the religion of his forebears and the new religion of many younger Jews: socialism.

"Are you a socialist too?" Ruth said.

"Yes. Are you?"

"Yes."

With that, conversation really took off as they discussed people they had known or read about, shared news of what was being said in the various cafés of the East Side, and asked each other what they thought of Abraham Cahan and other leading socialists of the area. As Ruth began to concentrate on the subject instead of the man, her eyes took on a luminescence and her gestures an animation that Tracy, if she had still been on the street, would have cheered.

Later, Ruth went up to Tracy's flat to see how she was and what had upset her. Tracy said, "It was someone I knew once. He died. The song reminded me."

"Can you tell me who it was?"

"Maybe someday." She cleared her throat. "I'm sorry about David."

"Sorry?"

"Maybe you should have a little drink before you try to talk to him. It'd relax you. And next time we'll curl your hair, all right?"

Ruth started to laugh. "But it's fine. It all went fine."

"You mean you actually *talked?*"

"Did we talk! For an hour at least, without stopping."

"Really?" Tracy grinned.

"And I owe it all to your grandfather and 'Danny Boy.' And to you, for crying your eyes out. I was so upset, I forgot I was shy and started acting normal."

"And he likes you?"

"He asked me to go with him to the Yiddish theater next week!"

Tracy clapped her hands together. "Well, saints be praised! And Gramp's got a dozen more ballads too, so if you and David need another boost. . . ."

"I'll know where to come," said Ruth.

They laughed and went back down to Ruth's bakery to continue their Sunday arguing.

Chapter Seven

Two weeks after Ruth's and David's courtship began, on a warm night in late September, Michael got into serious trouble. It was the dinner hour and Michael's father had just gone up to the flat. Michael, who had just come home too, was leaning against the lamppost in his customary hooligan pose smoking and talking to a couple of boys from his old gang. Tracy was on her way home from work and was coming down the street.

As Tracy approached her building she saw David come running out the door of his tenement shouting to Michael, "Get up there, quick!" Michael tossed his cigarette in the gutter and sprinted across the street and in the door, David following. Tracy, coming upon the scene, could not imagine what it was about. But a fat man who was also a resident of Michael's building came down to the stoop and explained it to her and to a group that was gathering. "Oh, Joe's just slapping Nell around again. The Jew kid, he lives under them, he must think it's a murder or something. Bunch of nervous nellies, them sheenies."

Tracy remembered Michael's saying that he was

afraid he'd kill his father someday. She also remembered the tone of voice in which he'd said it. Without thinking, she entered the building and started up the stairs. On the third-floor landing Michael and his father were grappling. As Tracy reached the second floor, she saw Michael take a final swing at his father. Forever afterward she would remember the power in that arm and the murderous expression on Michael's face. His father pitched backward and then thumped down the stairs, landing inches away from Tracy. David came running down after him. Tracy stared horrified at Joe's too-still form while David knelt down and felt for a pulse. Michael stood rigid on the landing above.

Doors opened on landings above and below them and people came in from the street. When David shouted, "Someone get a doctor!" two people darted out the door.

"Is he dead?" asked Tracy, finding her voice at last.

David said, "The family should be so lucky. He's out, though."

Michael still stood on the landing above. Behind him were a sister and some neighbors from across the hall. In the flat beyond Tracy could hear the mother's hysterical weeping.

Patrolman Roarke, who covered the area, arrived in minutes. Finding David at the scene, he questioned him first.

David said, "This man was beating up his wife. His son came in and found him. There was a struggle."

"Yeah?"

"And he landed down here."

"Uh huh. Go on."

"That's it," David said.

"Man outside said the kid threatened to kill the old man."

"I didn't hear that," lied David.

Roarke turned to Tracy. "You hear it, miss?"

"No." Which was the truth as far as the present occasion was concerned.

The cop's eyes now moved up the stairs to take in Michael. "Get down here, Ryan. The rest of yez stay where you are."

Michael walked down. His shirt was torn and his hair in wild disarray, but his face was expressionless.

"You threaten to kill your father?" asked Roarke.

Michael didn't answer.

"What's this gonna be, Ryan? A little altercation or assault with intent to kill?"

"I don't give a damn," muttered Michael.

David said, "You wanna arrest someone, arrest this bastard here as soon as he comes to."

"Who the hell you think you are, yid?"

"I wouldn't use that word," David said menacingly.

The cop bit his tongue as he remembered that just this day the kid had served as translator for a politician courting the Jewish vote on this street. He might complain to Tammany. "All right. Don't get touchy. But don't tell me how to do my job neither."

David jerked his head toward the stairs. "Go up

and ask that woman. Ask her what happened."

The cop grunted and nodded at Michael. "But he's coming with me." Daivd, Michael, and the policeman went up the stairs. Joe remained unconscious, Tracy looking down at him, unable to take a step closer. As the scene was described by David later, the cop had found Nell in a bad way. Black and blue, bleeding from the nose, she sat on a kitchen chair crying helplessly and stanching the blood. The twins were at her side, patting her skirts. The cop asked if she wanted to press charges against her husband, and to David's astonishment she had said no. The cop then patted the children's heads, said he'd send the doctor up, and steered Michael back into the hall.

"Nothing I can do, kid."

"She's scared," Michael said.

"Don't make no difference. She don't press charges, I got no case. Now take my advice and get going before your old man comes to and starts shooting his mouth off. The Jew kid says there was no threat, maybe there wasn't. Just a little misunderstanding, huh? Happens in the best of families. But you better get going before you do something lands you in Sing Sing."

After looking in on his mother, grabbing some cash he had hidden, and saying something reassuring to the twins, Michael left. He did not go far at first. Even the police knew where he was waiting, and neighbors could guess why his sister Maureen was carrying a satchel into the Mednick bakery. When Joe Ryan came to and felt the pain of the broken bones (a leg, an arm, and a finger), he was in no condition to talk to police anyway. An ambulance came along and took him to the hospital.

In the Mednick flat above the bakery Michael checked the satchel and made sure all his things were in it.

"Where will you go?" his sister asked him.

"I don't know, Mo."

"Back to Hell's Kitchen?"

"Maybe. Depends if he tries to get me arrested."

"Just to be safe," David said, "why not try Jersey? At least till the *momzer's* wounds are healed."

"Maybe," Michael said.

They were crammed into the small Mednick kitchen—Ruth, David, Tracy, Michael and his sister, and Ruth's parents. The parents spoke no English and did not understand what the group was saying, but they knew what had happened, for a boy downstairs who had been playing marbles near the scene of the crime told them all about it. An Irisher savage had attacked his wife and then his son had attacked him. Ruth's beau, David, had been there in the middle of it all. And now, thought Mr. Mednick, Ruth was in the middle of it too.

"Tell these people to leave," he said to Ruth sharply in Yiddish. "They'll bring trouble."

"Oh, Papa!" Ruth waved impatiently. "You don't understand."

"Criminals I understand. That man's face I understand." He was looking at Michael, whose eyes were huge and black, his face still contorted in anger.

90

Ruth drew in her breath. Could Michael have some of his father in him? she wondered. (Tracy at that moment was wondering the same thing.)

Ruth said to her father in Yiddish, "It's not Michael who's the criminal. Michael was defending his mother."

"I should care who he was defending? They're *goyim*. Animals. Tell the Irisher and his sister to leave. The skinny one can stay." For some reason Papa tolerated Tracy.

Michael understood little of the language, but the tone of voice he understood very well. "Tell your old man not to pop his cork," he snarled. "I'm leaving right now."

He walked quickly to the door of the flat. David followed him out, and Tracy followed David. Michael's sister Maureen, who had sensed nothing of this animosity, being too upset by Michael's predicament, turned to Ruth's mother and said solemnly, "Thank you for helping us."

Ruth's mother did not understand all the words, but she knew what "thank you" meant. She smiled at Maureen, but the father remained stony-faced. Ruth glared at him, then took Maureen's arm and prepared to leave the flat to join the others.

"Where are you going?" Mr. Mednick roared to his daughter.

"To be with David."

"That socialist? That troublemaker?"

"David a troublemaker? Just because he's interested in politics? Oh Papa, Papa, what's wrong with you?" Ruth went running out the door, ignoring her father's commands to stay home. He'd yell himself into apoplexy later, but he'd get over it after a while. In the meantime, being with David was more important than obeying her father. She continued down the stairs.

On the street Maureen kissed her brother good-bye. "I have to be getting home to Ma. Take care, Mike."

Michael nodded. "You too."

"You'll write, won't you?" David said. "You can send the mail to my flat. No one'll intercept it there." David's father did not interfere in David's affairs as Ruth's father did in hers.

"I better get going," Michael said. "Before they arrest me." To David and Tracy he said, "Thanks for lying to the cop."

David grinned. "So what's a little perjury between friends. C'mon, we'll walk you out of here. Give you an escort."

The four of them walked all the way to Fourteenth Street and there stopped at a saloon for a bon voyage beer. Ruth and David were not drinkers, and they simply nursed the beer along. Tracy was more at home with alcohol, but even she reacted to more than one beer. Michael, however, made up for them all, giving up on the beer early and switching to straight whiskey, which he was able to afford because he had money with him—savings he had taken from a hiding place in the flat before he left.

At one point David said to him, "This city's crazy. Laws so unfair that no one enforces them, a whole family under the heel of one maniac. And you're not able to do a thing about it. There has to be a way to change that."

"Try and find one," Michael said.

"There must be lawyers we could talk to. A judge. A Tammany man, a settlement worker, news reporter, someone."

"Wouldn't help," said Michael. "My old man never hurt anyone outside his family. Not recently, anyway. Got a record as clean as a snowbank. But I— well, the juvenile courts know my name."

Tracy knew that Michael had been in trouble before. Fights, drinking under age, and other adolescent stunts. Few boys grew up on downtown streets without getting into a scrape sooner or later, and Michael's record had been just about normal. There had been times when she thought him to be a mindless brute, but she'd felt that way about most of the boys. And compared to others in his crowd, Michael hadn't been bad, really. But the law wouldn't see it that way. To the law, Michael was a criminal and Joseph an innocent who didn't harm a soul outside his family.

"You know," David said, "we thought when we came from the old country that we'd left all that behind us. Injustice, I mean."

Ruth nodded. "But here at least you have justice in theory. There you didn't." Since she and David had met, Ruth had been thinking more of her past. He had encouraged her to do this, for he'd wanted to know everything about her. Yes, she knew full well what injustice was. She had known it in Poland where one could not even report the gangs who attacked you because there was no one to report them to. They'd come sweeping into their shtetls and villages, raping and murdering, slicing off limbs with swords. The law had done nothing, for officials were as anti-Semitic as the gangs themselves. A Jew dared not open his mouth for fear that his family would be slain in revenge during the next wave of terror. And there was nothing for it finally but to leave the shtetls and walk—what a walk—more than a hundred miles to a train. Ruth had been seven years old then. She remembered being cold and hungry, remembered how her feet had ached.

Yet Ruth did not hate gentiles categorically as her father did. For one reason, she'd been too young and too sheltered to be as affected as he was. She had never actually seen the slaughter, whereas her father had witnessed it more than once.

"Think of it," David had said the day Gramp Sullivan had sung "Danny Boy." "Generation after generation had lived the lives their parents had led. The customs, the language, unchanged for hundreds of years. And then came 1881, and suddenly it was all over. Alexander the Second was gone, and it was over. The world fell down around them. Literally. We were too young to appreciate that. We remembered only the excitement. But they—they saw their homes and shuls smashed and burned, saw their lives, everything they knew, burned with it. Then they had to leave people they loved and come here, for our

94

sakes. Imagine what courage that took. It would have been easier for them to die."

Could something like that have happened to Michael's father? Ruth wondered. Could that explain why he'd become what he'd become? She leaned across the table and asked him, "Was your father born in the old country?"

"No. He was born here."

"New York?"

Michael nodded. "The Five Points."

Good God, Ruth thought. That slum had been cleaned up some years ago, but in its day it had been the most notorious area in all America. Here thousands of potato famine victims had starved in rotting buildings and flooded cellars. Perhaps Michael's father had not come from the old country, but he must have lived as wretchedly as his parents who had starved in the huts of Ireland.

Ruth tried to picture Michael's mother and his father. Though she had never met either of them and knew them only from sight, she could visualize them on their wedding day in some decaying Five Points church. They would be smiling at each other. No thoughts of cruelty in that moment, she imagined. Only the eagerness to be together.

What had happened between then and now? Well, one baby and another baby, and a third, a fourth, a fifth, sixth, seventh, eighth. And jobs that were low in pay and hard to find. And flats with broken windows and crumbling walls. And illness—the full complement, of course—colds, croup, scarlet fever, measles, mumps. Children crying and crying through the long days and nights. The heat of summer, the brutal cold of winter, and never enough food. Never enough.

Ruth could imagine it. She had lived a part of it herself, though not the part about the eight children, since she was an only child. And sometime during those long, no-exit years, Joseph Ryan had turned into a bully. One summer day he might have come home to a flat heated to 110 degrees with steaming laundry. And his wife might have whined or said something cross or even said something innocent like, "I'm going to a novena tonight. Will you watch the children?" And that might have been enough to do it. Joseph Ryan would have been ready to strike at something, and he'd chosen his wife. And no doubt the children after that.

How unfair God was to women, Ruth thought. Frustrated as the men might be, the women had it worse. Pummeled as much by society as men were, they yet had to endure one extra wallop. The one men dished out to them after a long wretched day. Michael's father was physically violent; her own father did it with words.

To Michael she said, "Did he ever regret it?"

"What?"

"The beatings."

"Regret it?"

"You know, did he ever apologize? Weep with shame?"

"Weep? Yeah. Apologize, no. Once in a while if he

hurt us so bad we were bleeding, or if he was really sloppy drunk, he'd cry or pray over our bodies. Once he said a whole damned Act of Contrition. But usually he'd just walk out."

"If he's at all sensitive," Ruth said, "maybe he won't bring charges against you."

"Sensitive?" Michael laughed sarcastically. "That's my mother's favorite word. 'He don't mean it,' she says. 'He's sensitive. He wouldn't be like that, wasn't for the troubles. Wasn't for the sadness of his life.'" Michael paused, then said, "*His* sadness? What about her sadness, huh? What about that?"

From that moment on, Ruth liked Michael. Liked him as much as David did, though for different reasons. It wasn't just that he had defended a woman. Any thug could do what he had done. It was his going that one step further and actually asking himself what kind of life his mother had led. For this Ruth could forgive him his juvenile crimes, could even forgive his long ago street fights with Jewish gangs. All because he'd thought to ask the question.

Michael was saying, "She should have reported him, but she was afraid she'd be breaking her vows. I think she'd defend him even if he tried to hang her by the neck from the ceiling. She was brought up that way, you know." He shook his head in despair and Ruth realized how hopeless his situation was. The mother with whom he sympathized wasn't even on his side. She'd been browbeaten by the old man into thinking that suffering was her lot in life. Which was her decision to make, of course, but what about the

97

children? She couldn't protect them either—and this, more than anything else, was what was worrying Michael. He sat slumped over the table now, his hand propping his head.

Tracy was thinking that Michael was drunk. He had never in all these years run on so, even to her. She felt very bad for him, for the frustration he must be feeling. She felt many things for Michael—friendship, comradeship, sympathy, strong physical attraction. What she did not feel was admiration. Though she respected his physical strength and his courage, what Tracy admired most in men were the kind of abilities that translate to money and status. Since Michael had no such abilities that she could see, she did not especially admire him. But she liked him well enough, and she realized it most keenly when David suggested that they leave the saloon (he was too polite to also point out that Michael was getting drunk). The good-byes were solemn. Each of them shook Michael's hand. Ruth wanted to give him a sisterly hug, but was afraid that David would misunderstand. At last Tracy stood facing him alone and it was only then that she felt some emotion. A friend was leaving. A man who had shared her battle with the slums. A man who had touched her arm on that scorching roof. He was leaving, and though she knew he wouldn't go far and would be back often, she would miss him. She wished there had been more time to get to know him. Life moved by so fast, so fast, and it got faster as you grew older.

"Good-bye, Michael. Take care of yourself."

"You too."

"I'll miss you."

He nodded. "Same here."

"We had some good times, didn't we?" She couldn't really remember any, but it would make him feel better to believe they had existed.

"Well—" He shook her hand.

"Yeah," she said. "I don't like good-byes either."

But that was all life seemed to be, she thought. One good-bye after another.

Part

Two

Chapter Eight

Tracy sat in her boss's office, pencil poised over her paper, preparing to take dictation, just as soon as he got off the telephone. She was daydreaming, thinking again of her business. It was July of 1897, and two years had passed since Luke had given her the loan. Now half of it was gone, and Tracy was no closer to owning a business than she had been then.

She had needed some of the money to bury Gramp, who had died of pneumonia in the winter of 1896. And some had been spent on doctors for her father and the children, who had fallen ill with typhoid the following summer. And so it had gone, dollar by dollar, until she had only two hundred left. How she could start a typing school on that amount, she did not know. And to compound the problem, she was reluctant to leave her latest job. She had fallen in love with the boss's son.

She was working in another advertising agency and had managed to stay on for three months now. Ever since her first secretarial job she had wanted to get back into this jolly field. The work could be fun at times, the small staff merry, the surroundings bright with successful ads framed on the walls. The offices of Curtis and Price were on Broadway near Fourteenth Street. Mr. Curtis was an intellectual man of gentle birth. He gave the impression that he was embarrassed by his business and could better serve humanity as a classics professor but, alas, his crass society did not allow him that latitude. His son, Russell, who had come to work there for the summer before returning to Yale, was like his father in many ways. Tall, charming, and aristocratic, he too was uncomfortable pushing curling irons and crackers, but he did not hint to the staff that he was capable of more noble endeavors. He simply wrote his copy with a wry smile on his face. Were it not for the other partner, Mr. Price, Tracy thought, the agency would not have stayed in business a week.

Russell was attractive and gallant and had a good sense of humor. The day seemed to come to life when he walked in the door and stopped at Tracy's desk to offer witticisms or to tell her she had nice dimples. Unfortunately, Tracy wasn't the only one in the office who was crazy about him. Mr. Price's shorthand-typist, Louise, and two of the typewriters (the girls were given the names of their machines) were also quite smitten. Of all of them, only Louise had the remotest chance of getting him. Blonde and curvaceous, well-spoken, the product of a genteel family that had fallen on hard times, Louise Mitchell was practically in Russell's class. Whereas she, Tracy, with her unexciting hair, her thin (oh so thin!) body, her shabby clothes, and a background that was difficult to hide, was many rungs beneath him on the social ladder. A month ago, after first meeting Russell, she had seriously considered taking the entire two hundred dollars and doing herself over. But last week she had decided that as soon as he went back to college she'd open a business with whatever she had. With any luck, she'd prosper, and by June, when he came back to New York, she'd be comfortable and attractive enough to be taken seriously.

It was hard to believe in those dreams when she left the office and went back to her old East Side flat. For here nothing ever seemed to change. She sometimes had nightmares in which she saw herself as an old woman still traipsing up the three flights to the hungry household.

Some things had changed, though. Ruth and David were married and the parents of a little boy. Their families had moved across the river to Brooklyn, but Ruth and David remained on Monroe Street because of their work. David was co-owner of a small weekly newspaper that resembled the *Jewish Daily Forward* except that it was a fraction of the size, printed in English, and meant to appeal to younger folk of liberal persuasion. David's earnings provided the family with just enough to enable them to eat, but Ruth did not seem distressed by any of this. Indeed, she contributed articles to his paper on her favorite passions: women's suffrage, the labor movement, and the settlement house movement; and she didn't seem to care if her stomach growled as she scribbled.

Michael was living and working in New Jersey. Every month or so he came to New York to visit his family—but never to the old flat. Meetings were arranged with cousins in Brooklyn and Chelsea, and once in a while he came to Ruth's and David's place on the very street of his infamy. Michael's father had never pressed charges on his son but had threatened to do so if he ever saw Michael's face again, so reunions were held at Ruth's because the flat was convenient for Michael's family yet far enough down the street for Joseph not to have to see Michael. The meetings were pleasant and Tracy came to look forward to joining them.

Michael had changed. He was nearly twenty-three now, more mature and more friendly. He enjoyed his new job, which paid well and involved his long-ago passion, the horseless carriage. An expert bicycle mechanic, he now fixed an occasional automobile as well. It was definitely a machine that was here to stay, he said, though he wasn't sure if the electric type or the gasoline type would prevail.

His father lived on and raged on in the flat across the airshaft. Without Michael around, Joe was more tyrannical than ever, but neighbors had learned to ignore the beatings, for Nell still refused to make any formal complaint.

The death of Gramp had severely depressed Tracy. His gentle fatherly manner had held together the different factions of the household, and he'd always been there to listen and advise when anyone had a complaint. But he was gone now—like her mother and Luke. The sane and the decent seemed particularly susceptible to illness, she often thought.

But even as she grew more bitter, a part of her tried to escape it. She began seeking out happy and untroubled people even if they didn't have a brain in their heads. She laughed a lot more at foolish things and even sang foolish songs. Her most common remark to Ruth these days was, "Why do you have to be so *serious* all the time?" And she'd sometimes laugh helplessly watching the antics of her brothers and sisters or the stumbling progress of a drunk. But most especially did she laugh when Russell was around.

He'd been assigned to a cookie campaign this summer and was trying to come up with clever ideas. As Tracy began taking dictation from his father, Russell burst in without knocking, all smiles and high spirits, with his latest thoughts on the subject. He was jesting as usual—the job was something of a joke to him—and his father wasn't in the mood for it.

"Father, I feel that we must associate Bates cookies with exciting people or exciting adventures."

"Indeed?"

"For example: 'Bates: the cookie of the Klondike.'"

"Who the deuce was eating cookies in the Klondike?"

"Ah, Pater, ye of little faith. Can you prove that no one did?" Russell winked at Tracy.

Tracy began to laugh and Mr. Curtis, exasperated, addressed the air. "What am I doing in this business? Will someone tell me?" He rose, sighed, and said he thought he'd go for a walk.

Russell laughed and sat down at his father's desk. "Take a letter, Miss Sullivan," he said. His blond mane of hair gleamed in the sunlight streaming through the window.

"Yes, sir." Tracy realized that the letter would never be sent, but she went along with the joke, grinning to show off her dimples.

"To Mr. Henry Bates, director, etcetera. Dear Mr. Bates, etcetera. In the matter of Bates cookies there are a number of possible sales approaches. The Klondike, of course, is the most exciting, but let us not overlook possible associations with groups such as the Four Hundred, groups the hoi polloi is eager to emulate. Sample headline: 'Vanderbilt serves Bates Cookies at Breakers Housewarming. Sets Fashion at Newport.' We might also consider connecting Bates with rare ability or genius. 'Edison Chomps on Bates Cookies and within Twelve Hours the Moving Picture Is Born.' 'Alexander Graham Bell's First Words into the Telephone: "Any Bates Cookies in the House?"'"

Russell continued. "I tell you, gentlemen, your sales will increase a hundredfold. This is no ordinary cookie we'll be selling. This will be a cookie of magic properties, one bite of which can transport you to Newport or to Edison's laboratory. *That* is how we must promote Bates Cookies, gentlemen."

Tracy was laughing. "Will that be all, sir?"

"Except for one thing."

"Yes?"

"You have pretty dimples."

It never went beyond the gallant compliments, though Tracy often dreamed of the day that would happen. She mustn't hope too hard, she warned herself. Every time she had allowed herself to love somebody, that person had gone away. But it was no use telling herself these things. Tracy's dreams were more and more becoming tied to Russell.

She had other things to think of though. Mainly the business. When summer finally ended and Russell went back to Yale, she thought of it again—in earnest. For years she had dreamed, schemed, imagined herself rolling in money. Now, in 1897, she was an accomplished stenographer-typist, knowing everything one could possibly know about typing, dictation, filing procedures, and the like. True, there were dozens of girls more qualified by education and background to teach such skills, but those dozens didn't care as much about success. Success, she thought, was dependent less on talent than on need. Well, need she had. And it was time to make use of it whether she had the money or not.

Chapter Nine

The place was a former grocery store on West Third Street off thriving Broadway. A good location for the money, Tracy thought, for the rent was the cheapest she'd been able to find. She had canvassed the city for secondhand typewriters and ended up with six. She bought rickety tables from a junk dealer and with her brother Pat painted them brown. A typewriter was placed on each, and the effect was almost desklike. With Mary's help, she made long drapes and hung them in front of the plate-glass windows. Passersby must not gawk at the students as they had at the groceries stacked here two weeks earlier.

There were other things to take care of. In addition to license fees, Tracy had less official bills to pay. The landlord had to get a little something for his "trouble." The cops on the beat had politely requested a donation to their "patrolmen's organization." This donation was actually a payment that was split among policemen up the line, but in return they would look harder for thieves who loitered around the typewriters. The Blackhanders hadn't bothered Tracy. It was said that they preyed only on Italians. So she considered that she was all paid up, which was a good thing because money was running low.

Shortly after everything was in place, Tracy put a sign in the window in front of the curtains. It had been printed by the people who were doing David's paper. "Sullivan's Typing and Stenography School. All you need to know about today's modern office. Enroll for classes 12 noon to 3 P.M., 3 P.M. to 6 P.M. and 7 P.M. to 10 P.M. Fifty cents per class, payable in advance."

Everything about the school was designed to appeal to poor girls who wanted to move up. Tracy hadn't originally intended a lowly clientele, but that was all this place would be likely to attract, and she might as well set things up as though she'd planned it that way. Fifty cents per class wasn't too much to part with if one ended up a stenographer-typist instead of a garment worker. The location was convenient to the East Side, the evening hours were added for those who worked a full day, and the atmosphere was simple enough for the girls not to feel intimidated as they might have been in a fancier edifice.

Tracy was the only teacher. She could not, at this point, afford to hire anyone else. Nor could she afford to advertise or buy any extra paper. She had used every penny that remained of Luke's loan plus all her own petty savings. And she had not enough for a second month's rent, so this would have to work or they'd end up on the rolls of Catholic Charities.

111

Louise, the chief contender for Russell's affections, stopped in at lunchtime just before the school opened. Not realizing that Tracy was enamored of the same man, she had always liked Tracy and was concerned for her now. "Oh, Tracy, do you think this is right? Your whole life savings?"

"It's my decision," snapped Tracy, who disliked this woman because Russell paid too much attention to her. But at the same time it occurred to her that Louise would be a good future employee in the school. She had skills, education, good habits in dress and manner—and if she was lured down here, she'd be out of the office of Russell's father and hence out of everyone's thoughts, including Russell's. Tracy resolved to be sweet. "You'll have to excuse me," she said to Louise. "I'm so nervous, I can't think straight. But I'm hoping this works. Please wish me luck, Louise."

"Of course," Louise said. "Best wishes, Tracy." She had a hard time concealing the doubt in her face.

It was then that the first student entered the school. A dark thin girl of about sixteen. "Please? I'ma here to learna the type."

Italian, thought Tracy. Poor kid would never get anywhere until she learned where the vowels belonged and where they didn't. This was as hard for an Italian as it was for an Irishman to put a g at the end of a word. Or for a Jew to leave the g off. Until they learned these niceties of the English language, their horizons were limited, Tracy knew. Businessmen didn't approve of vowel-lovers or of people who

112

didn't know about g's. But it was not Tracy's duty to explain any of this. Her duty was to turn out shorthand-typists. The girl looked intelligent, and more important, she had the fifty cents in her hand. "Welcome to our school," gushed Tracy as Louise, still looking doubtful, walked away.

For five minutes Tracy was alone with the Italian girl. She sat her down at a typewriter and told her to look the machine over. Then Tracy went to the window, and pulling the curtain aside, she looked woefully out into the street, wondering if anyone else was going to show up. At last a breathless young woman came running up to the door. Simultaneously, Tracy opened it, and the student literally fell into her first class. She was a Jewish girl whose English was as bad as the Italian's. "You're just in time," trilled Tracy. "The class is about to begin!"

Only two students, she thought. But she wasn't daunted yet. These two would tell others—and by tomorrow there'd be three or four in this class alone.

She ran the course like a drill sergeant. First the keyboard: "ASDFG, ;LKJH. Again. Again. Again. *Now* type SAD, SAD, SAD. Come on. Come *on*. SAD, SAD, SAD. Got the rhythm? Hear it? Hear the rhythm? *Now*, LAD, LAD, LAD, LAD. I know you can't see what you're typing, but they promise they're going to manufacture a peekaboo typewriter soon. . . . Now, don't look at the keys for this one. Ready? SAD, SAD, LAD. Don't look at the keys!"

For an hour and a half the two students labored at this. The touch system had been discovered years before when some blind students, taught how to type, quickly became more proficient at the art than were the seeing who used only two fingers. Following this discovery, sighted typists began learning the machine as a blind person might.

After the typing lesson was complete, the students worked on stenography. For this, Tracy stood at a blackboard writing symbols over and over again, drilling them mercilessly so that at the end of the day they would feel that they'd accomplished something. It was hard for the girls. They could hardly speak and write the language, much less take it down in shorthand. Their confusion troubled Tracy. It wouldn't do to have them dropping out. Not yet. Not until her reputation was so well established that she could afford to lose them.

She interrupted the stenography lesson to deliver almost word for word a speech often rendered by her old common school teacher in Connecticut.

"Now, young ladies, I know this is difficult. All learning is difficult—that is why it is treasured so. But for some of you this will be the last chance you'll have. The *last*, my dear young ladies. Do this, and you'll have jobs you never dreamed of. Fail—run away—and you may be condemned to darkness for the rest of your lives!"

She had them, Tracy thought as the two students turned with new resolve back to their work. She must remember to use that speech for the two other classes today. And to use it periodically hereafter, maybe changing the wording here and there.

The stenography lesson ended and then it was time for what Tracy called "decorum," in which she had to give advice on how to dress (shirtwaist, plain hat, no frills), make telephone calls (she used a child's toy version of the real thing), address bosses, greet clients, and keep desks orderly. Later on in this half-hour session she would be teaching filing, the format of letters, basic office English, and other skills, thus rounding out the program nicely, she thought.

At the end of the session she smilingly bade the girls good-bye and said she'd see them next week. Tracy had assumed that most of the students could afford only once-a-week instruction, though she was hoping to get some who would take courses twice a week or even daily. This way, they could master skills more quickly and trumpet the news of their success to others. But she was pleased enough by the once-a-week and curious to see how many more she would get for the later sessions.

For the late afternoon session no one at all showed up. Tracy tried to tell herself that this was because of the hour. Most young girls were at work. But when only two came in for the evening session, she began to panic. Evenings were the best times for such schools. The only time many people had. If she couldn't pull them in now, then when in heaven could she do it?

She gave her lesson, but her voice was strained and hoarse with anxiety. From time to time her mind would slip from the subject. She had six typewriters and three sessions. That ought to have brought in eighteen students. Yet she'd had only four. Only four!

A student interrupted her thoughts. "Miss Sullivan?"

"Yes?" She stared blankly at a shy dark-haired girl.

"Hats you were telling us about?"

"Oh, hats, yes. Never wear a fancy one with cherries or feathers on it because. . . ." She trailed off, thinking that four students was only two dollars. If it kept on at that rate, then how could she pay next month's rent for this place? How could she support her family and pay *their* rent?

"Miss Sullivan?"

"Yes. Hats, yes. Never buy the fancy kind. Did I tell you that?" Tracy was close to tears. Now these girls would go home and tell their friends that Miss Sullivan was an idiot with a bad memory who couldn't even finish a sentence.

Somehow she bungled her way to the end of the session and said good evening to the girls with a strained smile. They wouldn't be back, she knew. She'd be lucky if she retained even one from the more successful early afternoon class. That meant only one to give a recommendation. And would she?

TRACY plodded to the school the next morning scowling. She hadn't slept the night before, and now she had a whole day's class ahead of her. Not only did she have to hold on to those students she already had (if any), but she must also make the course more exciting so that those students who came today

116

would spread the word. Exciting, hah! She had all the energy of a slab of tuna lying in the Fulton Fishmarket.

She hadn't told the family of yesterday's panic. She had told them only that business needed time to grow but that she had made a promising start. Then she had crawled into bed pleading fatigue and remained there feigning sleep until everyone else went to bed. Then she'd gone into the kitchen, made tea, and stayed up all night drinking it and worrying. Now, as she rounded the corner of Third Street, she warned herself that she must try to believe her own blarney. "Businesses need time to grow," she muttered aloud.

She saw it but didn't quite believe it. She blinked several times, wondering if she was hallucinating because of her fatigue. The plate-glass windows of the classroom had been smashed. All over the sidewalk in front of the building were shards of glass. A cop to whom she'd given nonharassment money was looking at the mess, and the butcher from the shop next door was standing next to him shaking his head.

"My windows!" Tracy shrieked when at last she realized that she wasn't dreaming.

"Must've happened before I came on duty," muttered the cop.

"Who did it? Who wrecked my windows?"

"Ah, that I don't know," said the cop. "But we'll investigate."

"But I *paid* you!" she shouted.

"What do you mean?" asked the cop.

117

"The contributions to the policemen's whatever-it-was."

"I don't know what you mean," said the cop.

The grocer, a small, Italian man, rolled his eyes heavenward. Then he said to the policeman. "She means nothing, officer. She is upset, eh? A young girl, just opened a business, she's upset. You understand how it is." To Tracy he said, "Come next door. You'll sit down, you'll feel better." He brushed his fingers across his lips in a gesture that Tracy correctly interpreted to mean, "Keep your mouth shut, young lady," and then he said again to the cop, "She is young. Please understand."

The policeman nodded. The Italian gestured to Tracy. And Tracy, confused, followed the man into his butcher shop. In back of the counter, amid sawdust and sides of beef, Mr. Vitale filled Tracy in on a few facts. He was the most amazingly diplomatic man she'd ever met. The blunt truths he was uttering were couched in language so polite that occasionally he had to repeat them so that Tracy could understand.

He said, "Patrolman Powers has a difficult job, eh? Every day he risks his life protecting good people. But the city cannot afford to pay him much. The taxpayers are so poor."

"But *I* paid him!" Tracy shouted. "I paid all *three* of those cops."

"And they remembered that," said Mr. Vitale.

"What do you mean? They let someone smash my windows!"

118

The butcher pointed out that Tracy's most valuable possessions, the typewriters, had not been taken. The ever-vigilant police on the street had sharp eyes when it came to stolen goods, especially goods belonging to people so generous to the police as Tracy was. But windows—ah, that was another matter. It took only a second to break a window, and a hardworking police officer could not be expected to be watching the school every minute. As for who had broken the window, why it had probably been the boys on the corner. They had broken many windows. Accidents did happen, Mr. Vitale acknowledged. But these were children who meant no harm. They were restless and a little wild. After all, they were poor, and many came from unhappy homes.

"And they were warning me that they expected to be paid not to do it again? Is that what you're trying to say?"

"They are poor," Mr. Vitale repeated.

"Well, I don't have a cent to pay *any* of those hooligans. I'm not making any profit on my business and now I have to replace the windows too. I was. . . ." She could not go on. She was struggling to keep the tears back.

Mr. Vitale was kind. He found a handkerchief and continued to talk to Tracy between stints at the counter with housewives coming in for their meat. He told her not to press charges against the boys, not even to frown at them when she passed. Indeed, she mustn't even indicate that she suspected them. With a smile she was to give the boys handbills advertising

119

her school and promise them money when business began to improve. She was also to ask them to keep an eye on the typewriters. She must say with a straight face, as though they understood nothing, that when a cop was busy elsewhere she needed people to watch out for her place. And in the meantime, Mr. Vitale concluded, she was to conduct classes as usual with a sign posted on the door saying that classes would continue in spite of the broken windows.

After a while, Tracy began to realize dimly that the man must know what he was talking about. After all, his own business flourished in this very same neighborhood, as did assorted grocery stores, candy stores, liquor stores, and dry goods stores, all with breakable windows. But it was easier for Tracy to understand the advice than to practice it. To *smile* upon those window-wreckers? To give them hand-bills and a promise of *money?* She wanted to *kill* the little monsters!

But in the end she did as Mr. Vitale had suggested. She apologized to Officer Powers for her "thought-lessness." She got David's printing firm to do up some handbills, promising to pay them later. She gritted her teeth and gave the handbills to the hooligans, promising to pay *them* later. The toughs passed those out and managed to produce two new students. There had been only two to four a day to begin with, so the newcomers scarcely represented advancement at all. She was still losing money. There was no cash to fix the broken windows and the sign on the door explaining the "temporary" inconvenience remained there for a week. Meanwhile the street boys were waiting for their pay, and patience did not seem their strong point.

In despair she went over to Ruth's one night in search of advice. Why weren't more students coming to the school? Where had she gone wrong? Should she lower the price of the lessons? Would that help fill the eighteen seats a day?

Ruth felt that this would be unwise. Tracy must not put education into the same category as a Hester Street bargain on pants. She was offering skills of lasting value that should not be treated cheaply. Fifty cents a lesson it was and fifty cents it should remain.

"Well, then, what should I *do?*" Tracy wailed.

David suggested the possibility that the poor Europeans she was trying to attract were puzzled by the concept of the school. They could not make the connection between machines that printed letters and money in the bank. If it were *sewing* machine skills she were selling, then they might understand. Quick ways of producing clothes were something *everyone* could understand. But typing letters in offices? That would be hard for immigrants to picture. They came from small villages and only had the vaguest idea of what went on in large offices.

"Then what should I *do?*" Tracy repeated for the third or fourth time that evening.

"I don't know," David said. "Find some way to show that this skill means advancement, more money."

121

"How do I do that?"

"An equation," he said, smiling. "Put a sign on the door saying typing equals dollars."

"You're a big help," muttered Ruth, giving her husband an angry glare.

"I'm sorry," David said. "I really don't know the answer. I'll run an article in the paper explaining it, but my circulation isn't very big."

Tracy sighed. How well she knew. It was hopeless, she thought. Even the butcher was running out of ideas. And how long before the hooligans began to lose their patience?

She stood one afternoon gazing upon the broken windows. The sign explaining that the inconvenience was only temporary would not fool people much longer. She had hung on to a few students, though. By some unexplained miracle *they* were able to see the connection between typing and advancement. But how did you show the equation to the others? Maybe if some students got wonderful jobs as a result of the instruction the news would spread quickly. But most of her students were once-a-weeks. There was no time to wait for them to prove themselves and give testimonials. If something didn't happen soon, Tracy would have to close up for good.

How could she advertise the uniqueness of the school? What was missing from the handbills that would make the difference? She thought of the agency she had worked at and wondered if Messrs. Curtis and Price would be able to tell her. Or Russell.

If she wrote him at Yale, maybe he would have an idea. But she knew instinctively that none of them would be able to solve a problem like this.

If only people could see how it worked, she thought. If they could see girls marching out of the school and into high-paying, higher prestige jobs. Even if they could just see the girls working the machines, their fingers moving surely over the keys. . . .

Tracy thought about that a moment. She had originally put up curtains so that the girls could not be seen. But the window was smashed now, wasn't it? What if the curtains had been damaged too? What if she suddenly discovered that she had to have them mended? Then the students would be learning in full view of the street. People could actually see and hear them hitting the keys. Not real students, though. They'd get nervous in a minute. She'd have to get some pretend students to sit in the class during the time the curtains were being "mended."

Tracy outlined the plan to Ruth and Mary later that evening. The meeting took place on the stoop of Tracy's tenement.

"I don't understand," said Mary. "You want us to pose as students?"

"Yes. You'd be out in the open. We'll pretend the curtains were torn. You and Ruth will be at your machines typing and smiling. You have to remember to smile and to say nice things because people passing by will be watching and listening."

"But I barely know what a typewriter looks like,"

said Mary. "I don't even know where *A* is."

"You'll know just as much as a beginner," Tracy said. "But actually you don't even have to go that far. Just hit the keys, that's all. Any old keys. Just bang at them and smile."

"Oh, Tracy!" Ruth said. "All this deception!"

"It's not deception," said Tracy to this hater of capitalist tricks, "it's a—well, it's showing in a *dramatic* way what these machines can do. Think of it as a kind of show or play."

"A play!" Ruth snorted. She wasn't fooled by Tracy's rationalizations. But she realized that immigrant girls really needed a good push to get them started in this promising field. "All right, a play," she said, nodding.

In the end, Mary and Ruth not only cooperated but also rounded up four more women (all Monroe Street housewives who had been promised wages later) to fill up the seats in the class. This was the late afternoon session in which Tracy had only one or two students, none of them on a Wednesday when the play was set to be held. She hand-printed a sign to post on the door reading, "Despite damage to the windows and curtains, the students in this class wish to complete their course of instruction. This is necessary so that they can secure the jobs recently offered them if they mastered these skills. We know you want the very best for them and we urge you to please respect their privacy." With help provided by Ruth and Mr. Vitale, Tracy also printed this in Yiddish and Italian.

Tracy "discovered" the torn curtains at the end of the early afternoon class. Feigning disgust, she took them down with the aid of a real student. Then she stormed into the back room, purportedly to whip up this sign for the door. If either of the two real students wondered how she was able to produce such professional lettering so quickly and in three languages too, they didn't ask. As Tracy ushered them out the door, she said emphatically that the class coming up was not to be denied instruction just because of this inconvenience.

Mary, Ruth, and the rest of the cast came filing in at five past three, just moments after the two real students had left. There had been a brief rehearsal at Ruth's that morning and all seemed to know their parts. Saying solemn hellos to Tracy, they went to their desks and sat quietly as Tracy delivered her opening remarks.

"I'm happy to announce that Rebecca Bernstein will begin next week as an assistant to Mr. Rivkin of Rivkin's Thread Company. Let's congratulate Rebecca, shall we?"

Five amateur actresses turned to the sixth and warmly applauded Miss Bernstein's acceptance in this nonexistent company. Tracy then told Rebecca (a fictional name) that she must be careful in her choice of costume on that first crucial day. "Don't dress like a factory girl. You're not a factory girl anymore. You're a lady now with a very important skill that Mr. Rivkin is willing to pay higher wages for. And you must dress with dignity."

Just in case this wasn't being understood by the passersby in the street, Tracy "allowed" the girls to chat exuberantly and loudly among themselves in English and in their native languages. They discussed Rebecca's coup for a while and then Tracy rapped on her desk sharply. "Back to work," she said firmly but with an indulgent smile.

They typed to Tracy's litany, their fingers sure, their faces wreathed in smiles. Later on, they pretended to take shorthand, their pencils dancing over the paper. Finally they listened raptly as Tracy discussed the "decorum" aspect of the course. All asked the right questions. And Tracy's answers seemed to impress them.

"I don't know too much about offices," Ruth said on cue. "Could you tell me about them, Miss Sullivan?"

Tracy did. Ruth discussed her answer with a "classmate," lapsing into Yiddish. A girl named Lena talked with another "classmate" in Italian. All smiled and even laughed in their exuberance. And the questions continued.

On the door was the sign in three languages urging onlookers to give the students privacy. But of course no one did. The crowd outside grew larger and larger.

At six o'clock the actresses left, and soon thereafter the curtains went back up. Success was not instantaneous. Tracy's little show attracted twenty more students to the school, but this averaged only three a day. Still, she was filling six seats a day now instead of two or three, and money was beginning to come in. As fast as it did, Tracy paid off her creditors. First the hooligans, then the actress-housewives, then another donation for the cops. She gave a tin of imported cookies to the butcher and a scarf to Ruth, who at first refused to take it.

"What do you think friends are for?" said Ruth. "Take it or I'll hang you with it."

"Gentle Tracy," Ruth said as she laughed and draped the scarf around her neck.

With what was left, Tracy paid for the rent on the school and the family's flat. There were only nickels remaining for food, but she wangled credit from a grocer, and by the second week, with two more students added, she paid him too.

Tracy was solvent.

As business began to pick up and daily seat occupancy moved closer and closer to the magic eighteen, Tracy decided that if she was going to take care of the school properly, she really ought to move in here. There was a tiny back flat that had come with the rent and had formerly been the residence of the bachelor grocer who had occupied these premises. Tracy had been using the space as an office and repository for papers and records because it was unheard of for a woman to live alone in a flat. But now she changed her mind. She needed a quiet place in which to work on lesson plans and to rest and sleep. When she added a morning course, she'd have to spend every waking minute overseeing the business, so when she rested she'd have to rest well.

She put off breaking this news to the family for as long as possible. Pa might have a stroke, and Mary would surely weep over the loss of her confidante even though Third Street was within walking distance of Monroe. But one evening in December Tracy could postpone the news no longer. That day had been a total of fifteen students. She'd made $7.50 in one day, more than she'd made in a *week* as a shopgirl! When she added more machines and a morning course, and when word of her school got around and every seat was filled, the daily take could conceivably go as high as eighteen dollars. And even if she had to pay an assistant (she was planning to ask Louise soon), the profit would still be considerable. In no time at all she'd have enough for a down payment on a house for the family.

"I have to talk to you," Tracy said to Mary that night. Mary always waited up for her sister and saw to it that she had a decent supper. The rest of the family was in bed. "I want to tell you my ideas," Tracy continued. "As soon as I have the money, I'm going to buy us a house in the country. You and Pa and the kids—and me, whenever I can get there. Won't it be nice to see trees again, and fresh flowers like the ones Ma used to—oh, Mary, don't cry. Mary, don't."

"I can't help it," Mary sobbed.

"And I'll bet you don't really believe it either. But just wait. The house'll have a bathroom too. Do you remember the bathroom at the big house?" They had both exclaimed over this when they went to visit the

128

factory owner at Christmas time. "Remember the water that ran in and out, and those big fat towels and all that soap? And, oh, the privacy when you had to—you know. No chamber pots, no clogged toilets. Everything so clean, smelling nice." Tracy smiled at the thought of such opulence. Then she said, "Oh, please stop crying, Mary."

"I'm crying because none of us ever appre-appreciated you," she sobbed.

"Oh, for pity's sake."

"You do love us, don't you?"

"You're all right," Tracy winked, trying to jolly her sister out of the sentiment. The truth of the matter was that she was doing these things in part because they were kin and in part to keep a promise to Ma that she'd watch out for them. But love them? Well, Mary she loved. And she was coming to respect her brother Pat. But Pa? No, she didn't love him. Kerry? She was a brat. Tommy? He'd end up in trouble if they didn't get him off the streets soon.

She told Mary that she would have to move out of the flat for a while and this brought a new deluge of tears. "Move out? Who will I talk to? Oh, you *can't*—"

"You've got friends all over the neighborhood and you can also come to the school. And I'll come here every Sunday for dinner." She wanted to add, "And when you move to the country you'll see me even less." But she didn't say it aloud, in part because she didn't want to think of that separation herself. But by that time, who knew? She might be rich enough to

129

leave the business in care of underlings while she and Mary walked the New England paths as they'd done when they were girls.

SHE moved bedding, clothes, and some pots and pans into the back rooms. Then she bought new typewriters just as fast as she could earn the money for them. By the middle of December she had ten. Then she hired Louise away from Curtis and Price, offering her ten dollars a week to teach three of the four daily classes. Tracy would teach the morning classes herself, but she would also try to be present at each of the others so that she could help the more accelerated students move on quickly. This way, the school would be able to establish a reputation not only for superior business education but also for efficiency in obtaining it. Though she did not like her employee, Tracy could see that the students were impressed with her, and this was certainly worth the price.

The money kept piling up. At fifteen to twenty dollars a day, even rent, overhead, and staff couldn't deplete it all. She bought new clothes for the family and herself and toys for Ruth's baby, and she took out an advertisement in David's paper more to keep it afloat than to get more business. And then, after a busy Christmas, she began to save in earnest for the house.

She had wondered if she ought to repay the loan to Luke's estate. But no—he had said that no one must ever know. And how else could she keep the news from them except by keeping the money? She couldn't even give it to Alison, for Luke's sister had died of pneumonia the winter before. How she missed them both. There was so much she wished she could show them. Luke had been so right about the business school. If only she could give him a kiss on the cheek and say thanks. Or to see him raise his wineglass and smile at her. The memory of that night in the restaurant was still vivid.

But thinking of Luke made her sad. It was better to think of Russell. Handsome, smiling Russell—how surprised he would be when he saw her next summer. She planned to go to the agency to pay the staff a visit, a vision in her fawn suit and matching hat that enhanced her hazel eyes. Rich, successful Tracy Sullivan. She must practice a few witticisms too, like a Vassar girl. And she must learn how to flirt properly. She'd never had time to learn before.

But underneath all the exuberance and newfound fancies beat a heart that hadn't softened one iota. When one of her students pleaded to be given credit, Tracy shook her head resolutely.

"No credit, Miss Steiner."

"Two weeks only. Such good things I'm learning. Please, Miss Sullivan. Two weeks only."

"I'm sorry."

"My father is sick. The doctor comes, we must pay him. The rent—"

"I can't make any exceptions. Come back when you have the money to pay."

"But maybe I don't come back. Maybe I'm into

the—how do you say?—into the darkness."

"You'll come back," Tracy said softly. And her head screamed, just go! Don't you understand? I can't make exceptions. Not one. Not a single one. Don't tell me about your father and the rent. I don't want to hear it. I've already lived it.

Another student had heard some of this, and when the distraught Miss Steiner left with tears in her eyes, she said, "How could you do it? How could you *do* it, Miss Sullivan?"

"This is a business, Miss O'Day. And that is how businesses are run. Now I'll let this impertinence pass this time, but if you dare to question my methods again—"

"Do you know what it's like to be poor, Miss Sullivan?"

"I know very well." And that was the whole point. But this fool didn't understand any of that. And chances were she'd end up on a soup line.

"Well, if you know, Miss Sullivan, and if you don't give that girl credit, you may end up poorer than ever."

"Indeed?" said Tracy, who was moving toward the girl preparatory to ushering her out the door.

"If you don't give this girl credit, she'll tell her friends. And pretty soon no one will have anything to do with this school. Because you'll have rivals all over New York with kinder hearts, and they'll take away your business and you'll—"

"Get out!" yelled Tracy. "Get the hell out!"

"Fishwife!" the girl screamed back. "Shanty slut!"

After she had calmed down, Tracy found Miss Steiner's address in her record book and wrote a warm note saying that her mood had been unusually black that day and of course Miss Steiner was welcome to credit. What kind of a world would it be if trust did not exist? And it was particularly gratifying to have a student like the honorable Miss Steiner. More students like Miss Steiner and she, Miss Sullivan, would not be as wary as circumstances sometimes compelled her to be. There were more profuse apologies and the urgent wish that Miss Steiner would grace the classroom again on Monday evening.

As for Miss O'Day, Tracy wished her good riddance. She would spread the word far and wide that Tracy was a cheapskate, but the presence of Miss Steiner would belie all she said and the rumors of Tracy's benevolence would drift through the city like a warm wind. And then, with any luck, that bigmouth O'Day would sink like a stone.

Ultimately Tracy handled the credit dilemma by limiting the amount owed to one dollar. Few, especially when they came near to completing the course, abused the privilege. A more serious problem was the question of placement. She had cheerfully admitted anyone who wanted to try, content only to take their money and fulfill her part of the bargain. But in February two tearful former students came to see her. Both were greenhorns who spoke fractured English. Neither had been able to find a job.

So Tracy became an employment agent too,

133

dashing around the city speaking to businessmen, telling them of her school, explaining that an excellent shorthand-typist who had trouble with English was preferable to a silver-tongued sophisticate who knew no shorthand and typed with two fingers. Sometimes she convinced prospective employers and sometimes she did not. A grammar lesson was added to the course. She made the mistake of telling Mary that she was going to screen her students more carefully, taking only the ones who would be likely to get jobs later on. And Mary, appalled, had said, "Tracy, don't you see? That's like—like what they do to *all* the poor. Defeat them before they've had a chance to try. I know *you'd* never do anything like that."

Oh, wouldn't I? thought Tracy. But when she tried to discourage a Greek girl only a month off the boat, her sister's words kept getting in the way. There was a conspiracy afoot to make her soft and foolish, she thought as she grudgingly admitted the Greek. She'd better be on her guard.

Chapter Ten

In May, Michael came home from New Jersey for a visit. Ruth and David brought him over to see the school. Tracy gave him a proud tour of the classroom, then the four of them walked with the Litvaks' small son through nearby Washington Square Park. Finally they returned to Tracy's living quarters behind the school. Using two kitchen chairs plus two brought in from the classroom, they crammed in around her stamp-size table and had dinner while Ruth's and David's boy slept on Tracy's bed.

"Such a businesswoman," said Ruth. "Next there'll be schools in every borough and she'll be living like Mrs. Astor pretending she never heard of the old gang from Monroe Street."

"I couldn't have done it without the gang," said Tracy, grinning, her mind feasting on Ruth's images, particularly the mansion on Fifth.

Michael said, "You got ten students each, four times a day?"

"That's right. Mondays are mostly for the once-a-weeks. They can't afford to pay more than that.

135

Tuesdays and Fridays are mostly the twice-a-weeks, and the other three days are for the three-timers. But some three-timers are slower than once-a-weeks, so we have to teach them at their own levels. It gets very complicated."

"Sounds like it," he said. "You got help?"

"A girl I used to work with."

He grinned, shook his head and said, "Wow."

Her living quarters were small. A kitchen, a small bedroom, and a water closet into which she'd had a plumber cram a small tub. The water was cold, and kettles of hot water had to be added to the bath, but at least she had a genuine bathroom and she felt as opulent as a Vanderbilt heiress. She had painted her quarters and then covered the walls with colorful sketches that had been cut from magazines and framed. There were bright print curtains, a brighter plaid tablecloth, a still brighter quilted bedspread, plus intense yellow walls in the bathroom. Blinding, Ruth thought. Dizzying. Yet Ruth could understand it. Tracy was trying to compensate for the gray tenement life she was now escaping and for the dreary school decor, which was obligatory for such places. This flat must represent Tracy's true taste. A little unsettling, thought Ruth.

Tracy told them that she had ordered a telephone for the school so that students could practice using the real thing. Her assistant Louise had an aunt who owned a telephone and for a modest fee would be happy to answer calls from the students and "play office." Tracy said too that she was looking into the

136

possibility of wiring the place for elecricity. Imagine it—those amazing bulbs that would make the place look like day even at night! It would be good for students who had trouble with their eyesight. And for her as well.

"Electricity yet," Ruth said. "Next she'll have Gramophones to play the lectures so she doesn't even have to talk."

"What a peachy idea!" Tracy exclaimed.

Michael said, "But what does the Gramophone answer when someone asks a question?"

"Spoilsport," laughed Tracy.

The dinner of Italian dishes had been provided by Tracy's upstairs neighbor, Mrs. Santini. A widow with a small daughter who earned her living taking in laundry, she'd been only too happy to give portions to Tracy in exchange for three needed dollars a week. Tracy ate what the family ate and sometimes dined with them. It saved her a great deal of time.

They had peppers and eggs, broccoli, a flat bread covered with sauce called pizza, and almond-flavored pastries for dessert. A little too spicy for Michael and the Litvaks, Tracy guessed, but they seemed to enjoy the novelty of Italian food. She felt good sitting here with her old friends talking about neighbors and David's latest stories for the paper. Even Michael seemed relaxed, and she guessed that the visit in Ruth's flat with his mother and family had gone well.

Michael told them that he was now in charge of a

bicycle repair shop in Newark and also fixed an occasional automobile. Too bad he didn't own the place himself, Tracy thought. And why couldn't he get out of the repair business altogether? With his brains he ought to be *buying* automobiles, not fixing them. His education might be no better than her own, but she had proved that success was possible even for such as they. When was Michael going to learn that? Or Ruth and David, for that matter. These two were still laboring over David's little paper, *New Trails*. They lived in a three-room flat on Monroe, half of which was filled with clippings and articles. What little they earned went for more magazines and books, and Ruth hadn't bought a new dress since her wedding.

Yet the Litvaks were happy. Ruth would care for her little boy and somehow write her socialist tracts at the same time, rising every hour or so to stir the soup. David would dash from his partner's printing press to the scene of a story, content to exist on a piece of cheese for lunch. They were both of them thin as telephone poles and dressed like beggars. David didn't own a decent hat. Tracy couldn't imagine why they were so content, could not comprehend how ideas could be more important than food and clothing.

But Tracy liked the Litvaks. There was never a pause in conversation when those two were around. Fired with plans to write exposés of everything imaginable, they were determined to see Utopia before they died. The replacement of Tammany with a more equitable charity system, a total reform of the schools, and the institution of factories where a fire never had a chance, where labor and management walked hand in hand, where Jews and Gentiles sang hymns to the new order and the words dago, sheenie, or mick never passed anyone's lips.

Tracy and Michael listened to all this with skepticism and not a little puzzlement. How could these two, the victims of such extreme prejudice, keep on ignoring the truth about human nature? When Michael put a question like this to David, David said, "We don't ignore it. We just want to improve on it."

Tracy remembered David bending over the body of Michael's unconscious father. How could you improve a man like that? she wanted to ask. But she couldn't ask in front of Michael. No one mentioned the man in Michael's presence.

Her mind drifted from Michael's situation to her own problems with family. She had enough money for a down payment on a small house, but where was she going to look for the place—and when? She wanted them settled before September so that Patrick, Tommy, and Kerry could start in a decent school.

The answer came to her before the end of the evening when her ears perked up at something David was saying about new ideas in labor relations.

"... in Massachusetts. A place called Madison Mills. This Katherine Madison says it can be done if people want to try."

Katherine Madison. Where had she heard that

name before?

David continued. "She sells the workers the houses and lets them buy stock in the mill. There was a big write-up about it in one of the business magazines."

It was a very innovative step, David explained to Tracy when she joined the conversation. A mill whose company houses were not rented but sold to the workers, where every cent given in rent was considered to be a payment toward the house. And no obligation to the mill owner once those houses were paid for. A worker could quit the mill and work anywhere he liked. In this particular Massachusetts town there were several options too. A factory and a machine plant, to say nothing of small businesses like groceries and shoemaker shops.

"What town is this?" Tracy asked, still trying to recall where she'd heard of this Katherine Madison.

"I don't remember. The article's back in the flat."

"A real Utopia?" Ruth said, a brow raised. She was the more skeptical of the pair.

"A start in that direction," her husband said. "Can you imagine a laborer owning a house and buying stock in a mill?"

"It's pretty hard to believe," said Michael.

"But leave it to a woman to think of it," said Ruth.

"Does she make any money?" asked Tracy, her mind ever fixed on priorities.

"Of course she does," said David. "When a laborer owns stock he cares more about the product, so everybody benefits."

How different things would have been, Tracy

thought, if Pa had owned that house in Connecticut and shares in the factory as well. They wouldn't have been so quick to fire him then.

"Her name's Madison?" said Tracy. "You know any more about her?"

He shook his head. "But she doesn't have any jobs, if that's what you're asking. There's a waiting list to get jobs in that place."

"A cotton mill?"

"Woolen."

Tracy nodded, then lapsed into daydream. A job for Pa, shares in a mill, a house that was paid for, the children graduating from high school and marrying farm folk from the area. Or maybe Tommy would go into a profession. Medicine, law, the priesthood. And Mary? Why, she would marry some lover of books— the high school teacher—and acquire yet another house. In time they'd all prosper, and Tracy most of all. Rich and classy, married to aristocratic Russell, she would blow into the town from time to time, resplendent in furs, while her kin cried their greetings, throwing open the doors of their elegant homes. . . .

The hour was growing late, David picked up two-year-old Aaron, and the family prepared to leave.

"When'll we see you again, Mike?" asked David.

"Summer, probably."

Ruth winked. "Sure it's all right to leave you two alone?"

"I'll be sure to scream if he gets fresh," Tracy said. Michael smiled but glanced at her quizzically as though to determine whether she really thought of him in that way. Tracy didn't notice his expression, and in fact she didn't think of him that way anymore. The incident on the rooftop was long forgotten, buried under the weight of the things that had happened since. As they finished the last of the wine, she sat politely through his description of some new type of automobile, wondering how he could be so absorbed with the subject, wondering if he would ever do anything sensible. Automobiles were toys for rich men. No working man could afford one. And even for the rich, she had heard, they were more trouble than they were worth, what with having to keep track of all the gadgets and charge it up or fill it with fuel. She had overheard a man say recently that the novelty of the auto had worn off. Motorcars were as dead as air balloons. But Michael didn't seem to know that yet.

Michael leaned on his elbow as he talked, and she noticed that he grew better looking as the years passed. She wondered if the girls chased him there in New Jersey. And what had ever happened to the married woman in Hell's Kitchen?''

"What do you think you'll do now?'' he was asking her.

"I want to save enough to move the family out of New York. Then I'd just like to pile up as much money as I can.''

"Regular Hetty Green, huh?''

"That's me.''

"Plan to marry? Have kids?''

"Someday." Sometime after June when she'd had a chance to work on Russell. "You need money to bring kids into the world."

"Yeah." He took out a cigarette and lit it. He was silent for a while, smoking. She rose and went to wash the dishes. After a while he said, "Tracy?"

She turned from the sink. "Huh?"

"It was nice. The evening."

"Oh. Thanks." She smiled. She was only half listening. She was trying to remember again who Katherine Madison was. Her distraction was not lost on Michael who said, "You look like you got a lot on your mind."

"Tons of things, but they all come down to money."

"That's your god, huh?"

"It's as good a god as any." This was something she was reluctant to admit to socialist Ruth, but Michael, she thought, might agree with her.

"Yeah," he said, and stood up. "Well, it's late. I have to catch a ferry."

"See you soon, I hope." She extended her hand.

He nodded and shook her hand.

"Don't get hurt by any backfires." She had heard how risky it was to start an automobile.

"I'll try not to," he said.

He was tall, she thought as she stood next to him. And dark, like an Italian. He resembled his father in this, for his mother was blue-eyed and blonde. They called Michael's coloring "Black Irish." Some said the original inhabitants of Ireland had been dark.

143

Others claimed it had started when the Spanish Armada got to Ireland. Luke had been even darker than Michael, she recalled. And as soon as she thought of Luke, she remembered who Katherine Madison was. Luke's supposed mistress. *That* was who Katherine Madison was.

Michael noticed the light coming into her eyes. "What is it?" he asked.

"I just remembered something."

"Something to do with me?"

"You?" She began to laugh, not at him but because she was so excited by her discovery. "Oh, no—something else."

"That's what I figured," he muttered, and because he was so near the door he walked out without any final good-byes.

Tracy was only peripherally aware of his abrupt departure. Her mind was on other matters. How would she do it? How could she get to Katherine Madison through Luke? A very delicate problem, and it had to be handled just right. It would be folly to let Katherine know that she'd heard the rumors. Katherine would see that as blackmail no matter how Tracy tried to explain that she wasn't intending to tell the world. No, the only thing to do was to simply let it drop that Luke had been her dear cousin. But how? When? Would Katherine even care? Assuming that she did, would she care enough to find a niche in this special town for this distant branch of Luke's family? David had said there were waiting lists to get work in that mill.

Tracy passed from table to sink, thinking. She washed the dishes and got into bed, thinking. It would take time to plan this, she finally realized, and she was too tired to consider the details now.

It was not until she was almost asleep that she remembered Michael. Had she said good-bye to him? She didn't remember, but she must have. She hoped that he'd had a good time.

Chapter Eleven

Tracy had kept on very good terms with her former boss, Mr. Curtis, father of the prized Russell. She had referred two students to Curtis and Price, and one of them had been hired. She had called on her former boss to get his "astute viewpoint" about the needs of employers in this modern age; about what he deemed to be proper telephone manners; about whether she should introduce elementary bookkeeping into her curriculum; and about other questions she already knew the answers to. If she could work herself into his good graces and perhaps even move him to take a fatherly attitude toward her, then she'd have an ally when it came time to conquer Russell's heart. On an early June visit to the agency, she determined during her general inquiries about the health of Mr. Curtis and family that Russell would be returning home from Yale on Saturday next. So as not to seem too obvious, she planned to stay away for a week at least and then casually drop in at the office, ostensibly to get more advice from her mentor.

As she stood one morning pressing the dress she planned to wear for the crucial visit to Curtis and

Price, she sighed, set the iron down, and gazed out the window into the maze of clotheslines in the backyard. She was so tired, she thought. It seemed as though she'd been running for years. Running, fighting, scheming, outsmarting—even the man she loved had to be connived for. How she envied those girls who had but to wait for life's delights to fall into their laps. Rich, soft, learned girls with none of the abrasiveness one saw in the poor. She had once told Ruth that the rich were nicer, and Ruth had said, "Well, if they are, it's because they've got a good reason." Tracy had said, "What difference does it make why it's true? Don't you agree that they're nicer?"

Soft voices, good manners, elegant carriage, a gentle way with children—this was what she had seen in the volunteers who came to the slums to help the immigrants. And she had longed to be one of them, longed to be serene enough not to have to shout, grab, connive, or scream. Could it be learned? she wondered. Once the family was settled and she was married to Russell, could she throw off her old self and become like them? Would people ever say, "Kind Tracy Sullivan . . . angel of mercy . . . lovely bearing . . . a gentlewoman . . . class"?

Later, as she was getting ready for the noon class, there was a rap on the door to the classroom. Early student, she thought, for Louise had her own key. Tracy went to open the door, and there stood Russell, all smiles and blond good looks, his hand extended.

"Miss Sullivan! How lovely to *see* you again."

"Mr. Curtis." She took his hand.

"Father told me of your little venture. We're very proud of you."

"Oh—yes. Thank you." She was grinning, but two small clouds had dampened her delight. The first was her appearance. If she'd known that he was going to come, she wouldn't have dressed in this dreary gray skirt and worn shirtwaist and she'd at least have powdered her nose. She was also disturbed by his tone. *"Little* venture?" She had expected a reaction more like Michael's "Wow!" But, after all, could she really expect a man of Russell's class to be impressed by a place like this?

"So you've hired Louise away from us too," he said.

Cloud number three. He remembered Louise. Was that why he was here? Oh, why hadn't she fired the girl a month ago? What was wrong with her brain these days? But she needed Louise. And after all, Louise was only an employee. She, Tracy, outshone her in rank, at least. And she had more money than Louise, for all the latter's genteel background. And she was smarter about business, for all the latter's academy education. These things were points in her favor, and Russell could hardly fail to take them into account.

"Tell me what you've been doing." She motioned Russell to sit in the instructor's chair behind her desk. She had only five minutes to work on him before the students and Louise began coming in. And the best way to get a man to like you quick was to ask him about himself.

"I have graduated," he said. "And now I go forth to seek my fortune." He smiled.

"Did you not plan to go to law school?" She was careful to keep her voice low and to articulate her words. She was careful also to keep her eyes fixed upon his. This was very important, someone had once said.

"I'm afraid that my alma mater will be deprived of my shining countenance. Alas, the law is a shade too tedious to challenge my eclectic mind." He was still smiling.

She didn't know what "eclectic" meant, but she was glad to hear that he wasn't returning to Yale. "Then what do you plan to do?"

"For the moment? To conceive more scintillating campaigns for Curtis and Price."

"You're going to work for your father? For good?"

"Or until one or the other of us succumbs to excessive doses of hyperbole."

"Hyperbole?" Was it a disease? Fumes from a wood stove?

"Exaggeration," he explained when he noticed her knit brow.

"Oh," she said doubtfully, having by this time lost the thread of the witticism. But she remembered to smile.

"You're looking lovely as always," he said.

"Thank you." Her heart gave a leap.

"Have you given further thought to our Bates Cookie campaign?"

He remembered that! It proved that he cared at least a little about her. She said, "We could tie it in with dancing and call it the Hoochie Cookie."

He laughed. "That's capital. Capital!"

She grinned with delight. She'd been saving that one for him. It had taken her a while to come up with it. First she'd asked Mary, who had a library card, to get her a book about recent events. Then she'd plowed through the material trying to find something that she could use in connection with an agency account. The Chicago World's Fair, which had occurred five years earlier, had featured Egyptian women who performed exotic dances that Americans called the hootchie-kootchie. More important, that fair had provided Tracy with what she considered to be a brilliant play on words. She had two other ideas, but she'd save them for later so she wouldn't use up her wit too fast. Oh, if only she were educated and these things could come to her as effortlessly as they did to him. But she wondered if she'd use her education in this particular way. Would she, of her own accord, spend her valuable time thinking up little jokes like this?

At that moment Louise came gliding in looking like a Gibson girl, all blonde hair and blue muslin. Her eyes glowed when she saw who had come. *Oh no*, Tracy thought, having hoped that some young man might have supplanted Russell in Louise's affections.

Russell greeted Louise warmly but didn't wink or make jokes with her as he had with Tracy. Probably

150

because Louise didn't have much of a sense of humor, Tracy thought smugly. She didn't realize how much such things mattered to Russell. He asked if the two young ladies wouldn't join him for lunch in a nearby restaurant. Tracy immediately nodded, but Louise reminded her that someone had to be here to teach the class.

"But you go ahead," said Louise, generously deferring to her employer. She looked bitterly disappointed, however.

"Oh, no." Russell held up a hand. "I asked you both and both it shall be. Perhaps for dinner?"

"We only have an hour before the evening class," Louise explained.

Oh, shut up, Tracy thought. I can *cancel* the evening class, you idiot.

"Then perhaps tomorrow," Russell said. "Surely you don't labor on the Sabbath."

"We don't," Tracy said hastily.

"Then it's settled."

The blue dress, Tracy thought. And think of a few amusing anecdotes to tell him. That would be difficult. There weren't many in her life. That is, many that would appeal to him. But she would try if it killed her, for she had to make Louise look dull beside her. A couplet she had been forced to memorize back in grammar school now flashed into her head and she smiled as a parody came to her:

The wit's the thing
Wherein I'll catch the conscience of the king.

Tracy was sure she cut a fine figure as she sat next to Louise, across the table from Russell. Slim and elegant in blue silk, her hair crimped stylishly, her face rouged and powdered (but discreetly, so as not to look too much like a shopgirl), she was as Gibson-girl-looking as Louise, she thought, if not more so. She had had the good sense to confer with the owner of a ladies' shop catering to the Fifth Avenue clientele. "I have an important dinner engagement," she had said, "and I thought a print scarf might complement a blue silk dress I have." When she described the dress, however, the expert had talked her out of a print and into a plain white. She had also advised Tracy on hat and gloves and ended up selling both to the anxious client. Tracy did not, however, ask the woman's advice as to just how much she ought to tamper with her face. It was presumed that a lady knew enough not to tamper too much, and Tracy was presenting herself as a lady. Thus only a dab of powder and a hint of rouge. Tracy thought she might look washed out, but a lady was supposed to look a little consumptive.

She was fortunate in being so thin that a wasp waist was easily achieved. Unfortunately, her bust and hips were also wanting in girth and only careful padding could create the coveted hourglass look. She had worked at her toilette all morning, thinking that the rich spent most of their time at such tasks. But it was all new to her, and though she enjoyed the novelty, she could not imagine doing this every day.

It took Tracy some time to get acclimated to the

conversation at the table. Louise and Russell spoke of artists and writers that Tracy had never heard of and chuckled over a newspaper humorist named Finley Peter Dunne whom Tracy had heard of but never read. They spoke at length about the Spanish-American War, now being fought, and both Russell and Louise frowned over the country's "jingoism." It wasn't until they were finishing their predinner drinks that Russell turned to Tracy, who had been silent until this time, and politely asked her what she thought ought to be done about the Philippines.

Tracy was in a panic. Like many Americans with hazy ideas about life beyond the Pacific Coast, she didn't know what the Philippines was. Was it a country or an army? An army, probably, under the command of someone named Philips. But suppose she was wrong? At last she said, "I'm not sure about the Philippines—about what we should do about it. I mean them. But I too am opposed to jingoism." (Whatever that was, and she hoped they would not go on to discuss it.)

They did not. They switched to an analysis of novelist Henry James whom Tracy had never read, whom she could not imagine getting excited about. What different worlds they lived in. In her world the stuffed breast of veal was far more stimulating than a reader's opinion of a writer's opinion of fictional people. To them this delicious meal was but a setting for their talk. Louise didn't even touch the grilled mushrooms, so absorbed was she in analyzing James's talent.

Tracy was feeling a growing irritation that she attributed to the fact that the talk seemed boring, passionless. But she reminded herself that passion belonged to the slums. If she wanted to rise in the world, she must learn to appreciate soft-spoken, analytical conversations.

They went on to talk of music, which was a subject that interested Tracy. But her idea of music was "There'll Be a Hot Time in the Old Town Tonight." These two spoke of Tchaikovsky and Paderewski and "the nationalist trend in themes." Asked if she had heard Paderewski when he'd been in New York on tour, Tracy said no and hastily turned back to her mushrooms and brussels sprouts, her mind frantically trying to think of something to say. She had heard of John Philip Sousa and even liked what she knew of his music, so she said at last in a voice suitably nasal, "I tend to favor Sousa myself."

"Yes, of course," Russell said. "Masterful martial music."

"'The Stars and Stripes Forever,'" Tracy said. "I tend to favor that."

"A most inspiring work," nodded Russell. And Louise nodded too.

Tracy, feeling a little more confident, returned to her brussels sprouts. She'd actually contributed an example of "the nationalist trend in themes"! When the talk turned to poetry, she found to her boundless delight that she was again prepared. They were comparing the romantics to the realists of recent years. Russell spoke approvingly of the romantics, "poets who aren't afraid of joy."

"Oh, I agree totally," Tracy gushed. "We need more poets who like joy. I'm sure you've read Ella Wheeler Wilcox."

"I've heard of her," Louise said.

"And read her, of course?" Tracy also turned to Russell.

"Not extensively," he said.

"Oh, but you'd *love* her poems. 'Laugh and the world laughs with you,'" Tracy intoned. "'Weep and you weep alone.'"

Russell and Louise looked at each other uncertainly, trying to determine whether Tracy was serious. And Tracy mistaking this for appreciation of her declamatory talents, continued: "For the sad old earth must borrow its mirth/But has troubles enough of its own."

She wished she could remember the rest of the poem, but she had forgotten what she'd memorized in school.

Russell was still staring at her, his brow knit as though trying to come to some decision. Finally he said, "Sometimes it's hard to tell when you're being serious and when you're being wry."

"What do you mean?" Tracy asked.

"Sousa and Wilcox. Do you take them seriously?"

She was confused. Wasn't she supposed to take them seriously? Had he thought she was joking? Why would she joke about it? Of course that stuff about laughing and weeping was awfully dramatic and a bit silly, but wasn't a line like "Hail to thee

155

blithe spirit" just as bad? Yet Mary had said that "Hail to thee . . ." was by a poet named Shelley who was supposed to be a genius. Then why wasn't Wilcox a genius? Weren't you supposed to like poetry whether or not it was silly, just because it was—well—*poetry?* But Russell seemed to be saying that some poetry was indeed silly. But which? And how could she distinguish? And what about music? Was John Philip Sousa all wrong too? If so, why? She couldn't imagine why.

Russell was still looking at her quizzically, and Tracy still didn't know what to say. At last she gathered her wits about her and drawled, "I just wanted to point out that Sousa and Wilcox have their place."

Russell laughed. "For a while there you had us fooled into thinking that you believed these two were the ranking artists of our generation. You're subtle, Miss Sullivan. Very subtle."

Louise laughed too and finally Tracy joined in, forcing the chuckles through a constricted throat. What a close call! How near to making a fool of herself she had come! And if she had insisted that she had in fact *liked* Wilcox, what on earth would he have thought of her? Of course he knew she came from the Lower East Side, but she had tried to give the impression that poor did not mean uneducated, witless, or tasteless. She'd wanted him to see her kind of poor as similar to Lincoln's. A temporary condition soon to be overcome by strength of character and brilliance of mind.

As the talk turned to politics again, Tracy developed a strategy for handling it. By analyzing Russell's facial expressions, she could tell in advance how he felt about a given topic and was able to prepare a suitable nod or frown that would not only indicate a general agreement with his ideas but would also convey the impression that there was heavy thought behind her agreement. Thus when he frowned over the methods of newspaperman Hearst, she frowned too, but in a more lingering way as though to say that Hearst's methods were not just bad but devious, dangerous, nothing to joke about.

"Before the war," Russell said, "Hearst sent a photographer to Cuba to find some stories of Spanish abuse so that he could sell more papers. The photographer wired Hearst that he could find no such stories and that he wanted to come home because there wasn't going to be any war. Hearst wired back, 'Please remain. You furnish pictures. I will furnish war.'"

"No!" Louise exclaimed. "He *didn't*."

Russell nodded. "Yes. That telegram exchange is fairly well documented."

Tracy said, "Oh, yes, I'd heard about it" (she hadn't), and was shaking her head in dismay long after the others had skipped to another subject. Russell seemed to be impressed by her distress. As he was impressed by her later delight over another bon mot of Finley Peter Dunne. She had learned how to fake her way through a genteel dinner. But she was so exhausted from the effort that she ached all over.

*   *   *

HE took them home in a hack, dropping Louise off first and Tracy last. She understood this to mean that he wanted time alone with her, perhaps to ask if he might see her again. As the hack drew up in front of the school, she toyed with the idea of asking him into her quarters for tea. But this wasn't a friend from the East Side. This was a high-class man. She'd get a lot further if she acted like high-class ladies acted and simply thanked him for the lovely evening and held out her gloved hand demurely.

He stepped around to assist her out and by careful concentration she managed the maneuver with all the grace of one who had never ridden an El or elbowed her way into a trolley. How fast she was learning it all! But would the knowledge stick? And would there come a day when being with him didn't tire her out so?

"It was a delightful evening," she said, offering her hand.

"The pleasure was mine. We must do it again soon."

"I should like that," she said, careful to look steadily into his eyes.

"You're an enigma, Miss Sullivan."

What the deuce was an "enigma"? It sounded like what the doctor prescribed for a purging. "Am I?" she said doubtfully.

"I can't quite figure you out."

"Indeed?" So "enigma" must mean mysterious.

"Indeed yes," he said. "Shall I see you safe inside?"

"Only to the door, sir." She smiled and kept her eyes coyly averted, wishing she could work up the appropriate blush.

"Of course." He grinned and waited while she extracted her keys from her handbag. "Well, it's been delightful, Miss Sullivan."

She smiled. "You may call me Tracy if you like."

"Tracy. And you shall call me Russell."

"I like that name," she said truthfully. "Russell."

"It's of French derivation."

"But you're not French, are you?"

"No. English and Welsh."

Sworn enemies of Ireland, she thought. What would Pa and Mary think when she married a Protestant? But would she marry him? Now that the year-long fantasy was flesh again, she had her doubts. Assuming she could get rid of Louise, would she still have a chance with Russell? He was so far above her in class, and there must be a dozen other ladies in New York who also melted in the presence of such charm. Why hadn't she thought of this before? What had made her think he would not be able to resist her? Probably it had been the confidence generated by her success in business. But she was beginning to see that success in romance required different skills.

"And so good-night," he said.

"Good-night." She glided into the classroom, then through the door to her own quarters, where she proceeded to disintegrate like the wonderful one-hoss shay. Off with the dress, off with the corset, off with the pinching shoes, the padding of bust and derriere, the stockings, the combs in her hair. Her face relaxed too. And her arms and legs felt looser. She had not realized how tightly she'd been bound up until the restrictions were removed. Oh, the joy of flopping into an armchair dressed only in a camisole and drawers, her brain relaxing along with the rest of her! She knew she could not laze around for long. Too soon she must begin keeping up with the daily paper, must take out a library card and acquaint herself with literature, must make reservations at a play or a concert. But tonight she would just sit here and let her poor head take a rest.

Chapter Twelve

Russell took the young women out again, but he persisted in treating them as a unit. There was a dinner in late June and a concert in early July, both ending just as the first occasion had ended with Russell shaking Louise's hand and later Tracy's. What his motives were, Tracy couldn't imagine. Was he so shy with women as to prefer safety in numbers? Or was he afraid that in showing preference for one he'd be hurting the feelings of the other? Which one did he favor? Tracy hadn't a clue.

But there were diversions to amuse her while she waited for the man to make up his mind, among these the attentions of two young men, both brothers of students. One took Tracy to dinner and Central Park, while another took her to Tony Pastor's vaudeville house, one of her favorite places. Both bored her a little, but she liked their admiration and she needed beaux to make Russell jealous, so she charmed them along. There was also an outing at Coney Island with the Litvaks and their baby plus Michael and the twins. They went swimming, saw the sights, took the children on rides, and stuffed themselves with franks, sodas, and ice cream. It was a delightful excursion for Tracy, and the others had a good time too. They sang songs all the way home on the trolleys and the group ended the day by joining the dancing at an Italian block party on Elizabeth Street. That is, Tracy, David, and the children danced. Michael and Ruth were more inhibited. They watched the others fake their way through Sicilian folk dances.

Ruth watched Michael's face as he followed Tracy's movement. His eyes were luminous and he smiled. He was obviously enchanted. Michael had always been fond of Tracy, probably because, Ruth thought, Tracy was the very opposite of Michael's mother. Tracy was vital, opinionated, able not only to stand on her own two feet but to pull her family up with her. She was the kind of woman Michael would have been likely to fall for. And how lucky for him that he had found her, as it were, in his own backyard. As for Tracy, she was pretty lucky too. She had a man who understood her and admired her.

"So when are you two going to make it official?" Ruth asked Tracy later as they walked down the sidewalk toward home. Ahead of them strode Michael, David, and the children, and Ruth was already visualizing the two families getting together for future excursions. "Tracy?"

"Make what official?" Tracy asked.

"You. Mike. Marriage. Babies."

"Marriage? Babies? Michael?" Tracy laughed. They sounded like a couple of language instructors.

162

Then she said, "But we don't want each other that way, Ruth."

"You *don't?*" Ruth was shocked.

"We like each other a lot, but that's all it'll ever be. I'd never marry a neighborhood boy, and he doesn't want a neighborhood girl."

"Why not?"

"I don't know. The one you marry should be a little mysterious, don't you think? Michael and I know too much about each other. I knew him when he was a hooligan and he knew me when I dressed in rags. We could hear each other yelling across the airshaft. We could see each other's laundry on the line. How romantic can you get when you're practically brother and sister?" Of course she had felt romantic once, that night on the roof. But it had been long ago, before she'd met Russell, and at that she had only wanted to kiss Michael, not marry him.

Ruth, the expert, intoned, "Married people are a lot like brother and sister. It's just as well you are used to it."

"Oh, no." Tracy shook her head. "That's not for me. I want some glamour, romance, violins over dinner." But mostly money, she thought, knowing better than to stress the point with socialist Ruth who'd be sure to launch into a speech.

"Glamour?" Ruth snorted. "You're a dreamer."

"Maybe so, but that's what I want. And I'm sure Michael wants it himself."

Ruth shrugged and said nothing more. Tracy might not want Michael, she thought, but Michael wanted Tracy. Ruth wondered when Michael was planning to tell the lady. And would he change Tracy's mind?

WHILE Tracy waited for some sign from Russell, summer was marching on. She had better go to Massachusetts to see Katherine. She had finally read the article David had mentioned and determined not only the name of Katherine's town (Lanston) but also the name of an inn where she might stay. It would only involve a two-day trip. She left on a Sunday afternoon and planned to return on Tuesday. Louise would only have to run the school alone for one full day and half of the next.

It was a long, intensely hot trip involving changes at New Haven and Springfield plus a wait of two hours in Springfield for the train to this model burg. A head-to-toe powdering with baking soda had eliminated the smell of perspiration, but she still looked and felt wilted by the time she reached the tiny Lanston inn. She had sent a note to Katherine Madison introducing herself as a businesswoman who had read the article on the mill with interest and wanted to discuss its features with Katherine. No hint that she was looking for a happy berth for a family and no hint that she had been related to Luke. All this she would reveal only when and if the time was right. Katherine had written back that Miss Sullivan was certainly welcome to visit the mill and that she would look forward to chatting with another business-woman.

After spending a restless night on a lumpy mattress at the inn, Tracy devoted a good hour to readying herself for the audience with Katherine. At last she was ready to go and went down the stairs to the main room, telling the sleepy innkeeper that she wouldn't be having breakfast after all. It was late and she was in a hurry. And in any case she couldn't have eaten. Tracy could never eat when she was nervous, and the Sullivan future depended on how things went today.

When Tracy saw the town in the morning light, she caught her breath. How lovely it was with its center green, its white Congregational church, its aristocratic houses on one side of the green and the small businesses on the other, where the inn was. Serene and shaded by great green trees, it was a town with its roots in another century, a town that meant tradition and security. Of course in the mill area it would be different. Here the smoke, the noise, the presence of Irish, Italians, and other old and late immigrants might remind her not only of New York but also of the factory owner in Connecticut who had turned his back on Pa and all of them. The feeling of those times came over her again. The stunned look on Pa's face when he said, "They let us go." Both him and Gramp.

"But it's not fair!" Tracy had shouted. "You were a good worker. You never missed many days."

"That's what I told them. They said it didn't make no difference. They got cheaper help."

"But it must make a difference. They care about us. They just can't push us out like that."

165

But they had. Coldly, with no apologies, no explanations except, "A factory is a business, Mr. Sullivan. That's all we can tell you. There are openings in other towns and many opportunities in the cities. . . ."

Tracy continued down the main street of Lanston. She wanted to believe that it would be different here. Store owners smiled and said hello to her. Little girls admired her city attire. A man in a milk wagon asked if he could help her, and she requested directions to the mill. She had to walk down a street that started elegant and ended shabby, then past the railroad tracks and over a bridge. Then she was in the industrial heart of the community, an area never depicted in Currier and Ives's New England paintings. Still it wasn't bad. Though there was one development of bleak, packed-together company houses, there was another where each house had plenty of yard space and room for gardens. They were at least on a par with the house they had left in Connecticut, and these you could actually buy! She stood in front of one house and remembered her mother, remembered herself as a schoolgirl running in the door and shouting, "I'm home, Ma. Any cookies?" Tears came into her eyes.

She would get it all back again if it killed her. Imagine a paid-for house only a stone's throw from the picturesque town center? Imagine Tommy and Kerry setting out for school over the bridge on a dewy spring morning fragrant with the smell of fresh flowers? And the summer picnics, the Independence

166

Day parades, the Christmas skating parties, the country dances, the walks in the woods with a sweetheart? Mary would walk in these woods with her high school teacher reciting poetry and dreaming to her heart's content. Pa would walk through town, perhaps with a kindhearted widow who'd reform him as Ma would have wanted. All the years in the slums would be forgotten. They'd be back with Ma again at least in spirit. Oh, she had to get through to Katherine today. She just *had* to.

Tracy walked up the flight of stairs leading to what she assumed were the mill headquarters. A workman directed her to Katherine's office, which consisted of an outer and inner chamber. In the outer chamber sat two rows of typists all properly dressed in shirtwaists and dark skirts. But none was as skilled as her own graduates, Tracy observed smugly. And none had decent posture either. Her girls had been taught to sit erect and to try to avoid touching their backs to their chairs. Fingers were to be held just so and arms tensed in a certain manner. These girls slouched and their palms practically dragged on the desk while an occasional finger seemed to groan its way to the key and then flop back again as though in exhaustion. Or so she fancied as she observed them disdainfully, feeling courage returning as she realized that she had no need to feel inferior to Katherine, that she, Tracy, was not only an accomplished businesswoman herself, but a trainer of true professionals.

There was a female secretary sitting to the right of Katherine's door. Leaning forward, she asked in a heavy brogue, "You'll be wanting to see Mrs. Madison?"

"I have an appointment," said Tracy, her nose at a higher angle than usual. If *she'd* trained the girl, she would not only have stood up but would also have greeted the caller by name. "Miss Sullivan? How do you do. I am Bridget O'Greenhorn, Mrs. Madison's secretary. Mrs. Madison is expecting you. Won't you come in?" *That* was the way things should be done!

The secretary knocked on Katherine's door and shouted, ""Someone's here to see you."

"Someone?" came a voice from behind the door.

"And what's your name, miss?" asked the secretary.

"Tracy Sullivan," said Tracy.

"Sullivan!" shouted the secretary.

"Sullivan?" queried Katherine through the closed door. "Oh, yes. The one from New York. I thought that was tomorrow. I'm going out of my mind today. . . ." The door opened as she spoke, and Katherine emerged, tendrils escaping from her upswept brown hair, glasses perched on the end of her nose, her face shiny and her brown frock limp. She stood slouched in the doorway, a hand on her hip, looking thin and harassed. Was this Katherine Madison, ruler of Madison Mills, lover of Luke? She looked like a housekeeper in a tenement building. All that was missing was an apron and a bucket of suds. Tracy felt majestic beside her in her crisp navy and white ensemble, with her smooth-finished face, her flawless hair.

Tracy extended a gloved hand first, since Katherine made no effort to do so in her distraction. Tracy said with a smile from which she tried to conceal the condescension, "How do you do, Mrs. Madison?"

"Yes. How do you do?" She shook Tracy's hand firmly. "Won't you come in?"

The office matched its mistress in its utter disarray. Piles of papers, swatches of materials, books, pens, and file folders strewn about. Katherine actually had to clear off a chair in order to give Tracy a place to sit. "Excuse me," she said. "It's proving to be a catastrophic day."

"I could come back this afternoon," said Tracy.

"No, no. It's fine. Now is fine." She smiled and to Tracy's astonishment lit a cigarette. Good grief, the woman even *smoked!* Katherine said, "So you wanted to discuss women in business. Are you with a feminist organization or a businesswoman's association?"

"No. Neither." Tracy had never actually rehearsed what to say, for she'd wanted first to determine what sort of person this mill owner was. She'd been prepared for a cold reception, a gracious reception, even a wary reception, but she had not expected anything so casual as this. That was the word to describe Katherine. Casual in the extreme. Therefore she, Tracy, must be informal too—but ever on her guard. She allowed herself to slouch a little in her chair. Then she said, "I'd read of your mill and I thought it would be an ideal place for my family."

"Your family?"

169

"I mean my father, brothers, and sisters. I'm not married."

Katherine smiled. "You did look rather young to have a family of your own. But I don't understand. Why do you want my advice? Do you mean you'd like me to give my opinion of the town?"

"No. I mean yes. But also—you see, my father was once a factory worker and I hoped you might have a position open in the mill."

"So you're asking for work? I mean for your father?"

"Yes."

Katherine looked surprised. Apparently the stunning navy outfit had led the woman to believe that Tracy was aristocracy looking around for a summer place in Lanston. Tracy explained that though she had recently started a business, her family wasn't wealthy, and she wanted them out of New York and in a town where the opportunity existed for them to work and to get ahead. She said she had enough money for a substantial down payment on a house and that she would pay Mrs. Madison on the spot if Mrs. Madison could give some guarantee of employment opportunities.

Katherine shook her head. "I'm afraid there's nothing. I'm sorry that article was ever printed because I get so many letters and telegrams asking—"

"But surely people resign once in a while."

"Yes, but not often, and I have waiting lists with so many names."

170

Then she'd have to get moved to the head of the list, Tracy thought. And there was only one way to do that. She leaned forward in her chair and took a deep breath. Forgive me, Luke, but I have no choice.

". . . and sorry you made the long trip," Katherine was saying.

"Oh, it wasn't a long—that is, it was just an excursion from Springfield," Tracy lied. "I had business in Springfield and I thought that as long as I was there I might as well come to see you." Tracy took another deep breath and said, "We met once and I always remembered you."

"We met?"

Tracy nodded. "When I was introduced, I was—well—I remembered it afterward. I'd never met a woman who ran a mill before and I was impressed." No one at the funeral had mentioned that Katherine ran a mill, but Katherine would not remember this, Tracy thought.

Katherine said, "Excuse me. I don't seem to recall. Who introduced us, and where?"

"Alison Sullivan. At the funeral of my cousin."

"The funeral of—you mean *Luke?*" She stubbed out her cigarette.

"Yes. You were there with a group of people."

Katherine's face grew pale and she swallowed hard. When Tracy saw this, she knew that the story was true. Every word of it must be true. Luke and this woman. What had they seen in each other for him to risk his wife and family and professional reputation? Katherine was much younger than Luke would have

171

been. She was pretty (and would have been prettier without the glasses, the slouch, and the cascading hair), but she was no great beauty as his wife had been. Well, maybe he hadn't wanted great beauty. Maybe he had wanted a woman who would love him as much as she loved herself.

Katherine, still pale, folded her hands and looked again at Tracy. "I'm afraid I don't recall the introduction. There were so many people. Luke was my brother's associate. I knew his sister very well too, of course. How is she?"

"Alison? She passed away last winter. She was—"

"Dead?" Katherine's mouth fell open. "Alison too?"

"She died of pneumonia. I didn't hear about it until afterward. Another cousin told Pa that—"

"*Alison?*" Katherine's voice broke, and tears poured down her face.

"I'm sorry," Tracy whispered, wishing this hadn't come up.

"I didn't keep in touch," Katherine said. "I just thought she'd always be there whenever I needed to—whenever I needed. . . ." She trailed off, crying and searching for a handkerchief.

Alison must have known about that affair, Tracy thought. Possibly many people had known. Had the wife?

It was quite a while before Katherine composed herself, placing her glasses on the desk. "Please excuse me. It was such a shock."

"I understand."

"So you're Luke's cousin. How were you related, Miss Sullivan?"

"My great-great-grandfather and his great-grandfather were brothers in Galway."

"I see."

"When I decided to go into business, I asked him to give me advice. He was a very kind man."

"He was that," she said, nodding. Then she scrutinized Tracy's face. "You say you remembered me because I owned a mill?"

"Yes."

"Is that all you know about me?"

"I know that Luke worked with your brother."

"And that's all?"

"Yes."

"I see. Did you live on the East Side?"

"Monroe Street."

"The East Side? And you'd never heard anything else about me?"

"Like what?" Tracy looked down at her hands. Should she admit it? Katherine seemed so suspicious anyway. But if she admitted it, then Katherine would know that Tracy was playing on her weakness.

"Had you heard talk, Miss Sullivan?"

Tracy didn't answer, but the color of her face did. She flamed under Katherine's close scrutiny.

Katherine nodded. "I thought so. And you decided that if you came to the woman who loved him, you'd get what you wanted."

Without thinking, Tracy blurted, "I didn't know what else to do."

Oh, *when* would she learn to harness her mouth? With this admission she knew it was all over. The lovely house, job, stocks, town—all down the drain. The woman had figured her out, knew perfectly well Tracy was counting on the fact that Katherine might do anything for a cousin of Luke's. But she wouldn't help a schemer—cousin or not.

Katherine stood up and Tracy rose too, anxious to leave as quickly as possible. Katherine opened the door and said to her secretary, "Cancel my appointments if I have any. Miss Sullivan and I will be at the house."

"At the house?" Tracy said.

"Mine. I want to talk to you."

TRACY had expected a mansion, but this was a small frame house no different from one of the company houses except that it was cluttered with expensive furnishings, books, Chinese fans, bric-a-brac. An extension of Katherine. Tracy's eye fell on an array of childish pictures framed on the wall.

"My daughter Julia," explained Katherine. "These were done a few years ago. She's eleven now."

"Is she here?"

"She's away with friends in the country."

Tracy nodded. "I read in that article that you had a daughter. You were widowed, weren't you?"

"That's a nice way of putting it. Actually my husband was murdered. During a strike."

Tracy hadn't known this. "I'm sorry." She decided not to ask for details. She was nervous, confused as to

174

why Katherine wanted to talk to her. But she must make some sort of talk, so she said, "Do you and your daughter live here alone?"

"Except for the housekeeper. She's in Boston today. And next month I'll have a man around again. That is, we'll be moving in with him. I'm remarrying."

"Oh? Uh—best wishes. Someone from this town?"

Katherine nodded. "Nick Taylor. A lawyer. I've known him most of my life."

"I see. Well. Best wishes."

"Yes. Thanks." Katherine motioned toward another room. "Come join me in the kitchen. Sit at the table while I make tea."

Just like the tenements, Tracy thought. Guests gathering in the kitchen. What did Katherine want to talk about?

Katherine told her as she brewed the tea and set out cakes. "We might as well be honest with each other, Miss Sullivan."

"Yes," sighed Tracy.

"You want something from me—"

"Yes."

"And I'm prepared to do my best."

Tracy's mouth fell open. "You are?"

"But first I want something from you."

Tracy gulped. "What?"

"No one knew about Luke but Alison. Others gossiped—all Elizabeth Street and the East Side gossiped—but no one knew for sure."

"I'm not trying to blackmail. I never planned to

tell anyone."

"I didn't think you did. In any case, it wouldn't hurt me. It would hurt Luke's family."

"I know that. But what did you want from me if not silence?"

"How can I explain it? I want you to talk about him. I want to see him through your eyes. I want to tell you about him too. Does that make sense?"

"That's all? That's all you want?"

"Isn't it enough?"

"In exchange for jobs and—"

"Yes. Yes. I'll arrange something. It may take time."

Jesus, Mary, and Joseph, Tracy thought, unable to believe either the motive or her good fortune.

Over tea, Katherine told Tracy about her relationship with Luke. Her father, Kent, a Civil War surgeon had rented an office to Luke when Katherine was very young. Kent had died, and years later his son became a surgeon, eventually occupying his father's office. Luke had stayed on through all these changes and had been very close to Katherine's family. Through the years Katherine had come to know him well, but not until she was twenty had she fallen in love with him. Because of religion he couldn't divorce his wife, so Katherine had married this Madison. Julia was born, and a few years later Edward Madison was killed by one of his workers during a strike against the mill. Tracy inferred that the husband had been a cruel boss, though Katherine did not actually say so. The murderer had also

176

burned their home, so Katherine had gone back to New York with Julia. The love affair with Luke had started then, in 1893. Once they had almost run away together, but in the end they had decided it couldn't work. Katherine came back to take over the mill and she did not see Luke again until the day he died.

"He came to New York for my brother's wedding and later he and I walked down to Alison's. . . ."

"She told me," Tracy said almost in a whisper. "How it happened."

"Did she mention me?"

"She never told me she knew. She just said he'd come to her flat with a friend."

Katherine nodded. "So that was the end of him. And when Alison died that was the end of—it broke the last link. And now I've met you. Can you understand why I asked you here? You make it all come alive again."

How she must have loved him, Tracy thought. Would she ever love like that? Reaching out to a stranger only because the stranger knew a secret. Turning what should have been a distaste for Tracy into a kind of reverence? It was plain that Katherine had no intention of secluding herself in her grief. She was planning to marry again, and she must have some affection for the man. But her love for Luke would always be there. Again and again she would search for ways to make him come alive. Would she, Tracy, *ever* love like that?

They talked for most of the afternoon. Katherine wanted to know about Tracy and her background. At one point she said, "I understand you, I think. You're so much like he must have been." She didn't say it, but Tracy sensed that Katherine was even forgiving her today's conniving. And all because Tracy was doing the kind of things Luke might have done.

So Luke had come to rescue her again, Tracy thought. He had reached beyond the limits of his own life and was coming to her through Katherine. Tracy very nearly wept.

Toward dusk Tracy said that it was time to leave for the inn, but Katherine asked her to stay the night and sent a neighbor child to fetch Tracy's bags at the inn. They had a supper of sandwiches and salad made earlier by the housekeeper and later had cakes and lemonade into which Katherine slipped a healthy tot of gin.

"I like my little nip," she explained. "Working women eventually get like men."

"I'll remember that," Tracy said.

Katherine said she would contact Tracy as soon as an opening came up. "I can't fire a man to make room for your father. That wouldn't be fair."

"I'm glad in a way. It means you'd never do it to Pa."

"You say there's a brother too?"

"Pat. He's fifteen. If there are any more openings—"

"But shouldn't he be in high school?"

It depends how long Pa can last at a job, Tracy thought. Aloud she said, "I hope he will go."

She learned that Katherine wasn't the only owner

of this place. There were in-laws and their descendants who also held portions of the mill. Katherine was only a part owner, but she was president and chairman of the board, and she had a genuine concern for the welfare of the workers. Tracy guessed that the operatives must adore her.

Just before retiring, Tracy asked Katherine if she knew what Luke's wife had been like.

"Beautiful and spoiled, very concerned with herself. But not malicious—just spoiled. I don't think Luke ever loved her. I think he wanted full respectability and this was the way to get it. So he probably chased her blindly without ever really knowing why. Later he met me. I understood him better, loved him so much more. But he couldn't marry me, and I think after all that it might have been for the best."

"The best?"

"We live in a romantic age, so it's hard sometimes to remember that there are things more important than love. I'm talking about survival. With me Luke would have had love, but he wouldn't have survived."

"But he *didn't* survive. Not for long."

"I'm not talking just about Luke. I'm talking about his whole family, his line, everything he'd worked for. What would have happened if he'd stayed with me? A charge of adultery, his career in jeopardy, family in disgrace. I know some men might do it. Men born to the manner, men who aren't greatly affected by scandal. But a man like Luke had to put survival ahead of everything. He had no choice.'' She paused. "I once hated him for it, but I've come to understand it.''

Tracy went to bed but lay awake most of the night. She was thinking primarily of her good fortune, but occasionally she thought of how sad it had been for Katherine and Luke. A man and woman married to people they didn't love. One of them—Luke— married for a reason he didn't understand. A hopeless love, a pointless death, a mourning stretched out over a lifetime, a groping for crumbs of remembrance even from conniving strangers. Tracy was young, and despite many misfortunes, she wanted to believe that life was more decent than that. But at least it had been decent to her this day. She fell asleep finally with a smile on her face.

Chapter Thirteen

Through August of 1898 it seemed that all Tracy did was wait. Every day she waited for a letter from Katherine saying that a job and a house had come though. Every day she waited for a knock on the classroom door and the sight of Russell's face. Possibly he had gone on holiday somewhere and just hadn't thought to mention it. What was she going to do about this situation? Pay another call on his father? It was Russell who should be paying a call on *hers*.

In late August Ruth suffered a bad cold complicated by summer complaint. For a time she was very sick, and David said it was because she'd been doing too much. He sent their little boy to her mother's in Brooklyn and shipped Ruth off to Tracy's where she wouldn't be compelled to care for either her housework on Monroe or her child in Brooklyn. She was to rest thoroughly for two straight days, he commanded. And he even provided a cot for her to sleep on, since there was no room in Tracy's bed.

The visit gave the young women a chance to talk as they had not talked in a long time. Tracy told Ruth of her plans to move her family to Massachusetts but made Ruth promise that she wouldn't say a word to anyone until the job came through.

"I want it to be a surprise. I've been trying to think of ways to tell them. Maybe I'll just show the papers to Pa. Very casual. 'By the way, Pa, I thought you'd like a house, so here it is.' No, no. I have a better idea. I'll find a picture of a New England town and hang it in the kitchen. Then I'll get Mary to read a poem about New England. Then, when they're all drooling—"

"Make sure she doesn't read Whittier or they'll be sneaking out the door."

Tracy laughed. "I remember from school. 'Snow-bound.' A million stanzas long." She paused. "Do you like poetry?"

"Some. Not that stuff."

"Ever heard of Ella Wheeler Wilcox?"

"The name. Never read her."

"'Laugh and the world laughs with you/Weep and you weep alone.'"

"Oh, that one. Makes me gag."

"But why? Why is it worse than Shelley and all them?"

"I don't know. Maybe because it's a lecture. Why do you even care?"

"A man I like said—"

"Aha!"

"Never mind 'aha.' What's wrong with the poem and what's wrong with John Philip Sousa?"

"Who?"

182

" 'The Stars and Stripes Forever.' Fellow who wrote it."

"*Nothing's* wrong. That's a grand tune," Ruth said.

"*I* thought so."

"But your 'man' didn't?"

"He just thought it wasn't real music. I guess he must mean tunes like Beethoven's."

"Let me guess. He's college, huh?"

Tracy nodded. She told Ruth about Russell and the dinners and lamented that she wasn't making as much progress with him as she'd hoped to.

"So you want to get instant education?"

Tracy nodded. "I wish."

Ruth sighed and shook her head. "I only have eighth grade and a little night school," she said. "I know a lot, I read an awful lot, but there're things I'll never know. There're things you just have to be born with. There're kids who are still in the cradle when their parents start telling them why some kinds of music are good and who Rembrandt is. So by the time they grow up they don't even have to think about it. It's all there." She paused. "I'll never be one of those. I can help my son learn more than me, but even he'll never be one of those. It takes generations."

"And I'll never be one either. Is that what you're trying to say?"

"Well . . ."

"All right. Maybe I only got to eighth grade, but it was a good school, much better than here. We read poems. We even read Shakespeare."

"So did we. 'Antony's Funeral Oration.' So tell me, what sense does that make to a kid? You don't read the play, just the oration. Do you know who Mark Antony was?"

"A Roman," Tracy said.

"Yeah, but what did he do?"

"I don't know. Told people to throw him their ears."

"See what I mean?" Ruth said.

"All right. Then I'll read the play. And I'll ask Mary to tell me all about poems."

"You can do that. You can do it day and night. But do it for yourself, not him. Because some day this *mensh* of yours will ask you if you think Shakespeare's stage directions are better than Shaw's and you'll be back where you started. I'm telling you, you have to be born to that life. You have to grow up with it. You have to go to fancy academies and college—"

"Well, I *can't* do that!" Tracy stamped her foot in vexation. "And I won't sit back and take second best just because I don't know about Shaw."

"What second best? Just because they're not Yankees with college education? Don't you want a man who understands you? Don't you want to feel comfortable with him? Like should stick with like, I always say." Or with Mike, Ruth thought, liking the rhyme and wishing she could say it aloud.

"Oh, you and your cracker-barrel philosophy!" Tracy shouted. "Is that why you stay in the slums when you know you could be rich and successful? You and David could be rich tomorrow if you didn't have this hopeless attitude."

"Hopeless? I'm a poor Jewish girl who barely escaped Poland with my life. I'm not in the Four Hundred and I don't want to be. I can't think of anything more boring than that Newport bunch. I'm living where people need me, people with real problems. And you expect me to sit around worrying about the difference between Sousa and Strauss?"

"You get a real boot out of making fun of me, don't you?"

"I'm not making fun of you. I just think it's so silly."

"Oh, you do, do you? Well you know what *I* think is silly? Your excuses. All this crying about the poor when the truth is you're afraid of any place that isn't the East Side."

"Are you crazy?"

"You're a blatherskite and a coward."

"And you're not? Running to hide with those uptown shlemiels? Talk about cowards! *They're* the ones who don't face the world. They sit on chairs in restaurants picking at their food and picking at things like Henry James's similes and for all I know picking their noses. But Tracy Sullivan thinks being with nose pickers is courage."

"You!" Tracy roared, for a moment at a loss for more words.

Ruth ranted on. "I'm sick and tired of being jeered at because I don't care about the things *you* want."

"And *I'm* sick and tired of seeing you smirk when I

say I want to be rich and successful."

"Then you won't have to see it!" Ruth stood up and stomped into the bedroom. She started throwing her things into her satchel.

"Where are you going?" Tracy asked as she stormed in behind her.

"Home. Where do you think?"

"You can't go home. You have to rest. I promised David."

"Rest?" Ruth shouted. "You call this *rest?*"

Tracy looked at Ruth's angry face and at the arm flying up and down as soap, toothbrush, and nightgown were retrieved and tossed into the satchel. No, it wasn't exactly a picture of tranquility, and the irony made Tracy smile. Soon she was at the brink of outright laughter, for Ruth was now charging around like a wild filly as she searched for her stockings. Tracy tried hard to suppress the mirth. This was a serious fight, after all. But the guffaws burst forth, one after another, and she was helplessly clutching her sides.

"What's so funny?" bellowed Ruth.

"You. I agree you're not resting." And Tracy was off again, tears running out of her eyes. Ruth stood glowering, her hands on her hips, until Tracy was in control. The laughter had driven much of the anger from Tracy. She said, "Oh come on, Ruth, don't go. Please."

"Now look—"

"I promised David."

"Then I'll explain to him," said Ruth.

186

"No, please. You're supposed to be recuperating. We'll just—we'll just set limits on what to talk about."

Ruth was puzzled. "Limits?"

"Yes. I'll tell you mine."

"Go ahead. This should be interesting."

"Don't keep reminding me where I come from. I already know, and I don't want to have to keep hearing it."

Ruth thought about this a moment and then said, "All right. And don't keep trying to get me to forget where I come from. Maybe you won't believe this, but I *like* where I come from."

Tracy nodded. The two studied each other gravely. Then Tracy cleared her throat and said she was going into the kitchen to make the two of them some tea. Ruth also cleared her throat and took her toothbrush out of her satchel. She laid it next to the washbasin on Tracy's secondhand pine dresser. Tracy went into the kitchen, relieved and yet a little uneasy. She was glad the friendship hadn't broken up, but she had wanted Ruth as an enthusiastic ally in her struggles. And now she knew that this was not to be.

Chapter Fourteen

In the early autumn Russell came back from a holiday on the Massachusetts shore and began seeing Louise exclusively. It started with tickets to plays and concerts on Saturday nights and soon included frequent calls at the school to see his girl home after the evening class was over. Tracy's pride took a brutal beating. But after pounding pillows and coming near to firing Louise, she began to think about the situation and realized that she'd been hanging onto a dream that had begun to die as long ago as the first time she'd dined with these two intellectuals. Was it Russell she'd really longed for or was it that part of him that had once made her forget temporarily her grim life on Monroe Street? When confronted with the whole of the man and the prospect of having to live up to his expectations, her enjoyment of him had lessened. Lately she'd been thinking of him as something of a project pursued only because she was too stubborn to give it up. Though she hated to admit it, that argument with Ruth had helped her to see this more clearly.

Still, Tracy's pride was badly hurt, and the

presence of Louise constantly reminded her of her defeat. Yet she wouldn't fire Louise. The woman was too good a teacher, too valuable to the business. By November Tracy had accepted the inevitable and had begun welcoming the attentions of other men.

Throughout this time, Tracy remained civil to Russell and Louise, neither of whom had ever suspected her passion. As the days went on, the civility became more natural. She could view dispassionately the sight of the two together and even trade pleasantries when Russell came by to pick up Louise. She scarcely reacted to the news that the two would be formally engaged at Christmas, except to worry that Louise might quit working—and who could she find to replace her?

As Tracy learned to look upon Russell as just another man, she began seeing flaws in him that she had missed while in the throes of love. The jokes about the agency weren't funny to her anymore. She saw them as a kind of childish rebellion against his background. He could afford to be contemptuous; his survival didn't depend upon his work. How far would his jokes have taken him if he'd been confronted with an empty school, a broken window, and a family utterly dependent on him? A foolish, spoiled baby was Russell Curtis. His only redeeming virtue had been the money in his family.

On a chilly Saturday in November, when the afternoon class was over and Tracy was preparing to close up for the weekend, Russell came by to pick up Louise. They were going to an early dinner before the play. Tracy greeted him cordially and told him that Louise had already gone home.

"But she said she'd meet me here," he said.

"I know, but she decided to change. A student got ink on her dress. She said to tell you she'd meet you at the restaurant."

"Which restaurant?" he said. "We never agreed on one."

"I have no idea," Tracy said impatiently.

"I'll have to ring her up. May I use your telephone?"

"Be my guest," she said, annoyance in her voice.

In order to give the name of the restaurant, Russell had to ring up not Louise but the candy store on her corner. Louise's family didn't yet have a telephone. The relative poverty of the family had initially caused Russell's parents some consternation, though they were fond of Louise herself. Mrs. Curtis in particular admired the young woman, proclaiming her beautiful, bright, genteel, and intelligent too. Even her working-girl status was not a liability, Russell's mother had asserted. To the contrary, a case could be made for its being a good thing, a sign of a plucky modern woman who could fend for herself in any emergency. Russell's parents were pleased about the coming engagement.

"Everything taken care of?" Tracy asked as Russell rang down the phone.

He nodded. "The boy at the candy store will give the message."

"Good. Well, if you'll excuse me, I'm going out

too and I'd better get dressed." She had promised
Mary she'd go over to the flat for supper. Then at ten
she was going to a surprise birthday party for a grocer
on this block. Her escort was the grocer's son, a night
school teacher Tracy had been out with once before.
He was much too poor to be taken seriously, but
Tracy liked him, was looking forward to the evening,
and was anxious to get dressed and out the door.

They were standing in the empty classroom.
Russell's eyes had moved to the door leading to
Tracy's quarters. He wondered what it was like to
live alone. Especially a girl as young as Tracy. He
found himself wondering too how she would look as
she got dressed, whether she was going out with a
man, and whether that man would come into the flat
when the evening was over.

Tracy was not the only woman he'd been curious
about in recent weeks, but she happened to be the one
he knew best apart from Louise. Though he loved
Louise and was eager to marry her, he was beginning
to fear the doors that would soon be clanging shut on
his freedom. In another few months he'd be a married
man, and there were so many things he hadn't done.

He had never, for example, kept company with
girls like Tracy, whom he still considered lower class.
Friends of his at Yale had often gone into the back
streets of New Haven and New York in pursuit of
what they called "free women." But Russell, in his
college years, had been content to court young
virgins and hadn't been able to understand his
friends' needs. There had been the Fifth Avenue

flowers who blushed at him behind fans and talked of the romance of Chopin. There had been college bluestockings whose seriousness made them all the more charming. There had been fresh-faced country girls who had left small towns in search of adventure. They lived with relatives or with boardinghouse "mothers" who watched over their virtue, and they talked to Russell about how "swell" the city was. And finally there had come Louise. She was Fifth Avenue, Smith College, and small town all rolled into one. So ideal had she been in his eyes that when he'd first fallen in love with her he'd been afraid to be alone with her, afraid he'd become tongue-tied or say the wrong thing. That was why he'd taken Tracy along on the first occasions he'd seen her.

But now that Louise's regard was assured and the wedding day was getting closer, Russell was beginning to wonder if he hadn't missed something by not joining his Yale cronies on their back street excursions. His roommate, Osgood, had told him once, "It's a different type of girl you get here, Russ. Freer, more fun, not so afraid of things."

"What do you mean?"

"They're not afraid to break rules. They're not afraid to show you their bodies. Or to get into bed with you and say they love you and then—well— prove it. I'm telling you, Russ, when I go from that kind of girl to the ones Mater has selected for me, I feel like crying. I feel like saying, 'Why don't you take Miss Vassar here and this house and this career you've planned for me and give it to some poor fellow

192

who really wants it?' I once told Father how I felt. He was awfully decent about it, said I'd get over it. But I don't know."

Russell's eyes were still fixed on the door to Tracy's quarters. She was staring at him, wondering why he had lapsed into what looked like a trance. She had once seen someone mesmerized in a vaudeville act and had been very impressed. She said, "Russell? Are you feeling well? Russell?"

"Huh? Oh, yes." But mentally he wasn't fine at all. He felt guilty for wondering about Osgood's women at a time when he should have been wondering where to buy Louise's engagement ring.

"Could you please leave, Russell? I have to get dressed."

They're not afraid. They're not afraid to show you their bodies. . . .

But Louise would be afraid, he thought. She was afraid when he kissed her too hard. He'd have to be gentle. He'd have to hope that in time she'd overcome her fright.

"Russell, did you hear me? I have to get *dressed!*"

"I'm leaving, Tracy."

"Good! I mean, good *night.*"

"Good night," he said hoarsely. And he walked out the door.

Maybe he's coming down with the grippe, she thought, as she hurried into her flat. It had been a busy day, and she had not even gotten to her mail. So as soon as she had dressed, she quickly riffled through it. And there it was—the next to the last

193

letter in the pile—the one she'd been awaiting for months. A letter from Katherine!

In a hastily written hand, Katherine said that there was a job for a weaver. Tracy's father could be trained intensely on the machines and master the skill quickly. As for a house, there were two possibilities. One former worker who already owned his house wanted to sell. And there was a new development of her own just being completed. Tracy could buy a house from the mill outright, deal with a bank, or arrange for the money to be deducted from her father's pay each week. Katherine strongly recommended the second house, which had front and backyards, a kitchen, a parlor, three bedrooms—*and* was spanking new. Tracy's brother Patrick could be employed too in another month or so when an old mill family was leaving for the West, but Katherine hoped the boy would decide to stay in high school.

"I didn't want to notify you until conditions were ideal," Katherine wrote. "But I think they are now. Don't you agree? Please come as soon as possible or others on the list will be storming at the gate. I look forward to another long chat with you, though of course, we'll have to be circumspect now. I'm remarried, as my new name will attest. . . ."

Tracy didn't walk to her family's flat. She flew there. Everyone was there but Pa. She sent Pat to get him out of Flanagan's, and he arrived looking disgruntled and deprived. "What's so important?"

"Oh, smile, Pa, please. It's wonderful news."

"Is it?" He sat down at the table looking skeptical.

Tommy and Kerry looked impatient. Mary was practically panting, but Pat looked doubtful. Yet it was Pat who said, "Come on, Tracy. Spill it."

"I got us a house," she said. "A house and a job for Pa and a good school for the rest of you and a place with prospects for Mary."

"Oh, Tracy!" Mary leaped to her feet and threw her arms around her sister. "Just like you promised!"

Pa said nothing but Pat asked, "Where?"

"In Massachusetts." She went on to tell about the town, the stock, and the opportunities. Mary was exuberant and so was Pat. Tommy looked confused. Kerry was frowning. And Pa, looking angry, was rising to his feet.

"You never tell me a thing!" he roared. "You just up and decide to change everyone's life and you go right ahead and do it. A hundred miles away? A stinking mill hand? If your mother, God rest her soul, was here—"

Kerry interrupted, shouting at Tracy, "And I ain't gonna leave my friends. You can't make me. She can't make me, can she, Pa?"

Tracy normally would have shouted, "Are you out of your heads? Don't you know what this means?" But she was in shock. She sat at the table shaking her head slowly. All those years of struggle, borrowing from Luke and keeping it secret, setting up the school, going up to see Katherine and ha ing to witness her grief—all that, and *this* was the reaction she got?

Mary, who was appalled, uncharacteristically

whirled on her father. "How can you say such things to Tracy? Don't you realize what she's done? This could be a whole new life—"

"I don't care what she done," said her father. "She don't tell me nothing, she don't ask me nothing. She just decides she's the boss around here and that's that. Well, I won't be having it. I won't be having it. If she thinks she can take me and stick me in some mill—"

"But Pa," Pat said. "She's buying the house. *Buying* it. Didn't you hear what she said?"

"Save your breath," Tracy said dully, getting up from her seat with the weariness of an old woman. She put on her coat, walked to the kitchen door, opened it, and started down the stairs. Mary was at her side immediately and behind her trailed Pat and Tommy. Mary said, "Don't pay any attention to Pa. It's his pride. He doesn't want to admit he's weak. And Kerry—all she understands is this street. She has no way of knowing—"

"Leave me alone," Tracy said.

"You can't go off like that." Mary and the boys continued to follow their sister down the stairs. Mary was thinking that Tracy was now paying for some of her tyrannical acts of the past. Pa and Kerry were incapable of understanding why Tracy had been forced to behave that way. Or maybe Pa understood but didn't want to admit it to himself. In this moment Mary, who had always defended her father, could feel nothing but contempt for him. First he abdicated responsibility, then he silently allowed his oldest daughter to take it on, and finally, at the worst possible moment, he attacked his oldest daughter because her methods had not been respectful and diplomatic.

"You buy the house," Mary said. "And we'll move in. And Pa—he can stay here and *rot* for all I care."

It was a statement so unlike Mary that Tracy could not help turning in amazement. They were now on the street. Pat was on one side of her, Mary on the other, and Tommy was skipping ahead as though clearing the way for an entourage.

"I mean it," Mary said. "He can stay here alone. And he can do his own cooking and cleaning into the bargain."

"What about Kerry?" Pat asked Mary.

"She'll come with us. I'll force her to."

"And the weaver's job," Pat said. "I can handle that myself."

"You're supposed to go to high school," Tracy said.

"You and Mary never went to high school."

"No, but that has nothing to do with it."

"I'm taking the weaver's job," he said.

And that was the way of it, Mary thought. The older children must sacrifice for the younger even when the younger (Kerry) wanted no part of the sacrifice. And if the father was a loafer, so be it. The children might look down on him, but they would provide. In time Pa would join them in Massachusetts, Mary knew. He'd be sulking, making all sorts of noises about how he was boss. The children would prop him up and go on working. That was the way of it. You went forward propelled by instinct alone.

All of Mary's and Pat's reassurances could not jolt Tracy out of her black mood. She walked along Monroe and up Catherine, still surrounded by the allies in her family, wishing they'd all go away and leave her to nurse her hurts alone, for nothing and no one could help her right now.

But she was wrong. When they reached the school, her little brother Tommy announced that he wanted to talk to Tracy alone. He followed her into her quarters and said, "You're a grand sister, Tracy, and don't let nobody tell you different." Then, embarrassed, he charged back out the door.

Tracy remembered the times she had whipped him and screamed at him. How much attention had she ever paid to Tommy? How much affection had there ever been? And yet he had said she was grand. She sat down at the table and began to cry.

Mary came in and started making tea. Pat came in and walked around looking uncomfortable. Finally Tommy came back and said, "How come everyone's so sad? We should be lighting firecrackers."

And so they should, Tracy thought, raising her head from the table.

Chapter Fifteen

Tracy took some classroom time off to help with the move. Pa had refused to go, but he made no attempt to stop the children. Instead, he spent his time crying at Flanagan's about his high-handed, disrespectful offspring and how they had destroyed his life. Ten-year-old Kerry sulked for a while but soon determined where her best interests lay and threw in her lot with the dissidents, though she complained when Tracy ordered her to help with the packing.

They were taking nothing but kitchen utensils, clothing, bedding, and mementos. The furniture would stay behind. The cost of moving it would be more than it was worth. They could buy something in Massachusetts, and in the meantime they could eat off the floor.

Mary would now be the head of the household and Pat the second-in-command. Pa could come or go as he liked. Though he still had rights where the children were concerned, it was doubtful that he would attempt to enforce them as Michael's father had. Pa might not like his children these days, but he knew in his heart what was best for them, and Tracy was sure he would not make trouble.

The evening before they were scheduled to leave, Tracy checked in with Louise at the school. Louise had been handling some of the classes alone and Tracy wanted to give her a few extra dollars. She arrived at 8:45, a few minutes before the evening class was supposed to end, and discovered that there was no class going on. Instead, a group of people were yelling, "Surprise!" There were Louise and the students; Mrs. Santini from upstairs; Mr. Vitale, the butcher who had saved Tracy's business from disaster; Mr. DiNarda, a grocer whose party she'd attended some nights earlier, and his son Tony, who was Tracy's friend. The wives of the butcher and grocer were here too as were their children and other children from the block. There was a cake on Tracy's desk and three bottles of wine. The neighbors, Louise explained, had come to celebrate with Tracy.

The last-minute party had been Mrs. Santini's idea. The good widow had just hours before rounded up local well-wishers and baked the cake on which was written, "Good luck, Miss Sullivan." Wine and juices had been brought in by other guests and the students had typed little notes of congratulation. There were toasts and impromptu speeches. Everyone knew how much the relocation of the family meant to Tracy. And Tracy, exuberant and tipsy with wine, cried and hugged them all and said she was glad she herself wouldn't be moving, for how could she give up such wonderful friends?

Into this emotional scene came Russell, here as usual to pick up Louise. He'd known nothing of this informal party, which had not been Louise's idea. But Tracy did not realize this, and so, in the general round of hugs, she included him. Feeling the crush of her arms and the press of her small but soft breasts, Russell turned red and began to breathe hard. When she had moved on to embrace someone else, he was forced to sit down at one of the student's desks in order to conceal the physical evidence of his reaction. He hoped that no one had noticed—but Mr. Vitale had; and during the time the party lasted, the butcher noted that the distinguished young businessman was looking not at the proper Louise but at her merry young boss. Mr. Vitale smiled. He'd seen this happen with many young men both here and in Italy. There came a time in life when their powerful need for sex blinded them to everything else. It looked like this gentleman was suffering from the condition.

The party lasted until well past midnight, and Tracy was still feeling the effects of the wine the next morning when the family piled into the train. But her head began to clear when they changed at New Haven. And by the time they reached Springfield, she felt fine.

Ever afterward she would be glad about the snow. It had snowed in New England earlier this week, and when the train bearing the Sullivans arrived in Lanston the snow was still there. Tracy did not take them at once to see the house. Instead, she checked their belongings at the station and made them follow

201

her up the hill to the town itself. There, surrounded by snow and cloudless skies, were the center green, the giant trees, and all the steep-roofed houses. It was early December, three weeks before Christmas, and everyone thought of this as they stood there.

"Oh, Tracy!" Mary exclaimed.

"Gosh," Pat said. "Like a picture."

Tommy and Kerry just stared and stared. It was all strange to them, for they could barely remember their Connecticut days. But they were quick to see the possibilities for fun, and soon they were sliding, throwing snowballs, rolling around in the abundant whiteness. They had seen snow before, but it had generally been filthy with ashes or manure. Never had they seen anything as pure as this.

"Come on, you two," Tracy shouted. "Don't you wanna go home?"

"Home?" Mary said. "Say that again."

"Home, home, home," Tracy laughed, picking up some snow and hurling it at Tommy. "Come *on!*"

The house was a surprise to Tracy too, for she had not seen it in advance. It was a story and a half high, white and clean, and a decent distance from its neighbor. The front and backyards were small, but they were covered with snow and so seemed exquisitely landscaped. There was a pile of wood sent over by Katherine, and Pat took some into the house.

The only thing missing was a bathroom. Someday, Tracy thought, she must have one installed. But the family did not seem disturbed by the absence of a built-in tub or toilet. They just ran from parlor to

202

bedrooms to kitchen and back, their eyes wide with realization that at last they'd have space and privacy. Pat made a fire in the kitchen stove and everyone came in, sat down on their bedding, and ate sandwiches and cookies left over from the trip while Mary made coffee. Tomorrow the rest of their goods would arrive by train and then Mary could begin fixing up while Pat went off to work and the two youngest children to school. In another week, Tracy predicted, Pa would probably be here too. But by that time she'd be gone.

At that moment, Tracy did not want to return to New York. It would be so much nicer just to stay here and set up a business school. But who would she train? Katherine's small crew? There were other industries in town, but she doubted that there would be students enough to fill half a class. Well, if she got too lonely, she could always come here for a weekend. Every week if she liked! She was her own boss.

How like a fairy tale it was! Her own business, her own flat, her own house in the country. And none of it likely to be taken away, cither. Now she could relax and maybe become the lady she had dreamed of being.

"That's Tracy Sullivan," they would say. "Beautiful and brilliant, responsible and generous, beloved sister, beloved friend, beloved human being . . ." And what about beloved wife and mother? Well, that would come too now that she had time to devote to the project.

Chapter Sixteen

She had been back in New York only two hours and was preparing for her evening class when Ruth came by, knocking at the back door. Little Aaron was with her, thoroughly wrapped against the December cold. Tracy could see that something was wrong, for Ruth looked terrible—pale and tense, clutching Aaron's hand as though she expected him to vanish any minute.

"What's happened?" Tracy asked, leading the two into her quarters.

"It's the Ryans," Ruth said, her voice shaking. She sat at the table holding Aaron in her lap.

Michael's father again? thought Tracy. "What happened this time?"

Ruth took a deep breath. "One of the twins—Annie—she's dead."

Michael's little sister? "Oh, no! Was it diphtheria?"

Ruth said quickly and in a flat tone, "She was beaten to death by her father."

Tracy went rigid, staring at Ruth.

"Early this morning. He was on a toot last night

and he woke with a hangover. I guess the children were playing or arguing. He gave them each a whipping and when he got to Annie, he must've gone berserk. He kicked her, jumped on. . . ." Ruth broke off.

"Mother of God," Tracy whispered. For a long time both of them were silent.

"They took him into custody," Ruth said finally. "We think Mrs. Ryan's lost her head. Michael's sisters were over there preparing the body and she was just screaming, trying to grab Annie's—"

"Oh, stop!" Tracy shouted, causing little Aaron to whimper in fright. She'd been plunged so quickly into the hell she'd only recently managed to escape that she could not assimilate it.

But she asked, "Where's Michael?"

"David went to get him in Jersey. He didn't want to send a telegram. How can you write something like this in a telegram?"

"Did they come back yet?"

"They weren't back when I left to come here."

"What about the rest of them?"

"Michael's sisters are over at the flat. Mo is expecting a child, you know. She was throwing up while they fixed up the body."

No more, Tracy thought, pressing her hands to her head.

"The two middle brothers were just walking around like chickens with their heads cut off. And the little one—the other twin, Matthew—he was just crying. And like I said, the mother's completely out of her head."

"Haven't the neighbors done anything?"

"They're bringing in food. We're taking up a collection for the funeral."

"So the bastard didn't leave them any money either?"

"Not much."

"I hope they don't hang him," Tracy said. "I hope they just cut him up slowly."

"Or use a rack," added nonviolent Ruth.

"They can't just let the girl go to a potter's field," Tracy said. "Michael must have money. He couldn't have been fool enough to send every penny to them."

"I'm sure he does," Ruth said.

"What time did David leave for Jersey?"

"Two or three hours ago."

Then Michael knew, Tracy thought, her stomach turning over as she put herself in Michael's place. What would his reaction be? She was afraid to know, afraid to see him at all. A sister dead, a father who was a murderer, a mother who was at best only temporarily insane—how could she stand to see Michael's pain? It would be easy for her to get out of it. She could say that her students needed her and that she must stay here for now but would go to the Ryans' as soon as possible (after the funeral). Yet she didn't do this. Instead, she rose and went for her coat, stopping on her way to drink some brandy straight from a bottle she always kept around. Ever since Katherine had admitted to her need for a nip now and then, Tracy had been seeing the advantages too. She expected Ruth to say something about this unfortunate habit, but Ruth did not appear to notice, and Tracy took a second swallow and a third. Then she said to Ruth, "I'm ready."

When they reached Monroe Street, Tracy said, "You're coming in with me."

"I can't bring Aaron into that. He'd be terrified. We were there this morning, but only in shifts. First I stayed home with the baby, then David."

"Can't you leave the baby with a neighbor?"

"I'm afraid to let him out of my sight."

"*He's* not going to die," Tracy said impatiently.

"But I'm afraid. Superstition. I'll get over it."

I wish you'd get over it right now, Tracy thought. She didn't want to walk in there alone. Wakes had always upset her, but when they were children they were unbearable.

She left Ruth at her building, which was half a block from the Ryans', then walked slowly toward hell. She had to pass her own former residence, and she wondered if Pa was up there. People were milling around in front of Michael's building. A fire in a barrel was keeping them warm, and they encircled it like moths, talking of the tragedy, lingering on the gory details and speculating on Joe Ryan's fate. Some said hello to Tracy and asked how the family was. She said fine and shoved past them, intent on getting it over with. As she started up the stoop, she met a little girl she knew and asked, "Is Michael here yet?"

"No," said the child.

"Oh, Michael," Tracy murmured to herself, mounting the stairs. "I wish you never had to know."

Tracy entered by way of the kitchen, which was jammed with people, including a cop, a reporter, a priest. In a room beyond she could hear the keening. Several neighborhood men, including Pa, were sitting and standing around the kitchen table guzzling whiskey while children and curiosity seekers milled about here and in the bedrooms. The heat from the stove and all the people was intense and the smell of perspiration strong. By slow degrees Tracy now worked her way through the intervening bedrooms and into the parlor. Michael's older sisters and the middle sister, Mo, were there. A woman Tracy didn't know was keening over the body. Michael's mother, eyes crazed, hands held aloft and bent like claws, sat in front of the body groaning like a woman in labor. The body was covered in a long white cotton dress. The face was bruised, bloated, ugly, and looked nothing like the child. Tracy remembered Anne at the age of three skipping along to mass on a Sunday, holding her sister's hand; remembered her in later years playing jump rope with her friends; remembered her best last summer at Coney Island riding along on Michael's shoulders as he strode down the beach.

Tracy did not look at the body for more than a second. Turning quickly to Mo, who was great with child, she murmured, "If there's anything I can do. . . ." Mo only stared at her blankly.

Where were they going to stay? Tracy wondered.

Where would half of them sleep? The body was in the parlor, and she didn't think anyone would sleep there. What would they do about the mother? And where was Matthew, the twin who had survived? He must be in shock. And where were the two middle boys? Tracy asked these questions of Kathleen, Michael's oldest sister, who simply shrugged and said, "I don't know. I got my own troubles. My kids are home alone in the flat and I'm scared they'll set it on fire."

The keening continued, shrill and chilling, yet somehow appropriate to this night. It was a wail of pain that sounded to Tracy like the cry of a little girl's outraged soul. Here in an area where misery and overcrowding were so much a way of life that a death was scarcely noticed, the custom of keening remained, she thought, to remind the world that this death mattered. It was as though the child were saying, "Listen now and remember me. Remember Annie."

Tracy went into the kitchen where Pa and some other men were feeling no pain. Someone should throw them out, she thought, and get the family together, plans made, funeral arrangements under way. The hopeless confusion in the place, the noise, and the heat were only adding to the anguish of the family.

She heard her own voice rising above the fray, "Pa, take these men over to our flat—your flat—if you want to get drunk."

"I told you last week and I'm telling you again,

Missy, you ain't ordering me around."

Angrily she turned to another man, one of Pa's cronies. "*You* do it then. Get them out of here. This isn't one of your usual wakes, in case you hadn't noticed?"

Chairs scraped and men rose to their feet. All except Pa, who was finally dragged to his. "C'mon, Tom, she's right," said the crony, and he finally succeeded in getting Pa out the door.

Tracy turned to an adolescent boy. "Get Dr. McNally. Maybe he can give Mrs. Ryan something to make her sleep." She looked around for the priest and saw him near the stove. "The funeral will be Wednesday morning, Father," she said.

"Are you a relative, miss?"

"A cousin," she lied. The young priest was new to the neighborhood and had never met her. "Is ten o'clock all right?"

"Are you sure you're authorized—"

"Who else is there, Father?"

"They say there's an older son."

"Michael isn't here yet. And God knows what shape he'll be in when he gets here." He was already long overdue, and she wondered why.

The priest said, "They don't have the coffin yet. They don't even know where they're going to bury her."

She turned to another man, a friend of Pa's. "Can you get an undertaker?"

"Is there money for one?"

"There will be when Michael gets here. Otherwise I'll pay for it myself. Don't worry about it. Just go, please." To the priest she said, "Where are the other children?"

"The boys? They're out somewhere. Walking. I don't know. Maybe it's the best thing."

Maybe it was, Tracy thought, wondering why she hadn't followed her initial instinct and stayed away from this ghastly place. But even as she questioned her sanity, she was asking neighborhood women to get together and make some arrangements about who was going to take care of the mother, oversee the boys, feed everyone, and care for them long enough to get through the funeral day after tomorrow. The neighborhood women seemed to have been looking for a leader, and in a few minutes they had decided that one of them would stay with Nell here at the flat and two others would divide up the boys and get them cleaned, fed, and calmed down. The sisters weren't a problem. All were older, married, and had their own flats.

Dr. McNally finally came in, looking harassed and confused. "Someone sick?" he said.

"Someone's dead," explained Tracy.

"I know all about that. But why did you call me?"

"Mrs. Ryan is out of her head. She needs laudanum."

"I won't give laudanum unless a patient's in acute pain."

"If you want to see pain, I'll *show* you pain."

Tracy gestured toward the parlor. *"Do* something!" Tracy shouted. And the babble in the sweltering kitchen stopped for a moment as people ·turned to look at her.

It was then that she saw Michael. He had just walked in, David behind him. Under his coat he wore a suit. David must have reminded him to wear formal attire and also reminded him to bring other essentials, including money. He was hatless, though, and his black hair was tousled from the wind.

"Michael." She said his name softly.

He nodded and studied her a moment as though getting his bearings. Before Tracy could go to him, his older sister came into the kitchen. She shouted his name and then others swarmed around him, talking hurriedly, crying. Tracy turned again to the doctor and urged him to help Mrs. Ryan. Then she slipped over to David and said, "How's Michael? Does he know everything?"

David nodded.

"What did he say?"

David shrugged. "Said he'd always known it would happen. Said that he should have finished his father off years ago. He also said he was surprised his mother had reported it. He would have expected her to hide the body somewhere and pretend nothing had happened."

"Michael *said* that?"

David nodded. "Do you blame him?"

"No," she murmured, then said, "Did he do anything crazy?"

212

"Not at first. We were at the repair shop. He told his boss there'd been a death in the family. We went from there to another street and leased a flat. He wants to move his family out to Jersey right away so he can take care of them."

"Does he have the money?"

"He has enough."

"For a funeral too?"

"I think so."

"So you two looked for flats all afternoon?"

"No. We found one right away. Then we went to his place. He changed and we left."

"Why did it take you so long to get here?"

"We made a stop first."

"Where?"

"The jail."

"Where his father is?"

David nodded. "I tried to keep him away, but Mike insisted."

"Mother of God! What did he do?"

"Tried to attack his old man—through the bars yet. The guard was ready to arrest him until I explained."

"How'd you get him calmed down?"

"Wasn't easy. I made him walk for blocks and blocks. Thought the cold would help."

Michael was walking toward them now, so Tracy ceased her questioning. He came over and said to Tracy, "They told me you were making arrangements."

"I had to. I didn't know where you were."

"Then the funeral's on Wednesday?"

"Yes, and the undertaker'll be here tomorrow. And Mrs. McNulty's staying with your mother. Mrs. O'Keefe is taking two of the boys. And Mrs.—"

"All right," he interrupted. "Thanks." Tracy heard someone shout, "Mike!" and turned to see his little brother, the other twin, rushing into Michael's arms. The boy was sobbing. Michael held him, but his face remained rigid. It was either shock, she thought, or the kind of strength that comes from knowing that everyone is depending on you and you can't break down no matter what.

She walked down to the parlor to see if the doctor had come to a decision on sedation, and while she was talking him into it, Michael appeared. As yet he had seen neither his mother nor the body of his sister. Tracy held her breath as he walked in. All eyes in the parlor turned toward him. His mother saw him and shrieked, "Mike—ee! He killed her! He killed my baby. He killed her!"

Tracy flattened herself against the wall as though to will herself through it. She couldn't bear this. Michael walked over to his mother, touched her arm, then stared down at the body of his sister. He did not kneel, did not pray, but simply stood there. As his mother began to wail, Michael turned to the doctor, who was standing near Tracy. "Give my mother laudanum." It was a sharp command that carried the hint of a threat.

"I'm sorry, but only physical illnesses warrant the

214

use of—"

"*Give* it to her!" Michael's body shook him with the impulse to strike out at the doctor—or at anyone.

"All right." The doctor's voice was almost a whisper. He must have been afraid that Michael was going to attack him, Tracy thought. He opened his bag and stepped over to Nell.

Michael slammed a fist into his hand and exhaled. In another minute, Tracy thought, he'd be tearing the flat to pieces. "Let's go back to the kitchen," Tracy said, taking his arm and holding fast to it. After a moment he nodded and followed her.

In time the flat began emptying out. The rosary had been said, the neighbors had gone home, Michael's younger brothers taken to other flats, his mother sedated and put to bed. His sisters went home to their own households and David finally left too. Only Tracy, Michael, his mother, and the neighbor taking care of her were left. Those four and the body of his sister. Michael had completed funeral arrangements, talked with the priest and police, and managed to keep his temper through it all. Now he stood near the kitchen door with Tracy as she prepared to leave.

"Are you still living at that school?" he asked.

"Yes."

"I'll walk you home."

"I'll be safe, for heaven's sake."

"I need the air," he said.

It was a fifteen-block walk in bitter cold weather,

but neither of them thought to take a trolley or a cab. Michael needed the air and Tracy wanted the numbing of the wind. They walked most of the way in silence. When they talked, it was not of the tragedy but of details like whether the boys had to have formal clothing for the funeral or whether Michael had to pay December's rent on the Monroe Street flat if he was moving the family from it in three days.

"Three days?" Tracy said. "You mean you're moving the day after the funeral?"

"I have to get back to work and I want them in Jersey when I do."

"Do you have enough money? Will the boys have to quit school?"

"I'll think about that when we get there."

She didn't tell him about her own family's move. Better not to describe the lovely little town at all. She'd been so fortunate compared to Michael. Newark was certainly better than the East Side, but a flat was a flat. She saw Michael's life and that of his family as doomed. Especially if Nell never recovered from this. What would it be like for Michael—a crazy mother and three wild brothers in a Newark flat? To say nothing of the disgrace of having a father on trial for murder. And mourning poor Annie besides.

When they reached her place, she asked him in for a drink. She hadn't gotten him drunk enough back at the flat, and he really did need something. He came into her quarters and sat down on the sofa near the stove. She poured them both brandies and sat next to him. They didn't talk much, but they drank steadily. Michael smoked cigarettes as well—one after another. Since it was past eleven, Tracy was growing very sleepy. Leaning back against the cushion, she closed her eyes.

Memories encroached on her. Ugly ones. Once she had seen a child fall off a fire escape to her death. Once she had seen a child trampled by a horse that was pulling an ice wagon. She had been in a crowd when a tenement was on fire and had seen a half-burned woman brought down. She had seen gangs attack other gangs, had seen men beat their wives, had heard a woman give birth in screaming agony only to learn that she had later died of the effort. She'd seen sick people of every variety, had seen her grandfather die of pneumonia, had seen typhoid ravage a neighborhood and her own family's flat. She'd seen people crippled by the slums, mutilated by the slums, even driven to suicide by the slums. And through it all she had thought, Someday I'll get away from it. She had gone, but here was Michael still chained to that hell.

She turned to him and spontaneously put her arms around him as though to shield him from more pain. Michael was unprepared for this. The brandy had been eroding his strength, and Tracy's sudden tenderness did away with it completely. He broke. It was a wrenching thing to witness, but Tracy didn't flinch. She held him, calmed him, blotted his wet face, comforted without words.

217

She could not have said later how grief finally turned into passion, but it happened. After a while she found herself lying beside him on the couch. He was holding her tight and kissing her hard. Their tongues were in each other's mouths. His hand moved from her back to her breast. He touched it and she moaned. He pulled her down from the couch to the floor where he hurriedly undressed her and she helped him. Lying down beside her at last, he pulled her close to him. She felt something hard against her thigh. Then she felt him on top of her, felt pain inside her—sharp but not enough to make her cry out. The pain passed quickly, to be replaced by a craving unlike anything she had ever experienced before. Her body went rigid and then she didn't feel it, and then she felt it again but concentrated all in one place. She cried out, was lifted higher by the pleasure, cried out again. Then it was over. Michael was next to her, panting, his eyes closed, his arm flung across her breasts.

From far off she heard the clop of horses and other city noises. But in this room it was very still. She thought he must be asleep, but he opened his eyes and turned his face toward her. She loved his face. She loved all of him, she realized. But she didn't think of anything else. Not why she might feel this way, or how they had gotten here, or how much she had drunk, or why this had happened.

"Are you all right?" he said.

"I'm all right. I love you, Michael."

"Do you mean that?" he said almost in a whisper.

"Yes. I love you. I don't want you to go home. Everything's taken care of there. Forget everything. Just stay with me tonight."

He said in a soft voice, "I love you too. I loved you for a long time."

Chapter Seventeen

She was aware of the headache before she even opened her eyes. Oh God, this was going to be a bad one. And she couldn't afford to be sick today because—why? There was work, of course, but something else had happened . . .

And then it came back to her all in a rush. All the horror, the grief, the drinking, and finally the passion. Her eyes opened, and she turned to find Michael. They were both on the floor, covered with a quilt she must have thrown over them in the middle of the night, after they had—oh God!

It wasn't that she was worried. There was no danger, after all. It had only been twice, she remembered, and she knew that the minimum for pregnancy was three times. What she regretted was the way it had happened. In grief and drunkenness they had devoured each other, had said things they hadn't meant. Or maybe they'd meant them at the time, in that particular circumstance, but would they have said such things otherwise?

Did she love him? Yes, she did, but it was the kind of love that came from growing up together, understanding each other, and at times, as last night, sharing the hurt of each other. But it wasn't the kind of love she wanted to build on. She wanted a future, security, money. She wanted to get as far away as possible from the slums. The last thing she wanted, having come so far, was to take on Michael's impossible situation. But she mustn't add to his problems by telling him that now.

He woke at last and, seeing Tracy, reached for her. She touched his arm but made no other physical overture, strongly tempted though she was. He asked, "What time is it?"

She squinted at the clock near the stove. "Eleven."

"I better get back to the flat," he said.

"Are you feeling well, Michael?" His eyes had dark circles under them.

"Are you?" He looked directly at her.

"I have no regrets, if that's what you mean."

She got up and put on a robe. He too rose and began to dress. He said, "We can be married just as soon as this is over."

"Married?" she croaked. Oh Lord, was he one of those honorable Irishmen who felt that a deflowering must be followed immediately by a wedding? "We don't have to be married, Michael."

"Don't you want to?"

"Well . . ."

"I want to marry you," he said.

"Because of what happened?"

"Not because of what happened. Because I want you to be my wife."

"You're in shock," she said. "I know *I* am and they're not even my folks, so I can imagine how you must— Last night was something done more in grief than. . . ."

"I know," he murmured as he began to button his shirt, "but I still. . . ." He stopped buttoning his shirt and looked at his hands as though trying to understand something. Was he feeling guilty because he had made love to a woman on the day his sister had been beaten to death?

He sat down on the couch, and she could see by his expression that he was remembering yesterday. Human beings, she thought, couldn't absorb horror constantly; they had to have respites in forgetfulness. Grief came over a person in waves, as it was coming over Michael now. His face was pale, and he was gripping the armrest of the sofa. She realized that he was holding feelings in so as not to upset her. Perhaps she ought to leave him alone for a while. She needed to go to the bakery anyway to get something for breakfast.

"I'm going to the bakery," she said.

He nodded.

"Anything you want?"

"No, thanks." He could barely talk.

When she returned from her errand, he looked tired, spent, but much calmer. She said softly, "Feel like eating?"

"No, thanks," he said. "A woman knocked. I thought it was you, so I answered. She said her name was Louise."

222

"My assistant."

"She said"—he shook his head—"I forget what she said, Tracy."

"She probably wants some certificates for the students."

"Yeah, that was it."

"I'll bring them over. I'll put the coffee on first so we can have some before we go back to your family's flat."

Tracy made the coffee and then opened the door to the classroom. Louise was talking to a student and Tracy motioned her over. Louise stared at Tracy strangely, but Tracy, in a kind of daze, didn't notice. "Here's the certificates," Tracy said. "For Anderson and Schwartz. Tell them congratulations, and I'll give them good recommendations. I'm not coming in today."

"Oh?" It was the fourth day in a row that Tracy had not been in. Last night she'd left a note pleading urgent business.

"The man you met just now—his sister was murdered yesterday."

"Murdered?" Louise drew in her breath. "What was her name?"

Tracy hadn't intended to give Louise any details, but she was distracted and upset. "Ryan," she said.

"Oh, yes." Louise perused her daily paper and had a good memory. "On the East Side. The father—"

"Yes," Tracy cut in sharply.

"Good grief. No wonder he looked so upset."

"Anyway, that's where I'll be till tomorrow after

the funeral, so if you'll—"

"Take whatever time you need," Louise said. "I'll take care of the students."

"Thanks."

Tracy opened the door to her quarters, never giving a thought to the reaction Louise might be having after finding a man in Tracy's quarters with his shirt half-unbuttoned and his hair in disarray.

THERE was another day to get through and the funeral after that. Michael's friends did more than any of the relatives in helping the family to endure the ordeal. Tracy mobilized the neighborhood housewives, Ruth comforted Michael's family, David organized the move, helping the family sort out belongings and contacting movers. They brought dignity back to the flat, saw to it that the children were clean and fed, got rid of reporters, assured the mother and the boys that Michael would make things better. No mention was made of the father, Joe. Aside from Michael, only Joe's brother had gone to see him in jail. The others would see him only if subpoenaed to the court. After the funeral there was a luncheon during which Nell showed signs of getting back to normal. She still wept a good deal, but she was able at times to talk rationally and even to thank a few people for their help.

"I think things'll be all right," Tracy told Michael after he'd walked her home and stopped for coffee.

He said, "It's a little late, though."

"Don't think about that. It's pointless."

224

He was silent for a while. Then he said, "I'll be leaving in the morning with them."

"I know."

"I won't be seeing you, so I think we should make plans."

"Plans?" Her heart thudded.

"I asked you to marry me."

She was silent.

"I know you want money and we'll have it. It'll just take time."

Money? From a bicycle repair shop?

"Tracy?"

"Yes. I—yes. I don't think this is the time to discuss anything so serious. We're both so tired."

"I'm not going to change my mind," he said.

"Michael, you're talking as though you wanted me for years and that's not true. You were very upset and I was here, so you—"

"I *did* want you. *Do.*"

"You had a strange way of showing it," she said.

"You had a strange way of not noticing."

"I *didn't* notice. You weren't very obvious. And what about the girl in Hell's Kitchen?"

"Who told you about that?"

"Have you ever heard of gossip?"

He sighed. "That was two years ago. And it wasn't serious."

"But I *was* serious?"

"Not then. I mean, I didn't realize it then even though I liked you. It was later I realized. The times we used to meet at David's. I used to hope we'd be like

225

them someday. But I knew you wanted money, so I was gonna wait till I had enough before I asked you. But the night I stayed with you, you said you loved me, so—well, I'm asking now." He paused. "Look, Tracy, you won't starve. I've made plans, good ones. I'm gonna have my own repair shop and I'm gonna learn more about autos. The ones they're making now—"

He talked on but her ears had shut off. Automobiles! Mother of God! There were only a few thousand automobiles in the whole country. How many could he repair? She loved him, yes, but she wasn't going to marry him. Putting up with his family would be bad enough, but he expected her to sink into poverty too? She shuddered.

He was waiting for some response. She hadn't heard a question, but she answered as though she had. "I have to have time to think." Please, please don't make me say it, she thought. Don't make me hurt you more.

"Time to think," he repeated. "What were you thinking about that night?"

"I wasn't. Wasn't thinking."

"You were a virgin," he said.

Meaning, she thought, that he assumed she was being very selective in choosing him to be the first. This was true, but it didn't mean she wanted to marry him.

She said, "Yes, you were the first. But—I still need time to think about this. It's such a big step, you know."

"I know," he said. "Well, all right. We'll talk about it some other time."

She fought back tears. Michael was being betrayed by everyone, she thought. by his father, who had murdered his favorite sister; by his mother, who hadn't acted until it was too late; by the law that had kept Michael away for such a long time; and now by her. There was no way to make him understand. Katherine had said it well when she had told Tracy that she thought survival was sometimes more important than love. But how could she explain it to Michael? How could she tell him that to marry him would be to snuff out all hope for the future?

She stood up and walked him to the door. "You'll write?" she said.

He nodded.

"And come back soon. New Jersey's only across the river."

"I know where Jersey is."

She reached out to touch his arm in farewell, and suddenly he pulled her against him, kissing her hard, reminding her of the passion of two nights before. In the frantic hours since, she hadn't had time to remember that night in detail, but now she remembered and her arms went around his neck, her breasts pressed against him, her tongue probed and darted. He moaned and reached for her breasts. She moaned too, but then she panicked and moved back. "No," she said.

"Tracy—"

"No, please."

227

He stepped back and stared at her. She could not read his expression. Anger? Disbelief? She could not read it. "Michael—"

"Have to go," he said.

"Wait a minute."

"So long," he said, and he left, slamming the door hard.

She walked slowly back to the sofa and sat down, missing him already. Tears threatened, but she fought them back. It was six o'clock and she had to get herself under control in time for the evening class. Lousie was coming down with a cold, she'd told Tracy yesterday, and hadn't known if she'd make it through the day. She'd made it, but Tracy would have to take over tonight.

Don't worry, Louise. I'm back now. Back to work, eye on the goal, hand on the rudder. Six o'clock of a fine winter's eve and all's well. But which eve? Tuesday? Wednesday? What was the month? She couldn't even remember the month. The past week had been as long as a decade. It must be December. Next year would be the last of the century. Days of auld lang syne . . .

She poured herself a brandy. She hadn't had anything to eat today, not even at the funeral luncheon. But she poured herself a brandy and then another. Then she drank some coffee to sober her up for work.

Chapter Eighteen

By ten o'clock that night, Tracy was ready to move to Lanston and forget she'd ever owned a business. Coaching ten students, all progressing at different rates, was difficult even for two people, much less one. This wasn't an ordinary classroom where students were sometimes ignored altogether. She had practically guaranteed results, guaranteed that everybody would end up a great success. And trying to train a girl who barely knew English to become a shorthand demon was very often impossible.

As she was saying good-night to her students, Russell came in. What was he doing here? she wondered. Didn't he know that Louise had a cold?

"Louise isn't here, Russell. She's home with a cold."

"Oh, yes. I'd forgotten that," he lied. "It's such a habit, my coming by to escort her home and I'd just—forgotten."

"I can understand why. Well, good night."

"Uh . . . Tracy?"

"Yes?"

He cleared his throat but said nothing. He was

weaving slightly. She thought that he might have been drinking.

"I've been drinking," he finally murmured.

"Uh huh?" She was careful not to add, "You're telling me?"

"Could I ask you to make me a cup of coffee?"

She put her hands on her hips. The colossal gall! There were delicatessens still open all over the place and he was asking a woman who'd been working all evening?

"Please," he said. "I'm drunk and I have to sit down for a moment."

He'd been drinking, yes, but he wasn't drunk. Tracy knew drunk when she saw it. But she was too tired to explain the distinction to him and too tired to argue. "All right," she sighed, "come into the flat and I'll make you a cup."

She thought nothing of asking a man into the flat. There had been several who had come and gone in the last few months, though only Michael had succeeded in leaving with more than good-night kiss. But as she motioned Russell in, she wasn't thinking of the possibility that he might make advances. She was thinking that he was a pain in the neck, and she wouldn't be making him coffee at all were it not for the fact that he was Louise's beau and she needed Louise for the business.

At last Russell was seeing the mysteries behind that intriguing door. The crash of colors jarred him at first. She had no taste whatsoever, he thought. But because he was stirred by desires he didn't quite understand, he found the place charming nevertheless. Tracy gestured toward the secondhand sofa and he sat down. On an end table next to the sofa was a half pint of brandy. He wished he could have some, but he'd just told her he was drunk.

Tracy put the coffee on to boil, then went back into the classroom to close up. While she was gone, Russell took a belt from the brandy bottle and then another. He didn't know what he was doing here. He knew only that he'd wanted to see this room ever since the night of the party. It was madness being here, he thought. What if she told Louise? Of all the women he might have developed these feelings for, why did it have to be Louise's boss? He didn't know, but he hoped he'd get over it, because he loved Louise very much.

"Coffee's perking," Tracy said as she came back into the room. "I don't have cream about. Would you like plain sugar?"

"A teaspoon would be fine."

She fixed the coffee, served it, and sat not next to him but in a chair facing the couch. "You're not drinking the coffee," she said, a little annoyed.

"I'm waiting for it to cool." He looked around. "This is a very pleasant home."

"Thank you."

"My own home doesn't have nearly so much charm."

She hadn't heard such blarney from him since the days when he'd complimented her on her dimples. She said, "You live with your parents, don't you?"

"Yes. Now I do."

"But you'll still live there after you're married to Louise, won't you?"

"Oh, of course. What I meant was . . . I wish sometimes that I'd lived on my own as you do."

"Why?" she said.

"Because . . . I've never known freedom. I've lived my life in a kind of—tunnel."

And what I wouldn't have given for his "tunnel," thought Tracy.

"I just wish I'd done more," he said. And he wondered why he was telling her this. All he'd intended to do was to see where she lived. He'd just been curious; that was all. But the extra drinks were beginning to hit him now, and though his mind kept warning him to shut up, his mouth kept moving. He told her of his restlessness, of the experiences he'd missed out on because he'd lived such a lockstep life. He told her he envied her because she'd lived and suffered and experienced life "close to the earth."

"And I guess you know all about the basic things," he said, leaning forward. "Birth and death and—and love. You must—you know a great deal."

Slowly all this was beginning to fall into place for Tracy. The allusions to love, to her "experience," the sick look on his face. Russell had been drinking, but she was cold sober because a headache from this afternoon's binge had decided her against taking more. She figured out that he was making some kind of advance. He looked as though he wanted to kiss her! When had this happened? she wondered. Did

232

Louise suspect that Russell had ideas like this in his mind? And why had it happened? Why was he suddenly finding Tracy Sullivan so desirable?

But that question was soon answered too. He began to talk in a slurred voice of someone named Osgood and of how he'd found happiness in the arms of women from "less fortunate" backgrounds and of how these warm women were such a contrast to the hard-to-get ladies of his own class.

"They know what life's all about. That's what Osgood said. He said those women aren't afraid to love. Truly love, truly love. Did I tell you his name was Osgood? He came from New London. That's not far from Yale, actually. . . ."

Tracy stopped listening to the incoherent blather as a suspicion formed. Had he come here looking for sex? She'd been thinking in terms of a kiss, but it sounded as though he were talking about actual in-bed *sex!* Those words he had used: "freedom," "experience," "less fortunate background," "close to the earth," not being "afraid to love." As hard as she'd tried to be a lady, he'd seen her all along as a tart from the slums. Nothing she had done had changed his ideas one iota. She, who had been a virgin until two days ago!

As he rambled on though, she began to realize that he hadn't intended to be condescending. He honestly respected the "unfortunates" for their "warmth" and their "bravery."

"You, for example, Tracy. You've got courage. I could never set up a business the way you did. I could

233

never in a thousand years do anything like that." He shook his head. "Never, no."

As though she needed him to tell her. But this part, she realized, was not blarney at all. He was far too drunk to be so calculating. She wondered when he had got so much drunker, then noticed that the level of the brandy bottle had gone down.

He talked and he talked, and in time Tracy's anger was tempered by a kind of comprehension. He finally admitted that he'd come here just to be with her, and since he hadn't made any actual physical advances, she believed him. He was just a confused mess, she thought, who didn't know what he wanted. She was annoyed that someone who had had so much could be so utterly dissatisfied. Him with his talk of "tunnels." He should have had Michael's rich, rewarding life.

Since he dared not take any more brandy, and since he was obliged to drink the coffee, Russell slowly began to sober up. At last he stood and thanked her for giving him the opportunity to talk. "I hope you didn't misunderstand," he said. "I like you and I may have said things that. . . . Look, Tracy, I don't really know what I'm saying or even what I'm doing here. So . . ."

But she knew. He wanted her body. Thin as it was, he wanted it, though his conscience was telling him he was mad. Yet her body had been around him for more than a year. At times she had all but flaunted it in his face. She remembered that day when she'd dressed for the restaurant dinner—padding the bodice and posing before the mirror, wondering if he'd notice her shape. She'd been so in love then—so hopeful that he'd return it—and he'd been completely indifferent to her charms. Yet now, without any encouragement from her, he found her so attractive that he was risking the girl he loved. Tracy shook her head.

But she wasn't fooled into believing that he wanted anything other than her body. His rambling remarks tonight had made that quite clear. Girls from the slums might be desirable, but they were never taken seriously. To Russell and his class, Tracy would forever remain the Monroe Street girl, who, no matter how many beautiful clothes she draped herself in, no matter how much money she made or how much culture she acquired, would remain Tracy, the Monroe Street girl, from the less fortunate background.

She had fought so hard for respectability. She had given up Michael for it. Yet none of this had done her any good. She remembered the day in Lanston when she'd settled the family in. She'd been so sure then that ladyhood was at last within her reach. What a fool she had been to believe that.

Russell was still standing there, still fighting his desires. She knew all about sexual pressures because boys on Monroe had spoken of them. Such pressures could completely obliterate common sense. Tracy thought about that for a moment. Suppose she gave him the passion he craved, fulfilled all the fantasies of the warm, loving woman? Wasn't it possible that in his frenzy he'd do things he might not ordinarily do? Wasn't it possible that she could keep him excited enough to get him in and out of City Hall before he knew what had hit him? Her eyes widened as the plan began to take shape in her mind.

She'd be Mrs. Russell Curtis; and then, by God, she'd be a lady. Then, by God, she'd have Russell's respect and everybody else's! She'd be Mrs. Russell Curtis, and never again would people see her as lower class. The pride her mother had instilled in her, the pride Tracy had carried in her heart, would finally be acknowledged by the world.

If it was sex he wanted, then sex she would give him. But she couldn't risk actual intercourse until she had some kind of commitment from him. If she did it now, it would be the third time, and that, according to girlfriends on Monroe Street, meant the possibility of pregnancy. No, she mustn't risk intercourse, but she could fulfill some of his other dreams. And as she did, she'd tell him that she loved him. She'd just leave out the part about the love having died long ago.

"Can you sit down a moment, Russell? There's something I have to confess."

Puzzled, he took a seat.

"I remember the day I met you," she said. "You were like—like a—a candle going on in a black room. You said, 'Don't you have pretty dimples?' and I blushed. I think I fell in love that very moment. But I understood that I wasn't the kind of girl you'd be interested in marrying because I didn't come from the proper background even though I tried so hard to better myself. So I hid my love, but it never died. To this day, when I look at you. . . . That's why I was so afraid to ask you in tonight."

She went on like this for a while, noting the various expressions crossing his face. It was easy acting out this speech, easy even to get that catch of emotion in her voice, because all she had to do was remember the times she had been so wildly in love and try to re-create her feelings.

Russell listened, his lips trembling with an emotion of his own. And then, like a cannon exploding, he leaped from the couch and swept her into his arms. She had trouble handling his ardor at first, but her adolescent experiences on Monroe Street had taught her much about satisfying men without actually permitting them to enter her body, and tonight she used that knowledge.

The couch would be too small for lovemaking, she thought. And the floor might be uncomfortable for him. So she led him gently into the next room and then fell, with him on top of her, onto the bed. In a frenzy he began to remove her shirtwaist. Then, feigning a moan of passion, she removed his tie and slid her hand under his shirt. He began tugging at her camisole and she began unbuttoning the shirt. It went on like this until he was completely naked and she was clad only in a petticoat. She permitted him to run his hands under the petticoat but would not allow anything else. Instead, she suggested in a breathy voice that he climax between her breasts. And he did so, clutching her fiercely and crying out so loudly that she was afraid the neighbors might hear. But she was obliged to moan too, with a passion she didn't feel, for she missed Michael so and wished it were he in this bed, and she felt wretched about what she was doing, not because of Russell, who deserved this deception, but because of Michael, who if he had known about this, would have been sick.

Russell lay inert on the bed, utterly spent. "I love you," he murmured.

"I love you too," she whispered. And she waited a while before proceeding to caress him again with all the warmth and the earthiness she could muster.

He became aroused again very quickly and this time he began to work in earnest on pushing up the petticoat.

"No, Russell, no! I'm afraid I'll get with child!"

"I'd marry you if you did."

"I can't, Russell. I can't risk it. But let me love you in other ways."

And she did—until nearly four in the morning by which time he was near to uncontrollable.

"Please, Tracy! I want to be inside you. I'm *sick* with the need to be inside you!"

"I can't. I love you very much, but I can't risk a fatherless child."

"But I'll marry you. I'd marry you right now. This minute if it were possible."

"Would you, my darling? I never dared to hope. . . ."

She decided to risk intercourse then. She knew he

had to mean what he had said because if he didn't really mean it, he could not come back anymore. And she knew he would rather die than be deprived of more nights like this. He had not been experienced. She had known that right away. He had probably been around girls whose idea of sex was to spoon on the sofa while the chaperone was out of the room. Now that he'd found the real thing, he was sure he'd been transported to Paradise. One of these days he would begin to cool down. He would realize that Paradise was the same Tracy Sullivan he had all but ignored all these months. But by that time he'd be married to her.

"All right," she whispered, her hands moving over his naked chest and downward. "I can't bear it anymore either. Oh, Russell, I've wanted you for so long. . . ."

Chapter Nineteen

"You're marrying *who?*" Ruth said.

"Russell Curtis, of Curtis and Price, Advertising."

"The Yankee who likes Sousa?"

"Hates Sousa. Likes Tchaikovsky."

"I should care what he likes? What about Michael?"

"Michael?"

"He loves you. Anybody can see that."

"I think maybe he needed me."

"He loves you, Tracy. And I think you love him."

"I care about him like a brother."

"Brother, my foot. An idiot I'm not."

"When did he leave for Jersey?"

"Day before yesterday."

Good, Tracy thought. She didn't want him hearing about this too soon.

Ruth said, "How did it happen? One minute you're helping Michael—bleeding for him, in fact—and the next minute you're marrying somebody else."

"Who I help and who I love have nothing to do with each other."

240

"Are you telling me you *love* Mr. College?"

"Yes."

"I don't believe it. For the past six months you haven't even mentioned him."

"Yes, I have. Now listen: I need you as a witness. We're going to City Hall day after tomorrow—"

"Day after—*Gott in himmel!* What did he do, get you pregnant?"

"Of course not. We just decided we wanted each other right now."

"One day after Michael left? *One day?*"

"Will you be a witness or not?"

"Oh, I'll be a witness, all right. When the fellow asks if anyone knows a reason why these two should not be joined together. . . ."

"You skunk!"

"Did you really expect me to say *mazel tov?* Did you really expect that? Only one day after Michael left?"

"Then I'll get, Mrs. Santini."

Ruth said nothing.

Tracy was sorry she had come. She wanted to get away fast before Ruth broke her resolve altogether. "Someday you'll understand," she said.

"Don't do this, Tracy. Or at least think about it a while."

"I've made up my mind," said Tracy, going toward the door.

LUKE would have understood it, Tracy thought. Katherine would have understood. The issue wasn't

241

love; it was survival. Yet she had loved Russell once, so she wasn't being totally crass today. She was making a choice that was practical and that was all. In the end it would be for the best. Michael would have his kind of woman and Tracy would have her kind of man. Never would they have to see their own love crushed by poverty.

This was what she told herself as she mounted the steps of City Hall with Russell at her side, Mrs. Santini puffing ahead of them, and the other witness, a college friend of Russell's named Martin Sanders, sprinting way out in front.

As the justice rattled through the ceremony, Tracy remembered that she'd always wanted a beautiful wedding. Elegant and romantic with a white dress, a colorful bridal party, good music, dancing, and champagne. Why, the christenings she'd attended had been more ceremonial than this! So had confirmations and first communions. And funerals—funerals had been the most lavish of all events, with priests, music, coaches, flowers, people in formal attire, and large meals afterward.

There was no celebration after the wedding was over. The witnesses had nothing in common with each other, one being a motherly Italian widow and the other a brash young sport. Mrs. Santini asked them over for coffee, but Russell's friend said that he had an appointment and Russell himself said they'd better tell his folks and get it over with.

His folks weren't the only ones who didn't know,

Tracy thought. Louise, who had returned to school today after a bout with bronchitis, didn't know either. How were they going to convince people that a long-standing love had driven them to this impulsive decision? Tracy hadn't wanted to think about that. And if Russell's folks were shocked, her own family would be ravaged. A Yankee and a Protestant? A wedding in City Hall? Did she want to end up in hell? they would ask.

How long would it take for the commotion to die down? How long before she and Russell were happy and comfortable with each other and settled in a lovely brownstone with two bathrooms, two children, and two servants? How long before the acceptance came and after that the parties and invitations, and after that her attainment of a good and gracious nature?

"WE WILL have it annulled," roared Russell's mother, a massive woman who reminded Tracy of a walrus.

"Mother, please don't forget yourself. Tracy is standing right here."

"I'm sure Tracy will agree that it would be best for all concerned. You both acted in haste, you didn't know what you were doing—"

"We knew what we were doing," said Russell. "There will be no annulment."

They were standing in his family's parlor in a brownstone on Thirtieth Street—the father, the mother, and the errant couple. A fire crackled in the hearth, and Tracy edged closer to it for warmth. She was cold and miserable and wishing she'd stayed single.

His mother said to Tracy, "Is there a baby involved?"

"Certainly not!" Tracy snapped.

"Would you consider submitting to a physical examination?"

"Joanne!" shouted Mr. Curtis, appalled.

Tracy whirled on the woman, her voice rising to fishwife heights. "I won't stand here and listen to this! I'm married to your son and I'm going to *stay* married to him. You may not like it, but there's nothing you can do about it. *I* can do something, though. I can leave this house!"

And she did, promptly, trailed out the door by Russell. They spent the night in a hotel and made plans to take an apartment. He had always lived at home, and had said he'd planned on bringing Tracy there. But not now, Tracy thought. And maybe not ever.

She spent her wedding night crying in his arms.

MRS. CURTIS'S reaction was tame compared to Louise's. Russell was reluctant to break the news himself, so he went off to the office on Monday, leaving Tracy to make the announcement. She waited until the six o'clock break between classes and then said it all in a rush so that it would be over with.

244

"Russell and I were married on Saturday."

Louise sat down hard on the instructor's chair, too stunned to speak.

"I know it must come as a shock—"

"How? What . . . what . . ." sputtered Louise, unable even to form a question.

"We—we were in love," Tracy said, looking away. "And we decided all of a sudden to—"

"In love? In *love?*" Louise began weaving back and forth. Then she stopped suddenly and looked up. "Oh, *wait* a minute. It's a joke, isn't it? You're only joking. For a minute I really—"

"I'm not joking," Tracy said, drawing off the glove of her left hand and exhibiting the wedding ring.

Louise's eyes widened and she began to wail. "Why did he—when did he—why didn't he tell me? He and I—my Russell—" she broke off and began to sob.

Tracy held her breath. She felt terrible, but she didn't know how she could help Louise. It would have been different if Louise were simply a friend. But this was the woman Russell had jilted for Tracy. How could Tracy console her?

Within minutes, however, that worry had fled. Louise, after crying for a while, turned on Tracy like a madwoman, screaming, "You! You!" There was no hint now of Louise's usual refinement. She was like an animal in pain, clawing the air. "Does he know you're a whore? Does he *know* that?"

"What did you call me?" Tracy screeched.

"The man I found in your flat that day—"

"'The man' was a *friend.*"

"A friend half undressed. I saw your combs on a blanket on the floor next to his necktie."

Sharp-eyed Louise. How fast she had scanned the room. Tracy's heart sank. Was she going to tell Russell?

"You saw no such thing," said Tracy. "You've got a dirty mind."

"Russell will hear about this."

"Fine! Go ahead and tell him. It's not true, and I have nothing to hide. But imagine what *his* reaction will be when he realizes how crazy you are?"

"I don't care about his reaction. It's a little late for that. But I do care about the truth."

"It *isn't* the truth. Michael was a *friend.*"

"A client, more likely."

"You pig! You dirty-minded *pig!* What proof do you have?"

"Proof, you say? The combs, the tie, the open shirt." But Louise said no more. She knew she couldn't produce this proof and that if she went to Russell anyway Tracy would deny everything. She would say sweetly that Louise, in her grief, was grasping at straws. She would even urge Russell to try to understand the poor hysterical woman. And Louise would end up looking like a candidate for Bellevue. There was no way to get revenge, Louise thought. No way at all. Not until a long time afterward would a way occur to her.

Tracy stood up straight and glided toward the door leading to her quarters. "Under the circumstances I shall have to dismiss you," she said.

"I hope you go to hell," shouted genteel Louise. "I hope you burn to a crisp!"

Tracy closed the door behind her.

Chapter Twenty

The baby, a son, was born nine months later. But Tracy did not calculate in months. She had read somewhere that the normal gestation period for humans was 270 days. It had been 280 since the night she had first slept with Russell, which meant that the child hadn't even been conceived until after the marriage. She did not tell Russell this. He might think he'd sacrificed his freedom for nothing. She kept the day count to herself but saw to it that people remembered she had been married in December. If there were still those who doubted her virtue, they could rest their minds now. Especially her fat and petty mother-in-law.

They were still living in an apartment—a modest one on the Upper West Side with five small rooms and a bathroom. The nursery had been fitted out and the bedroom equipped with paraphernalia for the birth. Though more women were going to hospitals these days, the majority had their babies at home.

In all these months Mrs. Curtis hadn't spoken to Tracy, though Mr. Curtis had come to call and Russell's sister, who lived in California, had sent a note. But now, as the nine months ended, Mrs. Curtis was having a change of heart. Why, the girl hadn't lied after all. Hadn't made a fool of her gullible son. And she, Joanne Curtis, was to be a grandmother! Why not just swallow her pride and accept the situation and be with the girl when the child came into the world? A new child, born in the last year of the century. It was a moment she *must* be a part of. Mrs. Curtis had a keen sense of destiny.

And so it came to pass that as Tracy lay screaming in the tenth hour of labor, her sheets drenched with sweat that was caused both by pain and by the August heat, her mother-in-law came waddling onto the scene. At first Tracy didn't know who this was. She had met the woman only briefly. When Mrs. Curtis revealed her identity Tracy winced and turned to the wall. Of all the times for the bitch to show up!

But her mother-in-law was strong, Tracy had to admit that. She didn't cover her ears or run away. She stood there through the whole ordeal, occasionally assisting the doctor and nurse, and during the final push she gripped Tracy's hand crying, "It's coming! It's coming! Be brave, my dear. Be brave!"

Afterward, Mrs. Curtis's thoughts were fixed on Stephen. Tracy might have been part of the wall-paper for all the woman cared. She gushed over him, said he looked just like Russell, said they all must come home to her now that the baby was here.

The change of heart threw Tracy into a state of confusion. On the one hand she didn't want to live with this walrus, but on the other she wanted the brownstone, the servants, the prestige and everything else. Russell was in the room looking at his son when his mother extended the invitation. He looked relieved, Tracy thought—as though his life in the apartment had been a kind of exile.

It hadn't been a bad life for Tracy. She and Russell got along after a fashion. He liked her in bed, and she liked the things he was able to give her. As for talk, there wasn't much of it, but she hadn't missed it yet. For the first four months she had continued at the school, hiring a former student to take over the position of Louise—who had disappeared. When Tracy's pregnancy had become apparent she had stopped working altogether but had hired another former student to assist the first. Thus she managed to stay in business—and she had been so preoccupied with this and with fixing up her home that she hadn't had time to worry about whether she and Russell had done the right thing.

But now he was indicating that things hadn't been idyllic for him. If he'd been unhappy, she was sorry. After all, she had tricked him into the marriage. It was guilt that finally tipped the balance, and she decided that the walrus would be worth putting up with if a happier Russell was the result.

"Of course I'll go," she told him later when he was alone with her.

"You won't mind my mother?"

"I'll try to get on with her. I know you want that."

"Yes, I do," he said. "Thank you, Tracy."

She smiled. "How do you feel, Pop?"

"He's—he doesn't look like a person yet."

She laughed. "Yes, he does. Like a drooling old man."

"This is the first newborn I've ever seen."

Where had he been? she wondered. On the East Side one saw newborns every day. One saw women breast-feeding too. Last week on Ruth's stoop she'd seen two women, each with a suckling baby—

"Ruth!" Tracy said suddenly. "She doesn't know."

"Excuse me?" Russell bent over the bed.

"Send a message to Ruth. She doesn't know the baby's come." Russell had already wired her family in Massachusetts, who had come to accept the marriage though everyone feared for Tracy's immortal soul. Pa was living with them now and actually holding down a job at the mill. How would he feel about being a grandfather?

"Did you hear me, Russell? Send a message to the Litvaks."

"*Must* we have that tribe in here tonight?"

"That tribe" referred to all Tracy's friends outside of Russell's circle and members of her family as well. He was uncomfortable with old chums from Monroe, with Tracy's assistants at school, and with Mrs. Santini and the merchants on Third Street. This was not, he was quick to assure Tracy, because he didn't like the Jews, the Irish, and the Italians. Why, Jews were among the most intelligent people in the world, and the Irish were charming and could sing and dance so well, and the Italians were so colorful and so merry. What he didn't like about immigrant groups

251

was their politics. And their habit of shouting to make a point. And did they have to talk so much, argue so much, and carry on like banshees over the smallest travialities?

She said, "I want my friends to come and see Stephen. You can go hide down at the club if you like."

"Very well."

"And I don't want you calling them 'that tribe' again. It makes me furious. Is that understood?"

"Don't pick a fight now. Our son's only four hours old."

"I'm not 'picking.' Just telling you."

"All right."

"That tribe" indeed, she thought as he left the room, remembering how it had been. Russell had no conception of what it was like to live on Monroe and streets like it, or why Ruth and David had the politics they did, or why the Irish "carried on like banshees." She remembered the keening at Annie's wake and thought for a while of Michael. He had heard about the marriage after it happened. At Tracy's request David had written and mentioned it. No sense letting Michael go on believing she would wait for him, Tracy had thought. Michael had not written back. Neither he nor David was a good correspondent. But in June he had come to Manhattan on business and had dinner with the Litvaks. He said that his family was settled and that he owned his own bicycle business. He said he'd been surprised at Tracy's marriage. Or at least this was Ruth's version of the story. What Michael had actually said and how he had said it, Tracy didn't know. Nor would the Litvaks be likely to tell her.

She wanted to see "that tribe" and Michael most of all. But she mustn't dwell on the past. There was no undoing it now. She must think about Stephen, her son, who wasn't yet real to her but would be soon. She was a mother. She, Tracy Sullivan Curtis, was a mother.

Part

Three

Chapter Twenty-One

"We lost the canned soup account," said Russell. He sat in a defeated attitude at the head of the table. At the other end was Tracy. In the middle was his mother. Eleven-year-old Stephen had asked to be excused until dessert was served.

"Why did you lose it?" asked his mother.

"Hanged if I know. I guess they didn't like my copy."

Tracy bit her lip. This was the third account he'd lost since Christmas! What would happen if it went on like this? Would she end up having to give up all the things she'd gained in these past twelve years?

It wasn't the first time she'd worried about losing everything. Even when things had gone well, in the early years of her marriage when the agency had been benefiting from the new businesses springing up all over the rapidly growing city, she'd had fears about waking up some morning and finding that it had all been a dream, that she was back on Monroe Street and endlessly scheming to get out.

"You've just got to be blunter," she told Russell now. "You've got to write copy that people understand. If you'd just—"

"I think I know my business better than you do," he snapped.

Like hell, she thought. But she didn't argue. An argument might result in his making a mistake tomorrow that would cost him yet another account. She sighed and turned her eyes from his woebegone face. The very sight of it was depressing to her.

With maturity Russell had lost the sense of playfulness he'd had in college. Once he was required to fill the shoes of his father, who had died five years before, Russell's role as court jester had come to an abrupt end. There were no more jokes about cookie campaigns, for his job now was to sell products in earnest. Tracy thought that he was getting more and more like his father. He was ashamed of the advertising business and wished he could be a professor or a writer of profound philosophy or allegorical short stories. His attitude about his work showed in his advertisements, which were so understated that they were almost apologetic. Lately he had taken to leaving the office early, coming home and writing poetry and fiction. He was unsure of himself, however, and hadn't worked up the courage to submit any of his work to magazines. Nor could he abide the thought that his sensitive renderings might be printed alongside advertisements for men's suspenders or cucumber soup even if those ads were the product of his own agency.

Now Russell's mother was saying, "Does losing the soup account mean the agency's in danger?" Like

Tracy, her mind was always fixed on money.

"No," Russell said, his voice doubtful. Tracy and her mother-in-law exchanged glances, both of them thinking the same thing: Thank heaven for Russell's practical partner, old Ed Price. With luck, *he'd* see to it that they didn't go under.

Tracy said to the cook, "We'll have dessert now, Mrs. Donovan."

"Yes, ma'am," said the tiny but energetic widow.

Tracy watched Mrs. Donovan leave, wondering if one of these days she'd be leaving for good, wondering if everything else would be going too. She was glad she'd held on to the secretarial school. If Russell ever lost the business, at least they'd be able to eat. But that would be about all they *could* do, since there was very little left in savings and stocks.

Was she never to have any peace of mind? Oh, and it was such a good world too! She had a beautiful and brilliant child whom she adored and who loved her in turn because, she suspected, they were very much alike in temperament. She had a four-story brownstone and all the clothes she wanted, and maids taking care of the house, and dressmakers taking care of the clothes, and everyone deferring to her, calling her ma'am, so anxious to please her and stay in her good graces. At last had come a time when she could afford to be sweet and generous like the ladies who had come down to the slums long ago. It made her feel so grand.

"Here, Mrs. Donovan," she would say to her cook, "here's a little coat for your grandson. Stephen's

259

outgrown it, you know, and I should hate to give it away to charity when I know how much little Kevin would appreciate it."

"Oh, thank you, ma'am. Thank you!"

"I'm glad to give it. Why, you're one of the *family*, Mrs. Donovan."

"Ah, Mrs. Curtis. It's a grand lady you are to be caring so about my Kevin."

A lady at long last! How wonderful it felt to go on shopping sprees at Wanamaker's or off to a party or dinner with Russell, dressed in an outfit that came straight from the fashion section of the newspaper. To sweep into a hall on his arm and have butlers bow and take her wrap, and have guests converge on her as she entered a drawing room to compliment her on the lace at her neckline or the detail of the embroidery on the sleeves.

And she'd never forget the day she and Russell had ushered Stephen into a private school that was close enough so that he didn't have to board (Tracy couldn't have stood not seeing him), but snooty enough to ensure him a ticket to Yale and eventually a ticket to the invitation lists of hostesses planning comings out for young heiresses. She, Tracy Sullivan, had produced such a son!

So many people had told her that money was the root of all evil. But they had either lied or not understood what real evil was. There was nothing wrong with the good life, though possibly there were prices to pay that she found a bit of a strain. Try though she might, she had never acquired a knowledge of the arts sufficient to impress Russell. She still labored halfheartedly because she knew it was important to him, but she detested having to analyze books, plays, and sopranos. Then too it was hard getting along with some of his acquaintances. She vastly preferred being with her students and old friends. Down at the school she still maintained her flat (now an office) and here she got to see Ruth and David and others not welcome in Russell's circles. But she was bitter over the fact that he didn't make it easy for her to entertain them at home.

Yes, her life did have its drawbacks, and maybe concentrating on these would make Russell's failures easier to take. But she couldn't do it. She could not resign herself to disaster. She wanted to pound Russell over the head and knock some *sense* into him.

"You've still got the auto account, haven't you?" his mother asked.

"Yes, and that's solid. People buying autos don't want hyperbole; they want facts. But I wish it were a gasoline and not an electric."

The automobile industry had burgeoned beyond any optimists' expectations, and Tracy rued the day she had scorned Michael's ideas. Michael was married now, a father, and working in Michigan. He had left his younger brothers in charge of the bicycle business in New Jersey and gone to the heart of the auto industry—Detroit. He now worked in that city or in some factory town near it—Tracy wasn't sure of the details—and sent his brothers money to help support their mother. He was no factory hand or foreman either but a manager with an office and secretary. Ruth had told Tracy all this and then summed up, "He's making money hand over fist."

Tracy had seen Michael only once in the past ten years. It was in 1908 when he'd come east after Ruth's and David's son died. Little Aaron had contracted a rare blood disease called leukemia and had lingered three months in agonizing pain. Michael's sister had written Michael that the child was near death, and Michael had walked out of the Michigan plant, then taken the first train available. He'd been too late for the funeral, but he'd come anyway—a gesture Ruth and David never forgot.

On that occasion Tracy had been too preoccupied with Ruth's grief to take much note of Michael. She had a vague impression of well-cut clothes and an aura of maturity that she'd attributed to fatherhood, but she couldn't remember much else about the visit, for Ruth had been in a bad way.

So many had died, Tracy thought. Ruth's son, Ruth's parents, David's father, and Russell's father. Michael's father had died in a prison fight and Tracy's own father had finally died in Lanston of cirrhosis of the liver. Even Luke's youngest son had died last week. A notorious playboy, who must have squandered every cent his father had left him, he had finally met his end while racing a Renault over the poor roads of Long Island. A female companion, six months pregnant, had been thrown from the car and also killed, and the report in the paper had made much of the scandal. Tracy had heard from cousins

262

that Luke's older son was the younger one's opposite number. He had become a priest in a wealthy uptown parish, where he was reported to be richer than most of his parishioners and less interested in saving souls than in drinking himself into oblivion. Tracy was glad Luke had not lived to see this. Luke, who had given up love that his clan might survive. Here the older son was a celibate and inebriate and the younger one was wrapped around a tree. The family line Luke had sacrificed Katherine for had been cut off entirely.

Stephen came back into the dining room in time to eat dessert. Eleven years old, he was still an only child, though Tracy and Russell had tried very hard for more children. As a baby he had looked like Russell (or so his grandmother had claimed), but as he grew older even she had to admit that the child must favor Tracy: thin face, brown hair, eyes even darker brown than Tracy's hazel ones, and a slender body. But he shared with Russell a potential for height, and the size of his hands and feet gave promise of a tall man.

He was a high-spirited child and an optimistic one, little daunted by the rebuffs children occasionally encounter. He was doing well scholastically while boasting a group of loyal friends. He took his seat at the table opposite his fawning grandmother and asked where the dessert was.

"Mrs. Donovan hasn't brought it in yet," said Tracy. "My, but, you're impatient."

"Not impatient. Just starving."

"How was school today?" asked his grandmother.

"The history teacher asked us what we wanted to be when we grew up."

"And what did you say?"

"The president of the United States."

"How modest," muttered Russell who didn't approve of what he called Stephen's "bumptious-ness."

"More power to him," said Tracy, and her mother-in-law grinned and nodded assent. Tracy still wasn't crazy about the woman, but lately the two of them had found themselves on the same side of the fence so often that they'd fallen into a kind of cautious alliance. Joanne's conspiratorial wink was the latest evidence of their changing relationship.

Russell said to his son, "And what makes you think you would be qualified to be president?"

"I understand what's wrong with the country and I know how to change it."

"Indeed?" Russell said. "What exactly is wrong, and how do you propose to surpass the honorable W. H. Taft?"

"I'm going to make the rich share more with the poor."

"Noble sentiment," Russell muttered. "And how shall you do this?"

"I'll make them give the poor more of their money."

"'Take up the white man's burden!'" Russell quoted Kipling and smirked. Then he said, "Tammany Hall's already helping the poor. With dubious methods and dubious results."

"What does 'dubious' mean?" asked Stephen.

As Russell proceeded to explain, Tracy frowned. It was typical of her husband to shoot the boy down at every opportunity. "He's such an infernal optimist," Russell would sometimes complain when Tracy asked why he did this. "He thinks the world will fall into his lap. It's my duty to point out that it won't."

"Why should *you* tell him? He's got the rest of the world to tell him. Can't you just let him be?"

"To what purpose? To come back at the age of twenty-five beaten down by reality, scourged—"

"Stephen *scourged?* Nothing would *ever* beat Stephen for long, unless it's you and you keep up this naysaying."

After they were finished with the meal and Russell and Tracy were alone in the parlor he said, "You know what bothers me most about him?"

"What's that?" asked Tracy with a sigh.

"He's not consistent. He's an idealist and a little materialist too, wanting money for the nickelodeon every week and trips to the shore."

"He's a *child*, for pity's sake!"

"And a greedy one. Materialism and liberalism just don't go together."

"They could," Tracy said. "Maybe he wants the masses to have material things too."

Russell sighed and gave her an exasperated look. "You miss the point."

"No, I don't. I think you just like to pick on him."

It was Pa and herself all over again, she thought.

The one determined to penalize the other for trying new ideas, for daring. But why should Russell be like Pa? He'd been spoiled all his life, he'd never lost a wife or been fired without cause or been obliged to return to a slum and a future of unemployment. Why should Russell be so weak that he felt obliged to cut a child down?

She suspected that many of Russell's problems were in some way caused by her. Would he ever have married her if she hadn't tricked him into it? But she'd tried to be a good wife and worthy of him. And Stephen, after all, was Russell's son too. She shook her head. What was the point in trying to explain it? What was the good in wishing the problem would go away? Once a parent took an attitude toward a child, that attitude never changed. Her experience with Pa had taught her that.

Her thoughts turned to her family. She hadn't heard from her brothers and sisters since Christmas. Pat was the only one living at the house now. Mary had married not a high school teacher but an up-by-his-bootstraps Sicilian immigrant who had bought a grocery store on Center Street in the town and also a ten-room house. Mary was now the mother of three, financially comfortable and still very much in love. Her marriage to "the ginnie" had caused Pa to go on a two-week drunk. He'd contracted pneumonia but had eventually recovered and hadn't died until two years later. In all that time he had never exchanged a word with his son-in-law.

Kerry, now twenty-four, had also married a man

from town. He had been handsome but foul-natured, so she had left him and moved to Boston, where she had married another man without divorcing the first. When all this came to light and the fights, threats, annulments, and divorces had been dealt with, Kerry had moved to Bridgeport, where she finally settled down with a third husband and gave birth to a baby girl. All this had caused Tracy no end of aggravation and put the first gray hairs on her head. At thirty-three Tracy felt she was too young for gray hairs and she cursed her youngest sister every time she plucked one out.

Brother Pat had fallen in love with Katherine's daughter and she with him. But Pat had been so concerned that people would think he'd chosen Julia only for her money that he had given up his beloved altogether. Julia had married someone else and moved to Providence and Pat still pined for her memory while continuing to work at Madison Mills as a superintendent. Katherine, who finally found out about this, said she simply could not understand it. Tracy had gone a step further and pronounced her brother insane. He was now a bachelor of twenty-seven living alone at the house.

Brother Tommy had moved back to New York and become a policeman. He lived near Tracy's typing school and was a frequent guest at the Curtis house, where he had endeared himself to Tracy's mother-in-law with his newly cultivated Irish charm and was much admired by young Stephen.

Tracy still felt responsible for all of them. For them

and for Stephen and for every student she'd ever graduated. But Russell had been the one *she* had wanted to lean on, the one she had selected because he'd seemed to embody the word "security."

She gazed across the parlor at his weak, petulant face and she sighed.

Chapter Twenty-Two

Tracy was at her office one day in January going through the employment section of the paper in search of openings for her students when Ruth came by with a dark-haired girl who looked as though she'd just gotten off the boat. Tracy groaned inwardly. Another greenhorn, she thought. Some things never changed.

The school had not changed very much either. It was still a store-front school catering to the poor. Tracy had often thought of expanding, but there was a lot of competition now, including some from schools and settlement houses that taught typing and shorthand free of charge—if not as efficiently as she did. And expansion would have involved spending too much time away from Stephen. To say nothing of money, which was in short supply these days.

"This is Tracy Sullivan," Ruth said in English, then lapsed into Yiddish for five minutes, which annoyed Tracy. Turning to Tracy finally, Ruth said, "A new student. My niece Rachel Lipski from Minsk."

"New student? *My* student? She can't even speak English."

"So she'll learn. In the meantime she can type, *nu?*"

"Type with what? The Hebrew alphabet?"

"I promised her, Tracy. I promised her in a letter that America wouldn't disappoint her."

"But she's been through Ellis Island, so she already knows you lied."

"Be serious. I swear she'll learn fast. Just teach her typing. Shorthand we'll save for later."

"You're such a *nudje*, Ruth." Tracy used quite a bit of Yiddish herself, having learned from Ruth and the students.

"So kill me later. Now I want my niece to learn how to type."

"Does she even know the English alphabet?"

"That much I taught her."

"Bully for you," Tracy sighed. "All right, I'll send her to the classroom but just for typing. Does she have a job?"

"She starts Monday. A big shirtwaist factory over on Greene Street. She'll be on time for evening classes."

"But will she *pay* me on time? That's the issue."

"Isn't it always? Of course she will."

"All right. There's a typewriter free right now. I'll try her out. If she seems comfortable we'll take her on next week for a regular class. Only for you would I do this."

"I know. You're a peach."

"Meshuggeneh is what I am," said Tracy, "and this is the last greenhorn you're sending me. The *last*. Mother of God, I ought to set up a department of English in here!"

Year after year the flood of immigrants had rolled into New York. The East Side, which had been crowded enough in the nineties, was now, in 1911, crammed to the bursting point. Some older residents had been forced out and had gone to live in Brooklyn where tenements were also flourishing. And still they came, hundreds of thousands each year: Italians, Greeks, Russians, Poles, Serbs, Germans, Croatians, Austrians, Arabs, Swedes, Armenians, Bohemians, Chinese, Irish, Spanish, Portuguese . . . They were dumped at Ellis Island and left to make their way as best they could. Many took trains to New England or the West, but others stayed in New York either because they had kin here or because some contractor or padrone had promised them work sewing pants, building subways, or erecting yet more tenements in which to suffocate. If the immigrant were a lone man he might stay in a boardinghouse. But the single women (and a great many men as well) preferred to board with distant family or friends until they got their footing in the New World. In the past few years more than fifty boarders had spent time with the Litvaks who had even moved into a larger flat to accommodate them. This Rachel was the latest and the tenth Ruth had brought to Tracy's school, though the others had at least been prepared with a little night school English.

There had been times in the past eleven years when Tracy had been forced to admit that she missed her former assistant Louise. None of the help since then could compare with her as far as patience and teaching skills were concerned. Of course Louise had shown her true colors that last day, and Tracy preferred to think that she might eventually have lost her self-control in a students presence. So it was just as well she had gone, Tracy thought. Where she had gone neither Tracy nor Russell ever found out, but Tracy hoped fervently that she would never reappear.

"Be kind to Rachel," Ruth urged her friend after Tracy returned from the classroom. "She's alone in the world. Her parents are dead and her brother—he was a radical socialist—was killed in the '05 revolution. She lived with her aunt in Kiev for five years. A real *yenta* from what I could gather."

"How long has she been with you?"

"Two weeks now. *Di Greine Kuzine.*"

"What?"

"'The Greenhorn Cousin.' My niece reminds me of the girl in that song."

"Where will she go after this?"

"She'll stay with us until she marries."

"Ruth, you've already got *five boarders* living there."

"And a baby on the way." Ruth patted her stomach. She had finally decided that the only way to assuage her grief over Aaron was to have another child.

"How can you stand all that commotion and write

272

for the paper too?"

"Never mind that. Just tell me how I'm going to fit Michael in at the dinner table."

"Michael? Michael Ryan?"

"Didn't I tell you? His mother died. He came back to Jersey for the funeral. We didn't know till yesterday when he telephoned David at the printing office. He wants to see us before he goes back to Michigan."

Tracy said, "So she's dead too. Another one dead." She remembered Pa's saying, "One by one, they all drop off." To Ruth she said, "Did Michael take it well?"

"He'd been expecting it for years. She used to tell them she'd be happier dead." Ruth sighed. "Ah, that family, what they didn't have to put up with! It's a wonder any of them kept their sanity. You know, Mike had mixed feelings about her. If she'd gone to the police earlier, if she'd let him take over when he wanted to—and then all those years out in Jersey she was just so sad all the time. She never rallied. So I don't think he's mourning. I think maybe he's glad she's in a happier place."

"When did you say he'd be here?"

"Tonight sometime."

"I'll miss him. I'm going to the theater with Russell and Joanne."

"Who's Joanne?"

"My mother-in-law."

"You always call her the walrus."

"Not lately," Tracy said. "We're seeing Barrymore

273

in *The Fortune Hunter*."

Ruth nodded. "Shall I tell Michael you asked for him?"

"Yes. When's he leaving?"

"Tomorrow."

"His wife's coming too, I imagine."

"No, she didn't come east with him. Stayed in Michigan with the daughter."

Tracy was surprised, but she only said, "Oh. Well, give Michael my best, all right?"

"I will," Ruth said.

BUT AT six o'clock Tracy was at Ruth's door, having told Russell and Joanne that she couldn't go to the theater because of pressing school business. To make it all look authentic she even dressed in a working woman's outfit—navy suit, white shirt-waist, unostentatious gray coat and matching hat. She was here, she told Ruth, because the theater performance had been canceled and she'd decided to take this opportunity to tell Rachel more about the school and to "say hello to Michael if he's around."

"He's not here yet, but Rachel will be glad to know how concerned you are." Ruth didn't even bother to try keeping a straight face. Imagine Tracy coming all the way down here to reassure a greenhorn she had almost refused to admit? Who did she think she was kidding? She was here to see Michael and no one else. Ruth had known Tracy would come here since the moment Ruth had told her that the wife had stayed in Michigan.

The new home was a large six-room flat. It had a bathroom and stoves in both kitchen and parlor—rare opulence for Monroe Street or any street on the East Side. Since the paper was now doing very well, Ruth and David now had the money to live almost anywhere in the city. They'd chosen to stay here because they had agreed that they should live among the people about whom they wrote. At the kitchen table sat Rachel and a man with a beard who was wearing a skullcap. Down in the parlor with David were two other boarders. A fifth was out with a beau at the Yiddish theater.

After introducing Tracy to the gentleman with the beard (he didn't speak English, so the greetings were brief), Ruth told Rachel in Yiddish that her dear and thoughtful friend had come all the way from Thirtieth Street just to see her and to urge her to stay in school. Overcome by such kindness, Rachel scrambled to her feet and thanked Tracy profusely in Yiddish. Tracy, who hadn't understood some of Ruth's language, was puzzled by the excess of gratitude, but she smiled and nodded too. Ruth talked on in Yiddish, telling the girl that Tracy could practically guarantee her the best employment available to young women in the city. A few months in Tracy's care and Rachel would be as proud and accomplished as any native American girl and earning better money than most. Then in English she said, "Isn't that so, Tracy?"

"Isn't what so?"

Ruth then proceeded to translate and Tracy,

275

cursing her friend, had a hard time maintaining the smile for Rachel. "I'm going to fix you, Ruth," she said through grinning teeth.

"What do you mean?" Ruth smiled back. "You said you'd come here for Rachel and I was profoundly moved. Let us join together now and sing 'Heaven Will Protect the Working Girl.'"

Tracy made a face. "I came to ask how she's *doing*, not to turn her into the wonder of New York."

"Tell that to Rachel," Ruth said. "Go ahead, break her heart."

"Not before I break your head," Tracy said, still smiling into Rachel's face.

And Rachel, thinking that they were having a pleasant conversation, grinned with satisfaction. America could be a lovely place after all.

It was then that they heard the rap on the door that had to be announcing Michael. Tracy stiffened for a moment, then turned to face Rachel full-on so that she could get her bearings. Ruth went to the door, grinning. Tracy's back was still toward the door when she heard Ruth shout in the brogue she sometimes liked to put on, "Would you look at him, now? Sure and he takes me breath away!" She said no more, and Tracy turned slightly to see Ruth giving Michael an enormous hug. She turned a little more and took in a few details. He looked imposing in a rich black greatcoat, and the hat he was holding in the hand not embracing Ruth was expensive too. The gaslight caught a few gray highlights in his hair. This was common in black-haired people, where even one strand could gleam like a beacon, but he was also older than she.

"And would you look who's here?" cried Ruth, disengaging herself from Michael and gesturing toward Tracy.

"Tracy," he said, nodding.

"Hello, Michael." She smiled nervously.

Ruth introduced her guest to Rachel and the boarder with the beard and then shouted for David, who bounded down the hall and greeted Michael with a hug only a little less restrained than Ruth's. Only then did the three of them offer condolences upon the death of Michael's mother. He acknowledged these with a nod and took the seat at the table toward which David was motioning him.

"A little schanapps?" Ruth said.

"Please," said Michael.

"You, Tracy?"

"Uh huh. Yes. A little."

The other two had only enough to cover the bottoms of their glasses, then they switched to a light sweet wine, prompting Michael to remark, "Still booze hounds, I see."

"We do all right," said David.

"Regular falling-down drunks," said Michael.

They went on with this banter—for longer than necessary, Tracy thought—trotting out playful insults of the past. Michael dared David to drink him under the table and David said he would, but only if the drink of choice was sweet wine. Michael made a face and David and Ruth laughed, while Tracy sat there impatiently wondering how long this nonsense was going to go on. She wanted to hear about Michael's life now.

He was different, she thought. Well-dressed, much more relaxed and good-natured than she'd ever known him to be. And this was only a day after burying his mother. What must he be like in better circumstances? She wondered if money made the difference. Or perhaps it was just due to age. Whatever the cause, he was no longer the wild-eyed youth who had tossed his father down the stairs, no longer the grieving young man she had held in her arms two years later. Was he still capable of the passion he had shown that night? Had he acted that way with his wife? Well, he must have acted *some* way because there was the daughter to prove it. She wondered how much he loved his wife.

At last the drunken-Irishman—sober-Jew clichés came to an end and the Litvaks demanded to know what Michael had been up to all these years. He'd written once in a while, but the notes had been very brief. He said he was a manger and rarely got into the plant anymore, but business was booming and in ten years' time the automobile would be priced within the range of the average man.

His speech, Tracy noticed, was much more precise than it had been in years past. And the East Side was vastly toned down. His grammar was almost perfect now, and he'd greatly expanded his vocabulary, as befitted his more exalted station in life. In fact, this was true of Tracy and the Litvaks too. David and

Ruth had never finished night high school, and Tracy hadn't progressed past the eighth grade, but by paying attention to such details as grammar and vocabulary they managed to convey the impression that they were quite well-schooled.

Ruth asked Michael about his brothers and sisters and then about his daughter in Michigan.

"Chris? She's fine. Getting big. She had a touch of grippe when I saw her at Christmas, but she got over it fast the way kids do."

"Saw her at Christmas?" Ruth repeated. "Don't you see her every day?"

"Well—no."

"Is she away at school?"

"She's away with her mother. We're—Meg moved back to the farm."

"Then you're separated?"

"Physically we are. It's not a legal thing, and it isn't that we don't like each other. She just missed the two hundred acres she grew up with and I—what would I do on a farm? I don't know a hoe from a milk pail."

"How far away is she?"

"About a hundred miles from Detroit."

"And how long have you been separated?" Ruth asked.

"Two years, maybe a little longer."

"Two *years?*" Ruth exclaimed. "You never wrote and told us."

"No reason to," said Michael, with Michael-like logic.

279

"Two years without a woman?" David said. Then he looked embarrassed, for he tried to be proper in mixed company. But Tracy was sure that Michael wasn't suffering. Being without a wife didn't mean being without a woman. Hell's Kitchen, Michigan-style.

"Have you thought of divorce?" Ruth asked.

"There's no reason to get one."

"She deserted you," David said.

Michael shook his head. "She was unhappy, but she didn't run away. We talked about it first. It wasn't desertion. She was very—what's the word?—sheltered when I married her. And I had to uproot her and move her to a factory town. These aren't the kind of communities you find in the east. They're strictly factory and mostly men. Meg hated it. I didn't blame her. She comes from one of those big farm families, the kind you see in Thanksgiving Day etchings, and she missed it. I would have gone back with her, but I'd built my career around motorcars and what in blazes would I do on a farm?"

"What if she finds someone else?" Ruth said.

"I'll worry about that when it happens." He cleared his throat and said to the Litvaks, "I've been doing all the talking, but I came to hear about you. So talk, already."

They chatted mostly about stories David had covered: strikes, epidemics, Tammany skulduggery, fires, gang wars, Black Hand murders, extortion rings, white slavery rings. But David's paper genera-ally concentrated on the problems of the common people—most especially the children of Old World Jews who were trapped between traditional values and the American way. Since the paper was printed in English, it had a Gentile following too and was becoming something of a labor tract for the younger, more militant generation.

As they talked they consumed Ruth's dinner of chicken, *latkes,* and stuffed cabbage washed down with plenty of wine and followed by sponge cake, poppy-seed cookies, and coffee. Michael didn't have much to say to Tracy, and she couldn't think of what to say to him, so they looked to Ruth and David to lead the conversation and consumed the meal without making their discomfort with each other too obvious. Boarders flitted in and out, one sitting at the table awhile, the others, including Rachel, taking their plates to the parlor so that the Litvaks could be alone with their guests. There was more coffee and more talk, and finally the hour grew late enough for Michael to feel obliged to suggest leaving.

"I know you've got to get up early with the paper," he said to David. "And I've got to catch a morning train."

"Where are you staying?" David asked.

"The Waldorf. Fifth and Thirty-third."

"The Waldorf!" Ruth exclaimed. "Well, la de *da.* How far we've come from Monroe Street."

Michael grinned. "I figured I'd try it once before I died."

Ruth returned to her brogue. "Then be gone with ye, boyo. Ye mustn't be wastin' a minute of th' grrrand life. And will ye be escortin' this lassie home now?"

"Really, Ruth," Tracy said hastily. "I can manage meself—I mean *my*self." And she started to laugh, the first time she'd laughed all evening. Michael chuckled too, and that broke the ice a bit. He said, "Better let me take you, Tracy. It's late."

There was much talk of when they'd see one another again and an appeal from Ruth to Michael to move back to New York where he belonged. "You're about as midwestern as George M. Cohan," she chided.

"Give me time. I'll learn to speak slow as a cowboy."

"Oh, phooey. You don't belong in that outpost." And she was still shouting this when Michael and Tracy walked down the hall.

The ride in the hansom was a strain. For five blocks there was total silence. Finally Tracy said to him. "Have a good time?"

"I always do when I'm with them."

"Me too," she said. "Ruth looks good, doesn't she?"

"Yes," he said.

"A new baby. That's what she needs."

"Uh huh." He nodded. "When is she due?"

"June sometime."

Silence. More silence. She realized that it was the first time in twelve years that she'd been alone with him. On his previous visit, after young Aaron's death, he hadn't escorted her home.

"Do you like Michigan?" she asked.

"It's less crowded."

"Don't you miss the east?"

"Once in a while."

"What sort of automobiles are you working on?"

"Utilitarian ones. But in my area we're developing tractors."

"Tractors?"

"Motorized vehicles that pull plows and other farm machines."

"Really?" she said, bored already. "Is it difficult to make them?"

"They're not like autos. You've got to move them over rough terrain."

"That must really be a challenge," she said.

"And I can guess how excited you must be," he said with a grin.

"I mean it. It's interesting."

"No doubt," he muttered wryly. "And what have *you* been doing these days? I assume you've given up the typing school?"

"Not at all. I still have it."

"What for? You must have all the money you need."

"I like the school," she said.

He nodded. "How's your son?"

"Growing up. He's eleven now."

"Does he take after you?"

"In some ways," she said.

"God help him," Michael muttered, then added with a smile, "just kidding."

"You'll never forgive me, will you?"

"I'll probably have a hard time forgetting it. As I recall, there were only two or three days between my proposal and your marriage to him."

"I didn't want to tell you about him that night. The night you and I—"

"Yes," he interrupted, clearing his throat. "Why wouldn't you tell me?"

"I thought I'd hurt your feelings."

"So you figured that by springing it as a surprise you'd hurt me less?"

"I was very confused," she said.

He was silent for a moment and then he said, "Well, I don't suppose it matters now."

Doesn't it? she thought. Somehow she wanted it to matter very much.

During the rest of the trip they discussed New York and its changing face. The Flatiron Building and other skyscrapers, the new subways tunneling under the city, the increasing number of electrified buildings, and the expanding trolley lines. Michael had not been here in three years and was mightily impressed. She wished he would talk of something personal, but he continued to comment on the new marvels.

At her house he stepped out of the hansom and escorted her to the door. She feared Russell might be getting home from the theater soon and she'd be forced to give some explanation. But this did not happen. Michael smiled and held his hand out. She shook it, her fingers trembling. He tipped his hat and walked back down the brownstone stairs with too much spring in his step to suit her. Not that she wanted him to *mourn* the parting exactly, but she would have liked to see some evidence that he still cared. After all, she still cared for him. She turned to wave at him, but he didn't look back. He got into the cab and the driver took off.

Tracy remained on the step until the hansom turned the corner.

Chapter Twenty-Three

Ruth's boarder Rachel became a favorite of Tracy's and though Tracy was still angry at Ruth for forcing her hand, she came to enjoy the challenge of transforming seventeen-year-old Rachel into an expert typist. One reason she liked the new student was that Rachel, having been misled by Ruth into thinking that Tracy was benevolence itself, grew almost worshipful of Tracy to the point where she imitated her walk and even phrases like "Mother of God!" which she uttered when she made a mistake on the keyboard. Tracy heard her once and explained through a student's translation what the phrase meant. The girl blushed when she realized that she'd been referring to a god that Jews didn't recognize and laughed over her blunder. But Rachel learned fast, adding night school to her heavy schedule, and by March could tell Tracy how much she loved the school in a little speech she had composed from her limited English. This prompted Tracy to invite Rachel into the office for tea, which caused the other students to grumble that Rachel was teacher's pet.

Rachel's progress and stories of other students

constituted the mainstay of the subjects Tracy talked about during dinner conversations, much to Russell's annoyance. This might have been more of a problem had her mother-in-law not also been more interested in real people than the fictional ones in well-reviewed plays. There were nights when the two chatted on about everyone from the milkman to Houdini and paid no attention whatever to Russell.

He was growing more and more self-absorbed these days, sinking deeper into his writing and commenting occasionally that he didn't belong to this age, that he was an alien, an outsider. The two women ignored much of what he said, including his misanthropic pronouncements and bald assertions that he was getting downright xenophobic. Thus it came as a shock to Tracy when he slammed down his fork on the table one evening and burst out, "How much more of this do you expect me to endure?"

"What?" Tracy blinked in astonishment.

"This chatter of the school as though it's Oxford or Harvard you're talking about. You exalt the slums as though you were one of the ashcan artists. Don't you have a single elevated thought? Can't you utter a sentence without peppering it with low Italian and Yiddish phrases?"

"What in blazes do you expect me to talk about?" she screeched. "Plato and Aristotle aren't in my classes!"

"Now children—" Mrs. Curtis began.

Russell interrupted. "Talk about anything. *Anything* but that school."

287

"'That school' may be supporting you someday at the rate you're losing accounts."

"Please stop!" Mrs. Curtis urged, and young Stephen nodded.

"If I'm losing accounts," Russell said, "it's because they're forcing me to conform to this coarse age you're so fond of, this Tin Pan Alley mentality!" And he stormed away from the table.

Mrs. Curtis sighed and Stephen said, "Why does Daddy hate his job so much?"

"Because he thinks he's too good for the masses!" Tracy shouted.

"Because he doesn't like to make people buy things," Mrs. Curtis explained more reasonably.

Stephen said, "But if people want things, why doesn't Daddy want to sell it to them?"

"He's a poet," Tracy muttered. "Poets don't taint themselves with business matters. They'd rather starve in garrets. Which is fine with me, so long as we don't have to starve along with him."

"Tracy, please!" said her mother-in-law. "The child doesn't understand."

"Yes, I do!" insisted Stephen.

"And your father's also a wit," Tracy said, ignoring her mother-in-law's pleas. "Or used to be. Spent all his time dreaming up clever little jokes. Oh, how charming I thought it was then. . . ."

"Stephen, why don't you go do your homework?" Mrs. Curtis said.

"Do I *have* to?" he whined.

"Yes," Tracy snapped. "Now *go!*"

When Stephen had stomped off, Mrs. Curtis said, "Russell's remarks were uncalled for."

"You don't say," Tracy muttered.

"But calling him a failure won't help matters. And certainly not in front of the child. Now if you want this marriage to improve you're going to have to start complimenting him once in a while."

"Complimenting! After what he said to me?"

"A little building up and he won't get so angry about little things."

Tracy sighed. "Joanne, I spent the first twenty years of my life catering to men. My father was a drunk and a freeloader, but I put up with it. I held my tongue. I bought him a house with the money I saved. And you know how he thanked me? By throwing the house in my face. Weak people don't like being pandered to. They only grow to hate the panderer."

Mrs. Curtis was silent for a while and then she said, "You may have a point. But what can you do about it?"

"I think we should let him flounder. Let him come face-to-face with the wolf at the door. Then he'll either buck up and get his priorities right or else—"

"Or else?"

"He'll buck up. He's got too much to lose if he doesn't."

TRACY was proved right within a week. Russell was scarcely speaking to his wife, but she noticed that he was spending more time at the office. And on

289

Saturday he came home for lunch and announced that he'd saved a key account with a clever promotion idea he'd come up with himself. Tracy didn't fawn all over him as his mother did. She simply nodded. Still angry at him, she was planning not to go with him to the theater tonight, though it was an engagement they'd planned two weeks earlier. She did not look forward to the prospect of the fight that would follow her announcement, but as it turned out she need not have worried. For by theater hour one of the worst catastrophes in the city's history had occurred.

She was walking through Washington Square, heading back to the school after a shopping trip on Fifth, when she heard the clang of fire bells and saw people running toward Washington Place. Tracy had never been one to follow fire wagons. In the slums fires raged in one place or another almost constantly, and she'd become inured to them long ago. But she was close to Washington Place now and could see at once that this wasn't just a burning mattress. Great clouds of smoke billowed into the sky, and the voices of the observers rose in shrill alarm. Pushing into Washington Place with other curiosity seekers, she saw the building and the flames. It was at the end of the block, on the corner of Greene Street. She knew this building as she knew almost all the sites in the area. She spent much of her time placing students in neighborhoods within walking distance of home so that they could save carfare. She tried to remember which offices she had

290

visited here. Meyers, Crown, and Wallach—that was it. Was this the place that was on fire? The police and fire wagons were crowding into the area, forcing her up onto the sidewalk and into the dense onlooking crowd.

"They're jumping!" someone was screaming.

Tracy craned her neck and saw it—girls leaping from windows eight and nine floors up. They descended, trying to keep themselves upright, some holding the hands of companions. She did not see them land, for crowds obscured her view of the far sidewalk.

Tracy blinked. She could not believe what she was seeing. No one could jump from such a height and live. Perhaps the fire department had nets and she just couldn't see them. Yes, that had to be the explanation. There were large nets all around the base of the building.

"Can you see?" she asked the man in front of her. "Do they have nets?"

"Do they have nets?" the man asked people in front of him who in turn asked others.

Nobody seemed to know. The bodies kept falling. The street was now dense with fire wagons, police wagons, screaming crowds, horses leaping up on their hind legs, frightened by all the commotion. Tracy saw a hook and ladder moved into place but then saw to her dismay that it didn't reach far enough. A girl made a long leap downward for it. She missed and fell into the abyss. Hoses were finally turned on the building, and she did not see anyone else jump. It was then that she heard the word "Triangle" echo through the crowd. At first it meant nothing, but quickly she made the connection. Triangle Shirtwaist. Was that what was burning? Of course. She could see a sign on the outside of the building near a window full of flames. She knew it to be one of the largest waist factories in the field because Rachel worked at Triangle and she had said—

Rachel worked at Triangle! The realization hit her with all the impact of the falling bodies. She screamed again, "Do they have nets? Do they have nets?" No one answered.

The crowds were being controlled by cordons of police. She saw a cop who looked like her brother standing a few yards away. Yes, it must be. Tommy worked at the Mercer Street station house.

"Tommy!"

He did not turn.

"Tommy! Tommy Sullivan!"

He turned but did not see her.

"Tommy! It's me! Tracy!"

He looked steadily in her direction, then came into her general area, waving his club to part the crowd. "Tracy?" he kept calling.

"Over here."

He saw her. "What are *you* doing—"

"What happened? Do they have nets?"

"There were nets for a few of 'em. But some of 'em broke 'cause they were jumping two and three at a time."

"Broke? Is anyone dead?"

"There's a lot dead. And probably more in the building. Why don't you get out of here? You'll be—"

"Did you see a thin dark-haired girl wearing a blue jacket? She didn't speak much English. She was about five feet four. She was—"

"Tracy, there're *dozens* of girls." His voice shook with impatience. Then he looked at her and realized why she was asking the question. "Don't tell me you knew someone who—"

"My student, Rachel. Rachel Lipski. Could you find out if—"

"Lipski. I'll find out what I can, but it may take hours. I can't get anywhere near the building yet."

"Please try, Tommy. She's Ruth's niece."

"Can't do it right now, Trace. The sidewalks are waist-deep in bodies and some of 'em are burned so bad that. . . ." He broke off. "I'm sorry. Didn't mean to—get out of here, Tracy, please."

She stared at him, unable to absorb it. She saw him turn again toward the building and then heard him mutter, "Looks like they got it under control now. C'mon, I'll get you through this crowd. You can't stay here or you'll be crushed to death."

He yanked her by the hand, and a few of the curious crowd watched him, thinking that the cop had a woman under arrest. He tugged her through the crowd as far as Washington Square and then said, "I'd better get back now."

"Find out as soon as possible," she said.

293

"Lipski. Rachel," he said.

"I'll be waiting at the school."

"All right. But don't expect to hear for hours."

She did not leave Washington Square at once but continued to stand there hoping news would somehow filter through to her. And incredibly something did. There was a girl sitting on the ground sobbing hysterically. Tracy asked her if she knew anyone at Triangle. It turned out that she was an employee at Triangle and had barely managed to escape the inferno.

"Do you know Rachel Lipski?" asked Tracy.

"Sì. She work on nina floor," said the girl in a heavy Italian accent.

"The ninth floor?"

The girl nodded and continued to sob.

"Did you see her? Did she escape?"

The girl looked blank.

"Escape. Get out. Did Rachel get out?"

"I no see. Don' know." The girl broke off, hysterical.

By this time a crowd had discovered the girl and pushed in around her firing questions. Tracy did her best to fend them off, for it was plain that she couldn't answer and wouldn't answer unless they all stopped badgering her. But it was no use. The crowd questioned, and the girl cried, and Tracy stood in the midst of it all, growing more and more light-headed as the realization of what she had seen and what might have happened to Rachel penetrated a heretofore numbed body. She was forced to sit down on the cold March earth and to lower her head to her knees, taking deep breaths to prevent a faint. Too unsteady to get up immediately, she continued to sit there stupefied and was still there ten minutes later when the Italian girl recovered enough to answer a few of the questions people were still putting to her.

The fire had started at closing time—4:30—in a pile of scrap material on the eighth floor where the girl had worked. No one knew what had caused it. Men had tried to douse the flames with pails of water, but the fire had soared high and the sparks had caught the lines of hanging paper patterns. These had burned and fallen on tables and sewing machines, igniting the highly flammable shirtwaist material, and still the men had flung the water. How long the men had continued doing this the young woman did not know. Some of the girls had headed for doors and others had gone to coat closets, but this one had charged straight for the fire escape. She had climbed from the eighth floor to the sixth then ducked inside and made her escape through the building stairway. At the door to the street she had been held back, for bodies were now falling from windows overhead and splattering on the sidewalk in front of her. When at last the way was clear, she was led through the bloody carnage and out into the street where she learned that the ninth and tenth floors had caught fire too. And now she was wondering if her best friend on the tenth was dead or alive.

All this was related in broken English interrupted

by sobs, and at last a well-dressed older woman took pity on her and led her away through the crowd. Tracy finally rose too and made her way slowly through Washington Square and then along West Third Street toward Broadway and the school. Since the school was only a few blocks away from Triangle, there were people here who had also been at the scene. As Tracy passed one group, she heard a woman saying that the crowds over there were now so dense that the police were beating them back with clubs so that they could remove the bodies to a sidewalk on Greene Street. From here they would probably be taken to the morgue.

Tracy plodded in through the classroom entrance, where her assistant and students who had already heard the news stood talking, some with tears streaming down their faces. The students in this day class did not know Rachel, but the two assistants did, and Tracy told them of her fears.

"But she probably escaped," Tracy said. "She might be at Ruth's right now. I'm going down there to check. One of you please stay here and wait for my brother. He may have news."

There was no question of taking transportation to Monroe Street. Every street around was glutted with the traffic of curiosity seekers, and except when vehicles made way for ambulances, the streets were impassable. So she walked, and the farther south she walked the more normally people were behaving. Incredibly there were areas here on the East Side, the home of most of the victims, where some hadn't heard of the disaster. They would hear soon enough. She was sure that some of those girls had been the sole support of households, just as she had once been. Not for these families a little business and a house in the country. For these there would be only burials and destitution.

She thought of girls like Rachel, victims of prejudice, starvation, or revolutions, who had made their way to America in the vermin-infested holds of ships, who had endured the indignity of Ellis Island and of the teeming city streets only to slave their lives away in sweatshops that were, and had always been, firetraps. All this—and yet some of them could smile (they were young, after all) and dare to hope that things would get better. She could see Rachel at the typewriter muttering "Mudder-o-Gud" with her new American-style spunk, could see her blushing when Tracy had corrected her, could see her proudly fingering a new blue jacket she had bought last week to look more fashionable. Had she returned to the coatroom to get that jacket instead of bolting for an exit at once? No! Rachel had to have survived. Surely many had gotten out as the Italian girl had.

Tracy reached Monroe Street and began racing toward Ruth's. After a moment she saw David hurrying in the opposite direction.

"David!" she cried when she came upon him. "Did you—"

"I heard. Don't tell Ruth; she doesn't know."

"Then Rachel didn't come back?"

"No. And it's almost six." He had heard the news

at his printing office shortly after it had happened. He had rushed home to see if Ruth knew, had rushed back to the printing office, and then back to the flat to see if Rachel was there yet. Now he was heading uptown to get the story at the scene.

"Don't tell Ruth," he urged. "I'm afraid the shock might affect her pregnancy. Better not go up there at all. You look terrible."

"I saw it," she said dully.

"You *saw* it?" He grabbed her by the elbow and propelled her around. "Come on. Walk with me. Tell me what you saw."

"I can't."

"Tracy, please."

"I can't. It was too horrible. Oh, David, Rachel may be dead."

"Maybe not. Maybe she's in a hospital. Or trapped in a crowd somewhere."

"My brother's going to check for us. He was there controlling crowds in front of the building."

"Tell me what happened. I know it's hard, but try, please."

As they hurried back along the route she had taken down there, Tracy told him what she had seen and what the Italian girl had said. David was a hardened reporter, who had been at the scene of some shocking disasters, but even he could not assimilate this.

"Murderers!" he shouted so that knots of people turned to look at him. "Murderers, all of them. The building inspectors, the *gonifs* running the sweatshops, all of them. What do they care about fire

298

hazards? What do they care about young girls? These children are just bodies fed into their money-making machines! You remember the shirtwaist strike last year? You remember those girls standing out in the freezing cold till they were ready to die of exposure and hunger? You think those animals cared? No, they let 'em freeze until the girls couldn't stand anymore and ended up working for the same old wages in the same old firetraps. Murderers!"

She walked as far as the scene with David, but whole blocks were jammed with crowds and police. David said he was going to use his press credentials to get through, and Tracy told him she'd be over at the school waiting for Tommy. She learned from people in the crowd that the bodies were being transferred to a temporary morgue in a pier at Twenty-sixth Street but that identifications could not be made for hours, since the doctors had to check through the bodies to determine whether any still lived and the police had to remove valuables and number the coffins. She also learned that the number of dead was around 120. Returning to the now-closed school, she asked her waiting assistant if Tommy had come. The assistant said no.

Tracy dismissed the assistant and waited. Six o'clock, seven o'clock, eight. No Tommy. At eight, Russell phoned and found out why she couldn't go to the theater. At nine P.M. David came in, ashen-faced, his clothing torn by the mobs that had surged around him. In a rush he told her that the crowds at the scene had been hysterical and uncontrollable and that the

299

police had beaten them off with clubs. No, he hadn't seen Tommy.

"I'm going downtown now," he said. "I stopped to see if you'd heard anything about Rachel."

"No, I was hoping you had."

He shook his head. "Maybe she's back at the flat by now."

"Let me know."

"I'll ring you when I find out." Because of their businesses, both of them had telephones.

"I'll be waiting," she said.

Another hour went by. She'd been sitting here half the night. Just after ten, David rang and said that Rachel wasn't there, that Ruth had found out about the fire and had wanted to go to the morgue to make the identification. But David refused to permit it, fearing that she would lose the baby if she had a shock like that. David himself couldn't go to the morgue right away, as he had to get the story into print and prepare follow-ups for a special edition tomorrow. He would try to get there later, but Ruth was very anxious to find out and could Tracy go over there and make an identification?

"The morgue?" she screamed. "You want *me*—"

"She was wearing a blue jacket with—"

"I *know* what she was wearing, but I can't. . . ." She broke off. There was silence on both ends of the phone until finally she said, "All right. All right, I'll go. But only if Tommy's not here by eleven."

She phoned home to tell Russell where she would

300

be tonight. In sepulchral tones he said, "I'd do it myself if I knew the girl."

Like hell he would, she thought. But she accepted his condolences and his warnings to be careful in the crowds over at the morgue, especially at night. She hung up and continued to hope for Tommy's arrival.

Chapter Twenty-Four

The temporary morgue was in a pier on Twenty-sixth Street, and the block between First Avenue and the East River was jammed solid with relatives and friends waiting to get in. When Tracy arrived there at 11:30 that night they still hadn't opened the doors. All around her she heard wailing, screaming, muttered prayers, the murmured names of daughters. Most of the victims had been Eastern Jews and Southern Italians. These groups were the mainstay of sweatshops, for recent immigrants were always willing to work at cheaper wages than were older ones.

Tracy took her place at the end of a long line and could see from the size of the crowd that she would not get in for hours. By that time David would have come, she thought. It was a cold March night, and she shivered under her coat, rubbing her arms with her hands.

At midnight the gates to the pier were finally opened, and weeping people were admitted twenty at a time. The crowd behind them shuffled forward and waited, shuffled forward again and again. Where was

David? she wondered. Where had Tommy been? Did they really expect her to walk into this ghastly place? The latest estimate of bodies was around 130.

But the problems of some in the crowd around her were worse by far than Tracy's. They were there to find daughters, wives, sisters—and some were looking for two and three members of a family. An Italian man was searching for two sisters and a mother. A Jewish girl was looking for a fiancé. (A few men had died in the fire, though the overwhelming majority had been women.) People wailed, wondered aloud, sometimes spoke of miracles. Perhaps the loved one was in a hospital with nothing but a few burns on the fingers. Perhaps she was wandering around the city in a daze, not yet having come to her senses. They spoke of miracles, but periodically fits of terrified weeping would overtake them. And they moved forward, forward, closer to the only place that would give them the answer.

Tracy had no idea what time it was. She had no watch with her and the poor in the line could scarcely have afforded them. She thought of calling out to a policeman, but these men had their hands full trying to answer the questions of hysterical relatives, trying to reassure them that their turn would come. It must be two or three in the morning, she thought, as she moved numbly behind the others to the door. It was so cold, so cold. Where was David? Where had Tommy been? And why in hell couldn't Russell have come here to stand in line with her?

The police were now moving down the line

questioning those who were waiting, asking if they were looking for anyone in particular or if they were just curiosity seekers. If looking for someone, could they give the name and description of the person? If not, they must step out of the line immediately. In this way, the police were able to weed many out of the crowd. Tracy realized that some people had come just to see a ghoulish sight. She saw a well-dressed couple flouce off down the street, apparently quite perturbed because their fun had been spoiled by this tiresome official.

At last she came close to the doors. And when a cop counted off the next twenty people Tracy was finally included. Knees shaking, she followed the others into the pier. A few held back, not really wanting to know, but then moved forward again, whimpering in their fright.

There were two long rows of wooden coffins provided by the city. The bodies in them were covered to the neck with white sheets. The heads, however, were propped up on boards so that faces (if they weren't burned beyond recognition) could be quickly identified. Arc lights sputtered overhead but did not provide enough illumination, so the police waved lanterns over the faces of the dead. It was a sight so ghastly that Tracy hung back, afraid to focus her eyes.

Women screamed and men sobbed, making hoarse, horrible sounds. Some people fainted and were removed to an emergency hospital. When identifications were made, the police would close the coffin and ticket it. Then the cop would give a ticket to the friend or relative, which would enable the mourner to remove the body.

Tracy took a deep breath and started down the line. The weary police swung the lanterns back and forth, lighting up bruised faces, burned faces, mashed faces. Some girls were mutilated beyond recognition, and the police held out trinkets or bits of cloth that had been found on the body. A woman ahead of Tracy stared at a necklace a cop was holding. Then she bent over the body, tore the sheet from it, screamed, and fell to the floor in a dead faint.

Twice Tracy thought she saw Rachel, and each time a close inspection proved that she was mistaken. But the third time she saw the black hair and familiar profile she also saw Rachel's fashionable new jacket. A cop was holding it.

Tracy looked at Rachel long enough to make an identification. The skull had been crushed; she must have jumped. But the face was recognizable. Too shocked for tears and too inured by this time to the horrible sights, she told the policeman in a dull voice that this was Rachel Lipski. She took the slip of paper he issued her and hurried to the coroner's office where she received permission to have the body removed. Back on the street again, she ran. Ran for blocks through the cold dark until she was exhausted and had pains in her chest and stomach. Hansom cabs were still around, though by this time it was 3:30, and at last she got into one and mumbled the address of David's printing office. Only then did she

305

start to cry—softly, so the cabbie wouldn't ask any questions.

At David's office, lights blazed and printing presses clanked. They were getting out a special edition of a paper that was normally printed only twice a week. David was there at a typewriter churning out a story with two fingers. His partner and two other men were scrawling stories in longhand. There were people in the crowded room who had come to ask for news. A young man was dealing with them.

"Rachel's dead," Tracy told David flatly. "Here's the slip for the undertaker."

"I thought so," he said, taking the slip and shaking his head. "I thought so."

He asked what conditions had been like up at the morgue. She cried and told him to go see for himself; she was not going to describe it. He made her sit down, and when she was recovered a little he shouted for someone and a young typesetter came out. David said, "Get Mrs. Curtis a cab, please." And to Tracy, "Go home and get some rest."

It was four when she arrived at the brownstone. She climbed into bed next to the snoring Russell and stared into space until the sun came up.

DAVID got no sleep either. At dawn he left the office, woke up an undertaker, and told him to go to the morgue for Rachel. After this, he talked to a rabbi, then he broke the news gently to Ruth and made her promise that she'd stay inside and rest until the services later that day. After that, he went uptown and covered the scene at the morgue, seeing what Tracy had seen but by daylight so that it wasn't quite as macabre. Coming back into the still-waiting crowds, David noticed that their numbers had been swelled by cheerful, well-dressed people who obviously had no business here. Cops kept sending these ghouls on their way, but as fast as some departed others showed up. David wrote in his notebook. "One reason the Triangle tragedy happened is that people adore a disaster and tolerate conditions that will lead to delightful sights like bodies burned down to the bone." Much of the idealism of his youth had long since fled. Any that was left was running out fast.

From the morgue David went back to the scene of the fire. It was Sunday and crowds filled Washington Square, a block from the building. There was a holiday atmosphere about the place and vendors took advantage of this by selling chestnuts, jellied apples, and other treats. Strollers walked about chatting and laughing. To them this place made for a good Sunday outing. Disgusted, David walked toward the building itself, getting past the police by flashing his credentials (his was a small paper but respected).

Very little of the building structure had been damaged; it was only the interior that had burned. He was planning to ask authorities if he could inspect the inside of the building, but before he could make inquiries he saw a hawker moving in the direction of the Washington Square. He was carrying a bag and shouting, "Now! While they last! Rings, necklaces, found where the girls landed. Earrings, bracelets. Yes, folks, gen-u-wine souvenirs of the dead girls. Now! While they last!"

David tore after the man, lunged at him, threw him to the sidewalk and, holding him down with a knee, took the man's bag and hurled it so that the rings, bracelets, and necklaces, none of them from girls' bodies, scattered all over the sidewalk and cobbled street. David was a big, powerfully built man, and the hawker was correspondingly small. Under David's weight he whimpered, waving his arms around and crying in turn for mercy and for the police. The area was dense with cops, Tommy Sullivan among them. He came over and pried David off, then sent the peddler packing, warning the man harshly that he might be the target of other angry people. The man stumbled down the street picking up the scattered jewelry, and David said to Tommy that he had no doubt the man would soon be in business again. Tommy agreed but explained to his old neighbor that there was nothing much he could do about it. Tommy was very busy and there was no time to discuss this further. David hadn't even told him that Rachel had been identified.

For a while David followed the peddler. Then he shook his head and turned away, scrawling in his notebook, "Some people must have evolved not from the ape but from the crow. Check Darwin for clues."

He talked to authorities about the possibility of touring the building and was told it was not yet safe. He interviewed police, firemen, and city officials in the area, clarifying details of stories he had heard the night before.

The total count of dead was now 146. The fire had raged through three floors—the eighth, ninth, and tenth. Most of those on the tenth floor who hadn't gotten out by elevator had escaped by way of the roof. From here they were able to reach the adjacent New York University buildings. Students there had flung ladders from their building to the roof of the inferno. On the ninth floor and on the eighth (where the fire had started) people hadn't been so lucky. Some managed to get out by elevator, others by stairs, and a few by means of the fire escape. But the fire had grown so fast that many exits were soon impassable. Compounding the problem was the fact that one of the exit doors had been locked. And the fire escape finally proved too skimpy for the weight of the fleeing workers. In time it tore away from the building, hurtling the girls into space.

David took pages and pages of notes thinking that one day he'd write an exposé of the garment industry as Upton Sinclair had done of the Chicago stockyards. One man he interviewed said that the building had conformed to safety standards, but a fireman said that those standards had been grossly inadequate. Some said that though a door was indeed locked, the key to that lock had been hanging on the knob. But these explanations did not cover the collapsing fire escape or the fact that employers had neglected to train girls in fire drills, or the carelessness with which clothing material was left around, or a dozen other factors having more to do with enacting new laws than with determining whether or not the old ones had been obeyed.

Some blamed City Hall for the tragedy. Others blamed the owners of Triangle—Isaac Harris and Max Blanck. These men had been responsible for blocking off exits at closing time, fearing their girls would pilfer goods if not inspected in one place by a watchman at the end of the day. But the keys to open the door had been hanging right there, these men insisted. Still others blamed the owner of the building itself, but Joseph Ashe would say later that his building had conformed to safety standards required by the government.

It was a typical New York disaster in that respect, David thought. No one fully responsible, everyone able to point the finger at someone else. Still, some action would be taken now. It always took a full-scale catastrophe to spur officials to reform. David knew there were scores of lofts elsewhere in the city that were even more dangerous than this one had been. He had been told last night of some that had no fire escapes at all. He had attended for years union meetings in which prospective strikers had cited these very dangers. And he'd been present at the shirtwaist strike only a little more than a year ago during which Triangle girls and others had listed better protection from fires among their demands. Nothing had happened then, he thought. Why should it happen now? Why not wait for the proof? The flaming bodies flying from windows? Now there would be action, he knew. There'd be a scream they could hear down in Washington. There'd be fire-proofing left and right and new labor laws by the dozens. Now a lot of things would happen. But a little too late for girls like Rachel.

ON SUNDAY AFTERNOON Tracy went down to see Ruth and with her attended the services for Rachel in a synagogue jammed with people from the neighbor-hood. The wails of the women reminded Tracy of Gaelic keening. Few of the neighborhood people had known Rachel, but all knew why she and the others had died, and the tears were mixed with an anger such as Tracy seldom saw among the exhausted and overworked people here. Ruth had told her not to go to the burial, for Tracy had had no sleep the night before. Ruth urged her to go home and rest, and Tracy decided that she would.

It was while she was walking down Monroe Street that she sensed a new moblike spirit. A gentle-natured man she knew was shouting in Yiddish, "Death to the capitalists!" The cop on the beat did not berate him. This prompted two women to wail and to scream, which in turn prompted three little boys to run down the street yelling, "Bomb City

311

Hall!'' Soon others joined the fray, shouting and overturning ash barrels. When Tracy passed the cop, whom she knew, he said, ''Guess I'll have to be breaking this up, but the truth is I don't blame 'em. Don't blame 'em a-tall.''

At home, after giving hasty accounts of the latest developments to her husband, son, and mother-in-law, Tracy fell into a troubled sleep, not awakening until nine at night, when Russell roused her to announce, ''Your brother's here.''

''Now? *Now* he's here? Well, better late than never, huh?'' She threw on a robe and went down to the sitting room where Tommy, looking exhausted, sat talking with Joanne.

''I couldn't get away,'' he explained. ''I've been in the same spot since yesterday at five.''

''Didn't you eat?'' Tracy said.

''Sandwiches while I was on the line. I found out about Lipski.''

''I already know. I went to the morgue and saw her.''

''You went to the *morgue?*''

She nodded.

He was still dressed in yesterday's uniform, and he was dirty and sweaty. Russell made him a drink and looked at him curiously. Tommy was his opposite number in many ways. He was not tall but thin and wiry. His hair was a ruddy brown, and his face was weather-beaten from months of walking a beat in all seasons. He looked older than twenty-three even on normal days, and tonight he looked twenty years older. Bloodshot eyes with dark circles under them, a day's growth of beard, and a tense look about the face as though steeling himself for more disasters.

Mrs. Curtis and Russell both had opinions on City Hall and the wickedness of the sweatshop system. They proceeded to declare them in outraged tones while Tracy and her brother looked at them wearily. Tracy believed that her mother-in-law was truly upset, but she couldn't quite believe it of Russell. Oh, he must have felt bad that young girls had died in the prime of their lives, and he'd never been fond of capitalists or governments. But he was a self-proclaimed xenophobe, a railer against common people and common ideas, so how much grief could he feel for a small group of peasants whose main idea had been to survive?

Mrs. Curtis asked Tommy some direct questions and he tried to answer them politely. No, not all the bodies had been identified, he said. Some were not recognizable even to close relatives, and in one instance a dentist had had to make the identification from teeth. But he didn't know too much about the morgue situation. He'd been on duty at the scene of the fire itself. Mrs. Curtis asked him how the crowds had behaved, and Tommy said they had been difficult to control.

"They'd come up to me, these mothers, these old women in shawls, and I wanted to say something kind to them, but I had to keep them back. I told them to go to the morgue and they'd scream, they'd faint. The word 'morgue,' you know. But some didn't understand. They didn't know any English. They just kept coming, shouting names of girls, pushing. They came through the ropes and then. . . ." He swallowed. "Some of the cops used clubs. They had to keep the crowds back and it was the only way. One club came down on a woman's head. She was crying a name: Elena. She fell. She was—I never found out who she was, but she must've been someone's mother. What if she was the mother of two of them, maybe three of them? There she was, this old woman—or maybe she wasn't old, maybe she just looked old—there she was on the street and she fell, limp like a rag doll. Someone picked her up and she fell down again. Just collapsed like that. Like she was dead. The cop who clubbed her, he felt bad and took her away to a hospital. By this time the mob was pretty controlled and he carried her over his shoulder like a rag doll. Just like that."

Tommy tried to continue, cleared his throat, tried again. "I'll always see their faces as long as I live. The mothers, the fathers, begging and begging us. All they wanted was news. Just news, that's all. But the clubs kept coming down: 'Get back, get back, get back, you scum.'"

He covered his face with his hands. The others looked at one another, but no one said a word or made a move. Tommy had not said exactly what role he himself had played in all this, and no one wanted

314

to ask. After a moment Tommy stood up abruptly and said he had to go. Mrs. Curtis asked if he'd like to spend the night here, but he said he would rather get home and change his clothes. Tracy saw him to the door and said, "Take care of yourself, Tommy. Get, some rest, something to eat. You'll feel better."

"What about you?" he said. "Think you'll have bad dreams about this?"

"For the rest of my life," she said.

"That's it. That's just it. If you could only forget it, if you could only—but some things happen and they never leave you no matter what."

FOR WEEKS following Triangle there were memorial services, newspaper editorials, union meetings, protests of every kind. Charities were quick to come forth with aid for families, and private donors all over the world sent help as well. A funeral procession for seven unidentified dead was attended by one hundred thousand people. In Albany, legislator Alfred E. Smith raised holy hell as David had predicted he would. Smith had been raised on Oliver Street, which was just the other side of Catherine. He was much admired by all the groups in his home turf and, though not a socialist, was known in David's circles as an allrightnick, an Irisher *mensh*. If anyone could do anything about new labor laws, Smith would.

Tracy was not quick to recover from the grisly experience. In the week following the tragedy she didn't even go to the school. She was not like Ruth, who could vent her rage in passionate prose for the paper. Tracy was neither a writer nor politically inclined. She did not believe that governments helped people very much. She believed that the poor would rise only by being smart enough to maneuver their way out and beyond their condition. Rachel could have risen that way if only she'd been given a chance, Tracy thought.

After about a week of sitting in the house, Tracy decided to get out of the city altogether and she went up to Lanston. She saw her own family, which was coping with March doldrums, and also Katherine, who was now a good friend of many years' standing, though she was still technically Pat's boss. Katherine's own mother, Beth, had died recently and so had her mother-in-law, Emily Taylor. So Tracy had to endure yet more mourning, and the trip was not exactly therapeutic. Katherine had also heard about the death of Luke's son and she concluded bitterly, "So that was the end of Luke's clan. And all I can say is, I'm sorry we did the right thing. We should have run off together."

"You had no way of knowing how things would turn out."

"We never do," Katherine said, "but we should learn to be cleverer about guessing. I trust that you're a little smarter about life than I was."

Oh, brilliant, Tracy thought. Giving up the man she loved and marrying the man she thought she ought to have, and later seeing one become successful and strong while the other became a pessimist on the brink of bankruptcy, driven there in part by herself. Brilliant.

Katherine said, "You *are* a little smarter, aren't you?"

"I wish I could say so," Tracy muttered.

And this was Tracy's holiday. She would have been better off in New York, she thought later.

Chapter Twenty-Five

On a warm afternoon in June Tracy was in her office making telephone calls to prospective employers of her students when one of her assistants came in and said, "There's two fellas in an auto outside."

"An auto?"

"And honking like mad. The passenger's your friend's husband. The driver I don't know."

Tracy walked out through the classroom exit and pulled the curtain away from the window. There in the front seat of a black funny-looking auto with a top over the front and a single seat sticking out of the back without any protection were David and Michael, the latter looking as proud as Casey Jones in the cab of his locomotive. Laughing, Tracy walked to the door and over to the car, shouting to Michael, "What are you doing here?"

"They sent me to speak with eastern dealers about tractor development. I drove from Detroit."

"In *this* thing?"

"You dare to jest at Ford's very latest model?"

"Who?"

318

"Ford. The Ford Motor Company. Never heard of it?"

"I've heard of Olds," she said.

"Profanity!" Michael shouted, and onlookers laughed.

David said, "Come on for a ride, Tracy. Ruth's too near her time to ride in this machine, so we figured we'd give you the opportunity."

"In that stupid-looking seat sticking out the back?"

"They call it the mother-in-law seat," David said.

"I'll go, only if *you* take that seat." And it was so done. Tracy climbed in beside Michael, and David moved to the seat behind. She wished she were dressed appropriately for the tour with a big floppy hat and a car coat and a long scarf to hold the hat in place. But she went in bareheaded, wearing only the outfit she had on (the day was seasonable), and shouted, "Let's go!"

They put-putted down Broadway toward Canal, David clowning in the rear seat, waving to crowds like a dignitary and shouting, "Reelect me, Phineas Farnsworth. I stand on my record!"

"I don't know that man back there," said Tracy to Michael. "Do you?"

"Never saw him before in my life."

From Broadway they turned into Canal and then headed into the tenement districts, where progress was impeded by slow-moving drays, children who hopped on the running board, and men shouting

319

questions about the engine, cylinders, and horse-power. And so to Madison Street, where they dropped David off at the printing office and stopped to watch a group of adolescents dancing ragtime to the accompaniment of a bearded banjo player.

"I'll drive you back," Michael said.

"Oh, so soon?"

"Don't you have to work?"

"I'm the boss. I can work whenever I please."

"How could I have forgotten?" he said in a droll tone. "All right, then. Where would you like to go?"

"East Side, West Side, all around the—"

"We'll try the West Side," he said. "Fewer crowds."

He didn't seem to enthusiastic about being with her, she thought. The whole idea of the ride had been David's. David was under the delusion that Tracy and Michael were still good friends in spite of Tracy's hasty marriage that long-ago winter. They might even have *been* good friends, she thought, had Michael been willing. Well, maybe he'd be willing now.

They drove down Canal Street and through Greenwich Village, then up through Chelsea and Hell's Kitchen and on into the uptown neighborhoods. While tooling along, Michael told her of the harrowing trip from Detroit.

"I didn't follow their suggested route," he said. "Thought I'd be smart and take a shortcut. I ended up in the wilds of Pennsylvania with no gasoline and a tire in its last gasp and no spares left. I slept in the car that night, then I walked ten miles to a farm to get some kerosene to feed her."

"Feed who?" Tracy asked distractedly.

"The car. There's a kerosene mixture you can concoct in an emergency. I was able to drive it to a town where they'd heard of autos. I got gasoline there and a few tires. . . ."

He told her more about his adventures and wound up by saying, "I like the manufacturing end of the business, but I think the industry ought to concentrate more on service. Places to get gasoline, places to get maps, tires, and things. What good is a motorcar if you can't find places to service it?"

"That's true," she said, wishing he'd talk about something more personal—like whether or not he was still separated or what kind of flat or house he was living in. Still, what he was saying was interesting. Up until now, autos had simply been carriages with motors in which people might tour or race or go for a Sunday afternoon excursion. They even looked like carriages and were often referred to by such names as phaetons and victorias. Half of them were electric, requiring recharging every few miles. And while they were being taken more seriously now than in the early years of the century, they were still mainly for fun. She seldom saw a machine as devoid of frills as Michael's black one. (It was called a Model T, she learned.) Most autos were made in brilliant colors and had expensive upholstery. She had rarely heard it advocated that autos be made for the common man, and never had she heard suggestions that service areas be set up for those planning to drive long distances. Trains were for distances, not autos. Autos were for gay tours of the area in which one lived. In the winter most weren't used at all but put away until spring. In the country they were stored in barns. In the city, in livery stables or carriage houses and occasionally in auto garages set up for the purpose of storage. But Michael was talking as though a day might come when autos could be driven all year long.

He asked if she'd like to go into the Bronx, where he could speed up a little (in congested areas the speed limit was fifteen; elsewhere twenty and twenty-five). She said the Bronx sounded like fun, and because she was feeling so good she sang "Waltz Me Around Again, Willie." Michael said she had a good voice, so she sang "Meet Me in St. Louis," verse and chorus. Her hair fell apart as they whizzed along, and she shoved hairpins at it and laughed. What a lovely turn the day had taken. She and Michael zooming through the Bronx, free as the clouds, with the city and the past far behind them. How wonderful it would be just to keep on going, flying down roads, singing and laughing.

> Wait till the sun shines, Nellie,
> When the clouds go drifting by.
> We will be happy, Nellie,
> Don't you sigh.
> Down lovers' lane we'll wander,

Sweetheart you and I.
Wait till the sun shines, Nellie,
Bye and bye.

"How do you remember all the words?" he shouted over the wind and the engine.

"If the tune is catchy I can remember them." Unlike the poems Russell loved, which had no tune at all.

"I've never heard you sing before."

"I've never ridden with you in an auto before. It practically commands you to sing, doesn't it?"

"Never thought of it that way."

"And you drove all the way from Detroit?"

"In Pennsylvania I hummed a few bars of 'John Brown's Body.'"

She laughed. "You thought you'd die out there?"

"My life passed before my eyes."

"Are you going to drive back?"

"Yes, but no more shortcuts."

"Are you happy out there in Michigan?"

"It's all right," he said. "Want to turn back now?"

She pretended she hadn't heard him. No, she didn't want to turn back. She wanted to stay with him. Before he could repeat the question, she exclaimed, "Oh, this is such fun!" and launched into the first song to pop into her head so that she couldn't hear the question if he did repeat it.

She's only a bird in a gilded cage
A beautiful sight to see.

You may think that she's happy and free from
    care,
She's not, though she seems to be.
'Tis sad when you think of her wasted life,
For youth cannot mate with age,
And her beauty was sold
For an old man's gold,
She's a bird in a gilded cage.

"Interesting song," he remarked.

"Haven't you ever heard it?"

"Oh, sure. But not sung by you."

"What do you mean?"

"I mean I've never heard you sing it." And then he said again, "Want to turn back?"

"Where are we?"

"Bronx somewhere."

"I'm in no hurry, you know."

"All right," he said. "We'll go to the Yonkers border."

"All right." She thought again of the song. What had Michael meant by that crack? And then it dawned on her. The marriage to Russell. But Russell wasn't old. He was a year younger than Michael. And he didn't have much gold either, though Michael didn't realize that. How petty of Michael to call attention to the lyrics. Yet the very pettiness was proof that he still cared. Yes, he *did* care! Oh if only they could run away for a while in this merry Oldsmobile or whatever this thing was called.

"Here's Yonkers," Michael announced after a while. "Have you had enough for one day?"

"I'll never get enough," she said recklessly. Why not let him know how she felt?

He missed her meaning. "I'll be running out of fuel pretty soon unless we find a store that sells it."

"Then we'll be stranded like you were in Pennsylvania? I couldn't think of a nicer fate than being stranded with you."

"Been giving blarney lessons at the school?"

"I mean it, Michael. I still care for you."

He pulled over and stopped the car. "Tracy, you shouldn't say things like that."

"Why not? I mean them. I still care. Don't *you* care?"

He didn't answer, and she said, "Are you going to go on hating me for choices I made when I was a child? I only married him so I wouldn't be tempted to run to you. I was a child. All I could think of was money. I'd struggled so many years for money."

"I know that," he said.

They were at the edge of a wood and she said, "Let's take a walk. I want to stretch my legs. And I want to talk to you without the engine drowning us out."

"All right, but not a long one. It'll be getting dark soon."

He was resisting her explanations. He was still angry and always would be, she thought. She understood why. How must it have felt after that

325

horrible funeral, after transporting his hysterical mother to New Jersey and trying to take care of that whole confused family—how much it have felt to discover that the one solid thing he had thought he could cling to had run off and married someone else? It had been a mistake, this ride. The best favor she could do herself would be to get back in the car and have him drive her straight home. Never mind that of the two men she had really cared about, Michael was the only one who had known her from early adolescence, the only one who thought her business was something to be proud of, the only one to appreciate her limited intellectual attainments. And he loved her friends because they were his friends too. And he'd like her stories of the girls in the class because they would remind him of his own struggles. They were so much alike. Ruth had recognized that all along. But she, Tracy, had been stupid and made him suffer, and it was plain that he'd never forgive her.

As they made their way down a bridle path, she tried again to explain. "I thought if I married you we'd have a hard time about money. You had all those people to care for and no real way of doing it. I thought we'd grow to hate each other. Like your father and mother."

"You thought I'd beat you black and blue?"

"No. Not that. But we'd hate each other. I didn't want it to end that way. I thought it would really be better just to remember the friendship and never have to see it change and become ugly. '

"I told you I'd have money."

"I didn't believe you. Really, Michael, I was a crazed child. I'd just managed to move my family into their first real house and things were looking so good and then, just a day later, there was your sister laid out, beaten to death, and all I could think of was I didn't want anything that reminded me of Monroe Street, not even the man I loved." She took a deep breath. "It wasn't the only time I've done that. I was always running away. I ran away after Triangle. Ruth wanted me to stay in town and go to a protest meeting and go on that memorial march, but all I wanted to do was get out, get away, and I went up to Lanston."

He said, "They told me about that girl in the fire. She was a student?"

"Yes. You met her that night at Ruth's."

"They mentioned it. I don't remember her. There were so many boarders."

"You would have liked her, I think." Tracy paused and then said in a faint voice, "She worked on the ninth floor."

"Yes. I heard the ninth floor was the worst."

"She must have jumped. The nets couldn't hold them because they were jumping two and three at a time. Oh, God, I hope they make someone pay for this. They've indicted the owners. . . ." She sat down on a rock and covered her face with her hands. "I saw them jump—I went to the morgue and identified the body. Michael, how do you get things like that out of your mind? How can you make yourself forget you ever saw it?"

"You can't. But when time passes, it fades. You even stop dreaming about it." He sat down on the ground beside her.

"Have you stopped dreaming?"

"Pretty much."

"Even of the good things?"

"Good things?"

"There were good times, you know. Like after your exile when you'd have those family reunions in Ruth's flat. We had some good times. And remember when the three of you came to see me at my school? I remember your reaction. You said 'wow!' Of all the things people have said about my school, that meant the most."

He smiled.

"I wish we could go back to those times. The four of us."

They were sitting only a short distance from the road, but it might as well have been the heart of a forest. The foliage was thick, and it was utterly still except for the chirp of birds. Michael had left his hat and suit jacket in the car and looked very relaxed sitting on the ground, his hair tousled, his shirt sleeves exposed under an expensive waistcoat. Most of the poor who had made good never got over the habit of treating their best clothes with reverence, but Michael didn't seem concerned about losing the

328

crease in his trousers or subjecting the expensive material to the abrasions of the rock he was now sitting on. Had he discarded all his early training? she wondered. Or just some of it?

She said, "Do you remember when it got so hot we'd have to sleep on the roof?"

"Is that supposed to be one of the 'good things'?"

"No, I hated it. Except for one time when I climbed over onto your roof. We talked half the night. Remember?"

He nodded. "Yes."

"You touched my arm. You thought I was asleep, but I wasn't. I wanted you to kiss me, but you were such a gentleman you walked away."

"If only I'd known how receptive you'd be."

"Think you would've had your way with me?"

"I might've tried," he said. "But you had the reputation of being a wildcat."

"Oh? The fellas used to talk?"

"You and your sister. They called you Tiger Tracy and the Virgin Mary."

She laughed. "There were a lot of other virgins around."

"None so sworn to protect the state."

She cleared her throat. "But there came a night when I didn't protect it anymore."

"Yes," he said, breaking a twig he was holding. "There did."

"No matter what you might think of me, Michael, remember that you were the first. Not Russell, not

329

anyone else. You. I think that should count for something."

"I've thought about that night a lot," he said.

"So have I."

Afterward she wasn't sure who had made the first move, but they were in each other's arms, and she didn't know if they were living a new event or trying to recapture one that had already taken place. It was different from the first time, though. He'd learned to take his time. Not that she needed much arousing, but it was marvelous the things he was doing to her body even as he undressed her. And it was good to see everything retreating as her world filled up with him. His touch was light and the kisses deep so that she had the sensation of melting into him. Her thighs loosened, lost their tone, but at the same time became extremely sensitive to the touch. Her moans became deeper when he kissed her breasts, flicking his tongue over the nipples so that they turned rock hard. Then it seemed as though his hands were everywhere, for all of her body was sensitized, waiting, and her moaning was deep and continued like a wail of pain.

Her head whipped back and forth on the ground, crushing the leaves beneath it, and her legs fell open to him. She reached out and touched it, touched him, hard and throbbing, and then she felt him come inside her, filling a place that had been empty too long. He moaned and held her tightly. She wrapped her legs around him as he rose and fell, quickening his speed. She felt her climax beginning and her body arched upward, upward. Just as she was about to spend herself, he pulled away from her, crying out hoarsely. She did not understand at first, then realized that he must be trying to prevent conception and had withdrawn at the last second.

The interruption left her panting and aching for completion. He was quick to sense this and helped her by using his hand. One touch of his fingers, and her nerves seemed to burn. She writhed, groaned, arched her body, cried out, and then lost consciousness for a moment. Gradually she regained awareness and realized that her body was utterly inert except for a steady throb between her legs.

"Tracy?" She felt his hand grazing her forehead and turned to him.

"Let's not leave this place," she said.

"It's getting late. You'll be devoured by mosquitoes."

"Who cares?" she said. But as the first few attacked, she changed her mind. They'd been biting for quite some time now, but in her frenzy she hadn't realized it. They helped each other dress but did not immediately leave the forest, preferring to sit here with their arms around each other, enjoying the quiet night air.

"You were beautiful," he said. "The way you enjoyed it."

"Oh." She blushed. "I did enjoy it." How must she have looked, though? Rather like an animal, she thought. She had never been particularly modest and certainly was not modest with Russell, but it must have been quite a performance Michael had witnessed. She recalled that Russell had rarely, if ever, seen her like that. Russell, who had always been very intent on his own climax, had remained inside her long after it was over because his intention was to create a child and not to prevent one. Sometimes with Russell she had had a climax too. More often she hadn't—and hadn't concerned herself with getting one. To touch oneself was dangerous and led to mind enfeeblement, and it had never occurred to her to ask Russell to do things with his hand. In the past, intercourse either had brought satisfaction or it hadn't. She had not known until now that the pleasure could be enhanced by a few deft strokes of a hand.

But the hands must be Michael's, she thought. He was her lover now. She wasn't sure what to do about the situation, but she was beginning to think of Michael's future trips to New York—the trysts in hotel suites, the savoring of each other's bodies, the long talks.

"I love you," she said.

He kissed her but remained silent. She wished he would say the words too. Even if he hadn't loved her earlier, surely he felt differently now, after they had lain together. But Michael didn't say such words easily, she thought. Why was it so much easier for a woman to utter sentiments like that?

They were silent for a while, Michael with his arm

around her, stroking her shoulder. Finally he said, "It was good—this."

"Yes." And then, "What should we do, Michael?"

"What do you mean?"

"Will we be together again?"

"You've got a husband," he reminded her.

"He'd never have to know."

"Are you unhappy?" he asked. "Is that why. . . ." he left the sentence unfinished.

"Yes, I'm unhappy. It was a mistake from the beginning. I've really wrecked my life, Michael, which is why I don't need you to remind me of what a rat I've been. If anyone's paying for it now, it's me."

"What's wrong?"

"He never loved me, and I never loved him either, though I thought I did once. We're so different. He's all wit and fancy and poetry and I'm—to hear him tell it I'm as dull-witted and common and blunt as those housewives who used to sit on the stoops on Monroe."

"You? Dull-witted?"

"Because I don't share his tastes, his sensitivities. He's in advertising—Ruth must have told you—and his job is to sell things with clever sales lines and little slogans. When he was young he thought it was fun and had a good time doing it. Now he's ashamed of his work, and when I try to tell him it's as worthy as any other work, he gets mad. How can I say such a thing? How can I compare a slogan for canned soup to a sonnet? Once I told him that at least a slogan for canned soup got people jobs in soup factories and filled stomachs—and a sonnet did neither. You can imagine what he said to me."

"It wouldn't be difficult," Michael said.

"We don't have much in common except for our son. I wanted more children. We both did. But I guess I must've gone barren or something."

"Did you see a doctor?"

"Yes. He said I seemed all right, but I don't know."

"The boy is how old?"

"Almost twelve."

"For twelve, thirteen years you've lived this way?"

"Lots of people live this way," she said. "Look at yourself? You and your wife don't even share the same house."

"But that's a lot better, I think."

"It probably is, but I don't think Russell would agree to me taking Stephen away."

He said, "You asked if we'd ever be together again. Would you be happy with an arrangement like this?"

"I'd be a lot happier if I were married to you, but that's out of the question until Stephen grows up. But—I'd like us to be lovers."

"It'd be risky for you."

"Would you move back to New York?"

"I can't right now. I'd visit a lot, though."

"And someday you'd come back?"

"Someday. I'd planned to anyway."

"Then we're in limbo for now?"

"You don't feel like limbo to me." He kissed her

hard on the mouth and fumbled with the buttons of her shirtwaist. Soon they were on the ground again. By this time the mosquitoes were out in force, but they didn't feel them.

"HOW DID I get through all those years without you?" she asked as they dressed.

"Want to try once more? Make up for lost time?"

"Aren't you a little tired?" she said.

"Not really, no."

"I don't want to go home, though."

"Won't they be expecting you?"

"Oh, I suppose. It's too late for me to be at the office. But oh, it's so depressing, those dinner conversations. Russell's barely holding on to the business, you know. We don't have much money. I have no idea what we'll do if he goes under. It's been better lately, but he—"

"I thought he was rich," Michael said.

"When I met him he was. And for a while things were good. But lately—"

"Is that why you're having problems?" he said. "Because of the money?"

"That's part of it," she said. "The major part, I guess."

It was very dark, so she sensed rather than saw a change in him. It was his sudden silence that gave her a hint that something was wrong. That and the slow, deliberate way his outline moved as he put on his vest.

"Michael, what is it?"

"You never change, do you? Always chasing after the bank account."

"The what?"

"Michael was poor so Tracy married Russell. Russell became poorer, but in the meantime Michael got richer. So Tracy decided—"

"That's not why I came to you."

"Isn't it?"

"You're joking, aren't you? You have to be joking. You don't believe I'm still a gold digger."

For answer he laughed harshly and said, "You might have admitted it straight out. You didn't have to go to the trouble of shedding your clothes and vowing eternal love."

Her rage was quick to attain full strength. She threw on the rest of her clothes carelessly as she shouted, "Go ahead! Believe what you like. Only while you're doing it maybe you ought to ask yourself a few questions. Such as how I planned to get my hands on your precious money while I was married to Russell and you were married to whatever her name is. What did you think I'd do, huh? Ask for a payment every time we slept together? Prostitute myself for your Michigan gold? Or did you think I was laying a trap for six or seven years from now when Stephen was old enough so I could leave Russell and marry you? Did you think I'd plot seven years for whatever money you might have? Hell, if I was going to go to lengths like that, I wouldn't waste my time on the likes of you. I'd go for bigger stakes. Lots bigger. There're plenty of millionaires around, and if that didn't work there are plenty with hundreds of thousands to play with. Why would I waste my time on small potatoes like you?" She began stomping through the woods ahead of him. They were almost at the car when she whirled around and shouted, "I'm beginning to think I was insane to have loved you at all. Insane! All you ever did was use me. Used my flat, my brandy, my body, every—"

"Used you!"

"You did. And you're using me now."

He grabbed her by the shoulders and whirled her around.

"Stop it!" she shouted. "Let go of me!"

But his fingers dug in tight. They hurt her. "Now listen. . . ." he began.

"Let go of me, you savage! That's all you are under those fancy clothes, a savage!" He'd wounded her more totally than anyone else, including her father. But Michael didn't loosen his grip on her arm, and she was wincing in pain. "I said let go of me! Take your hands *off* me! You're a brute and you always have been. It must run in the family!"

For a moment he just stared at her, unable to believe she had said those words. Then he dropped her arms so abruptly that they snapped back to her sides. He strode a few feet over to where the car stood and she ran past him and began to stumble down the road. He started the engine, yanking the crank handle so hard that he tripped backward. He put on the headlamps and got in the car. Driving to where Tracy was hurrying along, he left the engine running, leaped out of the car, picked Tracy up, and dropped her onto the seat. She started to open the door but he pulled her hand away and shot off down the road shouting, "Stay put, you damn fool. Or did you want to spend the night out here?"

The ride through the Bronx was silent. When he crossed the bridge and entered Manhattan, he stopped at a grocery for gasoline. She was tempted to leave the car then but decided that the quicker she got home the better off she'd be.

Before starting the engine up again, Michael turned and said to her, "You say I used you. From your point of view, I guess that was true. At the time my sister died I'd never given you anything, never even told you how I felt. So from your point of view I used you. But I did have plans. You just didn't want to listen. I wanted to give you what I had, but you didn't want what I had. If you'd waited you would have seen—well, anyway, I had to set the record straight."

"I might as well set it straight too," she said in a weary voice. "I didn't want to listen to your plans. I've already admitted that. And you're not a savage. I didn't mean what I said about your family."

"I think maybe you meant it more than you realize," he said.

"No, I was just—" She broke off, thought a

moment, and then said slowly, "It's just as well we found out some things now. Every bad argument we might have had would've ended with the words 'gold digger' and 'savage.'" The way they had once lived had made them do ugly things, she thought. Had turned him into a gang member and a tough who had nearly succeeded in murdering his father. Had turned her into a scheming money-hungry woman. And though they understood the reasons for these things, this understanding had not affected their basic judgments of each other. Had it been his past as much as his poverty that had caused her to reject him so long ago? Had she been afraid, without being fully aware of it, that Michael might be like his father, and that a child of theirs might be tainted with the blood of a murderer? Had she felt any of those things and had Michael suspected it?

The rest of the ride was quiet. He drove her to the end of her block and said, "Want me to drop you off here?"

"Here?"

"To avoid prying eyes."

"Oh. Yes." That's all she'd need to end this miserable episode: Russell hearing from the neighbors that a man had driven her home in an automobile. "Right here is fine."

He stepped around and opened the door for her. He said, "I'm sorry this happened."

"I'm sorry too." But that wouldn't change anything, she thought, and it was just as well that they not see each other again.

So it was done. They had finally wounded each other past all healing. She shook his hand stiffly, then turned and walked down the street, knowing that he was gone for good and wondering how she was going to fill the empty space in her life that had lately been filled with thoughts of him.

Part

Four

Chapter Twenty-Six

David Litvak was dead at forty-one. He had not died of disease, which was endemic in the area where he lived. And he had not died in the war that had been declared four months earlier. He was killed while investigating the murder of a German-American grocer on Market Street. David had suspected that war-crazed vigilantes had done it, for there were some who believed that every German in the land was a spy. David had apparently suspected right and was murdered for his curiosity. A single shot fired at his back as he was walking down Market Street on a hot summer night. The police had been mobilized in strength, for it was an unwritten law that criminals did not touch either the law or the press. But so far nothing had been turned up.

It was the end of August 1917. Anti-German hysteria had been quickly whipped up. Gone was the liberal, reforming mood that had characterized the first years of the century. Gone too was America's open-door policy. All over the nation came cries to stem the flood of immigrants or at the very least impose literacy tests on them. The mood was

America first and the mode was hate. Death to the Boches, hang Fritzie from the nearest tree, and never mind if Fritzie's family had been in America for two hundred years.

Superpatriots weren't advocating death for the other hyphenated Americans, but they tended to associate all foreign-accented people with the rot that afflicted Europe these days. Thus David, who was ideologically as far removed from Germany as any person could be, nevertheless was associated with the Hun conspiracy because he had inquired into the death of a German-American. David's death had not been mourned as it might have been a few years earlier. One small upstate newspaper, while deploring his murder, had questioned David's loyalty to the cause.

"The irony of it!" Ruth had shouted to Tracy just after the funeral. "David, the socialist, David the Russian-American getting branded as a Boche lover. Hasn't anyone heard that socialists, Russians, and Americans are on the Allied side?"

Ruth's reaction to her husband's murder differed greatly from her response to the death of her son so many years before. Then she had wept and hidden from the world. Now she was angry and confronted the world, raging through the shiva as she had once sat and cried.

She was planning to take over her husband's half of the paper. She now had two children to support— Joshua, six, and Sarah, five—and she was determined to get hold of herself and raise them, though she was not optimistic about the world she'd be raising them in. Six years before, when the owners of Triangle had been found not guilty, she had written an editorial for David's paper titled "Justice is Dead," and she had never changed her mind.

For the past week Tracy had been spending as much time as possible with Ruth. This evening she had come home for dinner before going back to Ruth's to spend the evening and probably sleep over. It was necessary to check with her own family often these days, since Stephen wanted to join the army and Russell wasn't doing much to talk him out of it.

Tracy no longer had her old ally Joanne around. Her mother-in-law had died of cancer in 1914, and Tracy missed her as she would never have believed she could. Russell, however, had mellowed considerably in the past six years. He did his job capably, without too many apologies, and he and his wife now got along better, in part because they spent so much time apart.

Russell smiled when his wife took her seat at the table tonight. "Home at last."

"For an hour at least."

"How is Ruth?"

"About the same."

Russell was still not crazy about Ruth or immigrants in general, but he tried to be a fair man and was very disturbed by the excesses that war hysteria had brought. He said, "I never thought I'd see the day when people defending citizens' rights were not only murdered but attacked by the press."

"And the Litvaks didn't even shop at that German grocer's," Tracy said. "He didn't sell kosher, so they scarcely knew the man. All David knew was that he was an American citizen."

German-Americans weren't the only ones being treated like enemy aliens these days. Many Irish were suspect too. Even though plenty of native Irishmen were in the trenches of France fighting alongside the British, the Irish in America were historically considered enemies of England and hence enemies of the Allied cause. Particularly suspect were those who had supported the ill-fated Easter Uprising of 1916, but anyone with a brogue was expected to prove his loyalty—by writing songs as Cohan had, or by signing up with the army, or by getting a son to sign up. Michael, who had a faint trace of a brogue (acquired from growing up among immigrant stock), had apparently passed some loyalty test. Tracy hadn't seen him in six years, but the Litvaks reported that he had gone to France with a group of auto experts experienced in designing motorcars and tractors to consult with French and British engineers on the development of armored vehicles—or tanks, as the Europeans called them. He was still away, and Tracy thought of how shocked Michael would be when he came home and heard that David was dead.

Before leaving for Europe Michael had been living in the east for six months. The Ford Motor Company, which had begun so inconspicuously that as late as 1911 Tracy had never heard of it, was now so well known that a whole collection of jokes and jargon had grown up around the man, the assembly-line method, and the Tin Lizzie itself. Michael owned a lot of stock in Ford, but he'd finally left the company and had gone into the service end of the industry. After setting up a small network of filling stations in Ohio, he had moved to New Jersey where, with his brothers, he was building another group of Ryan stations along well-traveled highways. The request of the government to assist in tank development had disrupted Michael's plans for the moment, though the Litvaks said that his involvement would be advisory only. He would make his recommendations to the arms manufacturers and then return to his own business.

Michael was divorced now, his former wife having wanted at last to remarry. He had hesitated to move east because it meant not seeing his adolescent daughter as often as he would have liked, but he was rich enough now to return to Michigan as frequently as he wanted—even in a chauffeured auto if he preferred it to the luxury car of a train.

All this the Litvaks had reported, for Michael still saw them occasionally. Tracy's failure to appear at these reunions had surprised Ruth until Tracy explained that she and Michael had had "words" six years earlier, and that while she didn't think she wanted to see him yet, she wouldn't mind hearing about him.

She was thinking of Michael when Stephen came in for dinner—late as usual, striding into the dining room with his usual confident smile. He was

347

eighteen now, self-assured, good-looking, and a devil with the girls. He was a good son too, and Tracy was proud of him. Until the war had come, Stephen had been planning to follow his father into Yale. He had grown more realistic over the years and no longer dreamed of being president of the United States. As he had told his parents a few months before, "I don't know what I want to be, but I don't have to decide now, do I? I guess my ambition is just to live as much as I can, but I'll find something, folks. Don't worry."

"He'll end up at the agency like me," Russell had predicted.

If he did, Tracy thought, he'd be the first Curtis in three generations to enjoy the job. Stephen had the gift of enthusiasm. Though he had ideals, he had not inherited Russell's elitism and identified more with his practical mother. What was wrong with material- ism if it made people comfortable and happy? he had said.

Stephen's practical mother was now concerned with keeping her only child out of war. War, to Stephen, wasn't so much a matter of keeping the world safe for democracy as a challenge he felt he must undertake. Like education and women, war was one of life's experiences, and Stephen was always anxious to expand his horizons.

Now he was saying to his mother, "What if it ends before I'm in it? What if my draft number never comes up? I'll never have the chance to prove I was a man."

"A man indeed," Tracy snapped. "You've been

348

listening to all that propaganda. It's just as manly to go to college and study to build a better world. Isn't that so, Russell?"

Russell launched into one of his Hamlet-like analyses. "Well, in a sense I agree. For this nation to sacrifice its best young minds for a specious cause is in a sense tragic. You know I supported isolation for the past three years. On the other hand, how could we ignore the Germans' sinking of our submarines? We had to do something. And now someone has to fight."

"Then let it be a family with a few sons to spare," Tracy said, giving Russell a scowl. "We only have one, and I won't have him dying for a few feet of French soil."

The argument was not resolved at dinner, but later Tracy went up to Stephen's room and closed the door. She said, "Stephen, you love and respect me, don't you?"

"I respect you more than anyone in the world." He had always idolized his mother. Tracy knew it and was now prepared to use it even if it meant playing upon Stephen's guilt.

"Stephen, I've had a very hard life. I lost my mother when I was young, I lived in tenements and nearly starved, I fought my way out of the East Side and finally married hoping that no child of mine would ever have to see the things I saw. But I could never get over my fears. I was always afraid we'd be hungry again or that we'd lose all our money. I was afraid you'd die of pneumonia or consumption. Or leukemia, like Ruth's baby, or diphtheria. I was afraid you'd get caught in a fire or be run over by a wagon. That's the way it is when you've lived the life I did. Not a minute goes by that you're not afraid your world will crash around your ears. If you go into the army I'll be sick with terror every minute of the day. Every *minute*, Stephen."

"If only you'd had other children," he said.

"We didn't. We wanted to, but we didn't, couldn't. You're all we've got. You're *it*, Stephen. And I love you so much. Is it so terrible, wanting you to stay alive?" Her eyes filled with tears. Normally she would have fought them, for she didn't like Stephen to see her weaknesses. Now she let them flow. He needed to see.

The tears did it. Stephen took his mother in his arms and consoled her. "There, there, Ma. I won't go, I promise. It's not worth seeing you go to pieces this way. I'll make the world safe for democracy in college. I'll even say I'm pre-med so Dad'll think my motives are noble."

"You've got your mother's devious mind," she said, laughing and crying at the same time.

"I've got my mother's instinct for survival too. I guess it's not exactly bully to stand in a trench with cannonballs sailing overhead. I daresay there're more pleasant ways to spend one's time. Like strolling with pretty girls along the byways of New Haven."

She said, "I'll buy you boxes of chocolates for the girls. Books of poetry to melt their hearts."

He laughed. "Not all fellows are lucky enough to

350

have their mothers supporting them in their dishonorable intentions."

"Be as dishonorable as you like," she said, "but stay in one piece."

THE BATTLE wasn't over by any means, Tracy thought, as she left the house to return to Ruth's. Stephen might change his mind, and even if he didn't, his draft number might come up. But it was at least a temporary victory, and she felt slightly reassured as she walked down the block looking for a cab. At the corner of the block she thought she saw someone familiar. She came up closer and squinted. It looked like her old assistant, Louise Mitchell, though all Tracy could see was a profile. An older, dumpier, dowdier Louise who bore not a trace of her Gibson girl origins. Louise turned around and for an instant their eyes met. Tracy was repelled by those eyes. Blue and hard and penetrating, they seemed to be looking right through her, Tracy turned quickly, pretending not to have seen the woman, and charged across the street waving at a cab rounding the corner. Louise stared and stared at Tracy's bustling form. "I'll get you yet," she muttered into her shabby scarf. "I'll get you, Tracy Sullivan."

The incident had such an effect on Tracy that she absentmindedly gave the cabbie the wrong directions and ended up at her school instead of at Ruth's. She did not go into the classroom, where an evening session was now being held by the two assistants who had been with her these past ten years, but instead began to walk toward Ruth's, since there were no more cabs about.

It was an evening for moments of truth, she thought. First the confrontation with Stephen and then that face-to-face encounter with Louise. Had the woman been living here these past nineteen years? If so, why hadn't Tracy seen her before this? Of course it was a big city, but surely not so big that Tracy would not have run into her in all that time. She felt uneasy. She walked along Broadway for a while, then cut across to the Bowery and headed downtown, passing familiar streets: Broome, Grand, Hester, Canal, Bayard, Division. And then onto Catherine where she passed East Broadway, Henry, Madison, and then came home.

Home? But *this* wasn't home. Thirtieth Street was home. Had Louise thrown her time sense off too? She looked around her. Monroe and its neighboring streets were now just a cluttered neighborhood between two great bridges: the Brooklyn Bridge soaring off to the right and the newer Manhattan Bridge to the left. It was as though the bridges were reminding the residents here that the world was moving on without them. Yet the people seemed indifferent to the taunting of these giant spans of steel. Here still were the little boys playing marbles, and there were the men with beards talking in Yiddish, and farther along were two Irish men talking about some baseball game, and here on the stoops were the housewives calling shrilly to their children, and here in front of the candy store were the adolescent boys—the latter-day Michaels—smoking their cigarettes and calling to a girl whose skirt was exhibiting quite a bit of stocking. How long ago it had been, Tracy thought, and yet how recently had she and Ruth, David and Michael stood on this street and performed their own versions of the mating ritual. Over there Gramp had sat on the stoop and sung "Danny Boy" while Ruth and David listened. And higher up, on the roof, she and Michael had lain together on a scorching summer night. And of all that cast of characters only Ruth was left now. There were one or two shopkeepers who had been here since the old days and a few entrenched families, but otherwise it was a street of strangers.

She passed the boys with the cigarettes, thinking of Michael and David. But David was dead. And Michael, if he did come back, would never fit in here. And she, Tracy, didn't fit in either, yet she found herself thinking of this street as home. Odd . . .

Ruth was sitting alone in the parlor when Tracy arrived. The children had gone to bed early, mourning the death of their father. Ruth asked if Tracy could talk about her own problems for a change. It would get Ruth's mind off her troubles. So Tracy told her friend about the discussion with Stephen, saying, "So I pulled out all the stops, fell on his mercy. Do you blame me?"

"No, I don't. I should've done that with David. He was always taking risks, snooping into Black Hand affairs, prowling around Tammany, and now tracking down vigilantes. I should have said, 'Look, you *momzer,* I've lost my parents and a child and I'll be goddamned if I'm gonna lose you too. Let somebody else be the hero. Somebody without a wife and kids.'" She sighed. "That's what I should have said, and I should've cried oceans too. Well, it's too late for me, but not for you, kid. Whine and cry and make Stevie feel guilty. Maybe he won't respect you so much, but you should care? He'll be alive and happy and bringing grandchildren over to see you."

Ruth looked toward the bedroom of six-year-old Josh. "They'll be after Josh someday too," she said. "You bear them, diaper them, feed them in the middle of the night, see them through croup and chicken pox, protect them from streetcars and bullies, listen to their chatter—and then, after eighteen years of this, Uncle Sam comes along and says 'I want him.' You'll notice I said 'Uncle.' Does a man bear and diaper him? So what does he care what happens to this body he's so anxious to send to the trenches. Men never invested a thing in those bodies."

On and on Ruth ranted, working her grief out by making speeches. Later in the evening many friends came and went, and they sat patiently beside Ruth's soapbox for as long as they could endure it— neighbors, former boarders, people from the paper. It had been like this for a week, people coming to console but actually listening to Ruth attack the world.

"Michael's over there now," Ruth was saying to Tracy and other friends. "Haven't heard from him in weeks; he should be back by now. He doesn't know about David. We got a letter from him yesterday. I mean *I* got it; it's not 'we' anymore. Mike must've seen it three or four weeks ago. It mentioned Ypres." This was a Belgian city that had been totally destroyed. "Half of the letter was blacked out. Censored so you couldn't make head or tail of it. You know why? Because if the truth about that war was known, no one in *any* country would be joining up. When he gets home we'll hear the real story. I've half a mind to print it in the paper. But no more heroics for me. If I print the truth, some crazy war hound will set my building on fire and kill the rest of us. You know what I'm gonna turn the paper into? A patriotic American's dream. No more muckraking, no women's suffrage, no mention of the Wobblies or the I.L.G.W.U. No Eugene Debs, no opinions on war. We'll run headlines on the doings of Charlie Chaplin and Buster Keaton, Mary Pickford, Fanny Brice. We'll have comics, serialized Westerns, and instructions on how to do the tango, and a guide to where to eat in Coney Island. We'll have Ty Cobb's scores, sketches of the rising skirt lengths, a feature on the Boy Scouts—and no one'll ever guess that Ruth Litvak ever had any opinions. No one will ever guess that I pray for peace every night. This way my kids'll grow to adulthood."

Tracy listened, and she knew Ruth wasn't joking. Exaggerating maybe but not joking. There would have to be changes in the paper. For one reason, sedition acts were being pushed through Congress. If

Ruth didn't mind her manners in print, she'd end up in prison. And *then* where would the children be?

There were about a dozen people in the parlor during this particular tirade of Ruth's. One of them, Mrs. Berrigan from across the hall, whispered to Tracy, "She's in a bad way, she is."

"She'll be all right," Tracy said rather defensively. She glanced at her watch. Eight-thirty. If the crowd would only leave, maybe she could get Ruth to bed.

There was a knock on the parlor door. Mrs. Berrigan went to answer. There, looking five years older than his forty-two, stood Michael. He was dressed in an expensive suit, but it was rumpled. There were dark circles under his eyes. Tracy saw him come in, but he didn't see her. He crossed the room to Ruth. Ruth stood up, crying his name and embracing him. Then she burst into tears and he held her.

The room fell silent. Tracy watched Michael, watched Ruth. Michael was saying, "My brother met me at the ship and told me. I came right here."

Ruth said between sobs, "The police'll never find them. Never find them, Mike."

"Maybe they will." He patted her back. "Give them time."

He was thin and tired-looking, Tracy thought, and there was a lot of gray in his hair. Half of it had probably been put there by the war he had just this day returned from. He hadn't yet seen Tracy. She was in a corner of the room and he was on the other side holding Ruth. He had succeeded somewhat in

356

calming her, but he must be grieving himself, Tracy thought, since he had just found out about David.

Ruth drew her hands down from Michael's shoulders, and Michael handed her a handkerchief. She blew her nose, swallowed a few times, and then said in a ragged voice, "Let me introduce you to my friends. Everybody, this is Michael Ryan, an old friend of ours. . . ."

Michael's eyes passed around the room and finally met Tracy's. He nodded without smiling, but it wasn't a curt acknowledgment. It was just solemn, as though he were saying to Tracy, "And now David too."

She rose and went over to him. "Let me get you a cup of coffee," she said.

Chapter Twenty-Seven

It was after ten at night. David's partner on the paper, a widower named Al Mendel, was sitting over coffee with Michael at the kitchen table asking him about the situation in France. Ruth and Tracy were listening and sometimes asking questions of their own. The visitors had gone home. Ruth was interested in Michael's stories, partly because they took her mind off David and also because they supported her own theory: that the war was a suicide attempt by a lot of crazed governments.

"Yes, I saw the big battlefields," Michael was saying. "The French and British we were working with thought we ought to see what we'd be up against. I don't know if tanks'll do the trick, but we'll see."

Tracy still didn't know what the war was all about, but because she had a son of age she had learned what she could over the years. In 1914 a Serbian assassin had shot and killed an archduke of Austria-Hungary, heir to the throne. The assassin was a Slav and the heir a Teuton, and Slavs and Teutons hated each other (why this was so, Tracy had never bothered to find out). So Germany (Teuton) declared war on Russia (Slav) and also on France (neither Teuton nor Slav but allied with Slavic Russia). To get at France, the Germans elected to go through Belgium because the border between Germany and France was heavily fortified. Because England had once pledged to defend Belgium, this brought England into the war. In time, others became involved in this massive conflict—Italians, Japanese, Turks, Bulgarians, Arabs, and God knew who else—but Tracy had never troubled to find out who stood where on the other fronts. Her only concern was the western front in which Germany was fighting France and England—and now America as well.

For nearly three years America had been neutral and had tried to carry on normal commerce with the belligerents. But German submarines had sunk any ships sailing in or near the combat zones, including those of neutral American liners or British ones, like the *Lusitania,* carrying Americans. So President Wilson, who had run for reelection on the slogan "he kept us out of war," decided shortly after beginning his second term to get the United States into one.

The western front, where the first Americans were arriving now, was a static one, Tracy knew. Germany had beaten its way through Belgium and a corner of France, wreaking appalling destruction and casualties. But here they had been stopped by the British and the French. There were trenches running five hundred miles from the North Sea to the Swiss border. In one set of trenches stood the Germans, and facing them from the West, the Allies. The armies lived among rats, lice, and barbed wire and were felled as much by disease as by bullets. Every so often one side would climb out of a trench and go "over the top" into what was called "no-man's-land" and try to make some headway. Battles had flared up—some tremendous in size—but ultimately the same stalemate had prevailed. David had saved a rhyme from *Life* magazine. Written by a man named Edwin Dwight, it was still tacked up with a group of clippings in a corner of Ruth's kitchen.

Five hundred miles of Germans,
Five hundred miles of French,
And English, Scottish, Irishmen
All fighting for a trench.
And when the trench is taken,
And many thousands slain,
The losers with more slaughter,
Retake the trench again.

In 1915 the Germans had tried to break through by using poison gas. Such methods worked very well until the gas was blown back by the wind into their own faces and the Allies made not only gas masks to protect themselves but also poison gas of their own. In 1916 the British had tried to break through with tanks, but winter had set in and made tank attacks difficult. Dirigibles had also been tried, and even bombs thrown from aeroplanes, but the armies were still stalemated, and now the American Expeditionary Force under Pershing was joining the Allies in the trenches of France. They could look forward to diseases of every variety and also to shell fragments, bullets, and filth. But the American lads had been told about gay Paree and the French girls, and many who had spent their lives on farms or in small towns looked forward to the grand adventure.

This was the sum of Tracy's knowledge of The Great War. It was as thorough as the average person's understanding of it. Rare was the individual who could fathom how the actions of one mad Serbian (many had not known at first what a Serbian was) could lead to a fight involving Arabs, Japanese, and Americans. But they took it on faith that their governments knew what they were doing, and some simply reasoned that since other major powers had had their fun with imperialism, Germany had decided it was her turn now. It was as good an explanation as any.

One of the first questions Tracy had asked Michael was whether any of the atrocity stories were true. For years they had been hearing that the Germans were fiends who cut off the breasts of Belgian women, the hands of Belgian children, and the heads of enemy soldiers. A recent story had it that the Germans had gathered the corpses of dead soldiers and sent them back to factories where the bodies were melted down into soap.

Michael shook his head. "I doubt that it's true. They have the same stories in France."

"Why wouldn't it be true?" Tracy said. "Men crazy

enough to throw shells and gas at each other are crazy enough to turn bodies into soap."

"It's propaganda," Al Mendel said. "Even the Cossacks weren't that grotesque."

Michael said, "The hands are propaganda too. I didn't see any handless children. Mostly I saw soldiers and tanks."

He had visited the two major battlefields on the western front—Ypres, near the North Sea, defended by the British; and Verdun, farther east, defended by the French. In 1916 the fighting around Verdun had resulted in something like seven hundred thousand casualties. For ten months there had been a major battle in some part of the field every day. The area around Verdun had been annihilated, reduced to a wasteland that resembled the Sahara, and in some places the casualties were so heavy that piles of corpses had served as barricades for the living. But no decisive progress had been made, and now, more than a year later, fighting still flared there.

The area around Ypres had been the scene of brutal fighting. It had been attacked and defended several times during the war and was a gutted mess with scarcely a tree left standing. Michael had seen a battle there, and it was still going on with staggering losses of troops.

Michael also said that he expected battles to get even worse. The Russians were assuring the Allies that they would see the war through to the end, but many experts doubted it. Russia, who had just forced the czar to abdicate, might want to make a separate peace with Germany soon. If this happened, then the Germans now on the eastern front would be released for the western front and no one could begin to imagine what would happen then.

"It's impossible to describe what it's like," Michael said. "And I don't like to do it in front of ladies."

"These two ladies have sons," Ruth said, "and Tracy's is of age and champing at the bit. The more she knows, the more she can tell him about, so never mind our fragile feelings." Ruth paused. "I listen to men talking about what hell war is and I can't help wondering if they'd thought of that before they joined the parade to arms. I don't understand your sex, gentlemen. You read books, same as we do. You read about Waterloo, Gettysburg, Borodino. You know well in advance what war is like, so why don't you stay away?"

Michael said, "Well, *I'm* not in the army, am I? But of course I'm forty-two years old. An adolescent boy doesn't want to believe what he reads. Or if he believes it, he shoves the information aside. If I hadn't been supporting a family, I would've gone to Cuba in '98. I was twenty-three then and that age group thinks it's invincible. Which is why both the Allies and the Germans depend on 'em. Who was it said there's a sucker born every minute? Well, when those suckers get to be eighteen, a government knows it's got an army." He paused, then said, "I'm glad my kid was a girl."

"But mine wasn't," Tracy snapped, angry at him for mentioning it.

"Therefore," Ruth said hastily, "you'd better arm Tracy with the truth so she can go home and tell Stephen."

For all the good it will do, Michael thought.

"Come on," Ruth said. "Tell us a few facts."

"I'd rather not," he said.

"*Tell* us!" Ruth demanded. "How can we argue against this war if we're not sure what we're arguing against?"

"All right," Michael said. "There's the gas. Everyone's got masks now, so it's not like it was. And they send it over in shells these days. Very neat. But some Canadians described what it was like back in '15 when the Boches weren't so efficient and the Allies weren't prepared."

"Go on," Ruth said.

"It's yellow—some say it's greenish—but it rolls forward like a fog or a cloud. These fellows first saw it near Ypres. They didn't know what it was. No one did. They had a smart officer who said to wet their handkerchiefs and put them over their faces."

Ruth said, "What if they didn't have water in their canteens?"

"They used urine," Michael said.

"Ugh!" Tracy made a face.

Michael said, "Yes, but that indelicacy saved a lot of lives. The ones who didn't—couldn't—produce water fast died quickly."

"How long does it take to die of gas?" Ruth asked.

"Five, six minutes."

"That's quick," Ruth said. "With bullets it

sometimes takes days. Three cheers for gas, everyone."

The three others looked at her. Al was frowning.

"They didn't always die," Michael said. "Some were blinded."

He described a battle he had seen near Ypres. Or rather, the carnage that was left. At considerable risk he and another American visitor had helped British stretcher bearers rescue the wounded. He'd seen men armless, legless, blown to bits. He'd seen heads in one place and bodies in another. He'd seen men with their intestines exposed, men with eyeballs blown from their sockets, men with no faces left.

Ruth said, "When you read about war do you read about dangling eyeballs or exposed intestines? You do not. First come the ideals and then come the crosses in the military cemeteries. But how much do you hear about the detail in between? I say we should take pictures of the wounded, plaster them all over the papers, the trolleys, the subways, the sides of buildings. The war would be over tomorrow."

Michael shook his head. "People would be shocked for a while, but then they'd grow accustomed to it. The first time I saw a wounded Tommy I was sick. The hundredth time I saw one he looked normal to me, part of the scenery."

Ruth clenched her fists. "Then what's going to persuade people to stop wars?" she said.

"Feeling the bullet," Michael said.

"Well, by then it's too late. We should illustrate in advance with dress rehearsals."

"I can imagine what Wilson would say to that," Al said. "Or the press. 'A radical woman in New York is trying to discourage future soldiers by luring them into Camp Litvak for a practice war. Here the unsuspecting eighteen- to twenty-five-year-olds are treated to muddy trenches, rats, lice, and dysentery. The pain of bullets and shell fragments is simulated by jabbing two and three hypodermics at the same time into the skin and then bleeding the man just enough to make him feel faint. Proprietor Litvak reports that the cure rate for war enthusiasts is astounding. No one wants to join the army anymore. However, avoiding the draft is illegal, so those who won't join up must go to prison along with Mrs. Litvak.'"

"They'd be better off, believe me," said Ruth.

"I think dress rehearsal's a good idea," said Tracy.

"So do I," said Michael, "but it won't work unless you can get camps going in other countries too."

"Nothing works," Tracy said, "except scheming to keep your kids out of it."

It was nearly midnight by the time the four decided that further analysis of society's ills would have to wait until another day. Al was tired and had to be at the paper early. Michael was tired too since he'd just this day arrived from France. Ruth had to be up at dawn with the children, and Tracy was planning to stay the night with her friend, so she should be going to bed soon too.

"Are you going all the way back to Jersey?" Ruth asked Michael.

"No, I'll stay in town."

"The best hotel, of course."

"Of course," he smiled. "The Plaza."

"Can you come back tomorrow? I need your advice about the will and some savings David had."

"I'll be here," Michael said. "Ten o'clock all right?"

"Any time that's convenient for you. I'm not going anywhere."

Neither was she, Tracy thought. Not until she'd spent a little more time with Michael. Soon enough he'd be vanishing for another five to ten years.

Chapter Twenty-Eight

As they walked up Broadway the next afternoon, Tracy said to Michael, "We'll be doing this forever. Every few years we'll meet at Ruth's and take a walk and talk about auld lang syne. Till we're old and gray."

"I'm gray enough already," he said.

"You're still young to me."

"The blarney never stops," he said.

"I felt so bad after the last time we saw each other. I thought we'd never speak again."

"I know," Michael said.

It was a warm August day. Michael had gone through Ruth's papers this morning, and now he was walking Tracy back to the school. They chatted about the old days and the new, reminiscing about David, speculating on Ruth's future. For the first time in many years Tracy was fully at ease with him. Now that she and Russell had settled down, she had ceased to seek romantic escape in Michael and was content just to have him as a friend. Her attitude surprised her. She had been sure there would be stirrings again, a desire to sleep with him one more time. He looked the same, after all. He hadn't changed much. Yet the feelings failed to come. That might be because she was afraid of it, she thought. The last time had ended so badly, and she didn't want a repetition. Then too it wasn't a romantic occasion for either of them. The death of his best friend (did men call each other best friends?) had greatly upset Michael, though he had tried to conceal his own pain from Ruth. He was saying to Tracy now, "All the time I was in France I would find myself thinking, 'What would Dave think of this? Gotta tell Dave about that.' I can't believe he's not here anymore."

As they walked up Broadway toward the school, they were unaware of a pair of eyes following them from an office window. The eyes belonged to Louise Mitchell, whom Tracy had seen the night before. Back in New York for the past six months, Louise now worked in an office near Tracy's school and lived in a boardinghouse not far from the Curtis brownstone. Only once had Tracy seen Louise, but Louise had seen Tracy often—seen her walking down streets wearing expensive clothes, seen her dashing up the stairs of her brownstone home, seen her laughing with her handsome son as the two waited for a trolley or climbed into a cab, seen her being picked up at the school by Russell. And now she was seeing Tracy with another man—a man Louise thought she recognized.

Louise had had a hard life and was a bitter woman. In 1900 she had moved to San Francisco and there married—but not a man to match the coveted

Russell. Her husband and child had died in the earthquake of 1906, leaving Louise, whose father had died the year before, virtually alone in the world. She had moved to Chicago, where she contracted consumption, and from there to Arizona, where recovery had been slow. Since then, she'd been so sickly that secretarial jobs were hard to keep, and she was lucky to have this one in a pants factory, though the pay was abysmal.

Louise was forty, poor, and alone, and she looked and felt old. Tracy was the same age, but youthful looking, rich, and successful, with a husband, a son, and apparently a former lover too. Louise envied and loathed her. For more than five months she had been plotting a way of taking revenge but had lacked the proof. Now, before her eyes, the proof had materialized.

There he was, talking with Tracy, Michael Ryan, the son of that murderer in the long-ago child slaughter case. He had spent a night with Tracy. How well Louise remembered the flat and the unbuttoned shirt.

When Louise had come back to New York and begun watching Tracy, Russell, and the boy, she had deduced that the Curtises only had one child. The boy looked to be in his late teens. Normally Louise wouldn't have been too suspicious. After all, Tracy had married Russell almost nineteen years ago. But the fact that the Curtises did not have any other children was most curious indeed. It was obvious that Tracy could conceive. But what about Russell?

More interesting was the fact that the boy didn't resemble Russell except in height. Russell's face had always been full. The boy's was lean. Russell was blond and the boy's hair was dark brown. Russell had blue eyes and the boy brown ones. Of course it could be claimed that the boy took after Tracy in hair and eye color. This was probably the story Tracy had handed her husband. But Louise had always been curious to see the other man again. For months she had been intending to find out where he was, but she'd been busy with other matters and had put off searching for the proof. Now she was seeing the proof from an office window. She had known Ryan at once not because she remembered him from that long-ago five-minute encounter. No, she knew him because she was used to watching his son, and this man was definitely an older version—from the loose-limbed walk to the angle his head assumed as he turned and said something to Tracy.

It would have astonished Louise to know that no one else had ever been suspicious. Ruth had once noted a resemblance, but she would not believe that Tracy could keep such a truth from Michael, so she had told herself that Stephen was simply Irish-looking and obviously took after someone in Tracy's clan. Tracy's family, who also knew Michael, had not suspected Tracy's involvement with him and so the question of paternity had never occurred to them. Tracy herself had never suspected that Michael might be Stephen's father. To this day, she believed that it took three times before a child was possible.

371

And she also knew that Stephen had been born ten days after the normal gestation period. She never considered that the baby might simply have been late.

Over the years—and especially in recent ones—Tracy had sometimes found herself thinking of Michael when looking at Stephen, but she never asked herself why, though there were resemblances in shape of face, shape of eyes, jaw, and nose. Like Ruth, Tracy thought of Stephen as Irish-looking and guessed that he must take after her mother's side of the family. An uncle had had facial features that were roughly similar.

Louise, however, was convinced that Tracy knew the truth. Or what she, Louise, considered to be the truth. And she resolved, as she watched the couple pass, that Russell would soon know about it too. Years before, Tracy had screamed at Louise that she could not prove that Michael had been her lover. Well, she'd had no proof then, but these nineteen years had provided her with it.

TWO WEEKS after his shiva visit to Ruth's, Michael received a telegram at his Newark office:

"Please meet with this office on a matter concerning the disposition of David Litvak's will." It gave a date, time, and address and it was signed L. Anderson. Michael had no way of knowing this person was a secretary in a boardinghouse. Similar telegrams were sent to Tracy, Russell, and Stephen, who was now at Yale. Tracy asked Ruth if she knew what the wire was all about. Ruth said she hadn't the foggiest idea who L. Anderson was.

Louise Mitchell (who had married an Anderson) had wracked her brain trying to figure out a way to get all the principals in this would-be drama together. She not only needed them together in order to point out the resemblances but also had a fantasy of creating a scene similar to those in the detective stories she loved. She knew that Tracy and Mrs. Litvak, the wife of that slain newsman, were still close, for she'd seen the two women walking together more than once. She hadn't known that Michael too was a friend of the Litvaks, but she reasoned that since he had probably come from the same neighborhood and was still a friend of Tracy's he might possibly have been acquainted with David. Just to be sure Michael came from that neighborhood, Louise had checked out ancient newspaper accounts of the Ryan child murder and discovered to her delight that one David Litvak had actually testified to police about the character of the slayer. But why, after all these years, would David be remembering Michael in his will? And why would Russell and the boy be included too? It didn't matter why. The point was that they'd all known David and would come out of curiosity.

Finding Michael's address hadn't been difficult. Louise had a friend who was a reporter, and she went to chat with some people in the old neighborhood. Sure enough, there was a sister of Mike Ryan still around and she had his address in Newark. In order to find the name and present address of Russell's son,

Louise paid a pretty girl to engage the handsome lad in conversation before he took a cab to wherever he was going. Which turned out to be Grand Central and Yale.

Four telegrams went out, and four people showed up in the boardinghouse parlor on the appointed day and hour. Three of them—the Curtises—had showed their wires to one another, unable to make any sense of them, Stephen the most puzzled of all since he'd had to come all the way in from New Haven. The fourth, Michael, had had no one to show it to and thought the whole thing strange because Ruth had said that David was leaving Michael books in the will. Tracy had told Ruth that she thought Ruth ought to attend the meeting, but Ruth had declined, saying she'd trust them all not to run off with David's millions.

Russell, Tracy, and Stephen arrived first. Russell caught his breath and said "Louise?" Tracy exclaimed, "Louise!" And Stephen said sotto voce, "Who the hell is Louise?"

For a moment the four just stared at one another. Then Russell asked Louise what she'd been doing these past nineteen years. Simultaneously Tracy was asking what Louise knew of David's will and when she had become a lawyer.

"All in good time," Louise said pleasantly. "The fourth—er—beneficiary hasn't arrived yet." Tracy thought her former assistant looked terrible. At least thirty pounds overweight, wrinkled as a prune, and grayer by far than Tracy. The years had not been kind to poor Louise. Tracy had seen it that night on the street, but now she was seeing it up close.

"I don't understand," Tracy finally said impatiently. "What are *you* doing here in a boardinghouse with David Litvak's will?" And what was David leaving Russell? she wondered. The two hadn't exactly been lifelong pals. Why was David leaving money to any of them? Ruth needed every penny for the children.

"I can't explain until the fourth beneficiary gets here," Louise said. And finally there came a knock on the door. "Ah, here he is now. Come in, Mr. Ryan. Come in."

Michael? Tracy thought. Yes, of course David would leave something to Michael.

"Mr. Ryan," gushed Louise. "How do you do? Are you acquainted with this little family here?"

Tracy said hastily, "My husband, Russell, and my son, Stephen. This is Michael Ryan, a friend of the Litvaks."

"How do you do?" said Russell, rising.

"Pleased to meet you," Michael mumbled, looking Russell over carefully, finally appraising the competition after all these years. Not a bad-looking fellow, Michael thought, but a little flabby. Didn't get enough exercise. Michael didn't pay much attention to Stephen, though he said hello.

Louise said, "Mr. Ryan is an emissary of Henry Ford."

"Not anymore," Michael corrected her. "I have my own business now."

375

"Well, speaking of business," Louise trilled. "Shall we get down to it?"

Michael took a seat and the parlor fell silent.

"Before we get to the Litvak will," Louise began, picking up an official-looking paper, "I have to discuss this letter from the Board of Health."

"Board of Health?" Tracy said, more confused than before.

"Certain questions concerning the birth certificate of your son. They asked me to straighten the matter out."

"What?" four people chorused.

"It seems the father of record may not be the natural father of one Stephen Curtis." Louise rustled the paper. "There's evidence to show that the natural father may be Michael Ryan. Which is why we've invited him here today."

As Tracy leaped to her feet to seize the paper, Louise said quickly, "Forgive me my little deception, everyone, but it was the only way I could think of to get you all together. There's no will, of course, and no letter. There's only an eyewitness to an unfortunate truth. And that's me."

They were all in various stages of shock. Tracy, who had risen for the paper, now collapsed into a chair. Michael looked as though he'd been hit with a brick. Stephen was staring wide-eyed at the dark-haired man next to him. And Russell looked astonished. After a moment of speechlessness Russell said, "You're saying that this man is the father of my son? That's preposterous. Stephen was born nine months after our marriage."

"Nine months and a few days perhaps," Louise said. "Though he could have been born at *any* time and *still* not be your son. How naïve you are, my dear Russell. However, Tracy *did* spend the night with this man just before she married you. I was there."

Tracy felt faint. It was partly shock and partly the realization that there was no way to deny that she'd been with Michael. Here sat Michael himself, a witness. Of course the paternity charge was absurd. Stephen couldn't possibly be Michael's child. He hadn't even been conceived until after the wedding. She had counted in days and could prove that to Russell. Still, the exposure of that night with Michael would hurt Russell now. Oh, the vindictive bitch! And what on earth would poor Stephen think? Imagine having to drag out a calendar and count off the days for her son?

Tracy rose and said, "Russell, she's out of her mind. She hates me because I took you away from her and she'll stop at nothing to—"

Louise interrupted. "Out of my mind, am I? Take a look at your son and take a look at Mr. Ryan here. Note the cheekbones, the mouth, the jaw. Note in particular the shape of the eyes. And if the participants are willing, you might also compare voice tones. There's a striking similarity, though of course Mr. Ryan has a touch of a brogue."

Tracy and Russell looked from Michael to Stephen. Michael looked at Stephen. Stephen looked at Michael. Louise looked at them all, enjoying their

377

various expressions. She said, "And just in case that isn't proof enough for you, there's the question of Russell's ability to conceive. Doesn't it strike any of you as odd that there is only one child after all these years? Isn't it possible that you, my dear faithless Russell, were never able to conceive at all?"

Russell shouted, "Let's go! You too, Ryan. I want to clear this up in private." To Louise he said, "You're a contemptible, disgusting old—"

"Before you go," Louise interrupted. "I'd advise you to check the newspaper files for Monday, December 5, 1898. You'll find mention of the death of a child. Mr. Ryan's sister. Tracy is mentioned in the article. She was one of the concerned neighbors—and without a doubt the most sympathetic of them all. Read the article, Russell. And you'll understand how this unfortunate event came about. Remember the date now. December 5, 1898. And see how close that is to the date of your wedding."

"Is it true?" Russell shouted at Michael.

Michael didn't answer. He was staring at Tracy.

"Is it true?" Russell shouted again.

Michael still didn't answer, but his silence was answer enough. Russell whirled on Tracy. "You slept with this man?" And Stephen, ashen-faced, stared at his mother, disbelieving.

"But Stephen is your son, not his," Tracy sobbed to her husband. "He was conceived after we were married. And I can prove it."

"Oh?"

"A normal baby takes two hundred and seventy

378

days to grow. Stephen was born two hundred and eighty days after we—after we first—"

"You counted? You counted *days?*"

"Not because I thought Michael might be the father."

"Then why?"

"To find out if I was pregnant the night you and I—the first—"

"The night we decided to get married?" he interrupted. Even in his rage he remained conscious of the proprieties.

"Yes, but I didn't get pregnant then, I *wasn't* pregnant then."

"How do you know?"

"Well, it's supposed to take two hundred and seventy days and it took two hundred and eighty. I got pregnant ten days *after* that night."

Louise said, "Perhaps the baby was just born late."

Tracy turned, knitting her brow.

"Two hundred seventy days is an average, my dear. Obviously Stephen's gestation was longer. But no harm done. He's a fine broth of a lad, isn't he?"

Stephen had covered his face with his hands and was pressing them against his skull as though to crush it. Not only was he finding out that this stranger might be his father, but he was also hearing his mother admit to sleeping with one man a few days before sleeping with another. The mother he idolized had done this thing. He didn't want to hear any more. He wanted, at that moment, to die.

Michael's shock was so overwhelming that he

379

could not at first move or speak. He knew it was the truth, all of it. One good look at Stephen's face told the story, and he didn't believe Tracy hadn't known. She must have known soon after the boy was born. If she'd had any courage, she would have done the right thing then. But why give up this man and all his money?

Russell was trembling, thinking that Tracy had married him knowing that there was a chance she might have someone else's child. All these years she had known whose child this was, and she had let him go on supporting the little mick, had even had the nerve to criticize his methods in raising him. Russell stared at Stephen. He too could see the resemblance to Ryan. This was Ryan's son, not his. He, Russell, had no son. He couldn't ever have a son. He couldn't ever have children at all.

It was a scene to warm Louise's heart. Scheming Tracy brought to justice at last and faithless Russell trembling, on the verge of tears. She felt a little sorry for Stephen and Mr. Ryan. They, after all, had never done anything to hurt her. But all wars had innocent victims, and Louise's only concern had been to win the war. But out of deference to the innocents she now decided to leave the group alone. She'd accomplished the objective; now it was over, and if the four wanted to speak without her interference they should be given the opportunity to do so. Of course it would be better if they left. The landlady would not want this parlor tied up indefinitely.

Louise departed. Michael remained seated. He was

very pale. Russell still stood stiffly against the wall. Stephen was feeling sick enough to throw up. Tracy was crying.

It was Russell who finally broke the silence. "Well, shall we reorganize the family?"

"You have no proof," Tracy sobbed.

"Take a look at him and tell me that's not proof."

"There's a slight resemblance, but Stephen is fairer."

Russell turned to Michael. "Well, now, Mr. Ryan, how does it feel to be a father?"

Michael, eyes stormy, rose and took a step toward Tracy. "Why the hell didn't you tell me?"

"I didn't know."

"You kept this from me for eighteen years? Eighteen *years?*"

"There's no proof," Tracy said, the tears coursing down her cheeks. "There's no proof that he's—"

Russell was saying to Stephen, "What's the matter with you? Aren't you going to say hello to your father?" And with that Russell began to cry.

Tracy jumped to her feet and ran to her husband. He shook her off, sobbing. "Don't touch me! Get your hands off me, you slut. As soon as I leave here I'm calling my lawyer. In the meantime you will remove yourself from my bed and board."

"What about Stephen? You can't disown him too."

"Oh, can't I?" Russell cried. "Can't I?" And still crying he ran from the room.

Stephen was the next to leave. He walked past

Michael and Tracy, keeping his eyes on the door, not answering when his mother cried, "Where are you going? *Tell* me!"

When he had gone, Tracy turned to Michael sobbing, "What am I going to do?"

"Seems to me you've done enough already," he said through clenched teeth.

"I didn't know. I swear I didn't."

Michael got up and started for the door.

"Where did Stephen go?" she asked. "Where's he going to go?"

"I have no idea," Michael said. He looked at her for a moment. Under all his fury he was still able to feel a kind of pity. She had lost everything, her son included.

"Will he come home to me?" she was wailing. "Oh, my God. Stephen!" She was crying so hard that she did not see Michael walk out. Nor did she know that Louise, who was wondering belatedly if Tracy might kill her, was at this moment making plans to move to another city. Savannah perhaps. Who would ever come looking for her in Savannah? There must be jobs there for experienced secretaries, and the weather would be better for her rheumatism.

Chapter Twenty-Nine

"I can't go on," Tracy sobbed to Ruth. "I want to die."

Ruth could understand that. What she couldn't understand was how Tracy could have been so stupid. Every school child knew that babies could be conceived on the first try. Where had Tracy got the notion that this was impossible? Well, from the neighborhood girls, of course. Ruth remembered a few of them. The ones who had told Tracy this could have taken prizes for imbecility. Why had Tracy never questioned it? Probably because most of the girls she had known were married, promiscuous, or virgins. If married or promiscuous they hadn't kept careful track of the number of times they had slept with a man before they discovered their pregnancy. If virgins, the question didn't apply. But surely she'd known at least one who had conceived after a single encounter. Perhaps Tracy had thought that this one was lying.

So Tracy had slept with Michael twice in one night, never believing that she could have his baby. And in all the years since she had never learned anything new about sex—or about this aspect of it. After all, it wasn't a subject discussed in genteel society, though a woman named Margaret Sanger, who lectured on a subject called "birth control," was trying to change that situation, risking the wrath of the law. Then too Tracy was so convinced about the 270 days that the question in her mind had never been who the father was. The question had been whether or not Russell would find out that she hadn't become pregnant until after the wedding she had seduced him into. (Tracy had finally spilled *that* shocking story to Ruth.)

For eighteen years Tracy had raised her son without considering that the father might be Michael. Normally Ruth would have thought that Tracy was lying through her teeth, but she knew Tracy better than anyone outside of her family and would have been quick to sniff out a lie. And now her friend's life had been blown to smithereens. She would have to move in here. Ruth would insist upon it. The two of them needed each other now.

There was a chance that Stephen would forgive his mother and decide to live with her in an apartment somewhere. But Ruth was almost certain of where Stephen would go. The army, of course. There wasn't a thing Tracy could do about it now.

AT FOUR O'CLOCK on the morning following Louise's revelations, Tracy's brother Tommy was asleep in his three-room bachelor flat on Bleecker Street. Tommy had surprised them as much by remaining a bachelor as Pat had surprised them by getting engaged in July to a Lanston girl. Tommy was still a policeman, still in the precinct where Triangle had happened, and still a great pal of his nephew Stephen. But he was annoyed at being awakened from a sound sleep by the young sport, who was blind drunk and barely able to stand.

"Stevie, what the hell—"

"Sorry to 'sturb you," Stephen slurred. "No money for a room."

"Aren't you supposed to be at Yale?"

"Yeah, but could I go to bed now? I wanna go to bed."

Tommy put the youth into his own bed and wondered if he should phone Tracy and Russell. Maybe he'd better wait till the sun came up. Stephen got up twice and Tommy heard him in the water closet throwing up. But eventually Stephen settled down and Tommy, on the couch in his tiny living area, tried to get back to sleep. Lucky for him he had the next day off. He was not a good cop when his sleep had been disturbed.

At ten the next morning when Tommy woke up he saw that his nephew was still dead to the world. He went to a drugstore and rang Tracy's house. No answer. He walked a few blocks to Tracy's school, but she wasn't there. Then he rang Russell at the agency, but *he* wasn't there. Tommy didn't know what else to do. He was going out in a little while. Today his sister Kerry was coming into town, and he was supposed to escort her to a Ziegfeld matinee.

Kerry was a stable Bridgeport mother now, married to a well-to-do druggist and able to come to the city whenever she wished for shopping trips, the theater, the latest movies. She even visited Tracy on occasion, though the two sisters still were not close. But Tommy was her chum from childhood, and she looked forward to doing the town from time to time with her favorite brother.

After a light lunch, Tommy dressed in his bedroom, glancing over at Stephen occasionally to see if the lad was stirring. No signs of life. What had happened? he wondered. An adolescent night on the town? Had he been too ashamed to go home and face his parents? Of course he would be. Russ didn't drink much, so what would he think if his son showed up stone blind?

Kerry arrived at one, all dressed up for the city in a green dress and a wide hat festooned with plumes. Tommy groaned inwardly. She'd drive the audience in the theater crazy with that thing on her head.

"We have a problem," Tommy said. "Nephew Stevie's here in the bedroom sleeping off a night on the town."

"The little devil," Kerry laughed. "Tracy know?"

"I can't find Tracy or Russ. They might not even know he's home from Yale."

"Better leave Stevie a note letting him know where we are. Maybe he'll just go back to school. We don't have to tell Tracy a thing."

Tommy nodded. "I'll let him off this once."

They were about to leave the flat when Ruth

Litvak, dressed in mourning, knocked on Tommy's door. Tommy, of course, knew all about David's death, but Kerry didn't yet know what had happened to the husband of her old neighbor, so there were kisses and condolences and it was a while before Ruth was able to state the purpose of her mission.

"I'm looking for Stephen. We thought he might be here."

"Yes, he is," Tommy said. "How did you know?"

"Tracy's at my place. She asked me to talk to him. I assume you know what happened?"

"No," Tommy said. "He just came here dead drunk and went to sleep."

"Oh," Ruth said, looking away.

"What did happen?" Kerry asked.

"Please—can I talk to Stephen?"

"Can't you tell us?" Kerry persisted.

"I'd rather talk to Stephen first if you don't mind."

From behind them came a sleepy voice. "Here I am, Mrs. Litvak." Stephen had slept in his clothes, and he stood in the bedroom door looking like a Bowery bum in rumpled pants and shirt and bare feet.

"Stephen, your mother's very concerned about you."

"*Is* she now. Well, fancy that. Tell her I'm fine. I'm just dandy."

"What on earth *happened?*" asked Kerry.

"You mean you don't know?" Stephen said. "Yesterday I found out I had another father. A Ford man with black hair and a brogue. Life is full of surprises, isn't it?" He yawned and went back to the bedroom muttering, "What happened to my shoes. Can't find my shoes."

Tommy and his sister turned to Ruth who said, "Let's all sit down."

Tommy sat on the floor, leaving his one item of furniture, a small couch, to Ruth and Kerry. Kerry said to Ruth, "Has Stevie gone berserk?"

"He heard something upsetting yesterday."

"What was it?"

"Do you remember Tracy's old assistant Louise?"

"Yeah," Tommy said. "The classy one with the pretty face. Left there a long time ago, didn't she?"

"Yes, and she's not so classy anymore. Yesterday she got the Curtises and Michael Ryan together and she told them that Michael was Stephen's father."

"Michael *Ryan?*" Kerry said. "Our old neighbor Michael? *That* Michael?"

"The same," Ruth murmured. "Of course there's no proof, but Russell believed the woman and he disowned Stephen. You can imagine how Stephen must be feeling, and his mother's worried sick about him."

"Michael is Stephen's father?" Kerry said, shaking her head.

"There's no proof," Ruth repeated. "Louise just claimed that he was."

"Tracy knew this?" Kerry said. "And never told anyone?"

"Tracy *didn't* know," Ruth said.

"How could she not know?" shouted Tommy. "Is

it true or isn't it? Did she and Mike get together or didn't they?"

Ruth said, "I'd rather not discuss this anymore."

Stephen, having found his shoes, came back into the room. "It's simple," he said. "Ma loved two men, see? So she had one. Then she had another. And finally I was born. She never troubled to find out which one I belonged to."

"Watch your tongue!" shouted Tommy. "I won't have you talking that way about your mother!"

Ruth said calmly, "You don't understand, Stephen. Your mother was convinced you were Russell's son."

"How could she be convinced? She slept with two men practically at the same time."

"Now see here—" began Tommy.

Ruth interrupted. "She had very strange notions about what it took to make a baby." Ruth opened her mouth to say more and then broke off. How could she explain it? Who in their right mind would believe it? And how could she go into detail in front of the brother and the son?

"What notions?" Stephen demanded. "What notions did she have?"

Would Tracy want her to explain? Ruth wondered. Would Tracy want this whole incredible story to come out? Yes, if it meant having Stephen's understanding. And after all, this was family Ruth was talking to, not strangers. But if it meant keeping Stephen out of the army Tracy probably wouldn't care if the whole world knew what she had done.

Still, there were other people's feelings to consider, so Ruth altered the story a little.

"Your mother was in love with Russell," Ruth lied. "The two were planning to marry. At about this time Michael Ryan lost his sister. Michael was an old friend, and he was extremely upset." (Ruth did not mention the fact that a murder had been committed.) "Tracy consoled him, and one thing led to another. . . . But your mother didn't think any harm would come of it. She believed—the neighborhood girls had told her—that in order to get with child a woman had to be with a man at least three times. After the incident with Michael happened, Michael went back to New Jersey and your mother married Russell just as she'd planned to. She never dreamed that the neighborhood girls might have been mistaken."

Kerry understood. She too had heard that it took three times before a baby was possible. But Stephen only laughed, a dry sarcastic laugh. "Good try, Mrs. Litvak, but I'm not a dunce."

"It's the truth," Ruth insisted.

"I doubt that very much."

So did Tommy, though he didn't say so. He was too stunned to speak. Michael Ryan?

Kerry said to Stephen, "Of course it's the truth. Do you think your mother would have married Russell if she'd had any doubts?" Kerry was none too fond of her sister, but she knew Tracy was loyal to kin. She could not imagine Tracy living all these years with such a secret. Tracy might lie about certain things,

390

but she'd never do anything that might ruin a child's life. After all, she hadn't wrecked the life of a sister she disliked, so why on earth would she hurt a son she loved?

Stephen said to the group, "I gotta get going."

"Where?" Tommy asked.

"Back to my former residence. Gonna pack up my troubles in my old kit bag."

"And join the army?" Ruth said.

"Yeah."

"But you can't!" Ruth shouted, knowing it was hopeless.

"Before you go," Kerry said to Stephen. "I'd like you to have lunch with me."

"I'm in an awful rush," he muttered.

"Not so rushed that you can't have a bite with your auntie. C'mon, Stevie. The war'll be there a long time." To Tommy she said, "Hope you don't mind if we cancel our plans."

"What?" Tommy had forgotten all about the Follies.

Aunt and nephew left. Tommy poured a whiskey for himself and another for Ruth who, surprising herself, took it.

"Why did she do it?" said Tommy.

"It's hard for you to understand it. You weren't here the day Joe Ryan beat his daughter to death."

"But wasn't she carrying sympathy to extremes?" Tommy remembered Ryan, though he had been grown up when Tommy was still a little boy. He hadn't seen Mike since '95 or '96. A surly bastard, as

391

Tommy recalled. What had Tracy seen in him? He said, "Anyone tell Stevie about that murder?"

"I don't know," Ruth said.

"What'd Russ say when he found out he had no son?"

"Stephen *is* his son."

"Yeah. I guess you're right. Russ did raise him."

"He also disowned him," Ruth reminded Tommy.

"He couldn't 've meant that. I'll talk to him about that." He paused. "He'll divorce Tracy, I guess."

"I imagine so."

"What a mess." Tommy shook his head. "What a mess."

OVER DESSERT in a Broadway restaurant Kerry said to her nephew, "I want to explain it, Steve."

"Don't bother. I already know what you're gonna say. I have to forgive her because she's my mother."

"You don't *have* to forgive her. But you should at least understand it."

"Sorry, but I don't. She's known this since I was born and she never told me."

"She *didn't* know."

"You believe that?"

"She did not know," Kerry said. And then, "What do *you* know about sex, smartie?"

"What I know I'm not gonna discuss with an aunt."

"But I'll wager you don't know a whale of a lot. Did your father talk to you about it?"

"Which father?" quipped Stephen.

"Russell, of course. Did he talk to you?"

"He's a Victorian. I found out things from the fellows at school."

"What did you learn?"

"That if you're intimate with a man you risk a child. Any idiot knows that."

"You said 'risk.' You didn't say 'have.'"

"Sometimes it doesn't work."

"Why?" Kerry asked.

Stephen colored. "You're my *aunt*," he said.

"Pretend I'm an uncle. Why doesn't it work?"

"I don't know. The cells don't always connect. I'm not sure why."

"Suppose someone had a theory. Suppose someone said a woman was barren two days out of every week. Would you believe that was the explanation?"

"Is it?"

"Never mind. Would you believe it?"

"It's as good an explanation as any, I guess."

"Exactly," Kerry said. "But it's not the right one."

"No?"

"No." Kerry's third husband, a pharmacist, had enlightened his wife long ago. She now told Stephen about ovulation and how conception was possible only a few days a month. Stephen colored, but he listened and she said, "Bet you didn't know that."

"No," he admitted.

"And your mother didn't know the facts of life either, Stephen. She believed a story told to her—and to Mary and me—by the street girls. A plausible story too. It's rare that a woman gets with child the first

393

time she tries. The odds are against it. Of course the odds weren't with Tracy that night, but. . . ." she paused. "Now that's the truth, Stephen. I would swear on my life that it was. Your mother would never deliberately do anything that would hurt you later."

But Kerry hadn't softened him. She could see that and in a sense she understood it. Stephen wasn't in a mood for explanations. His life had been upended and he was too bitter right now to think things out. She said. "So you're going to join the army?"

"Yes."

"Will you keep in touch with me? Write to me? Someone's got to know how you are, and if you won't contact your parents—"

"All right," he said impatiently. And he rose to leave.

"Promise to write?"

"Yes, yes."

"Good luck, Stevie."

"Thanks." He left the restaurant without looking back.

"I TALKED to Stephen," Kerry told Tracy later. They were in the parlor at Ruth's.

"*You* talked to him?"

"I know you don't think much of me, big sister, but I've got my good side too."

"I'm sorry," Tracy said hastily. "What did he say?"

"We discussed the facts of life. I told him how we'd

all been misinformed. You, Mary, and me."

"What did he say?"

"It'll take time, but I think he'll come around. Anyway, he's going to write."

"To me?" Tracy's heart leaped.

"To me. I made him promise."

Tracy was crushed. But at least he'd be writing to someone. She said, "I'm glad you made him promise."

Kerry hugged her sister. It was the first time she had ever done so. Ruth, watching them, reflected that in the past it had always been Kerry who was the problem child, while Tracy had been the competent sister, the straightener-out of messes. Now the situations were reversed and Kerry was in the role of arbiter and consoler. To her credit, Kerry didn't remind Tracy about this abrupt change of positions. And she was kinder about accepting faults than Tracy had ever been. Ruth respected her for this.

"I guess he's joining the army," Tracy said dully.

"Yes, he is," said Kerry.

"I'd better pray. I haven't prayed in years. I haven't felt right about it because I wasn't married by a priest. Once I went to confession, though. Just to talk to someone. The priest gave me penance and I said it even though I knew I'd never get to heaven. Oh, I wish I was still in the Church." She looked at her sister. "You're not either, are you?"

"After the bigamy and the divorce? Are you kidding?"

"But Mary is. I'll write to Mary and ask her to pray." She turned to Ruth. "You pray too. In the synagogue, all right?"

Ruth nodded. "All right."

"Tell God—tell Him I'll kill myself if anything happens to Stephen." She thought a moment and then said, "But maybe God won't care if I do."

Chapter Thirty

Stephen joined the army and went into training in Camp Upton, on Long Island. He told no one where he was going for basic, but most New Yorkers were trained there, and Tracy guessed that this was where he was, though she was afraid to write to him.

Russell left his business in the hands of his partner and went out to Nevada to establish residency for a divorce. In New York the only grounds were adultery, and since Tracy wasn't committing it now, he had no recourse but to go out of state. He had been deeply depressed and had considered ending it all, but in a sense things were easier than they had ever been. The son he hadn't understood was no longer his responsibility. The wife who had given him so many problems was gone. His financial problems had cleared up overnight, since he didn't have to worry about supporting a wife or a son at college. Now he could contemplate selling his share of the agency and using the money to support himself while he devoted his full time to writing. He would scribble away his twilight years, perhaps with a new woman at his side.

Before Russell left, Tommy had gone over to see him.

He had said he understood Russell's anger, but surely Russ could see that it wasn't the boy's fault. Stephen might not be Russell's natural son, but he was still a son, the same as if Russell had adopted him. Since Russell had had a couple of weeks to get over the shock, couldn't he go out to camp and see the boy?

Russell's reply astounded Tommy. "Why should I see him? He's not mine. I should have realized that long ago, but I wasn't using my head."

"But you *raised* him, Russ."

"So I did. But I thought I was raising someone who was only half Irish trash. Now I find out it was a hundred percent. By the way, I checked an old newspaper file. Did you know Stephen's grandfather was a murderer?"

Tommy turned and strode out of the plush brownstone parlor.

Tracy moved in with Ruth. She had cleaned her things out of what was now only Russell's house and sent some of it up to the house Pat occupied in Massachusetts. The rest she kept at Ruth's, where she sleepwalked through the days, occasionally rousing herself to go over and supervise the school. At night she cried herself to sleep.

Michael remained in New Jersey. He had bought another house (the one in Michigan was rented), and he settled in there while going ahead with plans for a network of New Jersey filling stations. Curiosity about the son he had never known made him tense and short-tempered most of the time, and he drank a good deal. He wasn't sure if he ought to establish a

398

relationship with the boy. Of course Russell had disowned him, but Michael didn't think the man would stick to that resolve. Still, he didn't know for sure, and if Russell didn't want the boy, Michael did. He wrote a letter to Ruth, asking if she knew where Stephen might be. She replied that he had joined the army and was probably at Camp Upton. The rest of her letter concerned the fall weather and the hope that the war would end soon. There was no mention of Tracy.

One day in November Michael wrote a letter to Stephen. He'd been drinking heavily that day and he wrote it on impulse, saying that he would like to talk to Stephen if possible and would meet him in New York at a time that was mutually convenient. He sent the letter to Pvt. Stephen Curtis, Camp Upton, New York, unable to give details in the address because he didn't know the regiment number, company letter, or anything else. He half-expected the note to come back ADDRESSEE UNKNOWN and so was surprised to receive a reply saying yes, Stephen would meet him in New York. The letter named a bar on the West Side. Stephen had a furlough next week and would meet Michael on Saturday at about seven o'clock in the evening.

Michael needed several stiff drinks to loosen him up for this encounter, and he drank them at the bar in gulps while he waited for Stephen. The bar, though on the fringes of the Tenderloin district, was definitely working class, and Michael could not understand why a Yale man would choose such a place unless he had stumbled in drunk one night by accident. It catered to neighborhood laborers who all seemed to know one another.

In a corner a rheumy-eyed piano player banged out ragtime tunes. At the tables men joked with a few shopworn women who looked like habitués of the place. Everyone here seemed to be a heavy drinker. Maybe they were just tanking up for the time when these places would be closed or serving Coca-Cola. Wartime prohibition would soon be going into effect, and temperance supporters were threatening to extend the dry period into peacetime as well. This Michael would have to see. A whole nation cold sober. It would last about ten minutes, he thought.

Stephen walked in the door, dressed in uniform. Michael signaled him, and as Stephen made his way past the tables a man shouted, "Hey there, doughboy, gonna go see them mamzelles? Kill a Fritzie for me, will ya soldier?" The pianist began to play "Over There," and Stephen nodded acknowledgment, forcing a smile.

"Hello, Stephen," Michael slid off the bar stool and held out his hand. Stephen took it as Michael said, "Would you like to sit at a table?"

"The bar is fine," Stephen said, taking a stool.

"Are you hungry? Bartender tells me they have good sandwiches here."

"Yes, as a matter of fact. I'm sick of monkey meat."

"What's that?" Michael asked. "Canned beef?"

"Uh huh. They must've saved it from the Spanish-American War." He took out a pack of cigarettes and

400

lit one. To Michael he said, "Want a butt?"

"I have my own. Thanks anyway."

The bartender took Stephen's order. A double whiskey straight and a turkey sandwich. The kid too was a drinker, Michael observed. It must run in the family.

"What do you think of the army?" Michael asked, not knowing what else to say at this point.

"Not much. Lousy hours, lousy grub, lousy C.O."

"Sounds wonderful."

"It'll be better when we get to France. What did you want to talk to me about, sir?"

"Nothing in particular. Just wanted to get to know you."

"No offense, sir, but what's the point?"

Michael was taken aback. "You're my son."

"Biologically maybe, but for all intents and purposes no. Don't take it the wrong way, sir. It's not your fault that you don't know me, but that's the way it is."

Michael winced. Then he said, "Is your legal father staying in touch with you?"

"Are you kidding? I haven't heard from him since that day."

"Then why should you object to your natural father wanting to see you?"

"I don't object," Stephen said. "I don't care one way or the other."

"You've made that clear," Michael said sharply. "I get the idea. All right?"

The men sat in sullen silence for a while, smoking

and concentrating on their drinks. Michael was by now pretty high on the whiskey. He usually knew how to pace himself and rarely got drunk, but he was now at the point where he really didn't care how stoned he got. The hotel was nearby, and he didn't have to worry about getting home, so he ordered another double.

The piano player was launching into maudlin Irish ballads. After a while Stephen broke the silence to remark, "There's a poem by Chesterton goes, 'For the great Gaels of Ireland/Are the men that God made mad/For all their wars are merry/And all their songs are sad.'"

Michael nodded. "Are you merry about this war?"

"Not hilarious exactly."

"Then why're you going?"

Stephen shrugged. "Adventure, patriotism. And the skirts, of course."

"Ah yes, Mademoiselle from Armentières. I tried to find her once."

"You were there?"

"In July and August."

"You weren't the one Ma was talking about, were you? She said she'd talked to someone who'd been there then. Told her a lot of atrocity stories."

"I was the one. We're both friends of the Litvaks. I guess the stories didn't scare you, huh?"

"Obviously not," Stephen said. "Have you seen a lot of my mother since the night I was—what's a good word?—started?"

Michael frowned, but he answered the question.

"No. I lived in Michigan for years. But as I said we're both friends of the Litvaks, so sometimes when I went to see them your mother was there too."

"And there was nothing between you all those years?"

"No," lied Michael. "It might interest you to know that most of the time I saw your mother it was at a funeral, a wake, or just after someone died."

"How Irish," Stephen said.

"Isn't it, though?"

"That's when I was conceived, wasn't it? After a funeral?"

"Before," Michael said.

"I remember that part. That fat slob telling my father to look up some date in a paper. Your mother died or something?"

"My sister."

"And my mother was comforting you?"

Michael nodded.

"So you'd say maybe you were a little out of your head?"

"You could say that," The boy wanted to be reassured that Michael hadn't taken advantage of Tracy with malice aforethought.

"My Aunt Kerry said Ma didn't know the facts of life too well."

"Oh?"

"She thought you had to be with a man three times before you could have a baby."

"She did?"

"Hard to believe, huh?"

Michael nodded. Everything about Tracy was hard to believe.

Stephen said, "So it never occurred to her that I could be yours. She thought it was impossible. That's what my aunt said. Do you believe that?"

"I don't know what to believe." Michael shook his head. "Who else besides Kerry knows what happened?"

"Mrs. Litvak and Uncle Tommy. I don't know who else. I haven't seen anyone."

"Not even your mother?"

"No."

"Does she know you're in the army?"

"I don't know."

"But she must," Michael said. "Ruth was the one who told me."

"Then she knows," Stephen said.

The piano player was now singing "Danny Boy." Michael turned and listened for a moment. Often when he heard this he remembered how Tracy's grandfather had sung it that day on the stoop.

"Strange," Michael said, "That song—and me seeing you off to war."

"Is that what the song's about? I always wondered."

"There are a lot of different explanations. Some say the son is leaving Ireland for America during the Famine. Some say he's going off to war. Some say it's a father seeing him off. Others a mother. And a few think it's a girl saying good-bye to a sweetheart."

"Which do you think it is?"

"A father seeing his son off to war. I've always thought that."

The piano player sang,

It's I'll be here in sunshine or in shadow
Oh Danny boy, oh Danny boy, I love you so.

"I'll have another," Michael said to the bartender.

"You, soldier?" the bartender asked Stephen.

"I'm still working on this one."

But should ye come when all the flowers are
    dying
If I am dead as dead I well may be,
Ye'll come and find the place where I am ly-
    ing,
And kneel and say an "Ave" there for me . . .

Michael picked up his fresh drink. "Tracy's grandfather sang it that day," he murmured. "I remembered I walked away. Knew I'd never be saying an 'Ave' for my father."

"What do you mean, sir?"

Michael realized that the boy didn't know. Hadn't that harpy in the boardinghouse said something about it? No, she'd only mentioned the death of a child and a date. Apparently Stephen had never inquired further.

"Why are you looking at me so strangely, sir?"

Michael shrugged. "No reason."

"Think maybe you've had too much to drink?"

"I *know* I have," Michael said.

"Maybe you better go home. Think I'll be shoving off too."

"Where're you staying?" Michael asked.

"Don't know yet."

"Let me get you a hotel room."

"No, thanks." Stephen stood up.

"Don't go!" Michael said in a harsh, pained voice. Startled, Stephen sat down again.

"You were just gonna walk out like that? I don't even *know* you, Steve."

"I thought we agreed it was pointless."

"*You* did. I didn't. *I* didn't agree." Michael pressed a hand to his head. He was dizzy from all the drinking and sick at the thought that this boy was going to walk out of here and into the trenches of France.

"You all right, sir?"

"You're not going to go off like that. Not like that. At least let me say good-bye." Michael blinked. The room was spinning around.

"You look pretty sick, sir. Let me get you back to your hotel."

"Don't you want me to say good-bye? I wanted my father to say it. Wanted him to say—you know, whenever I went anywhere—wanted him to say, 'Take care of yourself, son.'"

Stephen was only half-listening and had the impression that Michael was fondly reminiscing

406

about his father. "Just take my arm, sir. Can you step down?"

"FRESH AIR," Stephen said. "Feels good after all the smoke in that place."

"Yes."

They were walking toward Michael's hotel on Broadway. Michael was weaving slightly, but he didn't feel quite so drunk anymore. Stephen was acting strangely, he thought. No longer the brusque young smart aleck, the boy was being very solicitous all of a sudden. Michael didn't know why. He couldn't even remember leaving the bar. The last thing he could remember was asking Stephen not to leave.

"What happened in there?" he asked his son. "Did I pass out?"

"No. Don't you remember?"

"I'm afraid not."

"You just had a little too much. You didn't pass out or anything. You were telling me about your father and you— "

"My father? Jesus Christ!"

"Sounded like you missed him a lot."

Michael started to laugh and Stephen looked over in surprise. "Did I say something funny, sir?"

"Yes. Well, no, not really. It's just that my father wasn't a nice man. I can't imagine what I might have said."

"I didn't listen too hard," Stephen admitted. "I

was trying to get you on your feet. What do you mean he wasn't a nice man?"

"I'd rather not explain it."

"I wish you would."

"Why?"

"I don't know. I'm curious. He was my grandfather."

Michael sighed. The boy was bound to find out about it anyway. It might as well be from him. "Come up to my hotel room. You'll need to sit down for this, I think."

STEPHEN sat in a straight-backed chair and Michael on the edge of the bed. Outside it had begun to rain, and the downpour slapped against the hotel window. Stephen learned about Joe Ryan, about Michael's exile, and finally about the murder of the little girl. Michael spoke dispassionately and wound up by saying, "I didn't plan to tell you, but you would've heard about it eventually."

Stephen nodded. "And that was when you and my mother—"

"Yes. That night. She was very good to me and my family. Arranged the funeral, made sure my brothers were taken care of, and she—I walked her home that night and we went to her flat. That's when it happened."

"Did you love her?"

"Very much."

"Did you want to marry her?"

408

"Yes."

"And she wanted him?"

"Apparently."

"Even after that night?"

Michael nodded.

"I don't understand. Didn't she love you?"

"I don't know. I think in a way she did. But she had Curtis too."

"Where did you go after that?"

"To New Jersey, then to Michigan. I married out there. I'm divorced now. Did I tell you I had a daughter?"

"No." Stephen was surprised.

"She looks like you a little. Same eyes, I think. She's thirteen now."

Stephen shook his head. "I'm getting hit with so many things. A new father, a new family history, and now a half sister."

"Plus aunts and uncles," Michael reminded him.

"Yes."

"Does it bother you, knowing about your grand-father?"

"Yes, but only because of how it's affected you. What you said in the bar about your father—what you meant was, you *wished* he had been like that."

Michael nodded, and Stephen bit his lip. They had a lot in common, he and his real dad. Stephen had sometimes wished for a different Russell.

"I'm going to get you a room," Michael said. "There's only one bed here."

"It's all right. I'll sleep on the floor."

"Don't be ridiculous. I can afford a bed for you. Do you have to be back in camp early tomorrow?"

"I've got another twelve hours' leave."

"I've got my car here. I'll drive you back in the morning. Unless you have plans. Skirts, as you call them."

Stephen smiled. "Nothing important." He cleared his throat. "I'm glad we met, sir."

"So'm I. But Stephen—"

"Yes?"

"I think you should see your mother."

"Oh, please."

"Is it so difficult?"

"Why should you care? Aren't you angry with her too?"

"Intensely. But I know what it's like to be a parent."

"It's just that I lost respect. I used to respect her so much and then—"

"She's still the same person," Michael said.

"Yes. Well. But it'll be hard for me to see her just now."

"Then write."

Stephen nodded. "I'll think about it."

"I'll get you that room now."

"All right, sir."

"Don't call me, sir. Please."

"Shall I call you Mike?"

"Dad's what my daughter calls me."

"I'd feel funny."

410

"Whatever you prefer, then. Mike's all right."

"It's just that I used to call the other one Dad."

"No need to explain. Anything but 'sir.'"

"I'll think of something."

Michael grinned, crossed the room, and clapped Stephen on the shoulder.

Chapter Thirty-One

The winter of 1917–18 was wretchedly cold and dismal. David Litvak's murderer was found and pronounced criminally insane. The killer turned out not to be a member of a fanatical group or even to be associated with the death of the German grocer. He was a garden-variety lunatic who thought that Jews and the Jewish press would bring down the wrath of the Almighty and subject New York and its environs to a mammoth tidal wave. Ruth sank into a deep depression because her husband hadn't even died in the cause of human rights. He had died, it seemed, for nothing.

In early January President Wilson made a speech quickly dubbed the Fourteen Points. In it, his recommendations for peace were stated. If Germany would give back this, and Turkey would give back that, and other belligerents would just behave themselves, then peace would come and an association of nations could be formed, and serenity would settle over the troubled planet. Wilson was a good and idealistic man, but many thought he did not understand human nature, for the war continued unabated and seemed likely to get worse in the West because Russia, now under Lenin and the Bolsheviks, had made a separate peace, releasing the Germans for other fronts.

There were coal shortages in the land, and voluntary food rationing went into effect under the direction of a man named Hoover. Roommates Ruth and Tracy grumbled, but after all, they were Americans even though they disapproved of the war, so they tried out the wheatless Mondays and meatless Tuesdays. They had no trouble with the porkless Thursdays, since Ruth and the children were kosher and Tracy would have felt unclean eating the *trayf* in front of them. They were also stern with the children if they wasted food and were guilty of evoking the spectacle of the starving Belgian children if Josh didn't finish an apple or Sarah turned up her nose at oatmeal. They drew the line, however, at Anglicizing the names of German foods. To call sauerkraut "liberty cabbage" struck both Tracy and Ruth as crazy. Another patriotic task was to save peach and plum pits, which through some mysterious alchemy ended up as charcoal filters for gas masks. Both children, in their initial exuberance, ate their way through enough fruit to give them chronic diarrhea for a week. After that the practice was discontinued.

The presence of Ruth's children helped a little in getting Tracy's mind off her own child. She hadn't seen Stephen since September and would not be likely to see him again until the war was over—if he came back. With Ruth she took the children to puppet shows and liberty loan rallies, but her heart wasn't in it and the children soon sensed this. The school was another diversion for Tracy. It still brought in money, and she and Ruth earned enough between them to hire a daytime cook and house-keeper. The woman doubled as an afterschool companion for the children and provided the needed cheer in their lives.

When Russell filed for divorce in Nevada, Tracy did not contest. Michael remained in New Jersey. Tommy dropped by often, and Kerry came to town every week. One day she reported that she'd had a note from Stephen saying that he was now in France, was healthy, and hadn't seen any action.

"Did he mention me?" asked Tracy.

"In the letter?" edged her sister.

"*Did* he?"

"Well, there wasn't room. It was so rushed. I just made him promise that he'd write me, and he kept the promise. Otherwise why would he write to me?"

Tracy cried that night as she'd been crying for months, but now that she knew he was over there she became an avid newspaper reader. When the bulk of the Americans went into line and the casualties began cropping up in the papers, she was a nervous wreck from morning till night. By June, however, they hadn't heard bad news about any of the local boys. Tracy said to Ruth that maybe the New Yorkers were a bunch of klutzes and wouldn't it be wonderful if the generals decided that city boys weren't suited to

414

that rough sort of life? Ruth humored her along as best she could, neglecting to remind Tracy that some city boys had lived rougher lives than westerners. She also talked her friend out of reading the paper, saying that bad news would be likely to come via telegram, and why should Tracy torment herself like this? So by summer Tracy had stopped perusing papers, but she hadn't stopped thinking of what Michael had told her of the war. Many of her dreams were nightmares in which Stephen was bleeding to death and being eaten alive by rats in some trench.

In June Tracy finally got a letter from her son. It was short and not very personal, but it buoyed her spirits as nothing Ruth had ever seen before.

Dear Ma,
   Sorry I haven't written, but I've been so busy. It's no use explaining what I've been busy with since the censors will black most of that out. But I'm in a quiet sector and healthy even though the chow isn't so hot, and I'm pretty sure the war will end soon. Take care and don't worry too much.
      Love,
      Stephen.

First Tracy cried with joy, drenching half a dozen handkerchiefs. He'd used the word "love." He'd used that word! After that, she paced around the apartment, too excited to sit. Finally she decided to dance. She actually turned on the Victrola and danced the tango and the foxtrot with Josh and then with Sarah. Ruth thought that Tracy looked twenty again, smiling, radiant, all high color and dimples. After singing two Irving Berlin tunes, Tracy said that she and Ruth must be getting out more. David's partner, Al (now Ruth's partner), had been smitten with the opinionated widow for months, and Tracy thought that since the anniversary of David's death would be coming up soon, Ruth should consider an end to mourning and the possibility of marrying again.

"Marry Al?" Ruth bellowed. "Another newspaperman? Another target for some crackpot anti-Semite? Not on your life! And besides, what would happen to our working-girl ménage here?"

"I'll take my own apartment. I'll need one for when Stephen gets home." As she talked, Tracy was wrapping a scarf, some underwear and other items she'd been planning to send him as soon as she had his address.

Ruth said, "Stephen'll be nineteen when he comes home. If he doesn't go to college, he'll certainly marry."

"So I'll live alone then. I've done it once before."

How well Ruth remembered. And managed to get herself into a predicament that would alter the lives of four people and make *The Perils of Pauline* look as dull as an accountant's ledger.

But moments after planning these changes, Tracy suddenly crashed to earth. "Ruth?"

"What is it?"

"Do you think Stephen will come home?"

"I hope so."

"Sometimes I'm afraid to be too happy. I think God's going to punish me if I'm too happy."

"Are you Jewish?" Ruth said drolly.

"Be serious. It haunts me. Dancing with the children, singing and making plans. I think God may be expecting me to—you know—do penance. And I will. I'll do anything if only Stephen would—"

"Since when have you become so concerned about God? You ignored Him cheerfully enough all these years."

"Hush! Don't remind Him!"

"Tracy, I think you're crazy."

"I'm so scared. I'm so *scared*, Ruth."

As Tracy talked, the son she was worrying about was sitting in a café, his arm around a raven-haired young lady. It was only an overnight pass in this charming French village, but he was trying to make every minute count. He was here with some buddies who had also been deloused for the occasion, and they felt civilized for the first time in weeks with their clean bodies and uniforms, clean fingernails, clean-shaven faces. The girl was a British WAAC. Three years older than Stephen, she had lost a husband in Flanders two years before and was, in her words, "determined to carry on the fight." A beautiful and patriotic young woman whom he had met just an hour before, she touched Stephen's heart with her emotion. While rowdies at other tables sang dirty

417

verses of "Mademoiselle from Armentières," Stephen listened to Elizabeth recite the most popular of the war poems, written by a Canadian soldier named John D. McCrae.

In Flanders fields the poppies grow
Between the crosses, row on row,
That mark our place; and in the sky
The larks still bravely singing, fly
Scarce heard amid the guns below.

We are the dead. Short days ago
We lived, felt dawn, saw sunset glow,
Loved, and were loved, and now we lie
In Flanders fields.

Take up our quarrel with the foe:
To you from failing hands we throw
The torch; be yours to hold it high.
If ye break faith with us who die
We shall not sleep, though poppies grow
In Flanders fields.

Listening to this, Stephen felt his eyes begin to fill up. Patriotism had been drummed into him in the States, but none of it had the effect of this simple poem, which he, like Elizabeth, knew by heart. Now he sipped his whiskey and brooded upon the meaning of the words while gazing into the young woman's eyes. Others might think it indecent to be wondering what her lips felt like while he was supposed to be concerning himself with taking up the torch of the slain soldiers, but Stephen was getting accustomed to conflicting emotions of this sort and recognized that there was a place for ideals and also a place for lust. In one mood he could see himself as an all-wise President of the United States, in another as a lover powerless in the grip of his own carnal desires, and in yet another as a soldier pitting himself against the forces of evil and triumphing over cowardice as he avenged the dead of Ypres and Verdun. He had even learned to turn his semi-bastard state into an experience and had convinced himself that there was a reason for what had happened to him—a reason that would ultimately make him, if not a better man, at least a more complete one. As for his mother and his fathers, actual and legal, they too had played a part in nature's grand design, the meaning of which was not yet clear but the experience of which was profound. As a soldier about to go into battle, Stephen existed in a state of heightened awareness; the important thing was to feel—to experience—to see all life as a drama of importance. For the present, the drama consisted of this poem, this girl, this night . . .

"Stephen?"

"Yes?"

"What are you thinking about?"

"That poem—and you."

"You're awfully serious for a Yank."

"Am I supposed to be flattered by that or insulted?"

"I mean I don't see your type often."

"What type do you usually see?" And why did she see so many that she could type them?

She said, "The eat, drink, and be merry boys."

"Tell me more."

"Don't ask questions," she said.

He decided not to. What did he care about the others? What mattered was now.

The soldiers in the corner were getting drunker and bawdier. Mademoiselle from Armentières had by this time gone through many adventures. Stephen got a kick out of this song, as all the doughboys did, but he wondered if it wasn't too rough for someone like Elizabeth.

"I'll tell 'em to stop," Stephen said.

"Who?" asked Elizabeth.

"Those louts over there. They can't even rhyme."

"Oh, don't. They're harmless enough."

Elizabeth was giggling, and Stephen, after his initial surprise, gave way to laughter too. He understood her now. She was a female version of himself. Here on the edge of oblivion, she could respond with equal emotion to the image of poppies in a field and to the idea of couples giving each other indecent but heady pleasures.

"Where are you staying, Elizabeth?"

"In a *pension* with three other girls."

"Think they'd miss you if you didn't come back tonight?"

"I doubt it."

"I've got a room of my own."

"They told me the Yanks were rich."

"Will you go there with me?"

"You're young, you know."

"Not that young." Though in the past he had paid cash for such adventures.

He came equipped. The army had warned them about disease many times. He was quick in his execution of the act, and she was quick in her response. Then they lay with their arms around each other.

"Stephen?"

"Ummmm."

"I wasn't always like this."

"Don't explain."

"Just thought you should know."

"I'm not always like this either," he said.

"But it's different for a man."

"Why should it be different? I'm beginning to see that men and women are pretty much alike."

Dear Ma,

I'm sitting here under a tree "somewhere in France," as they say. It's hotter than Hades and I've emptied my canteen three times. Thanks so much for all the gifts and treats. I loved the chocolates best, of course. And please thank Mrs. Litvak for the books she included in the last package.

I want to tell you that things have changed for

me. I've had a lot of experiences and I learned a few things and I wanted to be sure you knew how I felt.

When you go into the army, you're stripped of your uniqueness. You're just a body and there's nothing special about you anymore. Everything you were as a civilian is gone-eradicated—and you're given a rank that you can't step out of no matter what—except by promotion, of course.

All this came as a terrific shock to me. And though I've more or less become used to the life, it wasn't until recently that I began to associate this state of things with life as it must have been for you in the days when you were poor. If your world was anything like the world of the army, if you ever had the feeling that there was no way to get out, if you thought that the most important thing in the world was survival but lived with the thought that everything you valued could, without any reason, be taken away, then I understand an awful lot I didn't realize before. I can understand the search for joy wherever you found it, the wanting to get away from the truth of the world. Mostly I understand that men and women aren't so different and that they behave the same way, especially in hard times.

I don't know if you're going to make sense of this letter, but I wanted you to know that I love you and miss you and most of all that I've grown

up enough to understand you.
    Love always,
    Stephen

Tracy's reaction to this surprised Ruth. She had expected cries of joy and the dancing of a lilt at the very least, but that was not what Ruth saw. Though Tracy had been moved to tears by Stephen's words, she was also filled with terror and read into several lines a portent of doom. "Wanted to be sure you knew how I felt . . ." (Just in case he couldn't come back to tell her in person?) ". . . wanted you to know that I love you. . . ." (Because he wouldn't have the chance to tell her later?)

"Oh, Ruth, he's not coming back. I know he's not!"

"Can't you look at the bright side, Tracy? He *understands* you now. This nightmare is over."

"It'll never be over. God's making me pay. He's fattening the calf, don't you see?"

"The *what?*"

"Building me up, filling me with hope so that the sacrifice will be that much greater. . . ."

She had gone round the bend, Ruth thought. And she spoke to her as a child. "Tracy, what's he making you pay *for?*"

"For hurting Michael, for marrying Russell, all those things."

Of all those things Tracy thought her worst sin was duping Russell. "I did it deliberately. Schemed and trapped him."

423

"You're not the first woman who's done that and you won't be the last. Anyway, all men and women misrepresent to a certain degree."

"What do you mean?"

"They charm each other before marriage, don't show their true selves. When I compare my behavior before I married David to my behavior afterward—"

"But that wasn't the worst of it," Tracy said. "The worst was that the baby wasn't even his son."

"Stephen *was* Russell's son. Biology doesn't make a relationship like that. Caring does. And if you ask me, Russell's disowning him was a much more serious crime than all your sins rolled into one. To drop Stephen just like that, without any reason, as though he'd never known him—*that* tells you what sort of man Russell was."

"I made him that way."

"No, you *didn't*. He *was* that way. He's a cold fish and he's been one all his life. You tried to be a good wife. I saw that when you moved in with the walrus. I saw that when you tried to convince him that advertising *was* a good field. And all those nights you attended the theater when you didn't feel like going. And entertained his friends, doing the lady act. You were as good a wife as anyone could have been to a man like that." She paused. "And if I hear one more word about sin and fatted calves, I'm going to send you to a psychoanalyst."

"A what?"

"It's like an alienist." Ruth explained the new word. "Have you ever heard of Sigmund Freud?"

424

"You mean the one who writes those dirty books?"

Ruth sighed. "Scientific, not dirty. Now not another word about sin, do you hear? You're no more a sinner than the rest of us. I know you'd prefer to outdo us all, even at that, but you can't. And since you can't, you're no more subject to damnation than anyone else. You have as much right to Stephen as I do to Josh and Sarah. Understand?"

Tracy nodded, but she hadn't understood a word.

Chapter Thirty-Two

In August Ruth received a surprise visitor at the paper. Michael was in town on business, still driving a flivver instead of the more expensive cars he could well have afforded. Ruth hadn't seen him for almost a year, though he had rung her up occasionally just to see how she was doing. He was still in New Jersey, still building gasoline pump stations left and right and planning to extend his network to upstate New York as well.

"I've never even seen one of your stations," she said. "You'll have to take me on a tour. I suppose you're rich as Rockefeller now."

"I do all right," he said.

"What brings you to tenement heaven?"

"Haven't seen you in months. I stopped by the flat, but you weren't there. A neighbor told me Tracy's living there now."

"Yes, she is. Almost a year."

"How are you, Ruth?"

Ruth shrugged, and for a while they made small talk about food scarcities and the weather. Finally he asked, "Do you hear from Stephen?"

"Tracy got a letter from him the other day."

He nodded. "I hear from him too."

"*You* do?"

"I had a drink with him last fall before he shipped out. Now we write once in a while." He paused. "I'm glad he and Tracy straightened it out."

"So'm I."

"Does she read the paper much?"

"Once in a while. I've talked her out of it."

"The Seventy-seventh—Steve's division—was in that fighting on the Vesle."

"That awful French river?"

Michael nodded.

"Well, she hasn't received any telegrams, so I assume he survived it." She paused. "Why are you really here, Mike? Just checking up on the merry widow or worrying about a son with someone else who cares about him?"

"Shrewd to the end aren't you, Litvak?"

"You'd be better off worrying with the mother."

Michael said nothing.

"Never forgive her, huh?"

Michael shrugged. "I don't know."

"She didn't know he was yours. I swear, Mike, she didn't."

Michael studied her face for a moment. "Maybe not."

"She'd feel better if she had your understanding."

"Maybe." He shrugged. "But tell me, how are you? I'm apt to go back to Jersey without ever finding out."

427

"Are you in a rush?"

"I'm always in a rush."

"You work too hard, Mike."

This was true, he thought. He was as busy these days as Bernard Baruch. One of the new war measures was something called daylight savings time, and it gave Michael still more hours in which to labor. Unaccustomed to leisure, he didn't know how to use it, even though he now had money enough to live like a gentleman. Instead of enjoying the twelve-room mansion he had bought last year, he used the house only for sleeping and spent the rest of his days in his Newark office, at the stations he owned or was building, or in New York on purchasing trips. The only time he went home early was when he had a woman to entertain. And tonight there was no one.

"Maybe I do work too hard," he said. "When you're finished here, I'll take you to dinner."

He came back to pick her up at six, and they went to an Italian place, taking a quiet corner table. Throughout the meal and the first bottle of red wine they reminisced about the old days. But at some point during the second bottle Ruth grew morose. She said that David had died for nothing and that she was having a hard time trying to absorb it. Could Michael try to make some sense of it?

"I wish I could," he said.

"I should have known better than to ask. You never were much of a rationalizer. The things that happened to you, Mike—how did you explain them?"

"I didn't."

"No God's mysterious ways and all that?"

He shook his head. "If I'd really believed in God—I've never been too sure either way—I wouldn't have thought of His ways as mysterious. I would've thought of 'em as vindictive."

Ruth laughed dryly. Every so often Michael's young self would crop out again. Though he was dressed impeccably now and usually soft-spoken, she could see and hear in him occasionally the ragged dark-eyed youth who had leaned against the lamp-post, his hands shoved in his pockets, his expression always cynical except when he and Dave talked about machines. She thought she understood Michael's love of the mechanical. Machines had neither human weaknesses nor the too-mysterious ways of the divine.

Eventually the talk got back to Tracy as Ruth had known it would. Michael asked if she was divorced and how she was getting on. Ruth answered truthfully, "She's not the woman you remember, Mike. The divorce, the worry about Stephen—it's breaking her."

He frowned and lit a cigarette. "I didn't think anything could break her."

"You were wrong." But Ruth made no more attempts to explain Tracy to Michael or to secure his forgiveness. She went on to talk about the world situation while Michael nodded blankly and continued to drink. Tracy broken? he thought. It was hard to believe. He remembered the first time he had met her, how she had tried to fight off that hooligan in the alley. He hadn't realized then that he was attracted to her, hadn't realized it for years. But gradually it had happened. And after Dave and Ruth had married, he began to think of Tracy and himself as the other couple. It had been foolish of him, he now realized. The same qualities that had made Tracy fight the slums had driven her to expect more of life than a flat in New Jersey. And he couldn't have had it both ways, couldn't have expected in the same woman both a drive to succeed and a docile acceptance of the only life he could have offered her then. But he had dreamed as the young will dream, had been as irrational as any of them. And that first time when she'd slept with him he was sure the happy ending was at hand. She had said she loved him. She had said, "Stay with me."

He had held on to those words during the days he was setting up the family in Jersey. He'd held on even though she had said she would have to think over his proposal. And then had come Dave's letter saying she was married. The news had numbed him, but at least it had been decisive, had turned him from a dreamer into a realist.

For a long time Michael had hated her, and when the moment came to choose a wife he had chosen someone very unlike Tracy. Meg had been a gentle, accepting girl who would not admit to her own unhappiness. It was he who took her back to the farm she missed so desperately and he who, years later,

430

played the villain in the divorce suit so that she could marry a man she really loved. Meg had been appalled. "But you *can't* say you deserted me. That isn't true. And you *can't* have photographers following you into a brothel. It would hurt your *reputation*."

"Do you want to marry the man or don't you?"

"Yes, but I'm the villain, not you, Mike."

"No judge would ever take you for a villain. I, on the other hand, won't give him a moment's doubt."

Ruth was saying, "Wilson thinks the whole world is as idealistic as he is. But the ugly truth is that everybody's leaders are conniving. America needs a conniving President to get along with all the other shrewdies."

"Um," Michael said.

"Aren't you listening, Irish? Or are you thinking of all your gasoline stations?"

Michael smiled. That was his life, all right. Gasoline stations. One trait he and Tracy had in common was their single-mindedness, though she had never understood what it was about cars that intrigued him. He wasn't sure he knew either, though he liked to tell himself that he, like Ford, had a vision of a world in which mankind's burdens would be lightened by the existence of cheap serviceable vehicles. But he had been less concerned with mankind than with power. Where Tracy's motive had been money, his had been mastery. Dave had once said to him, "You were sick of having the world drive you, so you decided to drive the world for a change."

Ruth was saying, ". . . thinks a powerful offense on all fronts could end it, but Al thinks it may go on as long as the Hundred Years' War."

The war, Michael thought. One situation he couldn't master, control—the fate of Stephen. Was that what had finally broken Tracy? Being in a situation over which she had no control? She, who had controlled things very well since she had been fourteen years old?

What a shock it had been, finding out he had a son. And the corollary of that: finding out that in a fundamental sense he had married Tracy after all. Today he had finally been persuaded that perhaps she hadn't lied to him that day in the boardinghouse. Thinking over the times he had seen Tracy since Stephen's birth he could not recall her ever giving any hints that she believed Michael was Stephen's father. Tracy was not one to hide her emotions well. Surely she would have betrayed something if she'd known. Yet when he had said he was glad he had a daughter who could not fight she hadn't in any way hinted that he had a son as well. To the contrary, she had glared at him as though to say, "Don't you dare brag about your good fortune!"

No, she couldn't have known. But it had taken him a year to believe it, and at that he had needed to hear Ruth confirm it today. A year was a long time, though, and so much of it had been filled with rage against her that it wasn't easy to break the pattern. Even now, though he no longer condemned her for withholding the truth, he cursed her for her stupidity. What had Stephen told him—that she thought it took three times before a baby was possible? The most moronic streetwalker knew better than that. Tracy's education in all areas had been sketchy, but she'd been so clever about business and money that he would not have expected her to be such an idiot about equally crucial matters. A child-woman, that was what she was. Maybe because her childhood had been wrenched from her so abruptly and she'd spent so much of her life trying to recapture it, even going so far as to move the family to a town like the one she'd been kicked out of. It was different with him. He'd never really known what it was to be a child.

Ruth said, "Mike, you've been daydreaming for fifteen minutes. That's not your way, so one of two things is possible. Either you're drunk or I'm a bore. Therefore you must be drunk."

He grinned. "I was thinking about Tracy."

"Oh?"

"You said she was broken. I don't believe it. She always had the resilience of a child."

"Maybe she'll have it yet. If Stephen comes home. But if he doesn't . . ." Ruth shrugged.

"Why is she living with you? Doesn't she have alimony?"

"No."

"But Russell never proved the boy wasn't his, did he? And even if he had—"

"She waived alimony."

Michael's mouth fell open. *"Tracy?"*

"It is rather surprising, I know."

"But why?"

"Guilt over what she did to Russell. Or what she thought she did. If you ask me, she paid for her mistake ten times over by being married to the lout."

Guilt, Michael thought. That was something that Tracy hadn't wasted time feeling in the past. Certainly not a guilt of such magnitude that she would sacrifice a major source of income. A new, self-effacing Tracy was being revealed to him tonight, and Michael didn't like the picture he was getting. In spite of her faults he preferred the cocky girl he had known. He remembered the old days when he had seen her walk up the street. She hadn't been tall, and she hadn't been a great beauty. Her clothes had been shabby, and she had not yet acquired any taste. But she had always been sure of herself, and she'd seemed attractive to him for those very reasons. Most men said they didn't admire that kind of woman. They liked them weak. They were supposed to enjoy it when women were helpless. So why had he loved Tracy and not the docile Meg? And why was he so appalled to hear that Tracy was changing?

Ruth could have told him, had she been able to hear his question. Long ago she had concluded that Michael had wanted a girl who was as strong as his mother was weak, a girl with more *chutzpa* than the girl who'd married dear old Dad. Michael had wanted this so much that he'd been willing to accept a carload of faults in the bargain.

Ruth said, "You look sleepy, Mike."

"Too much wine."

She nodded. "I'm feeling it too. Whenever I drink like this I get maudlin. I wonder where the years have gone. Where did they go?"

"There are some we should be happy to forget, so let's not waste time mourning them."

"Quite a roster of catastrophes, wasn't it?"

He nodded.

"And yet, I wish we had the time back. Good or bad, it's gone. We'll never see it again."

"Ruth, you're talking like an old lady."

"I *feel* like an old—"

"What's happened to you and Tracy?" he interrupted, exasperated. "Christ, you two were the strongest girls I knew."

"Too many defeats, I guess. And then the events of last year. You didn't expect me to stop mourning Dave, did you?"

"No, of course not," he said softly. "But you're not old. What are you, forty, forty-one? There are other men. There's a lot of work to be done. And you've always—"

"Listen to the optimist. Well, I'm in no mood to think about it. Even the bravest can get worn down, you know. Rocks erode to sand quickly where the waves are strong."

He sighed and signaled for the check. "You could move away from the East Side, you know."

She shook her head. "The paper's successful because we live what we write about."

"It'd be just as successful if you lived in the Bronx."

"No. Dave and I agreed long ago never to leave our readers."

"But Dave was killed by one of—"

"That maniac would've found him just as easily in the Bronx. I've never condemned the neighborhood like you and Tracy have. It's individuals who cause problems, not neighborhoods."

Michael drove Ruth back to Monroe Street but declined her invitation to come up for coffee. Someday he might want to see Tracy again, but not tonight. There was still too much anger in him, most of it admittedly based on the false assumption that she'd known about Stephen. Now that he knew the truth, the anger should have been gone, but it wasn't. It would take time.

Ruth said, "Good night, Mike, and thanks for a nice evening. We should do that more often. Maybe you could come to lunch or dinner at our place. Say in two or three weeks?"

"How would Tracy feel?"

"She'd like it, I think."

"I don't know, Ruth."

"Well, think about it."

"I will. Good night, Ruth."

436

"Good night. Drive carefully." She kissed him on the cheek as she had done so many times in the past, reminding him of the times with her and Dave and the years that were gone. Oh God, he thought. Now they had *him* doing it: starting to think like an old man. He decided then to ring up one of his New York girl friends. He'd prove that forty-three wasn't so old.

Chapter Thirty-Three

"Götterdämmerung" was the word Ruth's partner Al used to describe conditions in late September 1918. They'd had war, and of course the city was always pestilential, but now, to finish them off, they had a plague to rival the grandest in medieval history.

It was called Spanish influenza, and it was spreading around the world, felling the soldiers in battle too. No one knew what organism caused it, but it had a high mortality rate. There had been an outbreak in May, but it was so mild that no one thought much about it. The new outbreak astonished physicians with its virulence. When one of the neighbors fell ill with the disease, Ruth said to Tracy, "We've got to get the children out of the city right away."

"I know. We'll all go to Lanston for a few weeks."

"*I* can't go. I have the paper. And Al's in Washington."

"To hell with the paper. I'm closing the school, aren't I?"

"And I'm not even sure about Lanston, Tracy. New England's one of the hotbeds."

"But at least they won't be in crowds. Close the paper, Ruth."

"Could you take the children there for me?"

"Of course. But I think you're a fool."

The disease lasted three to five days. It was characterized by a dry cough, aching muscles, pain in the legs, the symptoms of catarrh, and occasionally nausea. Often recovery was uncomplicated, but frequently the disease left the body so severely depleted that pneumonias set in that were as deadly as the influenza itself.

"Take care of them for me," Ruth urged. "Keep them isolated. If you hear of one case up there, just one—"

"Yes?"

"I don't know." Ruth threw up her hands helplessly. "As soon as Al gets back from Washington I'll be up there."

"All right."

Tracy dashed off a wire to her sister and helped Ruth pack bags. Ruth could not help noticing what a different person Tracy was when she was able to act instead of being forced to wait. The two of them had been propping each other up for most of the year, and today Tracy was the stronger one.

It was just as well that she was preoccupied, Ruth thought. The news from Europe was that the Allies had begun a major offensive involving practically every trooper in France. So far, Tracy hadn't paid much attention, being so accustomed to banner headlines by this time that she didn't realize how significant these particular banners were. She did not scrutinize the articles as she had in the early days of American involvement, but she'd get the facts sooner or later. Ruth hoped it was later, after she got to Lanston, for in that remote town she wouldn't be seeing the numbers of New Yorkers on the casualty lists.

The train trip was long, but fun for the children. Tracy liked Ruth's kids, now seven and six, who were well-behaved and bright but not obnoxious as some smart children could be. They were curious, though, and subjected Tracy to a barrage of questions about the station, the engineer, how trains ran, how big New Haven was, and why there were farms here but not on Monroe Street. After they changed at Springfield, Tracy begged them to amuse themselves, and they finally did by chanting a favorite rhyme of the day.

I had a little bird named·Enza
I opened up the door and in-flew-Enza.

This Sarah repeated three times and Josh twice more. Tracy sighed and asked if they knew "Mary Had a Little Lamb." They did, and they also knew part of "Flanders Fields." In the midst of a reverie about Stephen, Tracy heard little Josh intone,

We are the dead. Short days ago
We lived, felt dawn, saw sunset glow

Loved, and were loved, and now we lie
In Flan—

"Stop!" shouted Tracy and the tears filled her eyes before she could stop them.

"There, there, Aunt Tracy," Sarah put her small arms around her pretend aunt.

"It's all right, children. It's all right. I just don't like that poem."

But by now the children were crying because they were being taken away from their mama and they still missed their papa. The three of them mourned and lamented all the way to Lanston, and there a smiling family met them, waving and smiling. Tracy had never been so glad to see anyone in her life.

"Mary! Mary!" Tracy shouted.

"Plain as any name can be!" Mary sang out, running toward the woebegone visitors coming down the platform. She already had lollipops in her hand for the children. Joe and Pat were behind her, ready to get the luggage. Pat's new wife was there too, and Tracy finally met her. Pat had married Joan last year just after Tracy's discoveries about Stephen's father. Tracy had wired that she was too ill to attend the ceremony and had since made excuses as to why she could not come up to meet the bride. Joan was short, plump, broad of face—and she was made to order for the children, who took to her smile as Stephen had taken to the colors.

"We want you at our house," Joan said to the

children, "and they want you at their house, so I guess we'll be fighting like cats and dogs for you. Will that make you unhappy?"

Unhappy? For these two still-grieving kids who had endured a year of long faces, to be fussed over like royalty was just the tonic they needed.

"The school here is good," Mary said. "And the teachers won't mind having new students for a few weeks. They'll feel comfortable at our houses too. We'll give them special plates. We can't get everything blessed by a rabbi, but at least we can keep milk and meat separate for them and—"

"Ruth doesn't expect all that."

"I know. But we'll try. It might be fun. And there's a synagogue in Dawn Hills. Sal will take them over Saturday."

"Oh," frowned Sarah. "Do we *hafta* go to shul?"

"Yes, you do," said Tracy. "I promised your mama and there'll be no arguing, and that's final."

Pat and Mary winked at each other. Their sister hadn't changed in twenty-five years. Still bossing children around.

Tracy was staying at Pat's house—actually her own house; she accepted a nominal rent from him now. After dinner, Mary and Pat's wife helped her put the children to bed. Before leaving for her own home, Mary came into Tracy's bedroom with her. As Tracy unpacked her suitcase, Mary sat on the bed and told her bluntly, "You look terrible."

"Aren't you the gallant sister."

"You've lost twenty pounds, and you look as

442

though you never sleep."

"It's worrying about Stephen and this plague we have and, oh, a dozen other things."

"Why didn't you come up here after it happened?"

"I just wanted to hide. Does Pat know the whole story? I know Kerry told *you* all the details."

"Pat knows, but the in-laws don't. Not even my husband. All they know is that you're divorced."

"Divorced from everything," Tracy said. "I don't even have a plan or a dream—except that Stephen will come home. I wish I could go to sleep and not wake up till it's over. And sometimes I wish I could just stay here and sort of fall apart."

"Fall apart then. We're here to take care of you."

"You've got your own worries."

"So did you when you were taking care of us."

In the end Tracy did permit herself to fall apart. With Pat's wife taking over the children, Tracy spent her days eating and drinking and sleeping a lot. Once she rode one of her brother-in-law's horses, and once Pat tried to teach her to drive his Chevrolet, but these diversions were too much like work to her. When it came to activities she preferred quiet walks, one of which she took with Katherine on a magnificent October day. Katherine was fifty-two now and had one son nearing draft age, as did Mary.

But Katherine was sure that Germany would be beaten soon and she spoke like an aging dowager, "I was born right after the Civil War and I feel that this war is closing some kind of epoch. I've seen so many changes, Tracy. It tires me just to think about them.

443

The coming of telephone and trolley. Moving pictures, Gramophones, the auto. The aeroplane and now the wireless. From Andrew Johnson and Reconstruction to Wilson and the Fourteen Points. From Jefferson Davis to Kaiser Wilhelm. And the rhythms—the way pace has picked up. Buggies to Chevrolets, waltzes to ragtime. Things are speeding up so fast that I expect the world to crash. Then maybe we'll see a new era. A gentler one."

"You think the twenties will be gentle?"

"I see them as serene. Like the eighties and nineties. The next generation won't be as frantic as we were."

"Or as warlike?" Tracy speculated optimistically.

Katherine nodded. "It's been the era to end all eras and the war to end all wars."

"Don't forget the plague to end all plagues." Tracy plucked a brilliant red leaf off a tree. "I know what you mean about an era ending. I'm back on Monroe Street where I began years ago. Like Luke that day returning to Elizabeth Street. The homing pigeons, that's us."

"Tracy, you're talking as though your life is over."

"I feel that way sometimes. I think I'm like Luke. I struggled to get out, used every means I knew. Then somehow everything exploded and I ended up on Monroe Street." She had told Katherine only about the divorce.

"But you're not poor. You don't *have* to live there."

"But if I leave, something will pull me back. It's in

444

the stars."

"Since when are you such a determinist?"

"Since when am I a lot of things? But I do know this: The cocky Sullivans are just homing pigeons who don't know how to live without their fire escapes and their ash barrels."

Chapter Thirty-Four

Homing pigeons were the only hope now for a battalion of men in the Argonne Forest in France. A group of men, Stephen among them, had gotten in advance of their lines as they pushed their way toward the Germans in one of the greatest offensives of the war—an attempt to break the Hindenburg line. Somewhere behind them were the infantry, artillery, supply trucks, tanks, motorcycles, ambulances, and rolling kitchens that made up the armies. But the battalion was now alone—cut off—and the situation was perilous. Germans had filtered in behind them, and they were now encircled—five hundred men whose numbers were diminishing rapidly as Germans picked them off from every angle. Food, medical supplies, and ammunition were running out, wounded men were moaning in funk holes, and burial parties had no time to cover the corpses, for the metal was flying every which way and German flame throwers were at work.

"Where the hell is our army?" grumbled Stephen's buddy Tony, a wiry youth from Baxter Street. (A great percentage of the men in the regiment here were

East Siders.)

"They'll get through," Stephen said without conviction.

"How'd it happen?"

"Ask the loot or the major. Far as I know we were on course," Stephen said.

"And we're supposed to be city rats," chimed in another buddy named Sam. "Can you beat this, huh? City rats in a forest yet and faster than the whole damned army."

"They'll never believe this at home," Tony said.

"Such an optimist," said Sam. "He thinks we're gonna get home."

There was no time for extended conversation, since the men were firing at Germans as they talked. They were hoping that American artillery far behind them would land on the Germans ahead of them. As for the Germans in back of them, there was nothing much to do except to shoot once in a while and hope that their own army would catch up and mop up.

At about noon the longed-for American artillery came, but it landed not on the Huns ahead. Through an error no one understood yet, it landed smack dab on top of the isolated American battalion.

"Holy shit!" screamed Tony, diving into a hole as the ground exploded in front of him.

"Those're our shells!" yelled Sam. "American shells!"

"Stupid bastards!" shouted Stephen. "How can we get them to stop?"

There was no way except by sending pigeons back

447

to the lines, and the battalion had only one left. He was released, a brave little flier named Bon Ami. Men watched him fly up, crossed their fingers, and said their prayers. The barrage went on and on. Tony was blown apart before Stephen's eyes. Sam got only a shell fragment, but it entered the head, and he died as quickly as Tony. Stephen remained in the funk hole with the remains of the buddies he'd known for a year. He did not think about what had happened to them. He'd been trained to shoot the Huns yonder and this was what he did. The Germans were throwing everything imaginable at the lost battalion, and what with the Americans unwittingly assisting them, it was a wonder that anything lived. The battering continued, heaving the ground up everywhere as though the earth were boiling. It went on four more hours, and then either the brave Bon Ami found its home or the Americans decided to save ammunition. It finally ended, except for sporadic German fire. By this time Stephen was numb.

"Hey, Curtis!"

A voice from somewhere.

"Hey, Curtis. You alive?"

Was he? Stephen didn't know anymore. He'd been in battle before down on the Vesle, but what he'd just seen was so unreal that it didn't seem as though he were on earth. Was it hell or purgatory? Was he alive?

"Hey, Curtis. Get outa there. C'mon, you can't stay there."

It was Freddie Amati, another private, and what he meant was that Stephen shouldn't be sharing quarters with the bloody pieces of dead buddies. But Stephen wasn't seeing the messes beside him, and he wasn't thinking of them as friends. He was still wondering whether he was alive.

"I think he's shell-shocked, sir," Amati said to someone.

"Nothing we can do about it now," came the lieutenant's voice. The doctors were back somewhere with the rest of the army. And the three medical assistants with the group were busy tending the appalling number of wounded.

Freddie slid into Stephen's funk hole, stood in front of his buddy, and slapped his face hard—not the most kindly of treatments, but it did the trick. "C'mon. C'mon, Curtis, snap out of it."

"I'm snapped. Your ugly puss would scare a dead man."

"Thought you were shell-shocked."

"Not that lucky. I was wondering whether I was alive is all."

"Let's get outa here. This place gives me the creeps."

"That's Sam over there, and that's Tony."

"The burial team'll get 'em. C'mon, c'mon."

"Right-o," Stephen said. "They gonna put Tony together or just throw the pieces on top of each other?"

"Keep talking that way, and I'll puke my guts out."

"After four hours in there, I'm beyond all that," said Stephen.

He was beyond any feeling at all, yet because of this, Stephen was of more use to the battalion that night than were those who could still feel any of what they had seen. Stephen didn't tremble or throw up or lament that he was never going to see home again. Instead, when he wasn't answering nighttime machine-gun fire, he kept his buddies amused with a Will Rogers style commentary rendered in a blacker humor.

"Remember all the times we said we'd rather starve than eat any more army grub? Well, men, God heard our prayers. And remember all those times we said we were sick of rifle practice? Happily I can now report to you that we won't be needing it soon. That's one of the good things about running out of ammunition. . . ."

Some of the men laughed, and others fingered their rosaries. Still others ignored Stephen and amused themselves by recounting their adventures both in and out of war, some lingering upon their encounters with women and others talking about ten-course meals they had known. When dark fell, Stephen made his way down to where the wounded lay and helped with their care. He made forays into no-man's-land for water and provided the wounded with the last available food: bird seed belonging to the pigeons, who would need it no longer. Cigarettes were getting hard to find. Stephen had only two left. He gave one to a man with a festering leg. "Want a fag, Turner?"

"Thanks."

The man took a puff and died.

The wounded moaned, they cried, they called for their mothers—but Stephen didn't listen. The trenches in which they lay stank of gangrene, but Stephen didn't smell it. He was apart from them, a visitor with no senses.

Much later that night there was a call for volunteers to try to reach the Americans. It was the third or fourth time that scouts had been sent, and so far no one had reported back.

"Curtis, how about it?"

"Delighted, major."

"Rose?"

"All right sir, but could you write to my mother?"

"Sure. O'Hara?"

"Do I have to, sir?"

"I can't force you, no."

"So long as it ain't an order," jested O'Hara. "Do I have time for a quick Hail Mary?"

"Make it quick," Stephen muttered. "And then let us away to that undiscovered country from whose bourn no traveler returns."

"What shit's that?" asked O'Hara.

"Shakespeare's shit," explained Stephen.

Four more people were volunteered for the mission, one of them Freddie Amati, who had slapped Stephen to sensibility earlier. Armed with pocket compasses, they were to follow a creek through the black night, dodging the machine-gun fire of the nest of Germans they'd be sneaking past.

Two were killed in the first quarter mile. Rose got

451

it a few yards later. O'Hara went down with a Hail Mary on his lips, and that left Stephen, Amati, and two others who soon rolled out of sight and did not reappear. In a few hours today Stephen had seen most of his friends eradicated.

"Where the hell are we?" Stephen whispered to Amati.

"About fifteen yards from Boches. Can you hear 'em?"

They heard them. And for half an hour they dared not move or speak.

"Curtis?" Amati finally whispered directly into his ear.

"What?"

"Wanna try again?"

"What the hell, why not?"

"If you make it out, will you give my regards to Broadway?"

"If you'll do the same for me. And tell my mother it didn't hurt."

"What?"

"The wound," Stephen said. "Whatever happens, tell her it was quick. I didn't feel a thing."

"Sure."

They edged a few feet out of the thicket. First they heard the twig snap, and then they saw the machine-gun flash.

"Damn!" Stephen swore, heaving himself to the ground. "A lousy twig."

Another flash, more sputtering fire.

"Curtis?"

452

No answer.

"Curtis?" Amati felt for his buddy in the dark, felt the blood on his head and on his chest, quickly reached for his pulse and felt it.

More fire. Amati rolled away. He would have to go back to the battalion. No way to get through this mess. There was something he was supposed to remember. Oh, yeah, he was supposed to tell Stephen's mother that it had been quick. Well, at least it was the truth.

Another flash. Amati was hit in the stomach. He fell to the earth and prayed that it would be quick for him too.

Chapter Thirty-Five

It was Ruth who received the telegram, for it had been sent to the Monroe Street flat. Though not addressed to her, she opened it anyway, hoping it said that Stephen was being transferred back to New York. She read it twice and then screamed, "Oh, Tracy, how am I going to tell you!"

She sat down on the couch and wept. She was already sick with influenza, though she did not want to admit it to herself, and the weeping exhausted her, raised her temperature even higher. She didn't know what to do and barely had the energy to think. Wire Tracy? No, no! Give her another night in Lanston. Wire Russell? That *momzer* wouldn't give a damn. Wire Michael? Yes, Michael. Someone had to be told. But not Tracy. Not yet. Give her one more day.

Ruth put on a shawl and descended the stairs with her message. She got as far as the stoop and could not move farther. She sat on a step, holding her head.

"Mrs. Litvak?" Mary McGuire, a neighbor, bent over her.

"I'm sick," Ruth said. "I have a message to send. It's very important."

The message requested Michael to come to New York but did not say why. Ruth wanted to break the news herself.

"Jimmy'll take it to the telegraph office." Mrs. McGuire shouted across the street to a son who was playing marbles. "Jim-ee!"

The message was taken away, but Ruth couldn't budge from the stoop.

"You should be in the hospital, Mrs. Litvak."

"I have to wait for someone."

"Who?"

"Michael Ryan."

"Ryan. Well when he gets here, I'll tell him where you are. You're going to the hospital."

MICHAEL read the telegram and didn't know what to make of it. All it said was "Come to New York." It didn't give a date or even an address. Was it just an impulsive invitation of Ruth's? Probably, but why hadn't she said "for lunch" or "for dinner"? Could she mean lunch? Would Tracy be there too?

It was ten o'clock in the morning. Michael had planned a heavy schedule today. Construction on three more service stations was being speeded up for completion by winter, and Michael had been planning to light a few fires under the gangs doing the work. Well, he supposed that could be put off. Michael dressed and went down to his car.

At the flat, there was no answer to his knock. Where was Ruth? At the paper? Of course. Why hadn't she said so in the wire? Irritated, he turned to leave.

"Are you Mr. Ryan?" A heavyset woman with stringy hair stood there.

"Yes, I am."

"Mrs. Litvak's been taken to the hospital." The woman named the hospital and gave the address. "Influenza, most likely. We took her off the stoop and put her right into an ambulance."

"My God! How bad is she?"

"I couldn't say, sir."

"Where's Tracy? Where are Ruth's children?"

"Mrs. Curtis and the little ones, they've gone to the country."

"The country?"

"Massachusetts somewhere."

That town Tracy'd settled the family in, Michael thought. What the hell was the name of it? And what should he do about Ruth? Next of kin? Both parents dead. Dave's parents dead, no brothers or sisters. Weren't there cousins in Brooklyn? Yeah, but who? Was that why she'd wired him? Was he as much kin as the cousins? Then she must have wired Tracy too. He asked the woman, who checked with the son. The boy said that there had only been one message.

Michael set off for the hospital, not sure what to do. Then he remembered Tracy telling him that Tommy was a cop in the Mercer Street area and he telephoned the precinct from a drugstore.

"Officer Thomas Sullivan, please."

It was five minutes before Tommy came on the line. "Sullivan here."

456

"Tommy, this is Michael Ryan, your old neighbor."

"Even more closely related than that, I understand."

"I don't have time for cracks. Ruth Litvak's been taken ill and I have to reach Tracy."

"Ruth? Sweet Jesus! What was it, influenza?"

"Yes. How do I reach Tracy?"

"Care of my brother Pat. Lanston, Mass."

"Lanston?"

Tommy spelled it out.

"Got it," Michael said.

"What hospital is she in, Mike?"

But Michael had already hung up and was on his way to the telegraph office.

MICHAEL'S telegram was short too. It said, "Ruth ill with influenza. Come soon as possible." It named the hospital and was signed "Michael." Tracy, whimpering in her panic, didn't stop to pack. She told her brother's wife not to say a word to the children, then she asked her brother-in-law Sal to drive her directly to Springfield in his Model T. This way she wouldn't have to make connections and could get to New York faster.

It was five by the time she went running through the hospital doors. The trip had been a horror, with delays and a breakdown and her own terror. Now her mouth was dry, and her heart was racing as she asked directions of nurses. Would she be too late?

Michael was sitting on a bench in a long chilly

457

corridor adjoining the wards. There appeared to be dozens like him, all waiting for news of a loved one. He was reading the paper, and next to him was a pile of magazines he had collected for the wait. Tracy had not seen him since the day in Louise's parlor, but she wasn't thinking about that.

"Michael, where is she? No one seems to know."

He rose and touched her arm. "Calm down. She's here. They won't let us in yet."

"How is she?"

"She's holding on."

Doctors and nurses hurried past them. The hospitals in the city were filled to overflowing, and volunteers had swelled the ranks of professional nurses.

She asked, "When can I see her?"

"At eight. You've got to wear a mask. I've got one for you here."

"Three hours? I have to wait three hours? Did you see her?"

"For five minutes."

"How was she? What did she say?"

"We didn't talk. She was asleep."

"Oh, God, what if something happens to her? The children—what'll happen to the children."

Michael said nothing. He'd been wondering the same thing.

"They have no one, Michael. No one—except some distant cousins in Brooklyn and the old country. I'll just have to raise them myself. I don't know what she wants, though. What college? And what about religion? Ruth's always complaining that the Orthodox are too strict. Should I try Reform?"

"Tracy, aren't you jumping the gun a little?"

"I have to know what to do. If she's awake I'm going to have to ask her. How should I do it, though? If I let her know that I think she's dying, maybe she really will die. But if I don't let her know, how shall I know what to do about the children? When Josh is Bar Mitzvahed he'll have to—"

"Josh is only seven years old. Will you calm down, for the love of God? A lot of people survive influenza."

"But what if she doesn't?"

"Then that's when we'll think about it. You can second-guess Ruth, and I'll second-guess Dave."

"Stop it! Stop talking that way! You're talking as though she's going to die."

"But you just said. . . ." He shrugged, knowing better than to try to make sense of her now.

The hours passed in an anguished monologue by Tracy, full of contradictions. Ruth was going to die. Ruth wasn't going to die. Tracy would move the children to Lanston. No, she'd move them to Brooklyn so she'd still be near the typing school. She'd raise the children Orthodox. No, she'd have them join Young Israel. The children should be told about their mother right away. No, maybe she should wait. Ruth was going to die and there was no hope. Ruth wasn't going to die, for what would she, Tracy, do without her?

It wasn't until about 7:30 that she asked Michael how he'd come to be here. He told her about the mysterious wire, and Tracy said, "I wonder why she thought of you first?"

"Probably because you had the children with you."

"Does anyone else know? Her neighbors? Her partner Al?"

"A whole crowd came up this afternoon, and the nurses asked them to leave because they needed the room."

"Including Al?"

"Someone told me he's sick with this too."

"Ruth was going to marry him," Tracy said, her eyes filling with tears.

Michael handed her a handkerchief. "I didn't know that."

"Neither did Ruth. But I decided it was the best thing for her."

For the first time today Michael grinned. "You never change, Tracy."

She looked at him and smiled too. "Funny," she said. "Every time we meet it's because of another disaster."

"That's what I told Stephen once. He said it was typically Irish."

Ruth had mentioned to Tracy that father and son had met at a bar one night. Now she said, "Do you like him, Michael?"

He nodded. "It was awkward at first, but I broke the ice by getting drunk. After he helped me out of the place, we were pals."

"Does he write to you?"

"A few times."

"He writes to me too. He's forgiven me."

"I'm glad," Michael said.

"Have you?" she asked.

"Have I what?"

"Forgiven me? For keeping him from you?"

"You didn't know he was my son."

"You mean you believe me now?"

He nodded. "So I don't think the word 'forgive' applies."

"Then what does?"

"I don't know. I know that you and I are going to be tied together through Stephen for the rest of our lives, and I hope a lot of what's happened can be—well—forgotten."

She nodded and was about to say she agreed, but a nurse came by and said to Michael, "You may see her now, but only for a minute."

Both Michael and Tracy stood up.

"Only one of you, please."

Michael deferred to Tracy. She put on a mask and followed the nurse down the corridor and into a ward. It seemed that hundreds of people were here, all of them stricken with influenza or pneumonia. They lay on high narrow beds with metal frames, and it looked as though all of them were dying.

Ruth, her breathing labored and uneven, was unconscious or asleep. Her black hair was coming undone, and part of it was fanned out on the pillow.

461

How strange to see Ruth this way, helpless for the first time in her life. Tracy took her cold hand. Ruth shifted slightly but did not awaken. Tracy whispered, "You're going to get well," but she did not believe it. Tears ran down her face and into her mask.

"I'm sorry," the nurse said after a moment. "That's all the time we're permitting."

"Is she going to get well?"

The nurse, a kindly middle-aged volunteer, pressed a finger to her mouth. "Shhhh." She signaled Tracy to move into the hall. "It's too soon to tell, but she's basically a healthy woman and she's got a good chance. I suggest that you go home—"

"Oh, I can't."

"If there's a change during the night we can notify you there. Do you have a telephone?"

"Yes, but—"

"Leave the number with me. I'll make sure the next shift gets it. We'll notify you if there's any change."

Tracy gave the nurse the number as Michael came up to them. He said to Tracy, "Come on."

"I'm afraid to."

"Come on. You're tired. And you're not going to help Ruth by sitting here freezing."

They didn't wait for an elevator but walked down the three flights of stairs. Out in the street it was chilly too, but it was more pleasant since it didn't reek of antiseptic as the hospital had. They walked over to Broadway, where they could more easily get a cab. There were a good many soldiers about, and

Tracy said to Michael, "I sometimes stand on the street and watch the soldiers pass. I close my eyes hard and wish that when I open them, one of them will be Stephen. That I'll walk up to this man and he'll turn around and it will be him."

Michael nodded. His throat hurt.

"I see him there," Tracy pointed. "And there near the chestnut man. And over there, the one getting on the streetcar. They're all Stephen."

Michael swallowed hard and took her arm as they crossed a street. He then moved away from the sidewalk and tried to flag down a cab. Next to Tracy, an accordion man was playing songs they had all become familiar with during these past months: "Till We Meet Again," "The Rose of Picardy," "The Long, Long Trail." As Michael waved the cab to the curb and Tracy headed toward it, she thought of the final lines in "The Long, Long Trail." And sitting down next to Michael, she said, "It almost never happens that dreams come true, but they write so many songs about it."

"I know."

"I wish I could believe them," she said.

Michael saw her safely upstairs to the apartment and she asked him in for a drink without hesitation. This was no time to be worrying about proprieties. He had said it back in the hospital: They were tied to each other through Stephen. And tonight through Ruth as well.

The apartment was clean, but there was evidence that Ruth had been sick. Unwashed dishes, blankets

463

on the couch, handkerchiefs in a basket beside the couch, two bottles of patent medicine. Next to the medicine was a telegram. As Michael took a seat in a chair across the room, Tracy picked it up and glanced at it. For a moment there was silence, and then Michael heard her scream.

He jumped up, caught her as she began to weave, eased her to the couch, and then read the wire himself.

The grief he felt was all for Tracy. He had liked Stephen, and he mourned him now, but it was Tracy who had raised the boy, cared for him, worried about him, loved him to distraction. And it was she who had lost him, Michael thought. He, Michael, had hardly known his son, though he had looked forward to being with Stephen after the war.

Michael held Tracy, rocked her in his arms, made her drink a shot of whiskey and then another. Sometimes she babbled about Stephen, about herself, about something she called "sin." Like Ruth, Michael assured her that this had nothing to do with her. But Tracy wouldn't listen.

He thought of what she had been once. And now here she was—defeated, crippled with grief and self-hate. Seeing her like this was almost too much for him to bear, but she had borne his tragedy long ago. She had gotten him through it, and he would get her through this night. Hour after hour he held her, and at last she fell into an exhausted sleep. Michael sat up through the early morning and at 7 A.M. telephoned

Tommy at work. Tommy said he would be right over. Michael didn't know who else to call. The school, of course. And he'd wire the family in Lanston. But that could come later. He covered Tracy with a blanket and went down to the street to wait for her brother and to clear his head.

On Monroe Street life was unchanged. Garment workers and men with pails and shovels marched off to their labors. Pushcart peddlers set up business. Ice wagons and coal wagons rattled along the cobblestones. Housewives leaned out of windows hoisting bread and ice up to the flats by rope. A new day was beginning. Michael stood on the street where he had been born and watched for a long time.

"Mike!" Tommy, in uniform, came running up to him. Michael hadn't seen Tracy's brother in twenty-some years, but Tommy was unchanged except for his weathered skin.

"How is she?" Tommy asked, panting.

"She's asleep now."

"What did the wire say exactly?"

"Missing in action."

"Missing? What does that mean?" Tommy thought a moment, then shrugged and said, "No sense getting our hopes up, huh? I know people who go on hoping even when it says 'dead' straight out. Still, once in a while even the dead show up. Nursed to health by a beautiful French girl."

"It's probably happened twice," Michael said. "And they wrote a hundred stories about it. That and the cases of amnesia.'' He sighed. ''But there's always that chance, isn't there? I wish I knew how it happened. Some details. He was in the Seventy-seventh. I don't remember the regiment number, but he might've been in that battalion they've been writing about in the paper. That lost battalion it took so long to catch up with. That was the Seventy-seventh, wasn't it?''

''I think so. I know there were a lot of New York boys in it. The papers were full of the story. The ones who were missing might've been scouts trying to find the American lines.''

''Which means they might've been captured,'' Michael said.

Tommy nodded. ''It's possible.''

They were silent for a while, and then Michael said, ''Tracy said something last night just before we came back here. She said she sees Stephen all the time in the streets. I know that feeling. I used to see my youngest sister. I used to see Dave. I guess it's a common thing.'' He cleared his throat. ''Could you imagine how it'd be if Tracy *did* see him?'' Michael looked off toward Catherine Street. ''She'd be hurrying up the block like she did when she was a girl. Hurrying, rushing to get somewhere, and then she'd see a soldier. Not a stranger this time but . . .'' Michael's voice broke. Tears filled his eyes and he couldn't finish the sentence.

Tommy swallowed hard and looked down. He could picture it too, clearly. The look on Tracy's face. Tommy glanced briefly at Michael. The fellow did care for Tracy, Tommy realized. Maybe Stephen hadn't been a one-night mistake after all. He said, "I'm going upstairs now. Will you stay around, Mike?"

"Until I sail for France," Michael said. "I've got connections that'll get me on a ship. I'm going to find out what happened."

Chapter Thirty-Six

"Tell me again how you were going to raise the children?" Ruth grinned across the parlor at Tracy. It had become a joke between them—or rather the only subject capable of getting a response from Tracy these days.

"I was going to raise them Young Israel or Reform."

"Knowing I'd be rolling over in my grave?"

"Well, how the deuce was I supposed to know what you wanted? You're always complaining about the strict laws."

"Let me repeat so you'll remember. Once an Orthodox, always an Orthodox, even if inside you're a socialist or an agnostic, even if you work on Saturday. No Litvak and no Mednick would switch to Reform unless Moses came down with a tablet and ordered it. Can you remember that for the next time you bury me?"

"I can't even remember the Sorrowful Mysteries and you expect me to make sense of Jews?"

"Then I have no choice but to raise them myself."

Ruth had recovered from influenza within a week.

468

Tracy, though grieving for Stephen, had managed to get to the hospital most days. Michael and Tommy had been around through the worst of that dreadful week, but Tracy would not let her sisters come to console her. She had written to Lanston that the country didn't need an "influenza Mary" since it already had a typhoid. The day the letter went out, Tracy came down with the disease and was hospitalized for three weeks, debilitated as much by grief as by influenza. By this time, Michael had disappeared. She didn't know where. And except for the visits of Ruth, her brother, and her students, she was alone in her grief and pain in an antiseptic hospital ward.

Somewhere in the midst of this, the war had ended. The armistice was signed, whistles blew, and bells rang out. Tracy remembered that clearly—the sound of bells coming through the hospital windows. In the weeks since, the outlook had grown a little brighter—for Ruth, at least. The war was over, she could do what she wanted with the paper now, the worst of the epidemic had passed, and she was planning to bring the children home next week. An East Side favorite, Al Smith, had just been elected governor of New York, and Ruth was glad about that. And women's suffrage had passed in the House. There was every chance for the Senate and state ratification one day soon. Ruth tried to interest Tracy in suffrage and, failing, tried to persuade her to do something challenging—like expanding her school. These were the only remedies for grief that Ruth could think of. But Tracy's only remedy would be to take a trip to Europe.

After things had settled down and the army found Stephen's body, she was going to go to France to find his grave. With advancing years Tracy was becoming Irish enough to find comfort in ceremonies. Saying a prayer at his grave would bring her closer to Stephen. It was the only thing she could look forward to these dismal December days.

It was a Sunday afternoon. Ruth and Tracy were sitting in the parlor, Ruth reading and Tracy mending a black skirt. There was a knock on the door, and Ruth went to answer. Michael was standing there, and she threw her arms around him. He kissed her and said, "I can't stay, Ruth. I'm late for a meeting."

"A cup of tea you've certainly got time for. We haven't seen you in months."

Michael shook his head. He nodded at Tracy, who was rising from the sofa. "Tracy, I want to talk to you, but I don't have time to sit down. Could you walk me up to Catherine? That way I'll at least be en route."

"En route to where?"

"A meeting I'm late for. Just walk with me to the corner. Throw your coat on and come with me. Please."

"It's freezing out there, Michael."

"It's not that bad. Come on."

Tracy went to the closet for her coat. "What do you want to talk about?"

"Training secretaries. I'm going to set up an office in Manhattan. I'll need the best."

"All right." Tracy sighed and buttoned her black coat and put on her black hat. Michael was relieved to see that she wasn't wearing a black veil as well.

They began walking down Monroe Street toward Catherine in the direction of Ruth's old bakery.

"So tell me," Tracy said.

"Tell me?" he said absently.

"No, *you* tell *me*. About the office. Hurry up. We'll be seeing a cab in a few minutes."

"Oh, the office. Yes. I'll need secretaries."

"And?"

"What did you say?"

"Michael, what in heaven's going on? First I don't see you for two months, then you show up out of the blue and drag me from my warm flat, and now I don't think you even know what you wanted me for." She turned to him, exasperated.

Michael was looking not at her but in the direction of the bakery, now owned by an Italian. Tracy turned too, to see what he was looking at. There was a soldier standing there, gazing at the window where the breads were always heaped high. In profile he looked just like Stephen, but then so many of them did, she thought. The height, the slouch, the angle of the head.

"Doesn't he look like Stephen?" she said to Michael.

"Very strong resemblance," Michael said. "The closer we get, the more like Stephen he looks. You

471

don't suppose—but no, that would be too much like one of those soppy sotires in a magazine."

"But *look* at him!" she exclaimed.

"Well, why not go up to him and see?" Michael's voice was shaking. She thought this odd. She looked from the soldier to Michael and then again at the soldier, who was still facing the bakery but looking at her out of the corner of his eye. Then she ran.

"Stephen!" He turned and she touched his face. There was a scar running from forehead to cheek. "Are you real? Oh, you *must* be. The scar. You *must* be real."

"I am, Ma." His cheeks were wet. He bent to hug her—stiffly, for his chest still pained him.

From a distance Michael watched. He and Stephen had planned this down to the last detail coming over on the ship. And it had worked out perfectly. Michael knew he would never again see a moment so perfect.

TRACY and Ruth stood in the parlor looking wonderingly at Stephen.

"You've convinced me," Ruth said. "I'm converted. I believe in the resurrection!"

Stephen laughed. "They never actually said 'dead,' Mrs. Litvak."

"But in this war that's what missing usually means."

"Not always. Not in my case, obviously, though I did come close, I have to admit."

"What happened?" Ruth asked.

He repeated for Ruth what he had told Tracy on

the way home from the bakery. "I was shot at night. The Boches found me the next morning. And my buddy, but he had died. They sent me to a dressing station and then to a field hospital, where they patched up my head and chest. When we were liberated, the Red Cross sent me to France. Pa was already there."

"Michael?" Ruth asked.

"Yes. He was there, in France. At first he was going to wire Ma, but then my chest got infected, and I said why tell her if I'm gonna die anyway? So we waited. I was sick a couple of weeks. When I finally recovered, he booked passage on a ship. He wanted to wire then, but I decided that with my luck some Boche airman who hadn't heard about the armistice would bomb the ship. So we waited till we got home. Just to be sure."

Ruth shook her head. "Incredible," she said. Then she turned around and said, "Where's Michael, anyway?"

"I don't know," Tracy said. "Right after I found Stephen, he disappeared."

"He went to phone Uncle Tommy," Stephen said. "That was part of the script too."

"What script?" Ruth said.

"Pa planned this day like a choreographed dance. Said he wanted it to be perfect for Ma. He said Ma had told him that she looked at soldiers all the time and kept thinking she saw me on the street. He said Ma didn't think dreams ever came true. He wanted this one to come true for her."

"Michael did that?" Tracy started to cry.

"Came all the way to France. Used his government connections to get the army to give him information. And when he found me, he bribed everyone so I'd get the best care. He talked the doctors into getting me a transfer to New York. All for this moment. Just so he could see your face, Ma."

"Why?" Tracy asked, still crying.

"I don't know," Stephen said. "He just told me it was something he had to do." Stephen paused. "He wouldn't admit that I could die. Even I was ready to admit it after a while. Two wounds, the infections, and then influenza."

Ruth said, "Influenza? You too?"

"At least he's immune for a while. At least I don't have to worry about *that*," Tracy said. "And you don't have to go back now, do you, Stephen?"

"My unit's still there, but I've been transferred here until I'm mustered out. With the war over, it shouldn't be long."

"So Michael refused to recognize that you could die?" Ruth said.

"He told me to buck up. I was in bad shape too. Not just the wounds but—things I can't talk about right now. He was good to me, sympathetic in his own way, but he was merciless. 'If you can't get well for yourself, Steve, do it for your mother. Do it for her. Now you've got to try, really try.' He'd go on that way for days, and I think I got well just to shut him up."

Ruth smiled. "But you're not well enough yet,

474

Stevie. You look like a skeleton. Come on, Tracy, we'll fatten him up."

"All right. You start cooking and I'll do the marketing." Tracy explained to Stephen, "We're roommates. Special talents. And it's the house-keeper's day off."

"We'll make enough for Tommy and Michael," Ruth said. "They'll be here in a while, I imagine. And I think I'll ring up Al too."

The women prepared the grocery list, and Tracy got ready for marketing. Automatically she put on the black hat. But then she threw it joyously across the room. "Burn it in the stove," she commanded Stephen, and she went winging out the door, hatless.

Michael was coming down the street, passing within a few yards of the building where he had once lived. She waved and called to him, then dashed across the street, missing by inches a quickly moving coal wagon. "Michael!"

He strode over to her. "I sent wires to Massachusetts," he said.

"Oh, Michael!" She threw her arms around him. "Thank you for bringing him home to me." He held her and she said, "How is he? It's so hard to tell."

"It was bad over there. It'll be a long time before he gets over the worst of it. The doctors warned me about nightmares, problems of readjustment. He saw most of his platoon shot to pieces in one day."

"My God!" She stood back from him.

"So it's gonna take time. He needs a lot of understanding. I didn't give him much of that, I have to admit. I just hounded him to get physically well and figured we'd worry about the rest of it later."

"We will," she said. "I want so much for him to be like he was before the war."

Michael shook his head. "He'll never be that boy again, Tracy."

"No. No, I guess you're right." She paused. "Michael, it's almost as though you willed this— brought him back to life, almost."

"Maybe I did." He stepped back. "Maybe I decided that we'd had enough."

"What do you mean?"

"The way it's been for you and me. For Ruth and Dave, for the people we knew. How much justice did we ever see? My father went free until my sister was dead. Maniacs went free until Dave was dead. At Triangle the owners went free even *after* the girls were dead. And now the world was going to go merrily on after my son was dead, after you were dead."

"But *I* wasn't."

"Yes, you were. For all intents and purposes you were. I remember how you looked when Stephen walked out of that boardinghouse parlor. Then Russell and finally me. Angry as I was, I knew how you must have felt. It was like the past had reached out after all those years and said, 'Here's one to remember me by.' I thought you'd recover from it, but you didn't." He took a deep breath. "The morning after the telegram came I went down to the street. I stood there and remembered the way you had

476

been once. But you were gone, just like Stephen, and I didn't think you'd be coming back. Tommy came by, and we talked about the telegram. He said, 'Missing? What does that mean?' I thought about that for a while and then I said to myself, 'This time, goddamn it, it'll mean what I *want* it to mean.'"

He continued. "I was challeninging God, I guess. Daring Him to give us one more funeral, just one more. It was getting to be ridiculous, you and me together only during catastrophes. That's when I decided to go to France." He cleared his throat. "Of course I didn't bring him back to life exactly. It was sheer luck, a bullet missing by inches. But I found him sick and shell-shocked, and I ordered him back to health. He'll tell you: I *ordered* it. I said I wasn't attending another funeral with his mother. So yes, in a way I made it happen. At least I made that street reunion happen."

"Stephen told me about it. It was a wonderful thing to do." She paused, then said in a trembling voice, "Will we be seeing more of each other now?"

"What do you think? We're both free and we've got a son."

"Yes, we have a son. This courtship ought to be easy. The family's already set up." She laughed.

They began walking back toward Ruth's. Michael's arm was around her. The street where they had lived so long ago was no longer an enemy. She had found Stephen and Michael here, and her street was a loved friend.

"Look at it," she exclaimed to Michael. "Those

overflowing ashcans, that billowing laundry, that housewife yelling out the window, that awning knocked down by the kids. Oh Michael, isn't it beautiful?"

He laughed. "A little rest, that's what you need. We'll have you back to normal in no time."

STAR BESTSELLERS

0352 309350	**WHISPERS** Dean R Koontz (GF)	1.95*
0352 310804	**ROGUE OF GOR** John Norman (Sci. Fantasy)	2.25*
0352 310413	**AFTERMATH** Roger Williams (GF)	1.60
0352 310170	**A MAN WITH A MAID** Anonymous (GF)	1.60*
0352 310928	**A MAN WITH A MAID VOL. II** Anonymous (GF)	1.75
0352 395621	**THE STUD** Jackie Collins (GF)	1.75
0352 300701	**LOVEHEAD** Jackie Collins (GF)	1.50
0352 398663	**THE WORLD IS FULL OF DIVORCED WOMEN** Jackie Collins (GF)	1.75
0352 398752	**THE WORLD IS FULL OF MARRIED MEN** Jackie Collins (GF)	1.75
0352 311339	**THE GARMENT** Catherine Cookson (GF)	1.25
0426 163524	**HANNAH MASSEY** Catherine Cookson (GF)	1.35
0426 163605	**SLINKY JANE** Catherine Cookson (GF)	1.25
0352 310634	**THE OFFICERS' WIVES** Thomas Fleming (GF)	2.75*
0352 302720	**DELTA OF VENUS** Anais Nin (GF)	1.50*
0352 306157	**LITTLE BIRDS** Anais Nin (GF)	1.25*
0352 310359	**BITE OF THE APPLE** Molly Parkin (GF)	1.50

STAR BESTSELLERS

0352 311010	**CARDINAL SINS** Andrew M. Greeley (GF)	1.95*
0352 310723	**THE ANALOG BULLET** Martin Cruz Smith (GF)	1.50*
0352 310715	**THE INDIANS WON** Martin Cruz Smith (GF)	1.50*
0352 312513	**LOVING FEELINGS** Kelly Stearn (GF)	1.75
0352 312823	**FLIGHT 902 IS DOWN** H. Fisherman & B. Schiff (Thriller)	1.95*
0352 397403	**DOG SOLDIERS** Robert Stone (Thriller)	1.95*
0352 312408	**THE WARRIOR WITHIN** S. Green (Sci. Fic.)	1.75*
0352 312491	**FRIDAY 13TH III** Michael Avallone (Horror)	1.60*
0352 312017	**SLUGS** Shaun Hutson (Horror)	1.60
0352 306866	**DEATH TRIALS** Elwyn Jones (Gen. Non. Fic.)	1.25
0352 398108	**IT'S BEEN A LOT OF FUN** Brian Johnston (Bio)	1.80
0352 311487	**BING THE HOLLOW MAN** Shepherd & Slatzer	1.75*
0352 303506	**THE UNINVITED** Clive Harold (unexplained)	1.50
0352 310022	**BARRY MANILOW** Tony Jasper (Music)	1.50
0352 301961	**A TWIST OF LENNON** Cynthia Lennon (Music)	1.25

* Not for sale in Canada   Prices are subject to alteration